SWING TIME

SWING TIME

ZADIE SMITH

RANDOM HOUSE
LARGE PRINT

Copyright © 2016 by Zadie Smith

All rights reserved.
Published in the United States of America by Random House Large Print in association with Penguin Press, an imprint of Penguin Random House LLC

Cover design by gray318

The Library of Congress has established a Cataloging-in-Publication record for this title.

ISBN: 978-1-5247-2319-4

www.randomhouse.com/largeprint

FIRST LARGE PRINT EDITION

Printed in the United States of America

10 9 8 7 6 5 4 3 2 1

This Large Print edition published in accord with the standards of the N.A.V.H.

For my mother, Yvonne

When the music changes, so does the dance.
—Hausa proverb

Prologue

It was the first day of my humiliation. Put on a plane, sent back home, to England, set up with a temporary rental in St. John's Wood. The flat was on the eighth floor, the windows looked over the cricket ground. It had been chosen, I think, because of the doorman, who blocked all inquiries. I stayed indoors. The phone on the kitchen wall rang and rang, but I was warned not to answer it and to keep my own phone switched off. I watched the cricket being played, a game I don't understand, it offered no real distraction, but still it was better than looking at the interior of that apartment, a luxury condo, in which everything had been designed to be perfectly neutral, with all significant corners rounded, like an iPhone. When the cricket finished I stared at the sleek coffee machine embedded in the wall, and at two photos of the Buddha—one a brass Buddha, the other wood—and at a photo of an elephant kneeling next to a little Indian boy, who was also kneeling. The rooms were tasteful and gray, linked by a pris-

tine hallway of tan wool cord. I stared at the ridges
in the cord.

Two days passed like that. On the third day, the
doorman called up and said the lobby was clear. I
looked at my phone, it was sitting on the counter in
airplane mode. I had been offline for seventy-two
hours and can remember feeling that this should
be counted among the great examples of personal
stoicism and moral endurance of our times. I put
on my jacket and went downstairs. In the lobby
I met the doorman. He took the opportunity to
complain bitterly ("You've no idea what it's been
like down here, past few days—Piccadilly-bloody-
Circus!") although it was clear that he was also con-
flicted, even a little disappointed: it was a shame
for him that the fuss had died down—he had felt
very important for forty-eight hours. He told me
proudly of telling several people to "buck up their
ideas," of letting such and such a person know that
if they thought they were getting past him "they
had another think coming." I leaned against his
desk and listened to him talk. I had been out of
England long enough that many simple colloquial
British phrases now sounded exotic to me, almost
nonsensical. I asked him if he thought there would
be more people that evening and he said he thought
not, there hadn't been anyone since yesterday. I
wanted to know if it was safe to have an overnight
visitor. "I don't see any problem," he said, with a
tone that made me feel my question was ridicu-

lous. "There's always the back door." He sighed, and at the same moment a woman stopped to ask him if he could receive her dry cleaning as she was going out. She had a rude, impatient manner and rather than look at him as she spoke she stared at a calendar on his desk, a gray block with a digital screen, which informed whoever was standing in front of it exactly what moment they were in to the second. It was the twenty-fifth of the month of October, in the year two thousand and eight, and the time was twelve thirty-six and twenty-three seconds. I turned to leave; the doorman dealt with the woman and hurried out from behind his desk to open the front door for me. He asked me where I was going; I said I didn't know. I walked out into the city. It was a perfect autumnal London afternoon, chill but bright, under certain trees there was a shedding of golden leaves. I walked past the cricket ground and the mosque, past Madame Tussauds, up Goodge Street and down Tottenham Court Road, through Trafalgar Square, and found myself finally in Embankment, and then crossing the bridge. I thought—as I often think as I cross that bridge—of two young men, students, who were walking over it very late one night when they were mugged and thrown over the railing, into the Thames. One lived and one died. I've never understood how the survivor managed it, in the darkness, in the absolute cold, with the terrible shock and his shoes on. Thinking of him, I kept to the right-hand side of the bridge, by the railway line, and avoided looking at the water. When I reached the South Bank the first thing I saw was a poster advertising an afternoon event with an Austrian film director "in conversation," it was starting in twenty minutes at the Royal Festival Hall. I decided on a whim to try to get a ticket. I walked over and was able to buy a seat in the gods, in the very back row. I didn't expect much, I only wanted to be distracted from my own problems for a while, to sit in darkness, and hear a discussion of films I'd never seen, but in the middle of the program the director asked his interviewer to roll a clip from the movie **Swing Time**, a film I know very well, I only watched it over and over as a child. I sat up tall in my seat. On the huge screen before me Fred Astaire danced with three silhouetted figures. They can't keep up with him, they begin to lose their rhythm. Finally they throw in the towel, making that very American "oh phooey" gesture with their three left hands, and walking off stage. Astaire danced on alone. I understood all three of the shadows were also Fred Astaire. Had I known that, as a child? No one else paws the air like that, no other dancer bends his knees in quite that way. Meanwhile the director spoke of a theory of his, about "pure cinema," which he began to define as the "interplay of light and dark, expressed as a kind of rhythm, over time," but I found this line of thought boring and hard to follow. Behind him the same clip, for some reason, played again, and my feet, in sympathy with the music, tapped at the seat in front of me. I felt a wonderful lightness in my body, a ridiculous happiness, it seemed to come from nowhere. I'd lost my job, a certain version of my life, my privacy, yet all these things felt small and petty next to this joyful sense I had watching the dance, and following its precise rhythms in my own body. I felt I was losing track of my physical location, rising above my body, viewing my life from a very distant point, hovering over it. It reminded me of the way people describe hallucinogenic drug experiences. I saw all my years at once, but they were not piled up on each other, experience after experience, building into something of substance—the opposite. A truth was being revealed to me: that I had always tried to attach myself to the light of other people, that I had never had any light of my own. I experienced myself as a kind of shadow.

When the event was over I walked back through the city to the flat, phoned Lamin, who was waiting in a nearby café, and told him the coast was clear. He'd been fired, too, but instead of letting him go home, to Senegal, I'd brought him here, to London. At eleven o'clock he came round, in a hooded top, in case of cameras. The lobby was clear. In his hood he looked even younger and more beautiful, and it seemed to me to be a kind of scandal that I could find in my heart no real feelings for him. Afterward, we lay side by side in bed with our laptops, and to avoid checking my e-mail I googled, at first aimlessly, and then with an aim: I was looking for that clip from **Swing Time**. I wanted to show it to Lamin, I was curious to know what he thought of it, as a dancer now himself, but he said he had never seen or heard of Astaire, and as the clip played he sat up in bed and frowned. I hardly understood what we were looking at: Fred Astaire in black face. In the Royal Festival Hall I'd sat in the gods, without my glasses on, and the scene opens with Astaire in long shot. But none of this really explained how I'd managed to block the childhood image from my memory: the rolling eyes, the white gloves, the Bojangles grin. I felt very stupid, closed the laptop and went to sleep. The next morning I woke early, leaving Lamin in bed, hurried to the kitchen and switched on my phone. I expected hundreds of messages, thousands. I had maybe thirty. It had been Aimee who once sent me hundreds of messages a day, and now at last I understood that Aimee would never send me another message again. Why it took me so long to understand this obvious thing I don't know. I scrolled down a depressing list—a distant cousin, a few friends, several journalists. I spotted one titled: WHORE. It had a nonsense address of numbers and letters and a video attachment that wouldn't open. The body of the message was a single sentence: **Now everyone knows who you really are**. It was the kind of note you might get from a spiteful seven-year-old girl with a firm idea of justice. And of course that—if you can ignore the passage of time—is exactly what it was.

PART ONE
Early Days

One

If all the Saturdays of 1982 can be thought of as one day, I met Tracey at ten a.m. on that Saturday, walking through the sandy gravel of a churchyard, each holding our mother's hand. There were many other girls present but for obvious reasons we noticed each other, the similarities and the differences, as girls will. Our shade of brown was exactly the same—as if one piece of tan material had been cut to make us both—and our freckles gathered in the same areas, we were of the same height. But my face was ponderous and melancholy, with a long, serious nose, and my eyes turned down, as did my mouth. Tracey's face was perky and round, she looked like a darker Shirley Temple, except her nose was as problematic as mine, I could see that much at once, a ridiculous nose—it went straight up in the air like a little piglet. Cute, but also obscene: her nostrils were on permanent display. On noses you could call it a draw. On hair she won comprehensively. She had spiral curls, they reached to her backside and were gathered into two long plaits, glossy with some kind of oil, tied at their ends with satin yellow bows. Satin yellow bows were a phenomenon unknown to my mother. She pulled my great frizz back in a single cloud, tied with a black band. My mother was a feminist. She wore her hair in a half-inch Afro, her skull was perfectly shaped, she never wore make-up and dressed us both as plainly as possible. Hair is not essential when you look like Nefertiti. She'd no need of make-up or products or jewelry or expensive clothes, and in this way her financial circumstances, her politics and her aesthetic were all perfectly—conveniently—matched. Accessories only cramped her style, including, or so I felt at the time, the horse-faced seven-year-old by her side. Looking across at Tracey I diagnosed the opposite problem: her mother was white, obese, afflicted with acne. She wore her thin blond hair pulled back very tightly in what I knew my mother would call a "Kilburn facelift." But Tracey's personal glamour was the solution: she was her own mother's most striking accessory. The family look, though not to my mother's taste, I found captivating: logos, tin bangles and hoops, diamanté everything, expensive trainers of the kind my mother refused to recognize as a reality in the world— "Those aren't shoes." Despite appearances, though, there was not much to choose between our two families. We were both from the estates, neither of us received benefits. (A matter of pride for my mother, an outrage to Tracey's: she had tried many times—and failed—to "get on the disability.") In my mother's view it was exactly these superficial similarities that lent so much weight to questions of taste. She dressed for a future not yet with us but which she expected to arrive. That's what her plain white linen trousers were for, her blue-and-white-striped "Breton" T-shirt, her frayed espadrilles, her severe and beautiful African head—everything so plain, so understated, completely out of step with the spirit of the time, and with the place. One day we would "get out of here," she would complete her studies, become truly radical chic, perhaps even spoken of in the same breath as Angela Davis and Gloria Steinem . . . Straw-soled shoes were all a part of this bold vision, they pointed subtly at the higher concepts. I was an accessory only in the sense that in my very plainness I signified admirable maternal restraint, it being considered bad taste—in the circles to which my mother aspired—to dress your daughter like a little whore. But Tracey was unashamedly her mother's aspiration and avatar, her only joy, in those thrilling yellow bows, a frou-frou skirt of many ruffles and a crop top revealing inches of childish nut-brown belly, and as we pressed up against the pair of them in this bottleneck of mothers and daughters entering the church I watched with interest as Tracey's mother pushed the girl in front of herself—and in front of us—using her own body as a means of obstruction, the flesh on her arms swinging as she beat us back, until she arrived in Miss Isabel's dance class, a look of great pride and anxiety on her face, ready to place her precious cargo into the temporary care of others. My mother's attitude, by contrast, was one of weary, semi-ironic servitude, she thought the dance class ridiculous, she had better things to do, and after a few further Saturdays—in which she sat slumped in one of the plastic chairs that lined the left-hand wall, hardly able to contain her contempt for the whole exercise—a change was made and my father took over. I waited for Tracey's father to take over, but he never did. It turned out—as my mother had guessed at once—that there was no "Tracey's father," at least not in the conventional, married sense. This, too, was an example of bad taste.

Two

I want to describe the church now, and Miss Isabel. An unpretentious nineteenth-century building with large sandy stones on the façade, not unlike the cheap cladding you saw in the nastier houses—though it couldn't have been that—and a satisfying, pointy steeple atop a plain, barn-like interior. It was called St. Christopher's. It looked just like the church we made with our fingers when we sang:

Here is the church
Here is the steeple
Open the doors
There's all the people.

The stained glass told the story of St. Christopher carrying the baby Jesus on his shoulders across a river. It was poorly done: the saint looked mutilated, one-armed. The original windows had blown out during the war. Opposite St. Christopher's stood a high-rise estate of poor reputation, and this was where Tracey lived. (Mine was nicer, low-rise, in the next street.) Built in the sixties, it replaced a row of Victorian houses lost in the same bombing that had damaged the church, but here ended the relationship between the two buildings. The church, unable to tempt residents across the road for God, had made a pragmatic decision to diversify into other areas: a toddlers' playgroup, ESL, driver training. These were popular, and well established, but Saturday-morning dance classes were a new addition and no one knew quite what to make of them. The class itself cost two pounds fifty, but a maternal rumor went round concerning the going rate for ballet shoes, one woman had heard three pounds, another seven, so-and-so swore the only place you could get them was Freed, in Covent Garden, where they'd take ten quid off you as soon as look at you—and then what about "tap" and what about "modern?" Could ballet shoes be worn for modern? What **was** modern? There was no one you could ask, no one who'd already done it, you were stuck. It was a rare mother whose curiosity extended to calling the number written on the homemade flyers stapled to the local trees. Many girls who might have made fine dancers never made it across that road, for fear of a homemade flyer.

My mother was rare: homemade flyers did not scare her. She had a terrific instinct for middle-class mores. She knew, for example, that a car-boot sale—despite its unpromising name—was where you could find a better quality of person, and also their old Penguin paperbacks, sometimes by Orwell, their old china pill-boxes, their cracked Cornish earthenware, their discarded potter's wheels. Our flat was full of such things. No plastic flowers for us, sparkly with fake dew, and no crystal figurines. This was all part of the plan. Even things I hated—like my mother's espadrilles—usually turned out to be attractive to the kind of people we were trying to attract, and I learned not to question her methods, even when they filled me with shame. A week before classes were due to begin I heard her doing her posh voice in the galley kitchen, but when she got off the phone she had all the answers: five pounds for ballet shoes—if you went to the shopping center instead of up into town—and the tap shoes could wait till later. Ballet shoes could be used for modern. What was modern? She hadn't asked. The concerned parent she would play, but never, ever the ignorant one.

My father was sent to get the shoes. The pink of the leather turned out to be a lighter shade than I'd hoped, it looked like the underside of a kitten, and the sole was a dirty gray cat's tongue, and there were no long pink satin ribbons to criss-cross over the ankles, no, only a sad little elastic strap which my father had sewn on himself. I was extremely bitter about it. But perhaps they were, like the espadrilles, deliberately "simple," in good taste? It was possible to hold on to this idea right up to the moment when, having entered the hall, we were told to change into our dance clothes by the plastic chairs and go over to the opposite wall, to the barre. Almost everybody had the pink satin shoes, not the pale pink, piggy leather I was stuck with, and some—girls whom I knew to be on benefits, or fatherless, or both—had the shoes with long satin ribbons, criss-crossing round their ankles. Tracey, who was standing next to me, with her left foot in her mother's hand, had both—the deep pink satin and the criss-cross—and also a full tutu, which no one else had even considered as a possibility, no more than turning up to a first swimming lesson in a diving suit. Miss Isabel, meanwhile, was sweet-faced and friendly, but old, perhaps as old as forty-five. It was disappointing. Solidly constructed, she looked more like a farmer's wife than a ballet dancer and was all over pink and yellow, pink and yellow. Her hair was yellow, not blond, yellow like a canary. Her skin was very pink, raw pink, now that I think of it she probably suffered from rosacea. Her leotard was pink, her tracksuit bottoms were pink, her cover-up ballet cardigan was mohair and pink—yet her shoes were silk and yellow, the same shade as her hair. I was bitter about this, too. Yellow had never been mentioned! Next to her, in the corner, a very old white man in a trilby sat playing an upright piano, "Night and Day," a song I loved and was proud to recognize. I got the old songs from my father, whose own father had been a keen pub singer, the kind of man—or so my father believed—whose petty criminality represents, at least in part, some thwarted creative instinct. The piano player was called Mr. Booth. I hummed loudly along with him as he played, hoping to be heard, putting a lot of vibrato into my humming. I was a better singer than dancer—I was not a dancer at all—although I took too much pride in my singing, in a manner I knew my mother found obnoxious. Singing came naturally to me, but things that came naturally to females did not impress my mother, not at all. In her view you might as well be proud of breathing or walking or giving birth.

Our mothers served as our balance, as our foot-rests. We placed one hand on their shoulders, we placed one foot on their bended knees. My body was presently in the hands of my mother—being hoiked up and tied down, fastened and straight-ened, brushed off—but my mind was on Tracey, and on the soles of her ballet shoes, upon which I now read "Freed" clearly stamped in the leather. Her natural arches were two hummingbirds in flight, curved in on themselves. My own feet were square and flat, they seemed to grind through the positions. I felt like a toddler placing wooden blocks at a series of right angles to each other. Flutter, flutter, flutter said Isabel, yes that's lovely Tracey. Compliments made Tracey throw her head back and flare her little pig nose awfully. Aside from that, she was perfection, I was besotted. Her mother seemed equally infatuated, her commitment to those classes the only consistent feature of what we would now call "her parenting." She came to class more than any other mother, and while there her attention rarely wavered from her daughter's feet. My own mother's focus was always elsewhere. She could never simply sit somewhere and let time pass, she had to be learning something. She might arrive at the beginning of class with, say, **The Black Jacobins** in hand, and by the time I came over to ask her to swap my ballet shoes for tap she would already be a hundred pages through. Later, when my father took over, he either slept or "went for a walk," the parental euphemism for smoking in the churchyard.

At this early stage Tracey and I were not friends or enemies or even acquaintances: we barely spoke. Yet there was always this mutual awareness, an invisible band strung between us, connecting us and preventing us from straying too deeply into relations with others. Technically, I spoke more to Lily Bingham—who went to my school—and Tracey's own standby was sad old Danika Babić, with her ripped tights and thick accent, she lived on Tracey's corridor. But though we giggled and joked with these white girls during class, and although they had every right to assume that they were our focus, our central concern—that we were, to them, the good friends we appeared to be—as soon as it came to break-time and squash and biscuits Tracey and I lined up next to each other, every time, it was almost unconscious, two iron filings drawn to a magnet.

It turned out Tracey was as curious about my family as I was about hers, arguing, with a certain authority, that we had things "the wrong way round." I listened to her theory one day during break, dipping a biscuit anxiously into my orange squash. "With everyone else it's the dad," she said, and because I knew this to be more or less accurate I could think of nothing more to say. "When your dad's white it means—" she continued, but at that moment Lily Bingham came and stood next to us and I never did learn what it meant when your dad was white. Lily was gangly, a foot taller than everyone else. She had long, perfectly straight blond hair, pink cheeks and a happy, open nature that seemed, both to Tracey and me, the direct consequence of 29 Exeter Road, a whole house, to which I had been recently invited, eagerly reporting back to Tracey—who had never been—a private garden, a giant jam-jar full of "spare change" and a Swatch watch as big as a human man hanging on a bedroom wall. There were, consequently, things you couldn't discuss in front of Lily Bingham, and now Tracey shut her mouth, stuck her nose in the air and crossed the room to ask her mother for her ballet shoes.

Three

What do we want from our mothers when we are children? Complete submission.

Oh, it's very nice and rational and respectable to say that a woman has every right to her life, to her ambitions, to her needs, and so on—it's what I've always demanded myself—but as a child, no, the truth is it's a war of attrition, rationality doesn't come into it, not one bit, all you want from your mother is that she once and for all admit that she is your mother and only your mother, and that her battle with the rest of life is over. She has to lay down arms and come to you. And if she doesn't do it, then it's really a war, and it was a war between my mother and me. Only as an adult did I come to truly admire her—especially in the last, painful years of her life—for all that she had done to claw some space in this world for herself. When I was young her refusal to submit to me confused and wounded me, especially as I felt none of the usual reasons for refusal applied. I was her only child and she had no job—not back then—and she hardly spoke to the rest of her family. As far as I was concerned, she had nothing but time. Yet still I couldn't get her complete submission! My earliest sense of her was of a woman plotting an escape, from me, from the very role of motherhood. I felt sorry for my father. He was still a fairly young man, he loved her, he wanted more children—it was their daily argument—but on this issue, as on all things, my mother refused to budge. Her mother had birthed seven children, her grandmother, eleven. She was not going back to all that. She believed my father wanted more children in order to entrap her, and she was basically right about that, although entrapment in this case was only another word for love. How he loved her! More than she knew or cared to know, she was someone who lived in her own dreamscape, who presumed that everyone around her was at all times feeling exactly as she was. And so when she began, first slowly, and then with increasing speed, to outgrow my father, both intellectually and personally, she naturally expected that he was undergoing the same process at the same time. But he carried on as before. Looking after me, loving her, trying to keep up, reading **The Communist Manifesto** in his slow and diligent way. "Some people carry the bible," he told me proudly. "This is my bible." It sounded impressive—it was meant to impress my mother—but I had already noticed that he seemed to always be reading this book and not much else, he took it to every dance class, and yet never got any further than the first twenty pages. Within the context of the marriage it was a romantic gesture: they'd first encountered each other at a meeting of the SWP, in Dollis Hill. But even this was a form of misunderstanding for my father had gone to meet nice leftist girls in short skirts with no religion while my mother really was there for Karl Marx. My childhood took place in the widening gap. I watched my autodidact mother swiftly, easily, outstrip my father. The shelves in our lounge—which he built—filled up with second-hand books, Open University textbooks, political books, history books, books on race, books on gender, "All the 'isms,'" as my father liked to call them, whenever a neighbor happened to come by and spot the queer accumulation.

Saturday was her "day off." Day off from what? From us. She needed to read up on her isms. After my father took me to dance class we had to keep going somehow, find something to do, stay out of the flat until dinner time. It became our ritual to travel on a series of buses heading south, far south of the river, to my Uncle Lambert's, my mother's brother and a confidant of my father's. He was my mother's eldest sibling, the only person I ever saw from her side of the family. He had raised my mother and the rest of her brothers and sisters, back on the island, when their mother left for England to work as a cleaner in a retirement home. He knew what my father was dealing with.

"I take a step toward her," I heard my father complain, one day, in high summer, "and she takes a step back!"

"Cyan do nuttin wid er. Always been like dat."

I was in the garden, among the tomato plants. It was an allotment, really, nothing was decorative or meant simply to be admired, everything was to be eaten and grew in long, straight lines, tied to sticks of bamboo. At the end of it all was an outhouse, the last I ever saw in England. Uncle Lambert and my father sat on deckchairs by the back door, smoking marijuana. They were old friends—Lambert was the only other person in my parents' wedding photo—and they had work in common: Lambert was a postman and my father a Delivery Office Manager for Royal Mail. They shared a dry sense of humor and a mutual lack of ambition, of which my mother took a dim view, in both cases. As they smoked and lamented the things you couldn't do with my mother, I passed my arms through the tomato vines, allowing them to twist around my wrists. Most of Lambert's plants seemed menacing to me, they were twice my height and everything he planted grew wildly: a thicket of vines and high grass and obscenely swollen, calabash-type gourds. The soil is of a better quality in South London—in North London we have too much clay—but at the time I didn't know about that and my ideas were confused: I thought that when I visited Lambert I was visiting Jamaica, Lambert's garden was Jamaica to me, it smelled like Jamaica, and you ate coconut ice there, and even now, in my memory, it is always hot in Lambert's garden, and I am thirsty and fearful of insects. The garden was long and thin and it faced south, the outhouse abutted the right-hand fence, so you could watch the sun fall behind it, rippling the air as it went. I wanted badly to go to the toilet but had decided to hold on to the urge until we saw North London again—I was scared of that outhouse. The floor was wood and things grew up between the boards, grass blades, and thistles and dandelion clocks that dusted your knee as you hitched yourself up on to the seat. Spiders' webs connected the corners. It was a garden of abundance and decay: the tomatoes were too ripe, the marijuana too strong, woodlice were hiding under everything. Lambert lived all alone there, and it felt to me like a dying place. Even at that age I thought it odd that my father should travel eight miles to Lambert's for comfort when Lambert seemed already to have suffered the kind of abandonment my father feared so badly.

Tiring of walking through the lines of vegetables, I wandered back down the garden, and watched as the two men concealed their joints, poorly, in their fists.

"You bored?" asked Lambert. I confessed I was.

"Once dis house full of pick'ney," said Lambert, "but dem children got children now."

The image I had was of children my own age

with babies in their arms: it was a fate I connected with South London. I knew my mother left home to escape all that, so that no daughter of hers would ever become a child with a child, for any daughter of hers was to do more than just survive—as my mother had—she was to thrive, learning many unnecessary skills, like tap dancing. My father reached out for me and I crawled on to his lap, covering his growing bald spot with my hand and feeling the thin strands of wet hair he wore combed across it.

"She shy, eh? You not shy of your Uncle Lambert?"

Lambert's eyes were bloodshot, and his freckles were like mine but raised; his face was round and sweet, with light brown eyes that confirmed, supposedly, Chinese blood in the family tree. But I was shy of him. My mother—who never visited Lambert, except at Christmas—was strangely insistent that my father and I do so, though always with the proviso that we remain alert, never allowing ourselves to be "dragged back." Into what? I wound myself around my father's body until I was at the back of him and could see the little patch of hair he kept long at the nape of his neck, which he was so determined to maintain. Though he was only in his thirties, I'd never seen my father with a full head of hair, never known him blond, and would never know him gray. It was this fake nut-brown I knew, which came off on your fingers if you touched it, and which I had seen at its true source, a round, shallow tin that sat open on the edge of the bath, with an oily wheel of brown running round the rim, worn down to a bare patch in the middle, just like my father.

"She needs company," he fretted. "A book's no good, is it? A film's no good. You need the real thing."

"Cyan do nuttin wid dat woman. I knew it from time she was small. Her will is a will of iron."

It was true. Nothing could be done with her. When we got home she was watching a lecture from the Open University, pad and pencil in her hand, looking beautiful, serene, curled up on the couch with her bare feet under her bottom, but when she turned round I could see she was annoyed, we'd come back too early, she wanted more time, more peace, more quiet, so she could study. We were the vandals in the temple. She was studying Sociology & Politics. We didn't know why.

Four

If Fred Astaire represented the aristocracy, I represented the proletariat, said Gene Kelly, and by
this logic Bill "Bojangles" Robinson should really
have been my dancer, because Bojangles danced
for the Harlem dandy, for the ghetto kid, for the
sharecropper—for all the descendants of slaves.
But to me a dancer was a man from nowhere,
without parents or siblings, without a nation or
people, without obligations of any kind, and this
was exactly the quality I loved. The rest of it, all
the detail, fell away. I ignored the ridiculous plots
of those movies: the opera-like comings and go-
ings, the reversals of fortune, the outrageous meet
cutes and coincidences, the minstrels, maids and
butlers. To me they were only roads leading to the
dance. The story was the price you paid for the
rhythm. "Pardon me, boy, is that the Chattanooga
choo choo?" Each syllable found its corresponding
movement in the legs, the stomach, the backside,
the feet. In ballet hour, by contrast, we danced
to classical recordings—"white music" as Tracey
bluntly called it—which Miss Isabel recorded from

the radio on to a series of cassettes. But I could barely recognize it as music, it had no time signature that I could hear, and although Miss Isabel tried to help us, shouting out the beats of each bar, I could never relate these numbers in any way to the sea of melody that came over me from the violins or the crashing thump of a brass section. I still knew more than Tracey: I knew there was something not quite right about her rigid notions— black music, white music—that there must be a world somewhere in which the two combined. In films and photographs I had seen white men sitting at their pianos as black girls stood by them, singing. Oh, I wanted to be like those girls!

At quarter past eleven, just after ballet, in the middle of our first break, Mr. Booth entered the hall carrying a big black bag, the kind country doctors once carried, and in this bag he kept the sheet music for class. If I was free—which meant, if I could get away from Tracey—I hurried over to him, following him as he slowly approached the piano, and then positioning myself like the girls I'd seen onscreen, I asked him to play "All of Me" or "Autumn in New York" or "42nd Street." In the tap class he had to play the same half a dozen songs over and over and I had to dance to them, but before class—while the rest of the people in the hall were busy talking, eating, drinking—we had this time to ourselves, and I'd get him to work through a tune with me, singing below the vol-

ume of the piano if I was feeling shy, a little louder
if not. Sometimes when I sang the parents smoking outside the hall under the cherry trees would
come in to listen, and girls who were busy preparing for their own dances—pulling on tights,
tying laces—paused in these actions and turned
to watch me. I became aware that my voice—as
long as I did not deliberately sing underneath the
volume of the piano—had something charismatic
in it, drawing people in. This was not a technical
gift: my range was tiny. It had to do with emotion. Whatever I was feeling I was able to express
very clearly, I could "put it over." I made sad songs
very sad, and happy songs joyful. When the time
came for our "performance exams" I learned to use
my voice as a form of misdirection, the same way
some magicians make you look at their mouths
when you should be watching their hands. But I
couldn't fool Tracey. I saw her as I walked off the
stage, standing in the wings with her arms crossed
over her chest and her nose in the air. Even though
she always trumped everybody and her mother's
kitchen corkboard heaved with gold medals, she
was never satisfied, she wanted gold in "my" category, too—song and dance—though she could
hardly sing a note. It was difficult to understand. I
really felt that if I could dance like Tracey I would
never want for anything else in this world. Other
girls had rhythm in their limbs, some had it in their
hips or their little backsides but she had rhythm in

individual ligaments, probably in individual cells. Every movement was as sharp and precise as any child could hope to make it, her body could align itself with any time signature, no matter how intricate. Maybe you could say she was overly precise sometimes, not especially creative, or lacking in soul. But no one sane could quarrel with her technique. I was—I am—in awe of Tracey's technique. She knew the right time to do everything.

Five

A Sunday in late summer. I was on the balcony, watching a few girls from our floor skipping Double Dutch down by the bins. I heard my mother calling me. I looked over and saw her entering the estate, hand in hand with Miss Isabel. I waved, and she looked up, smiled and shouted, "Stay there!" I had never seen my mother and Miss Isabel together outside of class, and could tell even from this vantage point that Miss Isabel was being hustled into something. I wanted to go and confer with my father, who was painting a wall in the living room, but I knew my mother, so charming with strangers, had a short temper with her kin, and that "Stay there!" meant exactly that. I watched this odd pair move through the estate and into the stairwell, refracted in the glass blocks as a scatter of yellow and pink and mahogany brown. Meanwhile the girls by the bins switched the direction of their skipping ropes, a new jumper ran bravely into the vicious swinging loop and began a new chant, the one about the monkey who got choked.

Finally my mother came upon me, examined

me—she had a coy look on her face—and the first thing she said was: "Take your shoes off."

"Oh, we needn't do it right now," murmured Miss Isabel, but my mother said, "Better to know now than later," and disappeared into the flat, re-appearing a minute later with a large bag of self-raising flour, which she began sprinkling all over the balcony until there was a thin white carpet like first snowfall. I was to walk through this barefoot. I thought of Tracey. I wondered if Miss Isabel visited each girl's house in turn. What a terrible waste of flour! Miss Isabel crouched down to watch. My mother leaned back against the balcony with her elbows resting upon it, smoking a cigarette. She was at an angle to the balcony, and the cigarette was at an angle to her mouth, and she was wearing a beret, as if wearing a beret were the most natural thing in the world. She was positioned at an angle to me, an ironic angle. I reached the other end of the balcony and looked back at my footprints.

"Ah, well there you are," said Miss Isabel, but where were we? In the land of flat feet. My teacher slipped off a shoe and pressed her foot down for comparison: in her print you saw only the toes, the ball of the foot and the heel, in mine, the full, flat outline of a human tread. My mother was very interested in this result, but Miss Isabel, seeing my face, said something kind: "A ballet dancer needs an arch, yes, but you can tap with flat feet, you know, of course you can." I didn't think it was true, but it was kind and I clung to it and kept taking the class, and so continued to spend time with Tracey, which was, it dawned on me later, exactly the thing my mother had been trying to stop. She'd worked out that because Tracey and I went to different schools, in different neighborhoods, it was only dance class that brought us together, but when the summer came and dance class stopped, it made no difference anyway, we grew closer until, by August, we found ourselves together almost every day. From my balcony I could see into her estate and vice versa, no phone calls had to be made, and no formal arrangements, and although our mothers barely nodded at each other in the street it became a natural thing for us to pass in and out of each other's building.

Six

We had a different mode of being in each flat. In Tracey's we played and tested new toys, of which there appeared to be an unending supply. The Argos catalog, from whose pages I was allowed to choose three inexpensive items at Christmas, and one item for my birthday, was, to Tracey, an everyday bible, she read it religiously, circling her choices, often while in my company, with a little red pen she kept for this purpose. Her bedroom was a revelation. It overturned everything I thought I had understood about our shared situation. Her bed was in the shape of a pink Barbie sports car, her curtains were frilled, all her cabinets were white and shiny, and in the middle of the room it looked like someone had simply emptied Santa's sleigh on to the carpet. You had to **wade** through toys. Broken toys formed a kind of bedrock, on top of which each new wave of purchases was placed, in archeological layers, corresponding, more or less, to whatever toy adverts were playing on the television at the time. That summer was the summer of the pissing doll. You fed her water and she pissed everywhere. Tracey had several versions of this stunning technology, and was able to draw all kinds of drama from it. Sometimes she would beat the doll for pissing. Sometimes she would sit her, ashamed and naked, in the corner, her plastic legs twisted at right angles to her little, dimpled bum. We two played the poor, incontinent child's parents, and in the dialog Tracey gave me to say I sometimes heard odd, discomfiting echoes of her own home life, or else of the many soaps she watched, I couldn't be sure.

"Your turn. Say: 'You slag—she ain't even my kid! Is it my fault she pisses 'erself?' Go on, your turn!"

"You slag—she's not even my daughter! Is it my fault if she pisses herself?"

" 'Listen, mate, you take her! You take her and see how you do!' Now say: 'Fat chance, sunshine!' "

One Saturday, with great trepidation, I mentioned the existence of pissing dolls to my mother, being careful to say "wee" instead of "piss." She was studying. She looked up from her books with a mixture of incredulity and disgust.

"Tracey has one?"

"Tracey has **four**."

"Come here a minute."

She opened her arms, and I felt my face against the skin of her chest, taut and warm, utterly vital, as if there were a second, graceful young woman inside my mother bursting to get out. She had been growing her hair, it had been recently "done," plaited into a dramatic conch-shell shape at the back of her head, like a piece of sculpture.

"You know what I'm reading about right now?"

"No."

"I'm reading about the sankofa. You know what that is?"

"No."

"It's a bird, it looks back over itself, like this." She bent her beautiful head round as far as it could go. "From Africa. It looks backward, at the past, and it learns from what's gone before. Some people never learn."

My father was in the tiny galley kitchen, silently cooking—he was the chef in our home—and this conversation was really addressed to him, it was he who was meant to hear it. The two of them had begun arguing so much that I was often the only conduit through which information could pass, sometimes abusively—"You explain to your mother" or "You can tell your father from me"—and sometimes like this, with a delicate, an almost beautiful irony.

"Oh," I said. I didn't see the connection with pissing dolls. I knew my mother was in the process of becoming, or trying to become, "an intellectual," because my father often threw this term at her as a form of insult during their arguments. But I did not really understand what this meant, other than that an intellectual was someone who studied with the Open University, liked to wear a beret, frequently used the phrase "the Angel of History," sighed when the rest of their family wanted to watch Saturday-night telly and stopped to argue with the Trotskyites on the Kilburn High Road when everybody else crossed the road to avoid them. But the main consequence of her transformation, for me, was this new and puzzling indirection in her conversation. She always seemed to be making adult jokes just over my head, to amuse herself, or to annoy my father.

"When you're with that girl," explained my mother, "it's a kind thing to play with her, but she's been raised in a certain way, and the present is all she has. You've been raised in another way— don't forget that. That silly dance class is her whole world. It's not her fault—that's how she's been raised. But you're clever. Doesn't matter if you've got flat feet, doesn't matter **because you're clever** and you know where you came from and where you're going."

I nodded. I could hear my father banging saucepans expressively.

"You won't forget what I just said?"

I promised I wouldn't.

In our flat there were no dolls at all and so Tracey when she came was forced into different habits. Here we wrote, a little frantically, into a series of yellow, lined, A4 pads that my father brought home from work. It was a collaborative project. Tracey, because of her dyslexia—though we didn't know to call it that at the time—preferred to dictate, while I struggled to keep up with the naturally melo-dramatic twist and turn of her mind. Almost all our stories concerned a cruel, posh prima ballerina from "Oxford Street" breaking her leg at the last minute, which allowed our plucky heroine—often a lowly costume fitter, or a humble theater-toilet cleaner—to step in and save the day. I noticed that they were always blond, these plucky girls, with hair "like silk" and big blue eyes. Once I tried to write "brown eyes" and Tracey took the pen out of my hand and scratched it out. We wrote on our bellies, flat on the floor of my room, and if my mother happened to come by and see us like this it was the only moment she ever looked at Tracey with anything like fondness. I took advantage of these moments to win further concessions for my friend—Can Tracey stay for tea? Can Tracey stay the night?—though I knew if my mother actually paused to read what we wrote in those yellow pads Tracey would never be allowed into the flat again. In several stories African men "lurked in the shad-ows" with iron bars to break the knees of lily-white dancers; in one, the prima had a terrible secret: she was "half-caste," a word I trembled to write down, as I knew from experience how completely it en-raged my mother. But if I felt unease about these details it was a small sensation when compared to the pleasure of our collaboration. I was so completely taken with Tracey's stories, besotted with their endless delay of narrative gratification, which was again perhaps something she had got from the soaps or else extracted from the hard lessons her own life was teaching her. For just as you thought the happy ending had arrived, Tracey found some wonderful new way to destroy or divert it, so that the moment of consummation—which for both of us, I think, meant simply an audience, on their feet, cheering—never seemed to arrive. I wish I had those notepads still. Of all the thousands of words we wrote about ballerinas in various forms of physical danger only one sentence has stayed with me: **Tiffany jumped up high to kiss her prince and pointed her toes oh she looked so sexy but that's when the bullet went right up her thigh.**

Seven

In the autumn Tracey went off to her single-sex school, in Neasden, where almost all the girls were Indian or Pakistani and wild: I used to see the older ones at the bus stop, uniforms adapted— shirt unbuttoned, skirt hitched up—screaming obscenities at white boys as they passed. A rough school with a lot of fighting. Mine, in Willesden, was milder, more mixed: half black, a quarter white, a quarter South Asian. Of the black half at least a third were "half-caste," a minority nation within a nation, though the truth is it annoyed me to notice them. I wanted to believe that Tracey and I were sisters and kindred spirits, alone in the world and in special need of each other, but now I could not avoid seeing in front of me all the many kinds of children my mother had spent the summer trying to encourage me toward, girls with similar backgrounds but what my mother called "broader horizons." There was a girl called Tasha, half Guyanese, half Tamil, whose father was a real Tamil Tiger, which impressed my mother mightily and thus cemented in me the desire never to have anything whatsoever to do with the girl. There was a buck-toothed girl called Irie, always top of the class, whose parents were the same way round as us, but she'd moved out of the estate and now lived up in Willesden Green in a fancy maisonette. There was a girl called Anoushka with a father from St. Lucia and a Russian mother whose uncle was, according to my mother, "the most important revolutionary poet in the Caribbean," but almost every word of that recommendation was incomprehensible to me. My mind was not on school, or any of the people there. In the playground I pushed drawing pins into the soles of my shoes and sometimes spent the whole half-hour of playtime dancing alone, contentedly friendless. And when we got home—before my mother, and therefore outside of her jurisdiction—I dropped my satchel, left my father cooking dinner and headed straight to Tracey's, to do our time-steps together on her balcony, followed by a bowl each of Angel Delight, which was "not food" to my mother but in my opinion still delicious. By the time I came home an argument, the two sides of which no longer met, would be in full flow. My father's concern would be some tiny domestic issue: who'd vacuumed what when, who'd gone, or should have gone, to the launderette. Whereas my mother, in answering him, would stray into quite other topics: the importance of having a revolutionary consciousness, or the relative insignificance of sexual love when placed beside the struggles of the people, or the legacy of slavery in the hearts and minds of the young, and so on. She had by now finished her A levels, was enrolled at Middlesex Poly, up in Hendon, and more than ever we could not keep up, we were a disappointment, she had to keep explaining her terms.

At Tracey's, the only raised voices came from the television. I knew I was meant to pity Tracey for her fatherlessness—the blight marking every other door on our corridor—and to be thankful for my two married parents, but whenever I sat on her huge white leather settee eating her Angel Delight and peacefully watching **Easter Parade** or **The Red Shoes**—Tracey's mother would tolerate only Technicolor musicals—I couldn't help but notice the placidity of a small, all-female household. In Tracey's home, disappointment in the man was ancient history: they had never really had any hope in him, for he had almost never been at home. No one was surprised by Tracey's father's failure to foment revolution or do anything else. Yet Tracey was steadfast and loyal to his memory, far more likely to defend her absent father than I was to speak kindly of my wholly attentive one. Whenever her mother bad-mouthed him, Tracey would make sure to take me into her room, or some other private spot, and quickly integrate whatever her mother had just said into her own official story, which was that her father had not abandoned her, no, not at all, he was only very busy because he was one of Michael Jackson's backing dancers. Few people could keep up with Michael Jackson as he danced—in fact, almost nobody could, maybe there were only twenty dancers in the whole world who were up to it. Tracey's father was one such. He hadn't even had to finish his audition—he was that good they knew right away. This was why he was hardly ever home: he was on an eternal world tour. The next time he would be in town was probably next Christmas, when Michael played Wembley. On a clear day we could see this stadium from Tracey's balcony. It's hard for me to say now how much credence I gave this tale—certainly some part of me knew that Michael Jackson, at last free of his family, now danced alone—but just like Tracey I never brought up the subject in her mother's presence. As a fact it was, in my mind, at one and the same time absolutely true and obviously untrue, and perhaps only children are able to accommodate double-faced facts like these.

Eight

I was at Tracey's, watching **Top of the Pops**, when the **Thriller** video came on, it was the first time any of us had seen it. Tracey's mother got very excited: without actually standing, she danced madly, bopping up and down in the creases of her recliner. "Go on, girls! Let's be having you! Get moving— come on!" We unstuck ourselves from the sofa and began sliding back and forth across the rug, me poorly, Tracey with a good deal of skill. We spun round, we lifted our right legs, leaving the foot dangling like the foot of a puppet, we jerked our zombie bodies. There was so much new information: the red leather trousers, the red leather jacket, what had once been an Afro now transformed into something greater even than Tracey's own ringlets! And of course that pretty brown girl in blue, the potential victim. Was she "half-caste" too?

Due to my strong personal convictions, I wish to stress that this film in no way endorses a belief in the occult.

So read the credits, at the beginning, these were Michael's own words, but what did they mean?

We understood only the seriousness of this word "film." What we were watching was not a music video at all, it was a work of art that should properly be seen in a cinema, it was really a world event, a clarion call. We were modern! This was modern life! Generally I felt distant from modern life and the music that came with it—my mother had made a sankofa bird of me—but it happened that my father had told me a story about Fred Astaire himself once coming to Michael's house, coming as a kind of disciple, and he had begged Michael to teach him the moonwalk, and this makes sense to me, even now, for a great dancer has no time, no generation, he moves eternally through the world, so that any dancer in any age may recognize him. Picasso would be incomprehensible to Rembrandt, but Nijinsky would understand Michael Jackson. "Don't stop now, girls—get up!" cried Tracey's mother, when for a moment we paused to rest against her sofa. "Don't stop till you get enough! Get moving!" How long that song seemed—longer than life. I felt it would never end, that we were caught in a time loop, and would have to dance in this demonic way for ever, like poor Moira Shearer in **The Red Shoes**: "Time rushes by, love rushes by, life rushes by, but the red shoes dance on . . ." But then it was over. "That was fucking priceless," sighed Tracey's mother, forgetting herself, and we bowed and curtsied and ran to Tracey's room.

"She loves it when she sees him on TV," confided Tracey, once we were alone. "It makes their love stronger. She sees him and she knows he still loves her."

"Which one was he?" I asked.

"Second row, at the end, on the right," replied Tracey, without missing a beat.

I did not try—it wasn't possible—to integrate these "facts" about Tracey's father with the very few occasions I actually saw him, the first of which was the most terrible, it was in early November, not long after we had watched **Thriller**. We were all three in the kitchen, trying to make jacket potatoes stuffed with cheese and bacon, we were going to wrap them in foil and take them with us to Roundwood Park, where we'd watch the fireworks. The kitchens in the flats on Tracey's estate were even smaller than the kitchens in ours: when you opened the oven door it almost scraped the wall opposite. To have three people in there at the same time, one person—in this case, Tracey—had to sit on the counter. It was her job to scrape the potato out of its jacket, and then my job, standing next to her, to mix the potato with grated cheese and bacon bits snipped with a pair of scissors, and then her mother put it all back in the jacket and returned it to the oven for browning. Despite my mother's constant implication that Tracey's mother was slovenly, a magnet for chaos, I found her kitchen both cleaner and more orderly than ours. The food was never healthy and yet it was prepared with seriousness and care, whereas my mother, who aspired to healthy eating, could not spend fifteen minutes in a kitchen without being reduced to a sort of self-pitying mania, and quite often the whole, misguided experiment (to make vegetarian lasagne, to do "something" with okra) became so torturous for everybody that she would manufacture a row and storm off, shouting. We would end up eating Findus Crispy Pancakes again. Round Tracey's, things were simpler: you began with the clear intention of making Findus Crispy Pancakes or pizza (from frozen) or sausages and chips and it was all delicious and no one shouted about it. These potatoes were a special treat, a Fireworks Night tradition. Outside it was dark, though only five in the afternoon, and all over the estate you could smell gunpowder. Each flat had its private arsenal, and the random bangs and small, localized conflagrations had begun two weeks before, as soon as the sweetshops started selling fireworks. No one waited for official events. Cats were the most frequent victims of this general pyromania, but every now and then some kid went off to Casualty. Because of all the banging—and how used we were to bangs—at first the sound of someone beating on Tracey's front door didn't register, but then we heard somebody half yelling and half whispering, and we recognized panic and caution fighting each other. It was a man's voice, he was saying: "Let me in. Let me in! You there? Open up, woman!"

Tracey and I stared at her mother, who stood staring back at us, holding a tray of perfectly stuffed cheesy potatoes in her hand. Without looking at what she was doing, she tried to lower the tray on to the counter, misjudged, dropped it.

"Louie?" she said.

She grabbed us both, pulled Tracey off the counter, we stepped in potato. She dragged us down the hall and pushed us into Tracey's room. We were not to move a muscle. She closed the door and left us alone. Tracey went straight to her bed, got in it and began playing **Pac-Man**. She wouldn't look at me. It was clear I couldn't ask her anything, not even if Louie was the name of her father. I stood where her mother had left me and waited. I had never heard such a commotion in Tracey's house. Whoever Louie was, he had now been let in— or forced his way in—and **fuck** was every other word, and there were great, crashing thuds as he turned the furniture over, and a terrible feminine wailing, it sounded like a screaming fox. I stood by the door looking at Tracey, who was still tucked up in her Barbie bed, but she did not seem to hear what I heard or even to remember that I was there: she never looked up from her **Pac-Man**. Ten minutes later, it was over: we heard the front door slam shut. Tracey stayed in her bed and I stood where I had been planted, unable to make any move. After a while there was a light knock on the door, and Tracey's mother came in, pink with crying, holding a tray of Angel Delight, the same pink as her face. We sat and ate in silence and, later, went to the fireworks.

Nine

There was a kind of carelessness among the mothers we knew, or it looked like carelessness to outsiders but we knew it by another name. To the teachers at the school it probably looked as if they didn't care enough even to turn up for Parents' Evening, where, at desk after desk, the teachers sat, staring into space, waiting patiently for these mothers who never came. And I can see that our mothers must have seemed a little careless when, informed by a teacher of some misbehavior in the playground, they would—instead of reprimanding the child—begin shouting at the teacher. But we understood our mothers a little better. We knew that they, in their own time, had feared school, just as we did now, feared the arbitrary rules and felt shamed by them, by the new uniforms they couldn't afford, the baffling obsession with quiet, the incessant correcting of their original patois or cockney, the sense that they could never do anything right anyway. A deep anxiety about "being told off"—for who they were, for what they had or hadn't done, and now for the deeds of their children—this fear never really left our mothers, many of whom had become our mothers when they were not much more than children themselves. And so "Parents' Evening" was, in their minds, not so distant from "detention." It remained a place where they might be shamed. The difference was now they were grown and could not be forced to attend.

I say "our mothers," but of course mine was different: she had the anger but not the shame. She went to Parents' Evening, always. That year it was for some reason held on Valentine's Day: the hall was limply decorated with pink paper hearts stapled to the walls, and each desk sported a wilting rose of crinkled tissue paper atop a green pipe-cleaner. I trailed behind her as she made her way round the room, hectoring teachers, ignoring all attempts on their part to discuss my progress, instead giving a series of impromptu lectures about the incompetence of the school administration, the blindness and the stupidity of the local council, the desperate need for "teachers of color"—which I think was the first time I heard the new euphemism "of color." Those poor teachers clutched the sides of their desks for dear life. At one point, to emphasize a statement, she thumped a fist on a desk, sending the tissue rose and many pencils scattering to the floor: "These children deserve more!" Not me in particular—"these children." How I remember her doing that, and how wonderful she looked, like a queen! I was proud to be her child, the daughter of the only mother in the neighborhood free of shame. We swept out of the hall together, my mother triumphant, me in a state of awe, neither of us any the wiser as to how I was doing at school.

I do remember one occasion of shame, a few days before Christmas, a late afternoon on a Saturday, after dance class, after Lambert's, and I was watching a Fred and Ginger routine, "Pick Yourself Up," at my flat, with Tracey, over and over. Tracey had an ambition to one day re-create that whole routine herself—this seems to me now like looking at the Sistine Chapel and hoping to re-create it on your bedroom ceiling—though she only ever practiced the male part, it never occurred to either of us to learn Ginger's part in anything. Tracey was standing in the doorway to the living room, tap dancing—there was no carpet over there—and I was kneeling by the VHS, rewinding and pausing as necessary. My mother was in the kitchen on a high stool, studying. My father—and this was unusual—had gone "out," with no explanation, just "out," at about four o'clock, with no stated purpose and no errand to run that I knew of. At a certain point I ventured into the kitchen to get two beakers of Ribena. Instead of seeing my mother bent over her books, earplugs in, oblivious to me, I found her gazing out of the window, her face wet with tears. When she saw me she jumped a little in her skin, as if I were a ghost.

"They're here," she said, almost to herself. I

looked over to where she was looking and saw my father crossing the estate with two young white people trailing behind him, a boy of about twenty and a girl who looked to be fifteen or sixteen.

"Who's here?"

"Some people your father wants you to meet."

And the shame that she felt, I think, was the shame of no control: she could not dominate this situation nor protect me from it as, for once, it had nothing much to do with her. She hurried instead to the living room and told Tracey to leave, but Tracey was deliberately slow collecting up her things: she wanted to get a good look at them. They were a sight. Seen up close the boy had shaggy blond hair and a beard, he wore dirty, ugly, old-looking clothes, his jeans were patched and he had lots of rock-band badges pinned to his frayed canvas rucksack: he seemed to be shamelessly advertising his poverty. The girl was equally peculiar but neater, truly "white as snow," as in a fairy tale, with a severe black bob cut straight across her forehead and diagonally high at her ears. She was dressed all in black, with a big black pair of Dr. Martens on her feet, and she was petite, with delicate features—excepting a large, indecent bosom which she seemed to be trying to obscure with all this black. Tracey and I stood staring at them. "Time you went home," said my father, to Tracey, and watching her go I realized how much my ally she was, despite everything, for without her, at that

moment, I felt totally undefended. The white teenagers sloped into our small living room. My father asked them to sit, but only the girl did. I was
alarmed to see my mother, whom ordinarily I knew
to be a completely non-neurotic person, dithering
anxiously, stumbling over her words. The boy—
his name was John—would not sit down. When
my mother tried to encourage him to sit down he
wouldn't look at or reply to her, and then my father
said something uncharacteristically sharp, and we
all watched as John marched back out of the flat. I
ran to the balcony, and saw him down there on the
communal grass, not going anywhere—he had to
wait for the girl—stamping around in a small circle, crunching the hoar frost underfoot. This left
the girl. Her name was Emma. When I came back
in my mother told me to sit next to her. "This is
your sister," said my father and went to make a cup
of tea. My mother stood by the Christmas tree,
pretending to do something useful with the lights.
The girl turned to me, and we stared frankly at
each other. As far as I could see we had no features
in common at all, the whole thing was ridiculous,
and I could see that this Emma person thought
exactly the same of me. Apart from the comically
obvious fact that I was black and she was white, I
was big-boned and she was narrow, I was tall for
my age and she was short for hers, my eyes were
big and brown and hers were narrow and green.
But then, at the same moment, I felt we both saw

it; the downturned mouth, the sad eyes. I don't remember thinking logically, I didn't ask myself, for example, who the mother of this Emma was or how and when she could possibly have known my father. My head wouldn't go that far round. I only thought: he made one like me and one like her. How can two such different creatures emerge from the same source? My father came back into the room with a tray of tea.

"Well, this is all a bit of a surprise, isn't it?" he said, handing Emma a mug. "For all of us. It's a long time since I've seen . . . But you see your mum suddenly decided . . . Well, she's a woman of sudden whims, isn't she?" My sister looked blankly at my father, and he at once gave up whatever he was trying to say and downgraded to small talk. "Now, I'm told Emma does a bit of ballet. That's something you two have in common. At the Royal Ballet for a little while—full scholarship—but she had to stop."

Dancing on stage, did he mean? In Covent Garden? As a principal? Or in the "corpse," as Tracey called it? But no—"scholarship" sounded like a school matter. Was there, then, a "Royal Ballet School"? But if such a place existed why hadn't **I** been sent to it? And if this Emma had been sent there, who paid for it? Why did she have to stop? Because her chest was so large? Or did a bullet go right up her thigh?

"Maybe you'll dance together one day!" said my

mother into the silence, which was the kind of maternal inanity in which she very rarely indulged. Emma looked up at my mother fearfully—it was the first time she had dared look at her directly— and whatever she saw there had the power to freshly horrify: she burst into tears. My mother left the room. My father said to me: "Go out for a bit. Go on. Put your coat on."

I slipped off the sofa, grabbed my duffel coat off the hook and let myself out. I went down the walkway, trying to put what little I knew of my father's past together with this new reality. He was from Whitechapel, a large East End family, not as big as my mother's but not far off, and his father had been a minor criminal of some kind, in and out of jail, and this, my mother once explained to me, was why my father put so much effort into my childhood: cooking, taking me to school and to dance class, packing my lunches and so on, all unusual activities for a father, at the time. I was compensation—retribution—for his own childhood. I knew too that he had himself been, at one point, "no good." Once we were watching TV and something about the Kray twins came on and my father said casually, "Oh, well, everybody knew them, you couldn't help knowing them, at that time." His many siblings were "no good," the East End in general was "no good," and this all helped consolidate my idea of our own corner of London as a little, clear-aired peak above a general quagmire, into which you might be dragged back into real poverty and crime from several directions. But no one had ever mentioned a son or a daughter.

I took the stairs down to the communal area and stood resting against a concrete pillar, watching my "brother" kick up little scraps of half-frozen turf. With his long hair and beard and that long face he looked like adult Jesus to me, whom I knew solely from a cross on the wall at Miss Isabel's dance class. Unlike my reaction to the girl—simply that some kind of fraud was under way—looking at the boy I found I could not deny his essential rightness. It was right that he should be my father's son, any-one looking at him would see the sense of it. What didn't make sense was me. Something coldly ob-jective took me over: that same instinct that al-lowed me to separate my voice from my throat as an object of consideration, of study, came to me now, and I looked at this boy and thought: yes, he is right and I am wrong, isn't it interesting? I could have, I suppose, thought of myself as the true child and the boy as the counterfeit, but I didn't do that.

He turned round and spotted me. Something in his face told me I was being pitied, and I was moved when, with effortful kindness, he began a game of hide and seek around the concrete pillars. Every time his shaggy blond head popped out from behind a block I had that out-of-body sensation: here is my father's son, looking just like my father's son, isn't that interesting? As we played we heard raised voices from upstairs. I tried to ignore them, but my new playmate stopped running and stood under the balcony and listened. At a certain point the anger flashed back into his eyes and he said to me: "Let me tell you something: he don't care about no one. He's not what he seems. He's fucked up in the head. Marrying that bloody spade!"

And then the girl came running down the stairs. No one ran after her, not my father or my mother. She was still crying and she came to the boy and they hugged and, still hugging, walked across the grass and out of the estate. Snow was lightly falling. I watched them go. I didn't see them again until my father died and they were never spoken of during my childhood. For a long time I thought the whole thing was a hallucination, or perhaps something I'd lifted from a bad film. When Tracey asked me about it I told her the truth, although with some elaboration: I claimed that a building we walked past daily, on Willesden Lane, the one with the shabby blue awning, was the Royal Ballet School, and that my cruel white posh sister went there, and was very successful but refused even to wave to me from the window, can you believe it? As she listened I witnessed a great struggle in her face to believe it, mostly expressed by her nostrils. Of course Tracey very likely had been inside that building herself, and would have known perfectly well what it really was: a down-at-heel event space where a lot of cheap local weddings were held, and sometimes the bingo. A few weeks later, as I was sitting in the back of my mother's ridiculous car—a tiny, white, ostentatiously French 2CV with a CND sticker placed next to the tax disk—I spotted a hard-faced bride, half swallowed by tulle and ringlets, standing outside my Royal Ballet, smoking a fag, but I did not let this vision penetrate my fantasy. By then I had come to share my friend's insusceptibility to reality. And now—as if we were both trying to get on a see-saw at the same time—neither of us pressed too hard and a delicate equilibrium was allowed to persist. I could have my evil ballerina if she could have her backing dancer. Maybe I never got out of this habit of elaboration. Twenty years later over a difficult lunch I revisited the story of my ghostly siblings with my mother, who sighed, lit a cigarette and said: "Trust you to add snow."

Ten

Long before it became her career my mother had a political mind: it was in her nature to think of people collectively. Even as a child I noticed it, and felt instinctively that there was something chilly and unfeeling in her ability to analyze so precisely the people she lived among: her friends, her community, her own family. We were all, at one and the same time, people she knew and loved but also objects of study, living embodiments of all she seemed to be learning up at Middlesex Poly. She held herself apart, always. She never submitted, for example, to the neighborhood cult of "sharpness"— the passion for shiny shell-suits and sparkling fake gems, for whole days spent in the hair salon, children in fifty-quid trainers, settees paid for over several years on hire purchase—although neither would she ever entirely condemn it. People are not poor because they've made bad choices, my mother liked to say, they make bad choices because they're poor. But though she was serene and anthropological about these matters in her college essays—or while lecturing me and my father across the dinner table—I knew in her real life she was often exasperated. She didn't pick me up from school any more—my father did that now—because the scene there aggravated her too much, in particular the way, each afternoon, time collapsed, and all those mothers became kids again, kids who had come to collect their kids, and all of these kids together turned from school with relief, free finally to speak with each other in their own way, and to laugh and joke and eat ice cream from the waiting ice-cream van, and to make what they considered to be a natural amount of noise. My mother didn't fit into all of that any longer. She still cared for the group—intellectually, politically—but she was no longer one of them.

Every now and then she did get caught up in it, usually by some error of timing, and found herself trapped in a conversation with a mother, often Tracey's, on Willesden Lane. On these occasions she could turn callous, making a point of mentioning each new academic achievement of mine—or inventing some—although she knew that all Tracey's mother could offer in return was more of Miss Isabel's praise, which was, to my mother, an entirely worthless commodity. My mother was proud of trying harder than Tracey's mother, than all the mothers, of having got me into a half-decent state school instead of one of the several terrible ones. She was in a competition of caring, and yet her fellow contestants, like Tracey's mother, were so ill-equipped when placed beside her that it was a fatally lopsided battle. I often wondered: is it some kind of a trade-off? Do others have to lose so we can win?

One morning in early spring, my father and I ran into Tracey under our block, by the garages. She seemed agitated and though she said she was only cutting through our estate on the way to her own I felt certain she'd been waiting for me. She looked cold: I wondered whether she had been to school at all. I knew she sometimes bunked off, with the approval of her mother. (My mother had been shocked to see them both, one school-day after-noon, coming out of What She Wants on the high road, laughing, carrying a load of shopping bags.) I watched my father greet Tracey warmly. Unlike my mother, he had no anxiety in connection with her, he found her single-minded dedication to her dancing sweet, and also, I think, admirable—it appealed to his work ethic—and it was very clear that Tracey adored my father, was even a little in love with him. She was so painfully grateful for the way he talked to her like a father, although sometimes he went too far in this direction, not understanding that what came after borrowing a father for a few minutes was the pain of having to give him back.

"Exams coming up, aren't they?" he asked her now. "And how's all that going?"

Tracey stuck her nose proudly in the air: "I'm doing all six categories."

"'Course you are."

"For modern, though, I ain't doing it by myself, I'm pairing. Ballet's my strongest, then tap, then modern, then song and dance. I'm going for three golds at least, but if it was two golds and four silvers I'd be well happy with that."

"And so you should be."

She put her little hands on her hips. "You coming to watch us then or what?"

"Oh, I'll be there! With bells on! Cheering my girls on."

Tracey loved to boast to my father, she unfurled in his presence, sometimes even blushed, and the monosyllabic no and yes answers she tended to give to all other adults, including my mother, disappeared, to be replaced by this running babble, as if she thought that any pause in the flow might run the risk of losing my father's attention altogether.

"Got some news," she said casually, turning to me, and now I understood why we'd run into her. "My mum's sorted it."

"Sorted what?" I asked.

"I'm leaving my school," she said. "I'm coming to yours."

Later, at home, I told my mother this news, and

she, too, was surprised, and, I suspected, a little displeased, at this proof of Tracey's mother's exertion on her daughter's behalf more than anything else. She kissed her teeth: "I really didn't think she had it in her."

Eleven

It took Tracey moving to my classroom for me to understand what my classroom really was. I had thought it was a room full of children. In fact it was a social experiment. The dinner lady's daughter shared a desk with the son of an art critic, a boy whose father was presently in prison shared a desk with the son of a policeman. The child of the postal officer shared a desk with the child of one of Michael Jackson's backing dancers. One of Tracey's first acts as my new desk mate was to articulate these subtle differences by way of a simple, compelling analogy: Cabbage Patch Kids versus Garbage Pail Kids. Each child was categorized as one or the other and she made it clear that any friendship I had formed before her arrival was now—in as far as it may have attempted to cross this divide—null and void, worthless, for the truth was it had never truly existed in the first place. There could be no real friendship between Cabbage Patch and Garbage Pail, not right now, not in England. She emptied our desk of my beloved Cabbage Patch Kid card collection and replaced

them with her Garbage Pail Kid cards, which—
like almost everything Tracey did in school—at
once became the new craze. Even children who
were, in Tracey's eyes, Cabbage Patch types themselves began to collect the Garbage Pail Kids, even
Lily Bingham collected them, and we all competed with each other to own the most repulsive
cards: the Garbage Pail Kid with snot streaming
down his face, or the one pictured on the toilet.
Her other striking innovation was her refusal to sit
down. She would only stand at her desk, bending
forward to work. Our teacher—a kind and ener-
getic man called Mr. Sherman—battled her for a
week but Tracey's will, like my mother's, was made
of iron, and in the end she was allowed to stand as
she pleased. I don't think Tracey had any special
passion for standing up, it was a point of principle.
The principle could have been anything, really, but
the point was she would win it. It was clear that
Mr. Sherman, having lost this argument, felt he
must come down hard in some other area and one
morning, as we were all excitedly swapping Garbage Pail Kids instead of listening to whatever he
was saying, he suddenly went completely out of his
mind, screaming like a lunatic, going from desk
to desk seizing the cards, sometimes from inside
the desk and sometimes from our hands, until he
had a huge pile of them on his desk which he then
shuffled into a tower laid on its side and brushed
into a drawer, locking it ostentatiously with a little

key. Tracey said nothing, but her piggy nose flared and I thought: oh dear, doesn't Mr. Sherman realize she'll never forgive him?

That same afternoon, after school, we walked home together. She wouldn't talk to me, she was still in her fury, but when I tried to turn into my estate she grabbed my wrist and led me across the road to hers. All the way up in the lift we were silent. It seemed to me something momentous was about to happen. I could feel her rage like an aura around her, it almost vibrated. When we got to her front door I saw that the knocker—a brass lion of Judah with its mouth open, bought on the high road from one of the stalls that sold Africana— had been damaged and now hung by a single nail, and I wondered if her father had been round again. I followed Tracey to her room. Once the door was closed she turned on me, glaring, as if I myself were Mr. Sherman, asking me sharply what I wanted to do, now that we were here? I had no idea: never before had I been canvassed for ideas of what to do, she was the one with all the ideas, there had never been any planning by me before today.

"Well, what's the point of coming round if you don't fucking know?"

She flopped down on to her bed, picked up **Pac-Man** and started playing. I felt my face getting hot. I meekly suggested practicing our triple time-steps but this made Tracey groan.

"Don't need to. I'm on to wings."

"But I can't do wings yet!"

"Look," she said, without raising her eyes from her screen, "you can't get silver without doing wings, forget about gold. So what's your dad going to come and watch you fuck it all up for? No point, is there?"

I looked at my stupid feet, that couldn't do wings. I sat down and began quietly to cry. This changed nothing and after a minute I found myself pitiful and stopped. I decided to busy myself organizing Barbie's wardrobe. All her clothes had been stuffed into Ken's open-top automobile. It was my plan to extract them, flatten them, hang them on their little hangers and place them back in the wardrobe, the kind of game I was never permitted to play at home due to its echoes of domestic oppression. Halfway through this painstaking procedure Tracey's heart mysteriously softened toward me: she slipped from the bed and joined me cross-legged on the floor. Together we got that tiny white woman's life in order.

Twelve

We had a favorite video, it was labeled "Saturday Cartoons and **Top Hat**" and moved weekly from my flat to Tracey's and back, played so often that tracking now ate the frame, from above and below. Because of this we couldn't risk forward-winding while playing—it made the tracking worse—so we forward-wound "blind," guessing at duration by assessing the width of the black tape as it flew from one reel to another. Tracey was an expert forward-winder, she seemed to know in her body exactly when we'd gone past the irrelevant cartoons and when to press stop to reach, for example, the song "Cheek to Cheek." It strikes me now that if I want to watch this same clip—as I did a few minutes ago, just before writing this—it's no effort at all, it's the work of a moment, I type my request in the box and it's there. Back then there was a craft to it. We were the first generation to have, in our own homes, the means to re- and forward-wind reality: even very small children could press their fingers against those clunky buttons and see what-has-been become what-is or what-will-be. When

Tracey was about this process she was absolutely concentrated, she would not press play until she had Fred and Ginger exactly where she wanted them, on the balcony, among the bougainvillea and the Doric columns. At which point she began to read the dance, as I never could, she saw everything, the stray ostrich feathers hitting the floor, the weak muscles in Ginger's back, the way Fred had to jerk her up from any supine position, spoiling the flow, ruining the line. She noticed the most important thing of all, which is the dance lesson within the performance. With Fred and Ginger you can always see the dance lesson. In a sense the dance lesson **is** the performance. He's not looking at her with love, not even fake movie love. He's looking at her as Miss Isabel looked at us: don't forget x, please keep in mind y, arm up now, leg down, spin, dip, bow.

"Look at her," Tracey said, smiling oddly, pressing a finger to Ginger's face on the screen. "She looks fucking scared."

It was during one of these viewings that I learned something new and important about Louie. On this occasion the flat was empty, and as it annoyed Tracey's mother when we watched the same clip multiple times, that afternoon we indulged ourselves. The moment Fred came to a rest and leaned against the balustrade Tracey shuffled forward on all fours and pressed the button down again and off we went, back to what-once-was. We must have watched the same five-minute clip a dozen times. Until suddenly it was enough: Tracey got up and told me to follow. It was dark outside. I wondered when her mother would be home. We walked past the kitchen to the bathroom. It was exactly the same as my bathroom. Same cork floor, same avocado bathroom set. She got down on her knees and pushed the side panel of the bath: it fell in easily. Sitting in a Clarks shoebox just by the pipes was a small gun. Tracey picked up the box and showed it to me. She told me it was her father's, that he had left it here, and when Michael came to Wembley at Christmas Louie would be his security man as well as one of his dancers, it had to be that way to confuse people, it was all top secret. You tell anyone, she told me, and you are dead. She put the panel back and went to the kitchen to start making her tea. I headed home. I remember feeling intensely envious of the glamour of Tracey's family life compared to my own, its secretive and explosive nature, and I walked toward my own flat trying to think of some equivalent revelation I could offer to Tracey the next time I saw her, a terrible illness or a new baby, but there was nothing, nothing, nothing!

Thirteen

We stood on the balcony. Tracey held up a cigarette, stolen from my father, and I stood ready to light it for her. Before I could she spat it from her mouth, kicked it behind her and pointed down at my mother, who, as it turned out, was right below us on the communal lawn, smiling up. It was a mid-May Sunday morning, warm and bright. My mother was waving a dramatically large spade, like a Soviet farmer, and wearing a terrific outfit: denim dungarees, thin, light brown crop top, perfect against her skin, Birkenstocks and a square yellow handkerchief folded into a triangle and worn over her head. This was tied at the back of her neck in a jaunty little knot. She was taking it upon herself, she explained, to dig up the communal grass, a rectangle about eight foot by three, with the idea of establishing a vegetable garden that everybody could enjoy. Tracey and I watched her. She dug for a while, pausing regularly to rest her foot on the lip of the shovel and to shout up to us about lettuces, the various strains, the right time for planting them, none of which interested us in the least, and yet everything she said was made somehow more compelling by that outfit. We watched as several other people came out of their flats, to express concern or query her right to do what she was doing, but they were no match for her, and we noticed and admired the way she dispatched the fathers in a few minutes—essentially by looking into their eyes—while with the mothers she met with resistance, yes, with the mothers she had to make a little more effort, drowning them in language until they understood how out of their depth they were and the thin stream of their objections was completely subsumed by the quick-running currents of my mother's talk. Everything she said sounded so convincing, so impossible to contradict. It was a wave washing over you, unstoppable. Who didn't like roses? Who was so small-minded they would begrudge an inner-city child the chance to plant a seed? Weren't we all Africans, originally? Weren't we people of the land?

It started to rain. My mother, not dressed for rain, returned indoors. The next morning before school we were excited to catch up with this spectacle: my mother, looking like Pam Grier herself, digging a large, illegal hole without permission from the council. But the spade lay exactly where she had left it and the trench filled with water. The hole looked like somebody's half-dug grave. The next day it rained again and no more digging was done. On the third day a gray sludge began to rise up and spill into the grass.

"Clay," said my father, digging a finger into it. "She's got a problem now."

But he was wrong: it was his problem. Someone had told my mother that clay is only a layer of the earth, and if you dig deep enough you can get past it, and then all you have to do is go to the garden center and get some compost and pour it into your large, illegal hole . . . We peered down into the hole my father was now digging: under the clay was more clay. My mother came downstairs and peered in, too, and claimed to be "very excited" about the clay. She never again mentioned vegetables, and if anyone else tried to mention them she seamlessly adopted the new party line, which was that the hole had never been about lettuces, the hole had always been a search for clay. Which had now been found. In fact, she had two potter's wheels, just sitting upstairs! What a wonderful resource for the children!

The wheels were small and very heavy, she had bought them because she "liked the look of them," one freezing February when the lift doors malfunctioned: my father braced his knees, squared his arms and lugged the bloody things up three flights of stairs. They were very basic, brutal in some way, a peasant's tool, and they had never been put to any use in our flat besides propping open the door

to the living room. Now we would use them, we
had to use them: if we didn't, my mother had dug
a large hole in the communal gardens for no reason
at all. Tracey and I were told to collect children.
We managed to convince only three kids from the
estate: to make up numbers we added Lily Bingham. My father scooped clay into carrier bags and
carted it up to the flat. My mother put a trestle
table on the balcony and dropped a large lump of
clay in front of each of us. It was a messy process,
we probably would have been better off doing it in
the bathroom or the kitchen, but the balcony allowed for an element of display: from up there my
mother's new concept in parenting could be seen
by all. She was essentially asking the whole estate a
question. What if we didn't plonk our children in
front of the telly each day, to watch the cartoons
and the soap operas? What if we gave them, instead, a lump of clay, and poured water over it, and
showed them how to spin it round until a shape
formed between their hands? What kind of a society would that be? We watched the clay being spun
between her palms. It looked like a penis—a long,
brown penis—though it was only when Tracey
whispered this idea into my ear that I allowed myself even to acknowledge the thought I was already
having. "It's a vase," claimed my mother, and then
added, as clarification: "For a single flower." I was
impressed. I looked around at the other children.
Had **their** mothers ever thought to dig a vase out

of the earth? Or grow a single flower to be placed inside it? But Tracey was not taking it at all seriously, she was still beside herself at the idea of a clay penis, and now she set me off, and my mother frowned at us both and, turning her attention to Lily Bingham, asked her what she would like to make, a vase or a mug. Under her breath, Tracey suggested, again, the obscene third option.

She was laughing at my mother—it was liberating. I had never imagined my mother could or should be a figure of fun, and yet Tracey found everything about her ridiculous: the way she spoke to us with respect, as if we were adults, giving us choices about things Tracey felt we had no business at all in choosing, and the license she gave us generally, allowing us to make all this unnecessary mess on her balcony—when everyone knew a real mother hated mess—and then having the cheek to call it "arts," the cheek to call it "crafts." When Tracey's turn came round and my mother asked her what she would like to make on the wheel, a vase or a mug, Tracey stopped laughing and scowled.

"I see," said my mother. "Well, what would you **like** to make?"

Tracey shrugged.

"Doesn't have to be useful," my mother pressed. "Art means not having to be useful! In West Africa, for example, a hundred years ago, there were some village women, they were making these strangely shaped pots, impractical pots, and the anthropologists couldn't understand what they were doing, but that was because they, the scientists, were expecting a quote unquote 'primitive' people to make only useful things, when actually they were making the pots just for their beauty—no different from a sculptor—not to collect water, not to hold grain, just for their beauty, and to say: **we were here, at this moment in time, and this is what we made**. Well, you could do that, couldn't you? Yes, you could make something ornamental. That's your freedom! Take it! Who knows? You might be the next Augusta Savage!"

I was used to my mother's speechifying—I tended to tune out whenever it was happening—and I was familiar, too, with the way she would drop whatever she happened to be studying that week into ordinary conversation, but I'm sure Tracey had never heard anything like it before in her life. She didn't know what an anthropologist was, or what a sculptor did, or who Augusta Savage was, or even what the word "ornamental" meant. She thought my mother was trying to make a fool of her. How could she know my mother found it impossible to speak in a natural way to children?

Fourteen

When Tracey got home each day after school her flat was almost always empty. Who knew where her mother was? "Down the high road," said my mother—this meant "drinking"—but I walked past the Sir Colin Campbell every day and never saw her in there. The times I did spot her she was usually in the street bending someone's ear, often crying and dabbing at her eyes with a hanky, or else sitting at the bus stop on the other side of the estate wall, smoking, staring into space. Anything but sit in that tiny flat—and I didn't blame her. Tracey by contrast very much liked to be home, she never wanted to go to the playground or to be in the streets. She kept a key in her pencil case, let herself in, went straight to the sofa and began watching the Australian soaps until the British ones started, a process which began at four p.m. and ended when the credits ran on **Coronation Street.** Somewhere in between she either got her own tea or her mother arrived with takeaway and joined her on the sofa. I dreamed of freedom like hers. When I got home either my mother or my father wanted to know "what had happened at school today," they were very insistent about it, I wouldn't be let alone until I told them something and so, naturally, I began lying to them. I thought of them at this point as two children, more innocent than me, whom it was my responsibility to protect from the kind of uncomfortable facts that they would either over-think (my mother) or over-feel (my father). That summer the problem became acute because the true answer to "How was school today?" was "There is a mania in the playground for grabbing vaginas." Three boys from Tracey's estate had initiated the game, but now everyone was playing, the Irish kids, the Greek kids, even Paul Barron, the completely Anglo-Saxon son of a policeman. It was like tag, but a girl was never "It," only boys were "It," girls simply ran and ran until we found ourselves cornered in some quiet spot, away from the eyes of dinner ladies and playground monitors, at which point our knickers were pulled aside and a little hand shot into our vaginas, we were roughly, frantically tickled, and then the boy ran away, and the whole thing started up again from the top. You could tell the popularity of a girl by who got chased longest and hardest. Tracey with her hysterical giggle—and deliberately slow run—was, as usual, number one. I, wanting to be popular, also sometimes ran slowly, and the awkward truth is I wanted to be caught—I liked the electricity that ran from my vagina to my ear even in anticipation of the hot little hand—but it is also true that when the hand actually appeared some reflex in me, some ingrained concept of self-preservation, inherited from my mother, always squeezed my legs together, and I tried to fight the hand, which was in the end always impossible. All I did was make myself even more unpopular by struggling for those first moments.

As to whether you wanted one boy or another boy to chase you, no, this wasn't anybody's concern. There was no hierarchy of desire because desire was a very weak, practically non-existent, element of the game. The important thing was that you were seen to be the kind of girl worth chasing. It was a game not of sex but of status—of power. We did not desire or dread the boys in themselves, we only desired and dreaded being wanted or not being wanted. An exception to this was the boy with terrible eczema, whom we all truly and sincerely dreaded, Tracey as much as anyone, because he left, in your knickers, little flecks of dead gray skin. When our game mutated from playground prank to classroom risk, the boy with eczema became my daily nightmare. Now the game went like this: a boy dropped a pencil on the floor, always at a moment when Mr. Sherman had his back to us and his eyes on the board. The boy crawled under the table to retrieve the pencil, came up to a girl's crotch, pulled her knickers aside and stuck his fingers in, leaving them there for as long as he thought he could get away with. The random element was now gone: only the original three boys played and they only visited those girls who were both close to their own desks and whom they assumed would not complain. Tracey was one of these girls, as was I, and a girl from my corridor called Sasha Richards. The white girls—who had generally been included in the playground mania—were now mysteriously no longer included: it was as if they had never been involved in the first place. The boy with eczema sat one desk away from me. I hated those scaly fingers, I was horrified and disgusted by them, and yet, at the same time, could not help but take pleasure in that delightful and uncontrollable electricity rushing from my knickers to my ear. Of course, it wasn't possible to describe such things to my parents. In fact this is the first time I have presented them in any way to anyone—even to myself.

Strange now to think that we were all only nine years old at the time. But I still look back on that period with a certain measure of gratitude for what I have come to see as my relative luck. It was the season of sex, yes, but it was also, in all the vital ways, without sex itself—and isn't that one useful definition of a happy girlhood? I didn't know or appreciate this aspect of my luck until well into adulthood, when I began to find, in more cases than I would have guessed, that among my women friends, irrespective of background, their own childhood sex seasons had been exploited and destroyed by the misdeeds of uncles and fathers, cousins, friends, strangers. I think of Aimee: abused at seven, raped at seventeen. And beyond personal luck, there is geographical and historical luck. What happened to the girls on the plantations—or in the Victorian workhouses? The closest I came to anything like that was the music store room and I did not come very close at all, and I have historical luck to thank for that, surely, but also Tracey, as it was she who came to my rescue, in her own peculiar way. It was a Friday at the end of the day, not long before school broke up for the year, and I'd gone to the store room to borrow some sheet music, it was for the song "We All Laughed," which Astaire sang so simply and so well, and I meant to give it to Mr. Booth on Saturday morning, to help us sing it as a duet. Another piece of my luck was that Mr. Sherman, my class teacher, was also the school's music teacher, and as keen on the old songs as I was: he had a filing cabinet full of Gershwin scores and Porter scores, and so on, kept here in the music cupboard, and on Fridays I was allowed to borrow what I wanted, to be returned on Monday. The space was typical of such schools at the time: chaotic, too small, windowless, many ceiling tiles missing. Old violin and cello cases were stacked up against one wall, and there were plastic tubs of descant recorders, full of saliva, their mouthpieces as chewed as dog toys. There were two pianos, one broken and covered in a dust sheet, one very out of tune, and many sets of African drums, for they were relatively cheap and anyone could play them. The overhead light didn't work. You had to work out what you wanted while the door was still open, pinpoint its location, and then, if the item was not in arm's reach, let the door shut and carry on in darkness. Mr. Sherman had told me he'd left the folder I needed on top of the gray filing cabinet in the far-left-hand corner, and I spotted the cabinet and let the door ease shut. The darkness was complete. I had the folder in my hand and my back to the door. A thin streak of light sliced the room for a few moments and disappeared. I turned—I felt hands on me. One pair of hands I recognized immediately—the boy with eczema—the other I soon understood belonged to this boy's best friend, a lanky, uncoordinated child called Jordan who was mentally slow, easily led and sometimes dangerously impulsive, a set of symptoms which had, back then, no particular diagnosis, or none that Jordan and his mother were ever given. Jordan was in my class, but I never called him Jordan, I called him Spaz, everybody did, but if it was meant as an insult he had long ago defused it by answering to it cheerfully as if it were his name. His status in our class was peculiar: despite his condition, whatever it was, he was tall and handsome. While we looked like children, he looked like an adolescent, his arms had muscle in them and his hair was sharp, shaved on the sides in a real barber's shop. He was no good at classwork, had no real friends, but he was a useful and passive sidekick for boys with nefarious plans, and was more often than not the focus of the teachers' attention, the smallest interruption from him had a disproportionate effect, and this was interesting for the rest of us. Tracey could—did— tell a teacher to "fuck off" without even being sent to stand in the hall, but Jordan passed most of his time in that hall, for what seemed, to the rest of us, small infractions—talking back, or not removing a baseball cap—and after a while of this we began to understand that the teachers, especially the white women, were scared of him. We respected that: it seemed like a special thing, an achievement, to make a grown woman fear you, though you were only nine years old and mentally disabled. Personally I was on good terms with him: he had sometimes put his fingers in my knickers but I was never convinced he knew why he was doing it, and on the walk home, if we happened to fall in step, I sometimes sang for him—the theme tune to "Top Cat," a cartoon with which he was obsessed—and this soothed and made him happy. He would walk along, head inclined toward me, making a low, gurgling sound like a contented baby. I did not think of him as an aggressor, yet here he was in the music cupboard, touching me everywhere, giggling in a manic way, following and imitating the more calculated laugh of the boy with eczema, and it was clear that this wasn't the playground game or the classroom game, it was a new and perhaps dangerous escalation. The boy with eczema was laughing, and I was meant to laugh, everything was meant to be a kind of joke, but each time I tried to keep some item of clothing up, they pulled it down and I was meant to laugh at that, too. Then the laughing stopped and something urgent took over, they worked in silence, and I went silent myself. At that moment the thin streak of light re-appeared. Tracey was at the door: I saw her in silhouette, framed in the light. She closed the door behind her. She didn't say anything right away. She just stood with us in the dark, silent, not doing anything. The boys' hands slowed down: it was the child's version of sexual absurdity—familiar to adults—when something that appeared so urgent and all-consuming a moment before now suddenly seems (often in conjunction with a light going on) small and pointless, even tragic. I looked over at Tracey, still burned into my retina in relief form: I saw her outline, the retroussé nose, the perfectly divided plaits with their satin bows. At last she took a step back, opened the door wide and held it open.

"Paul Barron's waiting for you at the gate," she said. I stared at her and she said it again, this time irritably, like I was wasting her time. I pulled down my skirt and hurried past. We both knew it was not possible that Paul Barron was waiting for me at the gate, his mother picked him up every day in a Volkswagen, his dad was a policeman, he had a permanently trembling upper lip and big, wet, blue eyes like a puppy. I had not spoken two words to Paul Barron my whole life. Tracey claimed he'd put his fingers in her knickers, but I had seen him play that game and noticed that he ran around the playground without aim, looking for a tree to hide behind. I strongly suspected him of not wanting to catch anybody. But his was the right name at the right moment. I could be messed with as long as I was considered a part of that element in the school which expected and deserved no better, but Paul Barron was a part of the other world, he couldn't be messed with, and this fictional connection with him, even for a moment, formed some kind of protection. I ran down the hill to the gate and found my father waiting for me there. We got ice creams from the van and walked home together. At the traffic lights I heard a lot of noise and looked across and saw Tracey and the boy with eczema and the one we called Spaz laughing and fighting and messing with each other, swearing freely and seeming to enjoy the public tutting and disapproval that now rose up and enveloped them like a cloud of midges from the queue at the bus stop, from the shopkeepers standing in their doorways, from mothers, from fathers. My own father, shortsighted, peered across the road in the direction of the disturbance: "That's not Tracey, is it?"

PART TWO
Early and Late

One

I was still a child when my path first crossed with Aimee's—but how can I call it fate? Everybody's path crossed with hers at the same moment, as soon as she emerged she was uncontained by space and time, with not one path to cross but all paths—they were all hers, like the Queen in **Alice in Wonderland**, all ways were her way—and of course millions of people felt as I did. Whenever they listened to her records they felt they were meeting her—they still do. Her first single came out the week of my tenth birthday. She was twenty-two at the time. By the end of that same year, she once told me, she could no longer walk down the street, not in Melbourne, Paris, New York, London, Tokyo. Once, when we were flying over London together en route to Rome, having a casual conversation about London as a city, its virtues and drawbacks, she admitted she had never been on the tube, not even once, and could not really imagine it as an experience. I suggested that tube systems were basically the same all over the world, but she said that the last time she had been on a train of any description was when she'd left Australia for New York, twenty years earlier. She was only six months out of her sleepy hometown at that point, she became an underground star in Melbourne so very quickly, and it took only six more months in New York to remove the qualifier. An indisputable star ever since, a fact that is for her devoid of sadness or any trace of neurosis or self-pity, and this is one of the striking things about Aimee: she has no tragic side. She accepts everything that has happened to her as her destiny, no more surprised or alienated to be who she is than I imagine Cleopatra was to be Cleopatra.

I bought that debut single as a present for Lily Bingham, for her tenth-birthday party, which happened to be a few days before my own. Both Tracey and I were invited to her party, we were handed the little homemade paper invitations by Lily herself, one Saturday morning at dance class, quite unexpectedly. I was very happy, but Tracey, maybe suspecting she'd been included out of politeness, took the invite with a sour look on her face and passed it straight to her mother, who was anxious enough about it to stop my mother in the street a few days later and pepper her with questions. Was it the kind of thing where you dropped your kid off? Or was she, as the mum, expected to come into the house? The invitation said a trip to the cinema—but who'd pay for this ticket? The guest or the host? Did you have to take a gift? What kind of gift were **we** getting? Would my mother do her a favor and take us both? It was as if the party was taking place in some bewildering foreign land, rather than a three-minute walk away, in a house on the other side of the park. My mother, with maximum condescension, said she'd take us both, and stay if staying was required. For the gift she suggested a record, a pop single, it could be from both of us, cheap but sure to be appreciated: she would take us down the high road to Woolworths to find something suitable. But we were prepared. We knew exactly what record we wanted to buy, the name of the song and the singer, and we knew my mother—who had never read a tabloid and listened only to the reggae stations—would be ignorant of Aimee's reputation. Our only concern was the cover: we hadn't seen it, didn't know what to expect. Given the lyrics—and the performance we had watched, open-mouthed, on **Top of the Pops**—we felt that almost anything was possible. She might be completely naked on the cover of her single, she might be on top of a man—or a woman—doing sex, she might be holding her middle finger up, as she had, for a moment, on a live children's TV show only the weekend before. It might be a photograph of Aimee executing one of her stunning, provocative dance moves, for love of which we had temporarily abandoned Fred Astaire, for the moment we wanted only to dance like Aimee, and imitated her whenever we had the privacy and opportunity, practicing the fluid roll of her mid-section—like a wave of desire passing through a body—and the way she jerked her narrow, boyish hips and lifted her small breasts from her ribcage, a subtle manipulation of muscles we did not yet have, under breasts we had not yet grown. When we got to Woolworths we rushed ahead of my mother and went straight to the record racks. Where was she? We looked for the white-blond pixie cut, the startling eyes, such a pale blue they seem gray, and that elfin face, androgynous, with its little pointed chin, half Peter Pan, half Alice. But we found no representation of Aimee, naked or otherwise: only her name and the title of the song along the left-hand side of the sleeve, while the rest of the space was taken up with the puzzling—to us—image of a pyramid with an eye hovering above it, which eye was contained in the point of a triangle. The sleeve was a dirty green color, and written above and below the pyramid were some words in a language we couldn't read. Confused, relieved, we brought it to my mother, who held it up close to her face—she was also a little short-sighted, though too vain for glasses—frowned and asked if it was "a song about money." I was very careful answering. I knew my mother to be far more prudish about money than about sex.

"It's not about anything. It's just a song."

"You think your friend will like it?"

"She'll like it," said Tracey. "Everybody loves it. Can we have a copy, too?"

Still frowning, my mother sighed, went to pick a second copy out of the rack, walked over to the counter and paid for the pair.

It was the kind of party where the parents left—my mother, always nosy about middle-class interiors, was disappointed—but it didn't seem to be organized like the parties we knew, there was no dancing or party games, and Lily's mother wasn't dressed up at all, she looked almost homeless, her hair hardly brushed. We left my mother at the door after an awkward exchange—"Don't you girls look glamorous!" cried Lily's mother, upon seeing us— after which we were added to the pile of children in the living room, all girls, none of them in the kind of pink-and-diamanté ruffled confection Tracey had on, but neither were they in a faux-Victorian, white-collared, black velvet dress like the one my mother had believed would be "perfect" and which she had "discovered" for me in the local charity shop. The other girls were in dungarees and jolly-looking jumpers, or simple cotton pinafores in primary colors, and when we entered the room they all stopped what they were doing and turned to stare. "Don't they look nice?" said Lily's mother, again, and walked out, leaving us to it. We were the only black girls and aside from Lily knew nobody there. At once Tracey became hostile. On the walk there we had argued over who was to give Lily our mutual present—naturally Tracey had won— but now she dropped the gift-wrapped single on the sofa without even mentioning it, and when she heard what film we were going to see—**The Jungle Book**—she denounced it as "babyish" and "just a cartoon" full of "stupid little animals" in a voice that seemed to me suddenly very loud, very distinct, with too many dropped "t"s.

Lily's mother reappeared. We piled into a long, blue car, which had several rows of seats, like a little bus, and when these seats had been filled, Tracey, me and two other girls were told to sit in the space at the back, in the boot, which was lined with a filthy tartan rug covered in dog hair. My mother had given me a five-pound note in case either of us was expected to pay for anything, and I was anxious about losing it: I kept taking it out of my coat pocket, flattening it against my knee and then folding it up into quarters again. Tracey meanwhile was entertaining the other two girls by showing them what we usually did when we sat in the back of the school bus that took us, once a week, up to Paddington Rec for PE: she got up on her knees—as far as the space allowed—placed two fingers in a V sign either side of her mouth, and thrust her tongue in and out at the mortified male driver in the car behind. When we stopped, five minutes later, on Willesden Lane, I was thank-

ful that the journey was over but disheartened at
the destination. I'd imagined we were heading to
one of the grand cinemas in the center of town,
but we were parked in front of our own little local
Odeon, just off the Kilburn High Road. Tracey
was pleased: this was home territory. While Lily's
mother was distracted at the ticket booth Tracey
showed everyone how to steal pick-and-mix without paying for it, and then, once we were in the dark
theater, how to sit balanced on a flipped-up seat so
that nobody behind you could see the screen, how
to kick the seat in front of you until the person
turned round. "That's enough, now," Lily's mother
kept mumbling, but she couldn't establish any authority, her own sense of embarrassment seemed
to stop her. She did not want us to make noise,
but at the same time she couldn't bear to make
the necessary noise it would take to stop us making noise, and as soon as Tracey had understood
this—and understood, too, that Lily's mother had
no intention of smacking her or swearing at her
or dragging her out of the cinema by her ear as
our mothers would have done—well, then she felt
herself to be quite free. She kept up her commentary throughout, ridiculing the plot and the songs
and describing the many ways the narrative would
violently diverge from both Kipling's and Disney's
vision if she herself were in the place of any or all of
the characters. "If I was that snake I'd just open my
jaw and yam that fool up in one bite!" or "If I was

that monkey I'd kill that boy soon as he turned up in my place!" The other party guests were thrilled by these interventions, and I laughed the loudest.

Afterward, in the car, Lily's mother tried to start a civilized conversation about the merits of the movie. A few girls said nice things, and then Tracey, again sitting in the very back—I had disloyally moved to the second row—piped up.

"Whassisname—Mowgli? He looks like Kurshed, don't he? In our class. Don't he?"

"Yeah, he does," I called back. "He looks just like this boy Kurshed in our class."

Lily's mother took an exaggerated interest, she turned her head right round as we paused at a traffic light.

"Perhaps his parents are from India."

"Nah," said Tracey casually, looking away, out of the window. "Kurshed's a Paki."

We drove back to the house in silence.

There was cake, though it was poorly decorated and homemade, and we sang "Happy Birthday," but then we still had half an hour before our parents were to pick us up and Lily's mother, not having planned for this, looked worried and asked what we'd like to do. Through the kitchen doors I could see a long, green space, overgrown with vines and bushes, and I longed to go out there, but this was ruled out: too cold. "Why don't you all run upstairs and explore—have an adventure?" I could see how struck Tracey was by this. Adults told us to "stay out of trouble" and to "go and find something to do" or "go and make yourself useful" but we were not accustomed to being told—instructed!—to have an adventure. It was a sentence from a different world. Lily—always gracious, always friendly, always kind—took all her guests to her room and showed us her toys, old and new, whatever we fancied, without any sign of bad temper or possessiveness. Even I, who had been to her house only once before, managed to feel more possessive about Lily's things than Lily herself. I went around showing Tracey the many delights of Lily's room as if they were my own, regulating how long she could hold this or that item, explaining to her the provenance of the things on the walls. I showed her the huge Swatch watch—and told her that she mustn't touch it—and pointed out a poster advertising a bullfight, purchased while the Binghams were on a recent holiday in Spain; under the image of the matador, instead of the matador's name, was printed, in huge, curlicue red letters: **Lily Bingham**. I wanted Tracey to be as amazed by this as I had been the first time I saw it but instead she shrugged, turned from me and said to Lily: "Got a player? We'll put on a show."

Tracey was very good at imaginative games, better than me, and the game she preferred to all others was "Putting on a Show." We played it often, always with just the two of us, but now she began to enlist these half-dozen girls in "our" game: one was sent downstairs to get the gift-wrapped single that would be our soundtrack, others were put to work making tickets for the upcoming show, and then a poster to advertise it, others collected pillows and cushions from various rooms to use as seats, and Tracey showed them where to clear an area for the "stage." The show was to be in Lily's teenage brother's room, where the record player was kept. He wasn't home and we treated his room as if we had a natural right to it. But when almost everything was organized Tracey abruptly informed her workers that the show would, after all, feature only her and me—everyone else was to be in the audience. When some of the girls dared to question this policy Tracey in turn questioned them aggressively. Did they go to dance class? Had they any gold medals? As many as she? A few of the girls began to cry. Tracey changed her tune, a little: so-and-so could do "lighting," so-and-so could do "props" and "costumes" or introduce the performance, and Lily Bingham could film it all on her father's camcorder. Tracey spoke to them as if they were babies and I was surprised how quickly they were mollified. They took their silly made-up jobs and seemed happy. Then everyone was banished to Lily's room while we "rehearsed." It was at this moment that I was shown the "costumes": two lacy camisoles taken from Mrs. Bingham's underwear drawer. Before I could speak Tracey was pulling my dress up over my head.

"You wear the red one," she said.

We put the record on, we rehearsed. I knew there was something wrong, that it wasn't like any dance we'd done before, but I felt it was out of my hands. Tracey was, as ever, the choreographer: my only job was to dance as well as I could. When she decided we were ready our audience was invited back into Lily's brother's room to sit upon the floor. Lily stood at the back, the heavy recorder on her narrow, pink shoulder, her pale blue eyes full of confusion—even before we had begun to dance—at the sight of two girls dressed in these slinky items of her mother's that of course she had probably never seen before in her life. She pressed the button that said "Record," and by doing so put in motion a chain of cause and effect which, more than a quarter of a century later, has come to feel like fate, would be almost impossible not to consider as fate, but which—whatever you think of fate—can certainly and rationally be said to have had one practical consequence: there's no need for me now to describe the dance itself. But there were things not captured by the camera. As we reached the final chorus—the moment where I am astride Tracey, on that chair—this was also the moment that Lily Bingham's mother, who had come upstairs to tell us so-and-so's mother had arrived, opened her son's bedroom door and saw us. That is why the footage stops as abruptly as it does. She froze at the threshold, still as Lot's wife. Then she exploded. Tore us apart, stripped us of our costumes, told our audience to return to Lily's room and stood over us silently as we got back into our stupid dresses. I kept apologizing. Tracey, who normally had nothing but backchat for furious adults, said nothing at all, but she packed contempt into every gesture, she even managed to put her tights on sarcastically. The doorbell rang again. Lily Bingham's mother went downstairs. We did not know whether to follow. For the next fifteen minutes, as the doorbell rang and rang, we stayed where we were. I did nothing, I just stood there, but Tracey with typical resourcefulness did three things. She took the VHS tape out of the recorder, put the single back in its sleeve and put both items in the pink silk drawstring purse her mother had seen fit to hang on her shoulder.

My mother, always late, for everything, was the last to arrive. She was taken upstairs to find us, like a lawyer coming to speak to her clients through the bars of a prison cell, while Lily's mother gave a very labored account of our activities, which included the rhetorical question: "Don't you wonder where children of this age even **pick up** such ideas?" My mother became defensive: she swore and the two women quarreled briefly. It shocked me. She seemed no different in that moment than all those other mothers confronted with a child's misbehavior up at the school—even a little of her patois came back—and I wasn't used to seeing her lose control. She grabbed us by the backs of our dresses and we all three flew downstairs, but Lily's mother followed us and in the hallway repeated what Tracey had said about Kurshed. It was her trump card. The rest of it could be dismissed, by my mother, as "typical bourgeois morality," but she couldn't ignore "Paki." At the time we were "Black and Asian," we ticked the Black and Asian box on the medical forms, joined the Black and Asian family support groups and stuck to the Black and Asian section of the library: it was considered a question of solidarity. And yet my mother defended Tracey, she said, "She's a child, she's just repeating what she's heard," to which Lily's mother said, quietly: "No doubt." My mother opened the front door, removed us, slamming the door shut very loudly. The moment we were outside, though, all her fury was for us, only for us, she pulled us like two bags of rubbish back down the road, shouting: "You think you're one of them? Is that what you think?" I remember exactly the sensation of being dragged along, my toes tracing the pavement, and how completely perplexed I was by the tears in my mother's eyes, the distortion spoiling her handsome face. I remember everything about Lily Bingham's tenth birthday and have no memory whatsoever of my own.

When we reached the road that ran between our estate and Tracey's my mother let go of Tracey's hand and delivered a brief but devastating lecture on the history of racial epithets. I hung my head and wept in the street. Tracey was unmoved. She lifted her chin and her little piggy nose, waited till it was over, then looked my mother straight in her eyes.

"It's just a word," she said.

Two

The day we learned that Aimee was to come, one day soon, into our Camden offices on Hawley Lane, everybody was affected by the news, no one was completely immune. A little whoop went around the conference room, and even the most hardened YTV hacks lifted their coffee to their lips, looked over at the fetid canal and smiled to remember an earlier version of themselves, dancing to Aimee's early, dirty, downtown disco—as kids in their living rooms—or breaking up with a college sweetheart to one of her soupy nineties ballads. There was respect in that place for a real pop star, no matter our personal musical preferences, and for Aimee there was a special regard: her fate and the channel's were linked from the start. She was a video artist right down to the bone. You could hear Michael Jackson's songs without bringing to mind the images that accompanied them (which is probably only to say that his music had a real life) but Aimee's music was contained by and seemed sometimes to only truly exist within the world of her videos, and whenever you heard those songs—in a shop, in a taxi, even if it was just the beats reverberating through some passing kid's headphones—you were sent back primarily to a visual memory, to the movement of her hand or legs or ribcage or groin, the color of her hair at the time, her clothes, those wintry eyes. For this reason Aimee—and all her imitators—were, for better or worse, the foundation of our business model. We knew American YTV had been built, in part, around her legend, like a shrine to a pixie god, and the fact that she should even deign now to enter our own, British, far lowlier place of worship was considered a great coup, it put everybody on our version of high alert. My section head, Zoe, convened a separate meeting just for our team, because in a sense Aimee was coming to us, in Talent and Artist Relations, to record an acceptance speech for an award she wouldn't be able to pick up in person in Zurich the following month. And there would surely be many indents to shoot for various emerging markets ("I'm Aimee, and you're watching YTV Japan!") and perhaps, if she could be convinced, an interview for **YTV News**, maybe even a live performance, recorded in the basement, for the **Dance Time Charts**. My job was to gather all such requests as they came in—from our European offices in Spain and France and Germany and in the Nordic countries, from Australia, from wherever else—and present them in a single document to be faxed to Aimee's people in New York, before her arrival, still four weeks away. And then, as the meeting wound down, something wonderful happened: Zoe slid off the desk she sat on, in her leather trousers and tube top—under which you could see a glimpse of a rock-hard brown stomach with a gem-like piercing at the belly button—shook out her lion's mane of half-Caribbean curls, turned to me in an offhand manner as if it were nothing at all, and said: "You'll need to collect her downstairs on the day and bring her to Studio B12, stay with her, get her whatever she needs."

I walked out of that conference room like Audrey Hepburn floating upstairs in **My Fair Lady**, on a cloud of swelling music, ready to dance the length of our open-plan office, spin and spin and spin out of the door and all the way home. I was twenty-two years old. And yet not especially surprised: it felt as if everything I'd seen and experienced over the past year had been moving in this direction. There was a crazed buoyancy to YTV in those dying days of the nineties, an atmosphere of wild success built on wobbly foundations, somehow symbolized by the building we occupied: three floors and the basement of the old "WAKE UP BRITAIN" TV studios in Camden (we still had a huge rising sun, egg-yolk yellow and now completely irrelevant, built into our façade). VH1 was wedged on top of us. Our external tubular heating system, painted in garish primary colors, looked like a poor man's Pompidou. Inside was sleek and modern, dimly lit and darkly furnished, lair of a James Bond nemesis. The place had once been a second-hand-car salesroom—before either music TV or breakfast TV—and the interior darkness seemed calculated to disguise the jerry-rigged nature of the construction. The air vents were so poorly finished rats crawled up from Regent's Canal and nested in there, leaving their feces. In the summer—when the ventilation was switched on—whole floors of people came down with summer flu. When you turned on the fancy light dimmers, more often than not the knob would come off in your hand.

It was a company that set great store on appearances. Twenty-something receptionists became assistant producers, just because they seemed "fun" and "up for it." My thirty-one-year-old boss had gone from production intern to Head of Talent in only four and a half years. During my own eight-month stint I was promoted twice. Sometimes I wonder what would have happened if I'd stayed—if digital hadn't killed the video stars. At the time I felt lucky: I had no particular career plans, yet my career advanced anyway. Drinking played a role. At Hawley Lane drinking was mandatory: going out for drinks, holding one's drink, drinking others under the table, never declining a drink, even if on antibiotics, even if ill. Keen, at that point in my life, to avoid evenings alone with my father, I went to all office drinks and office parties, and I could hold my alcohol, I'd been perfecting that very Brit-

ish skill since the age of thirteen. The big difference at YTV was that we drank for free. Money
sloshed around the company. "Freebie" and "open
bar": two of our most repeated office nouns. Compared to the jobs I'd had before—even compared
to college—it felt like being in an extended period
of playtime, in which we were forever expecting
the arrival of adults, who never appeared.

One of my earliest tasks was to collate the guest
lists for our departmental parties, of which there
was about one a month. They tended to be in expensive venues in the center of town, and there
were always loads of freebies: T-shirts, trainers,
MiniDisc players, stacks of CDs. Officially spon-
sored by one vodka company or another, unoffi-
cially by Colombian drug cartels. In and out of the
bathroom stalls we trooped. Next morning walks-
of-shame, nosebleeds, holding your high heels in
your hands. I also filed the company's mini-cab
receipts. People booked mini-cabs back from one-
night stands or to airports to go on holiday. They
booked them in the wee hours at weekends to and
from all-night off-licenses or house parties. I once
booked a cab to my Uncle Lambert's. An executive
became office-wide famous for booking a cab to
Manchester, having woken up late and missed the
train. After I left I heard there was a clampdown,
but that year the annual bill for transport was over
a hundred thousand pounds. I once asked Zoe to
explain the logic behind it all and was told that

VHS tape—which employees were often carrying upon their person—could be "corrupted" if taken on the tube. But most of our people didn't even know this was their official alibi, free travel was something they took for granted, as a sort of right that came with being "in the media," and which they felt to be the least they deserved. Certainly when compared to what old college friends—who had chosen, instead, banking or lawyering—were finding each Christmas in their bonus envelopes.

At least the bankers and lawyers worked all hours. We had nothing but time. My own calls were usually done and dusted by eleven thirty—bearing in mind I arrived at my desk around ten. Oh, time felt different then! When I took my hour and a half for lunch that's all I did with it: lunch. No e-mail in our offices, not quite yet, and I had no mobile phone. I went through the loading-bay exit, straight out to the canal, and walked along the water's edge, a plastic-wrapped, quintessentially British sandwich in my hand, taking in the day, the open-air drug deals and the fat mallards quacking for tourist bread crumbs, the decorated houseboats, and the sad young Goths hanging their feet over the bridge, bunking off school, shadows of myself from a decade before. Often I went as far as the zoo. There I'd sit on the grassy bank and look up at Snowdon's aviary, around which a flock of African birds flew, bone-white with blood-red beaks. I never knew their names until I saw them on their own continent, where they anyway had a different name. After lunch I strolled back, sometimes with a book in hand, in no particular hurry, and what's astonishing to me now is that I found none of this unusual or a special piece of luck. I, too, thought of free time as my God-given right. Yes, compared to the excesses of my colleagues, I considered myself hard-working, serious, with a sense of proportion the others lacked, the product of my background. Too junior to go on any of their multiple "company bonding trips," I was the one who booked their flights—to Vienna, to Budapest, to New York—and privately marveled at the price of a business-class seat, at the very existence of business class, never able to decide, as I filed away these "expenses," if this sort of thing had always been going on, all around me, during my childhood (but invisible to me, at a level above my awareness) or if I had come of age at an especially buoyant moment in the history of England, a period in which money had new meaning and uses and the "freebie" had become a form of social principle, unheard of in my neighborhood and yet normal elsewhere. "Freebism": the practice of giving free things to people who have no need of them. I thought of all the kids from school who could have done my present job easily—who knew so much more than me about music, who were genuinely cool, truly "street," as I was everywhere wrongly assumed to be—but who were as likely to turn up at these offices as go to the moon. I wondered: why me?

In the great piles of glossy magazines, also freebies, left around the office, we now read that Britannia was cool—or some version of it that struck even me as intensely uncool—and after a while began to understand that it must be on precisely this optimistic wave that the company surfed. Optimism infused with nostalgia: the boys in our office looked like rebooted Mods—with Kinks haircuts from thirty years earlier—and the girls were Julie Christie bottle-blondes in short skirts with smudgy black eyes. Everybody rode a Vespa to work, everybody's cubicle seemed to feature a picture of Michael Caine in **Alfie** or **The Italian Job**. It was nostalgia for an era and a culture that had meant nothing to me in the first place, and perhaps because of this I was, in the eyes of my colleagues, cool, by virtue of not being like them. New American hip-hop was brought solemnly to my desk by middle-aged executives who assumed I must have some very learned opinions about it and, in fact, the little I knew did seem a lot in this context. Even the task of chaperoning Aimee that day was given to me, I'm sure, because I was assumed to be too cool to care. My disapproval of most things was always already assumed: "Oh, no, don't bother asking her, she wouldn't like it." Said ironically, as everything was back then, but with a cold streak of defensive pride.

My most unexpected asset was my boss, Zoe. She had also begun as an intern, but with no trust fund or moneyed parents like the rest, nor even, as I had myself, a rent-free parental crash pad. She'd lived in a filthy Chalk Farm squat, remained unpaid for over a year, and yet came in every morning at nine—punctuality was considered, at YTV, an almost inconceivable virtue—where she proceeded to "work her arse off." A foster-care kid originally, in and out of the group homes of Westminster, she was familiar to me from other kids I'd known who'd gone through that system. She had that same wild thirst for whatever was on offer, and a disassociated, hypermanic persona—traits you sometimes find in war reporters, or in soldiers themselves. Rightfully she should have been fearful of life. Instead she was recklessly bold. The opposite of me. Yet in the context of the office, Zoe and I were viewed as interchangeable. Her politics, like mine, were always already assumed, although in her case the office had it quite wrong: she was an ardent Thatcherite, the kind who feels that having pulled herself up by her own bootstraps everybody else better follow her example and do the same. For some reason she "saw herself in me." I admired her grit, but did not see myself in her. I had been to university, after all, and she hadn't; she was a cokehead, I wasn't; she dressed like the Spice Girl she resembled, instead of the executive she actually was; made unfunny sexual jokes, slept with the youngest, poshest, floppiest-haired, whitest, indie-boy interns; I prudishly disapproved. She liked me anyway. When she was drunk or high she liked to remind me that we were sisters, two brown girls with a duty toward each other. Just before Christmas she sent me to our European Music Awards, in Salzburg, where one of my tasks was accompanying Whitney Houston to a soundcheck. I don't remember the song she sang—I never really liked her songs—but standing in that empty concert hall, listening to her sing without backing music, with no support of any kind, I found that the sheer beauty of the voice, its monumental dose of soul, the pain implicit within it, bypassed all my conscious opinions, my critical intelligence or sense of the sentimental, or whatever it is that people are referring to when they talk about their own "good taste," going instead straight into my spine, where it convulsed a muscle and undid me. Way back by the EXIT sign I burst into tears. By the time I'd got to Hawley Lane this story had done the rounds, although it did me no harm, quite the opposite—it was taken to mean I was a true believer.

Three

It seems funny now, pathetic almost—and maybe only technology can achieve this comic revenge on our memories—but when we had an artist coming in and needed to make a dossier on them, to give to interviewers and advertisers and so on, we would go down to a little library in the basement and pull out a four-volume encyclopedia called **The Biography of Rock**. Everything in Aimee's entry, major or minor, I already knew—Bendigo-born, allergic to walnuts—excepting one detail: her favorite color was green. I made my notes, by hand, collated all relevant requests, stood in the copy room by a noisy fax machine and slowly fed the documents into it, thinking of someone in New York—a dream city to me—waiting by a similar contraption as my document came through to them, at the exact same time I sent it, which felt so very modern in the doing of it, a triumph over distance and time. And then of course to meet her I would need new clothes, perhaps new hair, a fresh way of speaking and walking, a whole new attitude to life. What to wear? The only place I ever shopped back then was Camden Market, and from inside that warren of Doc Martens and hippy shawls I was very pleased to draw out a huge pair of bright green cargo pants of a silky parachute material, a close-fitting green crop top—which had, as an added bonus, **The Low End Theory** album cover art on the front of it picked out in black, green and red glitter—and a pair of space-age Air Jordans, also green. I finished with a fake nose ring. Nostalgic and futuristic, hip-hop and indie, rrriot girl and violent femme. Women often believe clothes will solve a problem, one way or another, but by the Tuesday before she was due to arrive I understood nothing I wore was going to help me, I was too nervous, couldn't work or concentrate on anything. I sat in front of my giant gray monitor listening to the whirr of the modem, anticipating Thursday and typing, in my distraction, Tracey's full name into the little white box, over and over again. It's what I did at work when I was bored or anxious though it never really relieved either condition. I had done it many times by then, firing up Netscape, waiting for our interminably slow dial-up, and always finding the same three little islands of information: Tracey's Equity listing, her personal web page, and a chat room she frequented, under the alias Truthteller_LeGon. The Equity listing was static, it never changed. It mentioned her stint the previous year in the chorus of **Guys and Dolls**, but no other shows were ever added, no fresh news appeared. Her page changed all the time. Sometimes I would check it twice in a day and find the song different or that the exploding pink firework graphic had been replaced by flashing rainbow hearts. It was on this page, a month earlier, that she had mentioned the chat room, with a hyperlinked note—Sometimes truth is hard to hear!!!—and this single reference was all I'd needed: the door was open and I began to wander through it a few times a week. I don't think anyone else who followed that link—no one but me—would have known that the "truth teller" in that bizarre conversation was Tracey herself. But then no one, as far as I could see, was reading her page anyway. There was a sad, austere purity to this: the songs she chose no one heard, the words she wrote—banal aphorisms, usually ("The Arc of the Moral Universe is Long but It Bends toward Justice")—no one but me ever read. Only in that chat room did she seem to be in the world, though it was such a bizarre world, filled only with the echoing voices of people who had apparently already agreed with each other. From what I could tell she spent a frightening amount of time in there, especially late at night, and by now I'd read through all her threads, both current and archived, until I was able to follow the logic of it all—better to say I was no longer shocked by it— and could trace and appreciate the line of argument. I became less inclined to tell my colleagues stories about my crazy ex-friend Tracey, her surreal chat-room adventures, her apocalyptic obsessions. I hadn't forgiven her—or forgotten—but using her in this way became somehow distasteful to me.

One of the oddest things about it was the fact that the man whose spell she appeared to be under, the guru himself, had once been a breakfast-TV reporter, had worked in the very building I sat in now, and when we were kids I can remember often sitting with Tracey, watching him, bowls of cereal in our laps, waiting for his boring grown-up show to be over and for our Saturday-morning cartoons to begin. Once, during my first winter break from university, I went to buy some textbooks in a chain bookshop on the Finchley Road, and while wandering around the film section saw him in person, presenting one of his books in a far-off corner of that mammoth shop. He sat at a plain white desk, dressed all in white, with his prematurely white head of hair, facing a sizable audience. Two girls who worked there stood near me and from behind shelving they peeked out at the peculiar gathering. They were laughing at him. But I was struck not so much by what he was saying as by the odd composition of his audience. There were a few middle-aged white women, dressed in their cozily patterned Christmas jumpers, looking no different from the housewives who would have liked him ten years earlier, but by far the greater part of his crowd was young black men, of about my own age, holding well-worn copies of his books on their knee and listening with an absolute focus and determination to an elaborate conspiracy theory. For the world was run by lizards in human form: the Rockefellers were lizards, and the Kennedys, and almost everybody at Goldman Sachs, and William Hearst had been a lizard, and Ronald Reagan and Napoleon—it was a global lizard plot. Eventually the shop-girls tired of their sniggering and wandered off. I stayed till the end, deeply troubled by what I'd seen, not knowing what to make of it. Only later, when I started reading Tracey's threads—which were, if you could put aside their insane first premise, striking in their detail and perverse erudition, linking many diverse historical periods and political ideas and facts, combining them all into a sort of theory of everything, which even in its comic wrongness required a certain depth of study and a persistent attention—yes, only then did I feel that I better understood why all those serious-looking young men had gathered in the bookshop that day. It became possible to read between the lines. Wasn't it all a way of explaining power, in the end? The power that certainly exists in the world? Which few hold and most never get near? A power my old friend must have felt, at that point in her life, she utterly lacked?

"Er, what the fuck is **that**?"

I turned round in my swivel chair and found Zoe at my shoulder, examining a flashing graphic of a lizard wearing, on top of his lizard head, the Crown Jewels. I minimized the page.

"Album graphics. Bad."

"Listen, Thursday morning—you're on, they've confirmed. Are you ready? Got everything you need?"

"Don't worry. It's going to be fine."

"Oh, I know it will be. But if you need some Dutch courage," said Zoe, tapping her nose, "let me know."

It didn't come to that. Difficult to piece back together exactly what it did come to. My memory of it and Aimee's have never had much overlap. I've heard her say that she hired me because she felt "we had an immediate connection" that day or, sometimes, because I struck her as being so capable. I think it was because I was inadvertently rude to her, a thing few people were at that time in her life, and in my rudeness must have lodged myself in her brain. A fortnight later, when she found herself in sudden need of a new, young assistant, there I was, lodged in there. She emerged anyway from a car with blacked-out windows in mid-argument with her then assistant, Melanie Wu. Her manager, Judy Ryan, walked two steps behind them both, shouting into a phone. The first thing I ever heard Aimee say was a put-down: "Everything coming out of your mouth right now is totally worthless to me." I noticed she did not have an Australian accent, not any more, but neither was it quite American or quite British, it was global: it was New York and Paris and Moscow and LA and London combined. Of course now lots of people speak in this way but Aimee's version was the first time I heard it. "You're the opposite of helpful," she said now, to which Melanie replied: "I can totally see that." A moment later this poor girl found herself in front of me, looked down at my chest, seeking a name tag, and when she looked back up I could see she was broken, struggling not to cry. "So we're on schedule," she said, firmly as could be managed, "and it would be great if we could stay on schedule?"

We four stood in the lift, silent. I was determined to speak, but before I managed it Aimee turned to me and pouted at my top, like a pretty teenage boy in a sulk.

"Interesting choice," she said, to Judy. "Wearing another artist's shirt when you're meeting an artist? Professional."

I looked down at myself and blushed.

"Oh! No! Miss—I mean, Mrs.—Ms. Aimee. I wasn't trying to make any—"

Judy let out a loud, single laugh, like a seal barking. I tried to say something else, but the lift doors opened and Aimee strode out.

To get to our various appointments we had to walk the halls, and they were lined with people, like the Mall during Diana's funeral. Nobody seemed to be working. Whenever we stopped in a studio people lost their cool almost immediately, irrespective of their position in the company. I watched a Managing Director tell Aimee that a ballad of hers was the first dance at his wedding. I listened, excruciated, as Zoe launched into a rambling account of the personal resonance "Move with Me" had for her, how it had helped her become a woman, and understand the power of women, and not be afraid to be a woman, and so on. As we got away, finally, along another hall and into another lift, to make our way down to the basement—where Aimee had, to Zoe's delight, agreed to record a brief interview—I worked up the courage to mention, in the world-weary way of twenty-two-year-olds, how dull I imagined it must be for her to hear people saying these sorts of things to her, day and night, night and day.

"As a matter of fact, Little Miss Green Goddess, I love it."

"Oh, OK, I just thought—"

"You just thought I had contempt for my own people."

"No! I just—I—"

"You know, just because you're not one of my people doesn't mean they're not good people. Everybody's got their tribe. Whose tribe are you in anyway?" She took a second, slow, assessing look at me, up and down. "Oh, right. This we already know."

"You mean—musically?" I asked, and made the

mistake of glancing over at Melanie Wu, in whose face I understood that the conversation should have ended many minutes earlier, should never have started.

Aimee sighed: "Sure."

"Well . . . a lot of things . . . I guess I like a lot of the older stuff, like Billie Holiday? Or Sarah Vaughan. Bessie Smith. Nina. Real singers. I mean, not that—I mean, I feel like—"

"Um, correct me if I'm wrong," said Judy, her own broad Aussie brogue untouched by the intervening decades. "The interview's not actually happening in this lift? Thank you."

We got out at the basement. I was mortified and tried to walk ahead of them all, but Aimee skipped in front of Judy and linked arms with me. I felt my heart rise in my throat, as the old songs tell you it can. I looked down—she's only five foot two— and for the first time confronted that face close up, somehow both male and female, the eyes with their icy, gray, cat-like beauty, left for the rest of the world to color in. The palest Australian I ever saw. Sometimes, without her make-up on, she did not look like she was from a warm planet at all, and she took steps to keep it that way, protecting herself from the sun at all times. There was something alien about her, a person who belongs to a tribe of one. Almost without knowing it, I smiled. She smiled back.

"You were saying?" she said.

"Oh! I . . . I guess I feel like voices are—they're sort of like—"

She sighed again, miming a glance at a non-existent watch.

"I think voices are like clothes," I said firmly, as if it were an idea I'd been thinking about for years rather than something I was at that moment pulling from the air. "So if you see a photo of 1968 you know it's '68 from what the people are wearing, and if you hear Janis sing, you know it's '68. Her voice is a sign of the times. It's like history or . . . something."

Aimee lifted one devastating eyebrow: "I see." She let go of my arm. "But **my** voice," she said, with equal conviction, "my voice **is** this time. If it sounds to you like a computer, well, I'm sorry, but that's just because **it's right on time**. You might not like it, you might be living in the past, but I'm fucking singing this time, right now."

"But I do like it!"

She made that funny adolescent pout again.

"Just not as much as Tribe. Or Lady-Fucking-Day."

Judy jogged up to us: "Excuse me, do you know what studio we're heading to, or do I have to—"

"Hey, Jude! I'm talking to the youth here!"

We'd reached the studio. I opened the door for them.

"Look, can I just say I think I really got off on the wrong—really, Miss—I mean, Aimee—I was ten when you first dropped—I bought the single. It's mental for me that I'm meeting you. I'm one of your people!"

She smiled at me again: there was a kind of flirtation in the way she spoke to me, as there was in the way she spoke to everybody. She held my chin gently in her hand.

"Don't believe you," she said, took my fake nose ring out in one swift movement, and handed it to me.

Four

Now, there is Aimee, on Tracey's wall—clear as day. She shared the space with Michael and Janet Jackson, Prince, Madonna, James Brown. Over the course of the summer she made her room into a kind of shrine to these people, her favorite dancers, decorated with many huge, glossy posters of them, all caught in mid-movement, so that her walls read like hieroglyphics, indecipherable to me but still clearly some form of message, constructed from gestures, bent elbows and legs, splayed fingers, pelvic thrusts. Disliking publicity shots, she chose stills from concerts we couldn't afford to attend, the kind in which you could see the sweat on a dancer's face. These, she argued, were "real." My room was likewise a shrine to dance but I was stuck in fantasy, I went to the library and took out old seventies biographies of the great MGM and RKO idols, ripped out their corny headshots and stuck them up on my walls with Blu-tack. In this way I discovered the Nicholas Brothers, Fayard and Harold: a photo of them in mid-air, doing the splits, marked the entrance to my room, they were leaping over the doorway. I learned that they were self-taught, and though they danced like gods had no formal training at all. I took a kind of proprietorial pride in them, as if they were my brothers, as if we were family. I tried hard to interest Tracey—which of my brothers would she marry? which would she kiss?—but she couldn't sit through even the briefest clip of black-and-white film any longer, everything about it bored her. It wasn't "real"—too much had been subtracted, too much artificially shaped. She wanted to see a dancer on stage, sweating, real, not done up in top hat and tails. But elegance attracted me. I liked the way it hid pain.

One night I dreamed of the Cotton Club: Cab Calloway was there, and Harold and Fayard, and I stood on a podium with a lily behind my ear. In my dream we were all elegant and none of us knew pain, we had never graced the sad pages of the history books my mother bought for me, never been called ugly or stupid, never entered theaters by the back door, drunk from separate water fountains or taken our seats at the back of any bus. None of our people ever swung by their necks from a tree, or found themselves suddenly thrown overboard, shackled, in dark water—no, in my dream we were golden! No one was more beautiful or elegant than us, we were a blessed people, wherever you happened to find us, in Nairobi, Paris, Berlin, London, or tonight, in Harlem. But when the orchestra started up, and as my audience sat at their little tables with drinks in their hands, happy in themselves, waiting for me, their sister, to sing, I opened my mouth and no sound came out. I woke up to find I had wet the bed. I was eleven.

My mother tried to help, in her way. Look closer at that Cotton Club, she said, there is the Harlem Renaissance. Look: here are Langston Hughes and Paul Robeson. Look closer at **Gone with the Wind**: here is the NAACP. But at the time my mother's political and literary ideas did not interest me as much as arms and legs, as rhythm and song, as the red silk of Mammy's underskirt or the unhinged pitch of Prissy's voice. The kind of information I was looking for, which I felt I needed to shore myself up, I dug out instead from an old, stolen library book—**The History of Dance**. I read about steps passed down over centuries, through generations. A different kind of history from my mother's, the kind that is barely written down— that is felt. And it seemed very important, at the time, that Tracey should feel it too, all that I was feeling, and at the same moment that I felt it, even if it no longer interested her. I ran all the way to her house, burst into her room and said, you know when you jump down into the splits (she was the only girl in Miss Isabel's dance class who could do this), you know how you jump into a split and you said your dad can do it, too, and you got it from your dad, and he got it from Michael Jackson, and Jackson got it from Prince and maybe

James Brown, well, they all got it from the Nicholas Brothers, the Nicholas Brothers are the originals, they're the very first, and so even if you don't know it or say you don't care, you're still dancing like them, you're still getting it from them. She was smoking one of her mother's cigarettes out of her bedroom window. She looked much older than me doing that, more like forty-five than eleven, she could even blow smoke out of those flaring nostrils, and as I spoke aloud this supposedly momentous thing I had come to tell her I felt the words turning to ash in my mouth. I didn't even know what I was saying or what I meant by it, really. To stop the smoke from filling the room, she kept her back to me, but when I had finished making my point, if that's what it was, she turned to me and said, very coolly, as if we were perfect strangers, "Don't you ever talk about my father again."

Five

"This isn't working."

It was only about a month after I'd started working for her—for Aimee—and as soon as it was said aloud I saw she was right, it wasn't working, and the problem lay with me. I was young and inexperienced, and didn't seem able to find my way back to that impression I'd had, on the very first day we'd met, that she might be a human woman like any other. Instead my gut reaction had been overlaid by the reactions of others—ex-colleagues, old schoolfriends, my own parents—and each had their effect, every gasp or incredulous laugh, so that now each morning when I arrived at Aimee's house in Knightsbridge or her Chelsea offices I had to battle a very powerful sense of the surreal. What was I doing here? I often stuttered as I spoke, or forgot basic facts she'd told me. I would lose the thread of conversations during conference calls, too distracted by another voice inside me that never stopped saying: she's not real, none of this is real, it's all your childish fantasy. It was a surprise at the end of a day to close the heavy black door of her Georgian townhouse and find myself not in a dream city after all but in London and only a few steps from the Piccadilly Line. I sat down next to all the other commuters as they read their city paper, often picking one up myself, but with the sense of having traveled further: not just from the center back to the suburbs but from another world back into theirs, the world that seemed to me, aged twenty-two, to exist at the center of the center—the one they were all so busy reading about.

"It's not working because you're not comfortable," Aimee informed me, from a big, gray couch that sat opposite an identical couch on which I sat. "You need to be comfortable in yourself to work for me. You're not."

I closed the notebook in my lap, lowered my head and felt almost relieved: so I could go back to my real job—if they'd still have me—and reality. But instead of firing me, Aimee threw a cushion playfully at my head: "Well, what can we do about that?"

I tried to laugh and admitted I didn't know. She tilted her head toward the window. On her face I saw that look of constant dissatisfaction, of impatience, which later I would get used to, the ebb and flow of her restlessness became the shape of my working day. But in those early days it was all still new to me, and I interpreted it only as boredom, specifically boredom and disappointment with me, and not knowing what to do about it, looked from vase to vase around that huge room—she packed every space with flowers—and at the further beauty outside, at the sun glinting off the slate-gray roofs of Knightsbridge, and tried to think of something interesting to say. I didn't understand yet that the beauty was part of the boredom. The walls were hung with many dark Victorian oils, portraits of the gentry in front of their grand houses, but there was nothing from her own century, and nothing recognizably Australian, nothing personal. This was meant to be Aimee's London home and yet it didn't have a thing to do with her. The furniture was of plush, generalized good taste, like any up-scale European hotel. The only real clue that Aimee lived here at all was a bronze near the windowsill, about as big as a plate and the same shape as one, at the center of which you could see the petals and leaves of something that at first seemed to be a lily on its pad but was actually the full cast of a vagina: vulva, labia, clitoris—the works. I didn't dare ask whose.

"But where do you feel the most comfortable?" she asked, turning back to me. I saw a new idea painted on her face like fresh lipstick.

"You mean a place?"

"In this city. A place."

"I've never thought about it."

She stood up: "Well, think about it and let's go there."

The Heath was the first place that came to mind.

But Aimee's London, like those little maps you pick up at the airport, was a city centered around St. James's, bordered to the north by Regent's Park, stretching as far as Kensington to the west—with occasional forays into the wilds of Ladbroke Grove—and only as far east as the Barbican. She knew no more of what might lie at the southern end of Hungerford Bridge than at the end of a rainbow.

"It's a big sort of park," I explained. "Near where I grew up."

"OK! Well, let's go there."

We cycled through town, winding round buses and racing the occasional courier, three of us in a line: her security detail first—his name was Granger—then Aimee, then me. The idea of Aimee cycling through London infuriated Judy but Aimee loved to do it, she called it her freedom in the city, and maybe at one traffic light in twenty the adjacent driver would lean forward on the wheel, put down his window, having noticed something familiar about the blue-gray, feline eyes, that dainty triangular chin . . . But by that point the lights would change and we'd be gone. When she rode she was in urban camouflage anyway—black sports bra, black vest and a grungy pair of black cycling shorts, worn at the crotch—and only Granger seemed likely to catch anybody's attention: a six-foot-four, two-hundred-and-fifty-pound black man wobbling on a titanium-framed racer, stopping every now and then to take an **A–Z** out of his pocket and furiously study it. He was from Harlem, originally—"where we got a grid"—and the inability of Londoners to likewise number their streets was something he couldn't forgive, he'd written off the whole city on account of it. For him, London was a sprawl of bad food and bad weather in which his one task—to keep Aimee safe—was made more difficult than it needed to be. At Swiss Cottage he waved us on to a traffic island and peeled his bomber jacket off to reveal a pair of massive biceps.

"I'm telling you right now I got no idea where this place is at," he said, slapping his handlebar with his map. "You get halfway down some tiny little street—Christchurch Close, Hingleberry fucking Corner—and then this thing's telling me: **turn to page 53**. Motherfucker, I'm on a bike."

"Chin up, Granger," said Aimee, in a terrible British accent, and pulled his big head down on to her shoulder for a moment, squeezing it fondly. Granger freed himself and glared at the sun: "Since when is it this hot?"

"Well, it's summer. England can sometimes get hot in summer. Should've worn shorts."

"I don't **wear** shorts."

"I don't think this is a very productive conversation. We're on a traffic island."

"I'm done. We heading back," said Granger, he

sounded very final about it, and I was surprised to hear anyone speak to Aimee this way.

"We are **not** going back."

"Then you best take this," said Granger, dropping the **A–Z** in the basket at the front of Aimee's bike, " 'Cos I can't use it."

"I know the way from here," I offered, mortified to be the cause of the problem. "It's really not far."

"We need a vehicle," Granger insisted, without looking at me. We almost never looked at each other. Sometimes I thought of us as two sleeper agents, mistakenly assigned to the same mark and wary of eye contact, in case the one blew the other's cover.

"I hear there's some cute boys up in there," said Aimee in a sing-song voice—this was meant to be an imitation of Granger—"They're hid-ing in the tree-ees." She put her foot to the pedal, pushed off, swerving into the traffic.

"I don't mix play with work," said Granger sniffily, getting back astride his dainty bike with dignity. "I am a professional person."

We set off back up the hill, monstrously steep, huffing and puffing and following Aimee's laughter.

I can always find the Heath—all my life I've taken paths that lead me back, whether I wanted it or not, to the Heath—but I've never consciously sought and found Kenwood. I only ever stumble upon it. It was the same this time: I was leading Granger and Aimee up the lanes, past the ponds, over a hill, trying to think where might be the prettiest, quietest and yet most interesting place to stop with a too-easily bored superstar, when I saw the little cast-iron gate and behind the trees, the white chimneys.

"No cycles," said Aimee, reading a sign, and Granger, seeing what was coming, began again to protest, but was overruled.

"We'll be, like, an hour," she said, getting off her bike and passing it to him. "Maybe two. I'll call you. Have you got that thing?"

Granger folded his arms across his massive chest.

"Yeah, but I ain't giving it to you. Not without me being there. No way. Forget about it."

As I got off my bike, though, I saw Aimee put out her adamant little hand to receive a small something wrapped in cling-film, closing her palm around it, which something turned out to be a joint—for me. Long and American in design, with no tobacco in it at all. We settled under the magnolia, right in front of Kenwood House, and I leaned against the trunk and smoked while Aimee lay flat in the grass with her black baseball cap low over eyes, her face turned up toward me.

"Feel better?"

"But . . . aren't you going to have any?"

"I don't smoke. Obviously."

She was sweating like she did on stage, and now grabbed at her vest, lifting it up and down to create a tunnel of air, so that I received a glimpse of that pale strip of midriff that once so mesmerized the world.

"I've got a coldish Coke in my bag?"

"I don't drink that shit and neither should you."

She got up on her elbows to take me in more fully.

"You don't look all that comfortable to me."

She sighed and rolled over on to her stomach to face the milling summer crowds going down to the old stables for scones and tea or through the doors of the great house for art and history.

"I have a question," I said, knowing I was stoned and that she wasn't but finding it hard to keep in mind the second half of that proposition. "You do this with all your assistants?"

She considered: "No, not this exactly. People are different. I always do something. I can't have somebody in my face twenty-four-seven who is going to act shy around me. No time. And I don't have the luxury of getting to know you in some slow, delicate way or being politely English about it, saying please and thank you whenever I want you to do something—if you work for me, you just have to jump to it. I've been doing this a while, and I've figured out that a few intense hours at the beginning save a lot of time and misunderstandings and bullshit later on. You're getting off easy, believe me. I had a bath with Melanie."

I attempted a goofy extended joke, hoping to hear her laugh again, but instead she squinted at me.

"Another thing you should understand is that it's not that I don't get your British irony, I just don't like it. I find it adolescent. Ninety-nine percent of the time when I meet British people my feeling is: grow up!" Her mind turned back to Melanie in that bath: "Wanted to know if her nipples were too long. Paranoid."

"Were they?"

"Were who what?"

"Her nipples. Long."

"They're fucking like fingers."

I spat some of my Coke on to the grass.

"You're funny."

"I come from a long line of funny people. God knows why the British think they're the only people allowed to be funny in this world."

"I'm not that British."

"Oh, babe, you're as British as they come."

She reached into her pocket for her phone and began going through her texts. Long before it became a general condition Aimee lived in her phone. She was a pioneer in this as in so many things.

"Granger, Granger, Granger, Granger. Doesn't know what to do with himself if he doesn't have anything to do with himself. He's like me. We've got the same mania. He reminds me of how tiring I can be. To others." Her thumb wavered over her brand-new BlackBerry. "With you I'm hoping for: cool, calm, collected. Could do with some of that around here. Jesus Christ, he's sent me like fifteen texts already. He just needs to hold the bikes. Says he's near the—what in hell is the 'men's pond'?"

I told her, in detail. She made a skeptical face.

"If I know Granger there's no way he's swimming in fresh water, he won't even swim in Miami. Big believer in chlorine. No, he can just hold the bikes." She poked a finger in my belly. "Are we done here? Got another one of those if you need it. This is a one-time deal—take advantage. One time per assistant. Rest of the time you work when I work. Which is always."

"I am so relaxed right now."

"Good! But is there anything else to do around here besides this?"

Which is how we came to be wandering around inside Kenwood House, followed, for a while, by an eagle-eyed six-year-old girl whose distracted mother refused to listen to her excellent hunch. I trailed red-eyed behind my new employer, noticing for the first time her very particular way of looking at paintings, how for example she ignored all men, not as painters, but as subjects, walking past a Rembrandt self-portrait without pausing, ignoring all the earls and dukes, and dismissing, with

a single line—"Get a haircut!"—a merchant sea-
man with my father's laughing eyes. Landscapes,
too, were nothing to her. She loved dogs, animals,
fruit, fabrics, and flowers especially. Over the years
I learned to expect that the bunch of anemones
we had just seen in the Prado or the peonies from
the National Gallery would reappear, a week or
so later, in vases all over whichever house or hotel
we happened to be in at the time. Many small,
painted dogs, too, leaped from canvases into her
life. Kenwood was the source of Colette, an incontinent Joshua Reynolds spaniel bought in Paris a
few months later, whom I then had to walk twice
a day for a year. But more than any of these she
loved the pictures of the women: their faces, their
fripperies, their hairstyles, their corsetry, their little, pointy shoes.

"Oh my God, it's Judy!"

Aimee was across the red damask room, in
front of a life-size portrait, laughing. I came up
behind and peered at the Van Dyck in question.
No doubt about it: there was Judy Ryan, in all her
horrible glory, but four hundred years ago, wearing an unflattering black-and-white tent of lace
and satin, and with her right hand—half maternal, half menacing—resting on the shoulder of
a young, unnamed page. Her bloodhound eyes,
terrible fringe, the long, chinless face—it was all
there. We laughed so much it seemed to me that
something changed between us, some formality or

fear fell away, so that when, a few minutes later, Aimee claimed to be charmed by something called **The Infant Academy** I felt free enough at least to disagree.

"It's a bit sentimental, isn't it? And weird . . ."

"I like it! I like the weirdness. Naked babies painting naked pictures of each other. I'm a sucker for babies right now." She looked wistfully at a boy child with a coy smirk on his cherubic face. "He reminds me of my baby. You really don't like it?"

I didn't know at the time that Aimee was pregnant with Kara, her second child. She probably didn't know it herself. To me it was obvious the whole picture was ridiculous, and the pink-cheeked infants especially repulsive, but when I looked at her face I saw she was serious. And what **are** babies, I can remember thinking, if they can do **this** to women? Do they have the power to reprogram their mothers? To make their mothers into the kinds of women their younger selves would not even recognize? The idea frightened me. I restricted myself to praising her son Jay's beauty in comparison to these cherubim, not very convincingly or coherently, thanks to the weed, and Aimee turned to me, frowning.

"You don't want kids, that it? Or you **think** you don't want them."

"Oh, I **know** I don't want them."

She patted me on the top of my head, as if there were not twelve years between us but forty.

"You're, what? Twenty-three? Things change. I was exactly the same."

"No, I've always known. Since I was little. I'm not the mothering type. Never wanted them, never will. I saw what it did to my mother."

"What did it do to her?"

To be asked so directly forced me to actually consider the answer.

"She was a young mum, then a single mum. There were things she wanted to be but she couldn't, not then—she was trapped. She had to fight for any time for herself."

Aimee put her hand on her hips and assumed a pedantic look.

"Well, **I'm** a single mom. And I can assure you my baby doesn't stop me doing a damn thing. He's like my fucking inspiration right now if you really want to know. It's a balance, for sure, but you've just got to **want** it enough."

I thought of the Jamaican nanny, Estelle, who let me into Aimee's house each morning and then disappeared to the nursery. That there might be any practical divergence between my mother's situation and her own did not seem to occur to Aimee, and this was one of my earliest lessons in her way of viewing the differences between people, which were never structural or economic but always essentially differences of personality. I looked at the color in her cheeks and where my hands were—out in front of me, like a politician making a point—and realized that our discussion had become rapidly and strangely heated, without either of us really wanting it to, as if the very word "baby" was a kind of accelerant. I put my hands back by my sides and smiled.

"It's just not for me."

We headed back through the galleries, looking for the exit, falling in step with a tour guide, he was telling a tale I'd known since childhood, about a brown girl—the daughter of a Caribbean slave and her British master—brought to England and raised in this big white house by well-to-do relatives, one of whom happened to be the Lord Chief Justice. A favorite anecdote of my mother's. Except my mother did not tell it like the tour guide, she did not believe that a great-uncle's compassion for his brown great-niece had the power to end slavery in England. I picked up one of the leaflets stacked on a side-table and read that the girl's father and mother had "met in the Caribbean," as if they'd been strolling through a beach resort at cocktail hour. Amused, I turned to show it to Aimee but she was in the next room, listening intently to the guide, hovering at the edges of the tour group as if she were part of it. She was always moved by stories that proved "the power of love"—and what difference did it make to me if she was? But I couldn't help myself, I began channeling my mother, commenting ironically on the commentary, until the guide became irritated and directed his group outside. When we, too, headed for the exit, I took over Aimee's tour, leading her through a low tunnel of ivy bent into an arbor and describing the **Zong** as if that great ship were floating right there in the lake right before us. It was an easy image to conjure up, I knew it intimately, it had sailed so many times through my childhood nightmares. On its way to Jamaica, but far off course due to an error in navigation, low on drinking water, filled with thirsty slaves ("Oh?" said Aimee, pulling a briar rose from its bush) and captained by a man who, fearing the slaves would not survive the rest of the journey—but not wanting a financial loss on his first voyage—gathered a hundred and thirty-three men, women and children and threw them overboard, shackled to each other: spoiled cargo on which insurance could later be collected. The famously compassionate great-uncle oversaw that case, too—I told Aimee, as my mother had told me—and he ruled against the captain, but only on the principle that the captain had made a mistake. He, and not the insurers, must take the loss. Those thrashing bodies were still cargo, you could still jettison cargo to protect the rest of your cargo. You just wouldn't be reimbursed for it. Aimee nodded, tucked the rose she had plucked between her left ear and her baseball cap and knelt suddenly to pat a passing pack of small dogs that were dragging behind them a single walker.

"Whatever doesn't kill you makes you stronger,"

I heard her tell a dachshund, and then, straightening up and facing me again: "If my dad hadn't died young? No way I'd be here. It's the pain. Jews, gays, women, blacks—the bloody Irish. That's our secret fucking strength." I thought of my mother—who had no patience for sentimental readings of history—and cringed. We left the dogs and walked on. The sky was cloudless, the Heath filled with flowers and foliage, the ponds were golden pools of light, but I couldn't rid myself of this feeling of discomfort and imbalance, and when I tried to trace its source I found myself back before that unnamed page in the gallery, a little gold ring in his ear, who looked beseechingly up at Judy's doppelgänger as we'd laughed at her. She did not look back at him, she never could, she'd been painted in such a way as to make that impossible. But hadn't I also avoided his eye, as I avoided Granger's eye and he avoided mine? I could see this little Moor now with absolute clarity. It was as if he were standing on the path before me.

Aimee insisted we end that peculiar afternoon by swimming in the ladies' pond. Granger waited once more at the gates, three bikes at his feet, angrily turning the pages of his pocket Penguin Machiavelli. A haze of pollen hovered just above the water, it seemed to be caught in the thick, drowsy air, though the water was frigid. I went in cringingly, in my knickers and T-shirt, inching myself down the ladder while two broad-beamed English women in sturdy Speedos and swim caps bobbed nearby, offering unsolicited encouragement to all who were in the process of joining them. ("Really rather nice once you're in." "Just keep kicking your legs till you feel them." "If Woolf swam here, so can you!") Women to the right and left of me, some three times my age, slipped right off the deck into the water, but I couldn't get any deeper than my waist and, stalling for time, turned round and pretended instead to be admiring the scene: white-haired ladies moving in a stately circle through the foul-smelling duckweed. A pretty dragonfly dressed in Aimee's favorite shade of green flitted by. I watched it land on the deck, just by my hand, and close its iridescent wings. Where was Aimee? I had a moment of paralyzing, weed-inflected paranoia: had she got in before me, while I was fretting about my underwear? Already drowned? Tomorrow would I find myself at an inquest, explaining to the world why I let a heavily insured, universally beloved Australian swim unaccompanied in an ice-cold North London pond? A banshee wail pierced the civilized scene: I turned back and saw Aimee, naked, running from the changing room toward me, launching herself in a dive over my head and over the ladder, arms out, back perfectly arched, as if lifted from below by an invisible principal dancer, before hitting the water clean and true.

Six

I didn't know that Tracey's father had gone to prison. It was my mother who told me, a few months after the fact: "I see he's gone in again." She didn't have to say more, or tell me to spend less time with Tracey, it was happening naturally anyway. A cooling-off: one of those things that can happen between girls. At first I was distraught, thinking it permanent, but in fact it was only a hiatus, one of many we would have, lasting a couple of months, sometimes longer, but always ending—not coincidentally—with her father getting out again, or else returning from Jamaica, where he often had to flee, when things got hot for him in the neighborhood. It was as if, when he was "in," or away, Tracey went into standby mode, pausing herself like a video-tape. Although in class we no longer shared a desk (we had been separated after Lily's party, my mother went up to the school and requested it) I had a clear view of her each day and when there was "trouble at home" I sensed it at once, it revealed itself in everything she did, or didn't do. She made life as difficult as possible for our teacher, not with explicit bad behavior like the rest of us, not by swearing or fighting, but by an absolute withdrawal of her presence. Her body was there, nothing else. She wouldn't answer questions or ask them, didn't involve herself in any activities or copy anything down, or even open her exercise book, and I understood, at such times, that for Tracey time had stopped. If Mr. Sherman started shouting she sat impassive at her desk, her eyes angled to a point above his head, her noise upturned, and nothing he could say—no threat and no degree of volume—had any effect. As I'd predicted, she never did forget those Garbage Pail Kids cards. And being sent to the headmistress's office held no fear for her: she stood up in the coat she had anyway never taken off and walked out of the room as if it made no difference where she went or what happened to her. When she was in this state of mind I took the opportunity to do those things that, when I was with Tracey, I felt inhibited from doing. I spent more time with Lily Bingham, for example, taking pleasure in her good humor and gentle way of being: she still played with dolls, knew nothing of sex, loved drawing and making things out of cardboard and glue. In other words she was still a child, as I sometimes wished I could be. In her games nobody died or was afraid or took revenge or feared being uncovered as a fraud, and there was absolutely no black and no white, for, as she solemnly explained to me one day as we played, she herself was "color blind" and saw only what was in a person's heart. She had a little cardboard theater of the Russian Ballet, bought in Covent Garden, and for her a perfect afternoon involved maneuvering the cardboard prince around the stage, letting him meet a cardboard princess and fall in love with her, while a scratchy copy of **Swan Lake**, her father's, played in the background. She loved ballet, though she was a poor dancer herself, too bandy-legged to have any real hopes, and she knew all the French words for everything, and the tragic life stories of Diaghilev and Pavlova. Tap dancing didn't interest her. When I showed her my well-worn copy of **Stormy Weather** she reacted in a way I hadn't anticipated, she was offended by it—hurt, even. Why was everybody black? It was unkind, she said, to have only black people in a film, it wasn't fair. Maybe in America you could do that, but not here, in England, where everybody was equal anyway and there was no need to "go on about it." And we wouldn't like it, she said, if someone said to us that only black people could come to Isabel's dance class, that wouldn't be nice or fair to us, would it? We'd be sad about that. Or that only black people could come into our school. We wouldn't like that, would we? I said nothing. I put **Stormy Weather** back in my rucksack and went home, walking beneath a Willesden sunset of petroleum colors and quick-shunting clouds, going over and over this curious lecture in my mind, wondering what she could have meant by the word "we"?

Seven

When things were frosty between Tracey and me I found Saturdays hard, and relied on Mr. Booth for conversation and advice. I brought new information to him—which I got from the library—and he added to what I had or explained things I didn't understand. Mr. Booth hadn't known, for example, that it was not really "Fred Astaire" but "Frederick Austerlitz," but he understood what "Austerlitz" meant, he explained it was a name that must have come not from America but from Europe, probably German or Austrian, possibly Jewish. To me Astaire **was** America—if he had been on the flag I would not have been surprised—but now I learned that he'd spent a lot of time in London, in fact, and that he had become famous here, dancing with his sister, and if I'd been born sixty years earlier I could have gone to the Shaftesbury Theater and seen him myself. And what's more, said Mr. Booth, his sister was a far better dancer than him, everybody said so, she was the star and he was the also-ran, **can't sing, can't act, balding, can dance, a little**, ha ha ha, well he showed them, didn't he? Listening to Mr. Booth, I wondered if it were possible for me, too, to become a person who revealed themselves later in life, much later, so that one day—a long time from now—it would be Tracey sitting in the front row of the Shaftesbury Theater, watching **me** dance, our positions reversed completely, my own superiority finally recognized by the world. And in later years, said Mr. Booth, taking my library book out of my hands and reading from it, in later years his daily routine was little changed from the life he had always led. He woke up at five a.m. and breakfasted on a single boiled egg that kept his weight at a constant hundred and thirty-four pounds. Addicted to television serials such as **The Guiding Light** and **As the World Turns**, he would telephone his housekeeper if he could not watch the soap operas, to find out what had happened. Mr. Booth closed the book, smiled and said: "What an odd fish!"

When I complained to Mr. Booth of Astaire's one imperfection—that he couldn't, in my opinion, sing—I was wrong-footed by how strongly he disagreed, usually we agreed about everything, and were always laughing together, but now he picked out the notes to "All of Me" in a minimal sort of way on the piano and said: "But singing isn't just about belting it out, is it? It's not just who has the most wobble or the highest note, no, it's about phrasing, and being delicate, and getting just the right feeling from a song, the soul of it, so that something real happens inside you when a man opens his mouth to sing, and don't you want to feel something real rather than just having your poor earholes bashed in?"

He stopped talking and played "All of Me" in full, and I sang along with him, consciously trying to deliver each phrase in the same manner that Astaire does in **Silk Stockings**—cutting some lines short, half speaking others—though it didn't feel natural to me. Together Mr. Booth and I considered what it would be like to love the east, west, north and south of somebody, to gain complete control of them, even if they loved, in return, only a small percentage of us. Usually I performed with one hand on the piano, facing out, because that's how the girls did it in the movies, and that way I could keep an eye on the clock over the church door and know when the last child had filed in and therefore when it was time to stop, but on this occasion the desire to try to sing in harmony with that delicate melody—to match Mr. Booth's way of playing it, not just to "belt it out" but to create a real feeling—made me instinctively turn inwards, halfway through the verse, and when I did I saw that Mr. Booth was crying, very softly, but certainly crying. I stopped singing. "And he's trying to make her dance," he said. "Fred wants Cyd to dance, but she won't, will she? She's what you'd call an intellectual, from Russia, and she don't **want** to dance, and she says to him: 'The trouble with dancing is **You go, go, go, but you don't get anywhere!**' And Fred says: '**You're telling me!**' Lovely. Lovely! Now look, dear, it's time for class. You'd best get your shoes on."

As we tied our laces and prepared to get back in line, Tracey said to her mother, within my hearing: "See? She loves all them weird old songs." It had the tone of an accusation. I knew that Tracey loved pop music, but I didn't think the melodies were as pretty, and now I tried to say so. Tracey shrugged, stopping me in my tracks. Her shrugs had a power over me. They could end any topic. She turned back to her mother and said, "Likes old buggers, too."

Her mother's reaction shocked me: she looked over and smirked. At that moment my father was outside, in the churchyard, in his usual spot under the cherry trees; I could see him with his pouch of tobacco in one hand and the cigarette paper in the other, he didn't bother to disguise these things from me any longer. But there was not a world in which I could make a cruel comment to another child and have my father—or mother—smirk, or side with me in any way. It struck me that Tracey and her mother were on the same side, and I thought there was something unnatural about this and that they seemed to know it, for in certain contexts they hid it. I felt sure that if my father had been present Tracey's mother would not have dared to smirk.

"Best keep away from strange old men," she said, pointing at me. But when I protested that Mr. Booth was not strange to us, that he was our dear old piano player and we loved him, Tracey's mother seemed bored as I talked, crossed her arms over her huge chest and looked straight ahead.

"Mum thinks he's a nonce," explained Tracey.

I walked out of that lesson gripping my father's hand, but I didn't tell him what had happened. I didn't think of asking either of my parents for help in any matter, not any more, if anything I thought only of protecting them. I went elsewhere for guidance. Books had begun to enter my life. Not good books, not yet, still those old showbiz biographies that I read in the absence of sacred texts, as if they **were** sacred texts, taking a form of comfort from them, though they were hack work done for quick money, barely given a second thought by their authors, surely, but to me, important. I kept certain pages folded and read lines over and over, like a Victorian lady reading her psalms. **He isn't doing that right**—that was a very important one. It was what Astaire claimed he was thinking whenever he watched himself onscreen, and I noted that third-person pronoun. This is what I understood by it: that for Astaire the person in the film was not especially connected with him. And I took this to heart, or rather, it echoed a feeling I already had, mainly that it was important to treat oneself as a

kind of stranger, to remain unattached and unprej-
udiced in your own case. I thought you needed to
think like that to achieve anything in this world.
Yes, I thought that was a very elegant attitude.
And I became fixated, too, upon Katharine Hepburn's famous Fred and Ginger theory: **He gives
her class, she gives him sex.** Was this a general
rule? Did all friendships—all relations—involve
this discreet and mysterious exchange of qualities,
this exchange of power? Did it extend to peoples
and nations or was it a thing that happened only
between individuals? What did my father give my
mother—and vice versa? What did Mr. Booth and
I give each other? What did I give Tracey? What
did Tracey give me?

PART THREE

Intermission

One

Governments are useless, they can't be trusted, Aimee explained to me, and charities have their own agendas, churches care more for souls than for bodies. And so if we want to see real change in this world, she continued, adjusting the incline on her running machine until I, who walked on a neighboring one, seemed to be watching her dash up the side of Kilimanjaro, well, then we ourselves have to be the ones to do it, yes, we have to be the change we want to see. By "we" she meant people like herself, of financial means and global reach, who happen to love freedom and equality, want justice, feel an obligation to do something good with their own good fortune. It was a moral category but also an economic one. And if you followed its logic all the way to the end of the revolving belt, then after a few miles you arrived at a new idea, that wealth and morality are in essence the same thing, for the more money a person had, then the more goodness—or potential for goodness—a person possessed. I mopped up my sweat with my vest and glanced at the screens in front of us: seven miles for Aimee, one and a half for me. At last she was finished, we stepped off our machines, I passed her a towel, we walked together to the editing room. She wanted to review an early cut of a promo we were making for prospective donors, which didn't yet have its music or sound. We stood behind the director and editor and looked on as a version of Aimee, a silent version, broke soil on the school project, large spade in hand, and laid the foundation stone with the help of a village elder. We watched her dance with her six-year-old daughter, Kara, and a group of beautiful schoolgirls, in their green-and-gray uniforms, to music we could not hear, each stamp of her feet raising great clouds of red dust. I recalled seeing all these things happening months earlier, in reality, in the very moment that they happened, and thought how different they appeared now, in this format, as the editor moved things about with the ease his software allowed, inter-splicing Aimee in America with Aimee in Europe and Aimee in Africa, placing familiar events in a new order. And this is how you get things done, she announced, after fifteen minutes, satisfied, standing up, ruffling the young director's hair and heading for the showers. I stayed and helped finish the edit. A time-lapse camera had been placed on the building site, back in February, and so now we could watch the whole school go up in a few minutes, as ant-like laborers, moving too fast to be distinguished from each other, swarmed over it, a surreal demonstration of what was possible when good people of means decided to get things done. The kind of people able to build a girls' school, in a rural West African village, in a matter of months, simply because that is what they have decided to do.

It pleased my mother to call Aimee's way of doing things "naïve." But Aimee felt she had already tried my mother's route, the political route. She'd gone to bat for presidential candidates, back in the eighties and nineties, hosting dinners, making campaign contributions, haranguing audiences from the stages of stadiums. By the time I came into the picture she was finished with all that, just as the generation she'd once encouraged to the ballot box, my generation, were finished. Now she was committed to "making change happen on the ground," she wanted only to "work with communities at a community level," and I honestly respected her commitment, and only occasionally—when some of her fellow good people of means came up to the Hudson Valley house, to lunch or to swim, and to discuss this or that venture—would it become very hard to avoid seeing the things my mother saw. At those times I really felt my mother at my shoulder, an invisible conscience, or an ironic commentary, pouring poison in my ear from thousands of miles away, as I tried to listen to all these various good people of means—famous for playing the guitar or singing or designing clothes or pretending to be other people—chatter over cocktails about their plans to end malaria in Senegal or bring clean wells to Sudan and so on. But I knew Aimee herself had no abstract interest in power. She was motivated by something else: impatience. To Aimee poverty was one of the world's sloppy errors, one among many, which might be easily corrected if only people would bring to the problem the focus she brought to everything. She hated meetings and long discussions, disliked considering an issue from too many angles. Nothing bored her more than "on the one hand this" and "on the other hand that." She put her faith instead in the power of her own decisions, and these she made with her "heart." Often these decisions were sudden, and were never changed or rescinded once she'd made them, for she believed in her own good timing, in timing itself, as a mystical force, a form of fate, operating at the global and cosmic level as much as at the personal. In fact, in Aimee's mind these three levels were connected. It was the good timing of fate, as she saw it, that burned down the British headquarters of YTV, on 20 June 1998, six days after she visited us, the wiring going wrong somehow, in the middle of the night, sending a fire ripping through the place, destroying those miles and miles of VHS which had been, up till then, preserved from the corrupting influence of the London Underground. We were told it would be nine months before the offices were habitable again. In the meantime everybody was moved to an ugly, featureless office block in King's Cross. My commute was twenty minutes longer, I missed the canal, the market, Snowdon's birds. But I spent only six days in King's Cross. It was all over for me the moment Zoe brought a fax to my desk, addressed to me, with a phone number on it, which I was to ring, with no explanation. From the other end came the voice of Aimee's manager, Judy Ryan. She told me Aimee herself had requested that the brown girl in green come to her offices in Chelsea and be interviewed for a possible position. I was stunned. I paced outside that building for half an hour before I entered it, shaking, all the way up in the lift and through the hall, but when I walked into that room I saw the decision already made, right there on her face. There was no anxiety for Aimee, and no doubt: none of this, in her view, was coincidence or luck or even happy accident. It was "Fate." "The Great Fire"—as the employees christened it—was only part of a conscious effort, on behalf of the universe, to bring the two of us together, Aimee and me, a universe which at the same moment declined to intervene in so many other matters.

Two

Aimee had an unusual attitude to time, but her approach was very pure and I came to admire it. She wasn't like the rest of her tribe. She didn't need surgeons, didn't live in the past, fudge dates or use any of the usual forms of distraction or distortion. With her it really was a matter of will. Over ten years I saw how formidable that will could be, what it could make happen. And all the labor she put into it—all the physical exercise, all the deliberate blindness, the innocence cultivated, the spiritual epiphanies she was able somehow to experience spontaneously, the very many ways she fell in and out of love, like a teenager—all of this came to seem to me effectively a form of energy in itself, a force capable of creating a dilation in time, as if she really were moving at the speed of light, away from the rest of us—stranded on earth and aging faster than her—while she looked down on us and wondered why.

The effect was most striking when one of her Bendigo siblings visited, or when she was with Judy, whom she'd known since secondary school.

What did these late-middle-aged people, with their fucked-up families and wrinkles and disappointments and difficult marriages and physical ailments—what did any of this have to do with Aimee? How could any of these people have grown up with her, or once slept with the same boys or been able to run in the same way at the same speed down the same street in the same year? It wasn't only that Aimee looked very young— although of course she did—it was that an almost unbelievable youthfulness pulsed through her. It went right down to the bone, affecting the way she sat, moved, thought, spoke, everything. Some, like Marco, her bad-tempered Italian chef, were cynical and bitter about it, they claimed it was only money that did it, that it was all a side-effect of money and no work, never any real work. But in our travels with Aimee we met plenty of people with a lot of money who did nothing, far less than Aimee—who, in her own way, worked hard—and most of them seemed as old as Methuselah. And so it was reasonable to assume, and a lot of people did, that it was her young lovers that kept Aimee young, this was after all basically her own argument for years—that and the lack of children. But this theory could not survive the year she canceled the South American and European tours, and the arrival of her son, Jay, and, two years later, baby Kara, and the quick dispatching of one middle-aged father and boyfriend, and the obtaining and subsequent even swifter dispatching of the second father and husband, who was, true enough, not much more than a boy himself. Surely, people thought, surely this much experience, crammed into a few years, will leave its mark? But while the rest of the team came out of that whirlwind exhausted, completely wrung out, ready to lie down for a decade, Aimee herself proved largely unaffected, she was more or less as she had always been, full of a terrifying amount of energy. After Kara was born she went straight back into the studio, back to the gym, back on tour, more nannies were hired, tutors appeared, and she emerged from it all, a few months later, seeming like a mature twenty-six-year-old. She was almost forty-two. I was just about to turn thirty, it was one of those facts about me that Aimee had decided to obsessively retain, and for two weeks beforehand she kept insisting that we'd have a "ladies' night," just the two of us, phones off, total focus, mindfulness, cocktails, none of which I expected or had asked for, but she wouldn't let it go, and then of course the day came and no mention at all was made of my birthday, instead we did press for Norway all day, after which she ate with her children, while I sat in my room alone and tried to read. She was still in the dance studio at ten when I was interrupted by Judy, sticking her head, with its unchanged feather-cut, remnant of her Bendigo youth, round the door, to tell me, without looking up from her phone, that I was to remind Aimee we were flying to Berlin the next morning. This was in New York. Aimee's dance studio was big as a ballroom, a mirrored box with a barre of walnut that stretched all the way round. It had been dug out of the basement of her townhouse. When I walked in she was sitting in the horizontal splits, completely still, as if dead, her head thrown forward, a long fringe—red at the time—covering her face. Music was playing. I waited to see if she'd turn to me. Instead she sprang up and began running through a routine, all the time facing her own reflection in the mirrors. It had been some time since I'd seen her dance. I rarely sat in the crowd for the shows any more: that aspect of her life felt very distant, the artificial performance of someone I had come to know too well at a deeper, granular level. A person for whom I scheduled abortions, hired dog walkers, ordered flowers, wrote Mother's Day cards, applied creams, administered injections, squeezed spots, wiped very occasional break-up tears, and so on. Most days I wouldn't have known I worked for a performer. My work with and for Aimee happened in cars, mostly, or on sofas, in airplanes and offices, on many kinds of screens and in thousands of e-mails.

But here she was, dancing. To a song I didn't recognize—I hardly ever went to the studio any more, either—but the steps themselves were familiar, they hadn't changed much, over the years. The greater part of her routine has always consisted primarily of a form of strident walking: a powerful, pacing step that marks the boundaries of whatever space she's in, like a big cat methodically prowling around her cage. What surprised me now was its undimmed erotic force. Usually when we compliment a dancer we say: she makes it look easy. This is not the case with Aimee. Part of her secret, I felt as I watched her, is the way she's able to summon joy out of effort, for no move of hers flowed instinctively or naturally from the next, each "step" was clearly visible, choreographed, and yet as she sweated away at their execution, the hard work itself felt erotic, it was like witnessing a woman cross the line at the end of a marathon, or working toward her own orgasm. That same ecstatic revelation of a woman's will.

"Let me finish!" she cried out, to her reflection.

I walked over to the far corner, slid down the glass wall, sat on the floor and reopened my book. I'd decided to establish a new rule for myself: read for half an hour an evening, no matter what. The book I had chosen was not long, but I hadn't got very far in it. Reading was basically impossible when you worked for Aimee, it was seen, by the rest of the team, as deeply impractical and I think in some sense fundamentally disloyal. Even if we were flying a long stretch—even if we were heading back to Australia—people were either answering Aimee-related e-mails or flicking through a stack of maga-

zines, which could always be disguised as work, for
Aimee was either in the magazine you had in your
hand or very soon would be. Aimee herself read
books, sometimes decent books, recommended by
me, more often self-help or diet nonsense that Judy
or Granger put in front of her, but Aimee's reading
was something separate, she was Aimee after all
and could do as she pleased. Sometimes she took
ideas from the books I gave her—a time period or
a character or a political idea—which would then
end up, in a flattened and vulgar form, in one
video or song or another. But this did not change
Judy's opinion on reading in general, for her it was
a kind of vice because it took up valuable time we
might otherwise spend working for Aimee. Still
sometimes it was necessary, even for Judy, to read
a book—because it was about to become a movie
vehicle for Aimee, or was otherwise necessary for
a project—and in these situations she would use
our long-haul flights to read a third of whatever
it was, with her feet up, and a lemon-sucking look
on her face. She never read more than a third—"I
get the basic idea"—and when she'd finished
she would give one of four possible judgments.
"Zippy"—which was good; "Important"—which
was very good; "Controversial"—which could be
either good or bad, you never knew; or "Lidder-
ary," which was pronounced with a sigh and an eye
roll and was very bad. If I tried to make a case for
whatever it was Judy would shrug and say: "What

do I know? I'm just a little bogan girl from Bendigo," and this, said within Aimee's earshot, killed any project dead. Aimee never underestimated the importance of the heartland. Though she'd left Bendigo behind—did not sound like her people any more, had always sung with a faux-American accent and often spoke of her childhood as a form of living death—she still considered her hometown a potent symbol, almost a form of bellwether. Her theory was that a star has New York and LA in their pocket, a star can take Paris and London and Tokyo—but only a superstar takes Cleveland and Hyderabad and Bendigo. A superstar takes everybody everywhere.

"What you reading?"

I held up the book. She drew her legs back together—from where they had landed, back in the splits—and scowled at the cover.

"Never heard of it."

"**Cabaret?** It's that, basically."

"A book of the movie?"

"The book that came before the movie. I thought it might be useful, since we're heading to Berlin. Judy sent me in here to crack the whip."

Aimee made a face at herself in the mirror.

"Judy can kiss my bogan arse. She's been giving me such a hard time recently. Think maybe she's menopausal?"

"Think maybe you're just annoying?"

"Ha ha."

She lay down and lifted her right leg up in front of her, waiting. I went over and knelt before her, bending her knee into her chest. I was so much more heavily constructed—broader, taller, weightier—that whenever I stretched her like this I felt I had to be careful, that she was fragile and I could break her, though she had muscles I could not imagine having and I had seen her lift young male dancers almost as high as her head.

"The Norwegians were dull, weren't they?" she muttered, and then an idea came to her, as if none of our conversations of the past three weeks had happened at all: "Why don't we go out? Like, right now. Judy won't know. We'll go out the back way. Have a few cocktails? I'm in the mood. We don't need a reason."

I smiled at her. I thought about what it must be like to live in this world of shifting facts that move or disappear, depending on your mood.

"Something funny?"

"Nope. Let's go."

She took a shower and got dressed in her civilian outfit: black jeans, black vest and a black baseball cap pulled low, which made her ears stick out through her hair and gave her an unexpectedly goofy look. People don't believe me when I say she liked to go out dancing, and it's true we didn't do it often, not in the later years, but it did happen and it never created much fuss, probably because we went late, and to gay places, and by the time the boys spotted her they were usually high and happy and full of an expansive sort of goodwill: they wanted to be protective of her. She'd been theirs years ago, before she was anybody's, and looking after her now was a way of demonstrating that she still really belonged to them. Nobody asked for autographs, or made her pose for pictures, no one called the papers—we just danced. My only job was to demonstrate that I couldn't keep up with her, and there was no need to fake this, I really couldn't. At the point where my calves burned and I was as wet with sweat as if I'd stood under a hose, Aimee would still be dancing, and I would have to take my seat and wait for her. I was doing just that, in the roped-off area, when I felt a great thwack on my shoulder and something wet on my cheek. I looked up. Aimee stood over me, grinning and looking down, sweat dripping from her face on to mine.

"On your feet, soldier. We're shipping out."

It was one in the morning. Not so late, but I wanted to go home. Instead, as we approached the Village, she lowered the partition and told Errol to keep going right past the house, to head for Seventh and Grove, and when Errol tried to protest Aimee stuck out her tongue and raised the partition. We pulled up outside a tiny, scuzzy-looking piano bar. I could already hear a man with a grating Broadway vibrato singing a number from **Chorus Line**. Errol wound down the window

and glared at the open doorway. He didn't want
to let her go. He looked at me pleadingly, in solidarity, as two people in the same boat—in Judy's
eyes we would both be held responsible tomorrow
morning—but there was nothing I could do with
Aimee once she'd set her will on something. She
opened the door and pulled me out of the car. We
were both drunk: Aimee overexcited, dangerously
re-energized, me exhausted, maudlin. We sat in a
dark corner—the whole place was dark corners—
with two vodka martinis brought over by a barman of Aimee's age so overwhelmed to be serving
her it wasn't clear how he was going to get through
the practical matter of putting the drinks in front
of us before he collapsed. I took the glasses out
of his shaking hands and endured Aimee telling
me the history of Stonewall, on and on, Stonewall this, Stonewall that, as if I'd never been to
New York and didn't know a thing about it. At
the piano a group of white women at a bachelor-
ette party sang something from **The Lion King**;
they had horrible, shrill voices, and kept forgetting
the words. I knew it was childish but I was in an
absolute rage about my birthday, my rage was the
only thing keeping me awake, I was feeding off it
in that righteous way you can if you never mention
out loud the wrong you are being done. I sank my
martini and listened without comment as Aimee
moved on from Stonewall to her own early days as
a jobbing dancer, in Alphabet City, in the late sev-

enties, when all her friends were "these crazy black boys, queers, divas; all dead now," stories I had heard so many times I could almost repeat them myself, and I was despairing of finding any way of stopping her talking when she announced she was "going to the dunny," in an accent she used only when very drunk. I knew her experience of public toilets to be limited but before I could get to my feet she was twenty yards ahead of me. As I tried to pass through the drunken bachelorettes the piano player looked up at me hopefully and grabbed my wrist: "Hey, sister. You sing?" At the same moment Aimee skipped down the basement steps and disappeared from view.

"How about this right here?" He nodded at his sheet music and passed a weary hand over the ebony sheen of his bald head. "Can't listen to these girls no more. You know it? From **Gypsy**?"

His elegant fingers were to the keyboard, and I was singing the opening bars, the famous preamble, in which only the dead stay home, while people like Mama, oh, they're different, they won't just sit and take it, they've got the dreams and the guts, they won't stay and rot, they'll always fight to get up—and out!

I rested a hand on the piano, turned in toward it, closed my eyes, and I can remember thinking I was starting small, at least, that's what I consciously intended to do—to start small and keep it small—singing under the notes so as not to be noticed, or not noticed too much, out of the old shyness. But also out of deference to Aimee, who was not a natural singer, even if this fact was unspeakable between us. Who was in fact no more a natural singer than the bachelorettes sitting in front of me sucking down mai tais on their bar stools. But I was a natural, wasn't I? Surely I was, despite everything? And now I found I couldn't stay small, my eyes stayed closed but my voice lifted, and kept lifting, I got louder and louder, I did not feel I had control of it, exactly, it was something I'd released that now rose up and away and escaped my reach. My hands were in the air, I was stamping my heels into the floor. I felt I had everyone in the room. I even had a sentimental vision of myself as one in a long line of gutsy brothers and sisters, music-makers, singers, musicians, dancers, for didn't I, too, have the gift so often ascribed to my people? I could turn time into musical phrases, into beats and notes, slowing it down and speeding it up, controlling the time of my life, finally, at last, here on a stage, if nowhere else. I thought of Nina Simone dividing each note from the next, so viciously, with such precision, as Bach, her hero, had taught her to do, and I thought of her name for it—"Black Classical Music"—she hated the word **jazz**, considering it a white word for black people, she rejected it totally—and I thought of her voice, the way she could extend a note beyond the point of tolerability and force her audience to concede to it, to her timescale, to her vision of the song, how she was completely without pity for her audience, and so relentless in pursuit of her freedom! But too involved in these thoughts of Nina I didn't see the end coming, I thought I had another verse, I sang over the concluding chord, when it came, and continued some way ahead before I realized, oh, yes, yes, stop now, it's over. If there had been riotous clapping I couldn't hear it any longer, it seemed to have stopped. I only felt the piano player patting me, two quick pats, on my back, which was sticky and cold with the dried sweat of the previous club. I opened my eyes. Yes, the uproar in the bar was over, or maybe it had never been, everything looked as it had before, the piano player was already talking to the next performer, the bachelorettes were happily drinking and talking as if nothing had happened at all. It was two thirty in the morning. Aimee was not in her seat. She was not in the bar. I stumbled around that cramped and crowded space twice, kicked open each stall in the awful toilets, my phone at my ear, ringing and ringing and getting her answerphone. I struggled back through the bar and up the stairs to the street. I was making yelping noises of panic. It was raining, and my hair which had been blow-dried straight now began to curl back up, with terrific speed, every raindrop that hit me spurred a curl, and I reached into it and felt lamb's wool, the damp spring of it, thick and alive. A car horn went. I looked up and saw Errol parked where we had left him. The back window went down and Aimee leaned out of it, slow-clapping.

"Oh, **bravo.**"

I hurried to her, apologizing. She opened the door: "Just get in."

I sat next to her, still apologizing. She shifted forward to speak to Errol.

"Drive to midtown and back."

Errol took off his glasses and pinched the bridge of his nose.

"It's almost three," I said, but the partition went up and off we went. For ten blocks or so Aimee said nothing at all and neither did I. As we passed through Union Square she turned to me: "Are you happy?"

"What?"

"Answer the question."

"I don't understand why I'm being asked the question."

She licked her thumb and wiped some mascara I had not realized was running down my face.

"We've been together, what? Five years?"

"Almost seven."

"OK. So you should know by now that I don't want the people who work for me," she explained slowly, as if talking to an idiot, "to be unhappy working for me. I don't see the point in that."

"But I'm not unhappy!"

"Then what are you?"

"Happy!"

She took the cap off her head and pulled it over mine.

"In this life," she said, falling back against the leather, "you've got to know what you want. You have to visualize it, and then you have to pull it down. But we've talked about this many times. Many times."

I nodded and smiled, too drunk to manage much more. I had my face wedged between the walnut and the window and from here I had a fresh view of the city, from the top down. I'd see the roof garden of a penthouse before I saw the few, stray people still out at this hour, splashing through puddled sidewalks, and I kept finding in this perspective uncanny, paranoid alignments. An old Chinese lady, a can collector, in an old-fashioned conical hat, pulling her load—hundreds, perhaps thousands, of cans gathered together in a huge plastic sheet—under the windows of a building I knew to contain a Chinese billionaire, a friend of Aimee's, with whom she had once discussed opening a chain of hotels.

"And in this city you really need to **know** what it is you want," Aimee was saying, "but I don't think you **do** know, yet. OK, so you're smart, we get that. You think what I'm saying doesn't apply to you, but it does. The brain is connected to the heart and the eye—it's all visualization, all of it. Want it, see it, take it. No apologies. I don't apologize **ever** for what I want! But I **see** you—and I see that you spend your life apologizing! It's like you've got survivor's guilt or something! But we're not in Bendigo any more! You've left Bendigo—right? Like Baldwin left Harlem. Like Dylan left . . . wherever the fuck it was he was from. Sometimes you gotta get out—get the fuck out of Bendigo! Thanks be to Christ we both have. Long ago. Bendigo's behind us. You get what I'm saying, right?"

I nodded many times over, though I had no idea what she was saying, really, apart from the strong sense I usually had with Aimee that she found her own story universally applicable, and never more so than when drunk, that in these moments we all of us came from Bendigo, and we all of us had fathers who had died when we were young, and we had all visualized our good fortune and pulled it down toward us. The border between Aimee and everybody else became obscure, hard to make out exactly.

I felt sick. I hung my head like a dog into the New York night.

"Look, you're not going to be doing this for ever," I heard her say, a little later, as we entered Times Square, driving beneath an eighty-foot Somali model with a two-foot Afro dancing for joy on the side of a building in her perfectly ordinary Gap khakis. "That's just fucking obvious. So the question becomes: what are you going to do, after this? What are you going to do with your **life**?"

I knew the right answer to this was meant to be "run my own" this or that, or something amorphously creative like "write a book" or "open a yoga retreat," for Aimee thought that in order to do these sorts of things a person only had to walk into, say, a publisher's office and announce their intent. This had been her own experience. What could she know about the waves of time that simply come at a person, one after the other? What could she know about life as the temporary, always partial, survival of that process? I fixed my eyes on the dancing Somali model.

"I'm fine! I'm happy!"

"Well, I think you're too much in your own head," she said, tapping hers. "Maybe you need to get laid more . . . You know, you never do seem to get **laid.** I mean: is it my fault? I set you up, don't I? All the time. You never tell me how it goes."

Light flooded the car. It came from a huge digital ad for something or other but inside the car it felt delicate and natural, like the break of day. Aimee rubbed her eyes.

"Well, I've got projects for you," she said, "if you want projects. We all know you're capable of more than you're doing. At the same time, if you want to jump ship, now would be a good time to do it. I'm serious about this African project—no, don't roll your eyes at me; we need to iron out details, of course I know that, I'm not a fool—but it's gonna happen. Judy's been talking to your mum. I know you don't want to hear that either, but she has, and your mother is not as full of shit as you seem to think she is. Judy feels that the zone . . . Well, I'm loaded right now and I can't remember where it is right now, tiny country . . . in the west? But she thinks that might be a really interesting direction for us to go in, it's got potential. Says Judy. And turns out your honorable member of a mother knows a lot about it. Says Judy. Point is, I'm going to need all hands on deck, and people who **want** to be here," she said, indicating her own heart. "Not people who are still wondering **why** they're here."

"I want to be there," I said, looking at the spot, though under the influence of vodka her little breasts doubled themselves, then crossed, then merged.

"I turn now?" asked Errol hopefully, through a microphone.

Aimee sighed: "You turn now. Well," she said, returning to me, "you've been acting screwy for months, since London. It's a lot of bad energy. It's the kind of bad energy that really needs to be grounded otherwise it just keeps passing round the circuit, affecting everybody."

She made a series of hand gestures here that suggested some previously unknown law of physics.

"Something happen in London?"

Three

By the time I'd finished answering her we'd looped back and reached Union Square, where I looked up and saw the number on that huge ticking board speeding forward, billowing smoke out of the Dantean red hole at its center. It gave me a breathless feeling. A lot of things that happened in those months in London had made me breathless: I'd finally given up my flat, for lack of use, and stood at a crowded hustings waiting all night to watch a man in a blue tie ascend the stage and concede victory to my mother in a red dress. I'd seen a flyer for a nostalgic nineties-hip-hop night, at the Jazz Café, and wanted urgently to go, but could not think of a single friend I might take, I'd simply traveled too much the past few years, was not on any of the usual sites, did not keep up with personal e-mail, partly out of lack of time and partly because Aimee frowned on our "socializing" online, fearing loose talk and leaks. Without really noticing it, I'd let my friendships wither on the vine. So I went alone, got drunk and ended up sleeping with one of the doormen, a huge American, from Philadelphia, who claimed to have once played professional basketball. Like most people in his line of work—like Granger—he had been hired for his height and his color, for the threat considered implicit in their combination. Two minutes of smoking a cigarette with him revealed a gentle soul on good terms with the universe, ill-suited to his role. I had a little pouch of coke on me, given to me by Aimee's chef, and when my doorman's break came we went to the bathroom stalls and took a lot of it, off a shiny ledge behind the toilets that seemed specifically designed for the purpose. He told me that he hated his job, the aggression, dreaded laying hands on anyone. We left together after his shift, giggling in a taxi as he massaged my feet. When we got back to my flat, in which everything was packed up in boxes, ready for Aimee's huge storage facility in Mary-lebone, he got hold of the aspirational pull-up bar that I'd put up above my bedroom door and never used, attempted a pull-up, and ripped the stupid thing from the wall, and part of the plaster, too. In bed, though, I could hardly feel him inside of me—shriveled up by the coke, maybe. He didn't seem to mind. Cheerfully he fell asleep on top of me like a big bear and then, with equal cheeriness, at around five a.m., wished me well and let himself out. I woke up in the morning with a nosebleed and the very clear sense that my youth, or at least this version of it, was over. Six weeks later, on a

Sunday morning, as Judy and Aimee frenetically texted me about the archiving, in Milan, of a portion of Aimee's stage wardrobe, years 92–98, I sat, unbeknownst to them both, in the walk-in clinic of the Royal Free Hospital, awaiting the results of an STD and AIDS test, listening to several people, far less lucky than I turned out to be, being taken into side rooms to weep. But I didn't speak to Aimee of any of this. Instead I was speaking of Tracey. Tracey of all people. The whole history of us, the chronology sliding woozily back and forth in time and vodka, all resentments writ large, pleasures either diminished or destroyed, and the longer I spoke the clearer I saw and understood—as if the truth were a sunken thing rising up through a well of vodka to meet me—that only one thing had happened in London, really: I'd seen Tracey. After so many years of not seeing Tracey I had seen her. None of the rest mattered. It was as if nothing in the period between the last time I saw her and this had happened at all.

"Wait, wait—" said Aimee, too drunk herself to disguise her impatience with another person's monologue—"This is your oldest girlfriend, right? Yes, I know this. Did I meet her?"

"Never."

"And she's a dancer?"

"Yes."

"Best type of people! Their bodies tell them what to do!"

I had been sitting on the edge of my seat, but now I deflated and lay my head back on its cold corner pillow of blacked-out glass, walnut and leather.

"Well, you can't make old friends," announced Aimee, in such a way that you might have assumed the phrase originated with her. "What would I do without my dear old Jude? Since we were fifteen! She fucked the dude I took to the school dance! But she calls me on my shit, yes she does. No one else does that . . ."

I was used to Aimee turning all stories about me into stories about her, usually I simply deferred to it, but the drink had me bold enough to believe, at that moment, that both our lives were in fact of equal weight, equally worthy of discussion, equally worthy of time.

"It was after I had that lunch with my mother," I explained, slowly. "The night I went out with that Daniel guy? In London? The disaster date."

Aimee frowned: "Daniel Kramer? **I** set you up with him. The financial guy? See, you didn't tell me anything about that!"

"Well, it was a disaster—we went to see a show. And she was in that fucking show."

"You spoke to her."

"No! I haven't spoken to her in eight years. I just told you that. Are you even listening to me?"

Aimee put two fingers to her temples.

"The timeline is confusing," she murmured. "Plus my head hurts. Look . . . God, I don't know . . .

maybe you **should** call her! Sounds like you want to. Call her now—fuck it, **I'll** talk to her."

"No!"

She grabbed my phone out of my hand—laughing, scrolling through my contacts—and when I tried to reach for it she held it out of her window.

"Give it to me!"

"Oh, come on—she'll love it."

I managed to climb over her, snatch the phone and press it between my thighs.

"You don't understand. She did a terrible thing to me. We were twenty-two. A terrible thing."

Aimee raised one of her famously geometric eyebrows and sent up the partition that Errol—wanting to know which entrance to the house we were heading for, front or back—had just sent down.

"Well, now I'm genuinely interested . . ."

We turned into Washington Square Park. The townhouses around the square stood red and noble, their façades warmly lit, but everything inside the park was dark and dripping, empty of people, aside from the half a dozen homeless black men in the far-right corner, sitting on the chess tables, their bodies wrapped in trash bags with holes for the arms and legs. I put my face to the window, closed my eyes, felt the flecks of rain and told the story as I remembered it, the fiction and the reality, in a jagged, painful rush, as if I were running across broken glass, but when I opened my eyes it was to the sound of Aimee laughing again.

"It's not fucking funny!"

"Wait—are you being serious right now?"

She tried pulling her top lip back into her mouth and biting down on it.

"You don't think it's possible," she asked, "that maybe you're making a big deal out of not so much?"

"What?"

"Honestly the only person I feel sorry for in that scenario—if it's true—is your dad. Poor guy! Super-lonely, trying to get his rocks—"

"Stop it!"

"It's not like he's Jeffrey Dahmer."

"It's not normal! That's not a normal thing to do!"

"Normal? Don't you understand that every man in this world with access to a computer, including the President, is right at this moment either looking at vaginas or has just stopped looking at vaginas—"

"It's not the same—"

"It's **exactly** the same. Except your dad didn't even have a computer. You think if George W. Bush looks up 'Teen Asian Pussy'—then what? He's a fucking serial killer?"

"Well . . ."

"Good point—bad example."

I chuckled, despite myself.

"I'm sorry. Maybe I'm being stupid. I don't get it. Why are you angry, exactly? Because she told you? You just said you thought it was bullshit!"

It was startling, after so many years of my own twisted logic, to hear the problem ironed out into Aimee's preferred straight line. The clarity disturbed me.

"She was always lying. She had this idea my father was perfect, and she wanted to ruin him for me, she wanted to make me hate my father like she hates hers. I couldn't ever really look him in the eye after. And it was that way till he died."

Aimee sighed. "That's the stupidest fucking thing I ever heard. You went and made yourself sad for no reason at all."

She reached out to touch my shoulder, but I turned my back on her and wiped a rogue tear from my eye.

"Pretty stupid."

"No. We all have our shit. You should call your friend, though."

She made a little pillow of her jacket and lay her head against her window, and by the time we'd crossed Sixth Avenue she was already asleep. She was the queen of power naps, had to be, to live as she did.

Four

Earlier that year, in London—a few days before the local elections—I'd had lunch with my mother. It was a gray, humid day, people moved across the bridge joylessly, beaten down by the drizzling rain, and even the grandest monuments, even Parliament, looked grim to me, sad and underwhelming. It all made me wish we were already in New York. I wanted all that height and sun-struck glass, and then after New York, Miami, and then five stops in South America and finally the European tour, twenty cities, ending in London once again. In this way, a whole year could pass by. I liked it that way. Other people had seasons to get through, they had to drag themselves through each year. In Aimee's world we didn't live like that. We couldn't even if we'd wanted to: we were never in one place long enough. If we didn't like winter we flew toward summer. When we were tired of cities we went to the beach—and vice versa. I'm exaggerating a little, not by much. My late twenties had passed in a weird state of timelessness, and I think now that not everyone could have fallen into a life like that, that I must have been somehow primed for it. Later I wondered whether we were chosen primarily for this reason, exactly because we tended to be people with few external ties, without partners or children, with the very minimum of family. The way we lived certainly kept us that way. Out of Aimee's four female assistants, only one of us ever had a child, and only then in her mid-forties, long after quitting. Climbing aboard that Learjet, you had to be untethered. It wouldn't have worked otherwise. I had only one rope now—my mother—and she was, like Aimee, in her prime, although unlike Aimee my mother had very little need of me. She was flying high herself, a few days from becoming the Member of Parliament for Brent West, and as I turned left, heading toward the Oxo Tower, leaving Parliament behind me, I felt, as usual, my own smallness next to her, the scale of what she had achieved, the frivolousness of my own occupation in comparison, despite all she'd tried to direct me toward. She seemed more impressive to me than ever. I held tight to the barrier, all the way, until I was across.

It was too damp to sit out on the terrace. I searched the restaurant for several minutes, but then spotted my mother, outside after all, under an umbrella, sheltered from the drizzle, and with Miriam, though there had been no mention, in our phone call, of Miriam. I didn't dislike Miriam. I didn't have any feeling about her really, it was hard to have feelings about her: she was so small and quiet and serious. All her dull features were gathered in the middle of her little face, and her natural hair was wound into sista dreads, genteelly graying at their tips. She had a little pair of round, gold-rimmed glasses which she never removed and made her eyes look even tinier than they were. She wore sensible brown fleeces and plain black trousers, no matter the occasion. A human picture frame, her only purpose to set off my mother. All that my mother ever really said about Miriam was: "Miriam makes me very happy." Miriam never spoke about herself—she only spoke about my mother. I had to google her to discover she was Afro-Cuban, by way of Lewisham, that once she'd worked in international aid but now taught at Queen Mary's—in some very lowly adjunct position—and had been writing a book "about the diaspora" for longer than I'd known her, which was about four years. She was introduced to my mother's constituents with a minimum of fuss at some event in a local school, photographed, tucked into the side of my mother, a timid dormouse standing by her lioness, and the journalist from the **Willesden and Brent Times** got exactly the same line I'd been given: "Miriam makes me very happy." Nobody seemed especially interested, not even the old Jamaican men and the African evangelicals. I got the sense that her constituents did not really think of my mother and Miriam as lovers, they were simply those two nice

Willesden ladies, who had saved the old cinema and fought to expand the leisure center and established Black History Month throughout the local libraries. Campaigning, they made an effective pair: if you found my mother overbearing, you could take comfort in Miriam's unassuming passivity, while people who were bored by Miriam relished the excitement my mother created wherever she went. Looking at Miriam now, nodding quickly, receptively, as my mother speechified, I knew that I was also glad of Miriam: she was a useful buffer. I went over and put a hand on my mother's shoulder. She did not look up or stop talking, but she registered my touch and raised a hand to lay over mine, accepting the kiss I pressed to her cheek. I drew out a chair and sat down.

"How are you, Mum?"

"Stressed!"

"Your mother's very stressed," confirmed Miriam, and began quietly to list all the many causes of my mother's stress: the envelopes that had to be stuffed and the flyers yet to be posted, the closeness of the latest polling, the underhand tactics of the opposition, and the supposed double-dealing of the only other black woman in Parliament, an MP of twenty years' standing, whom my mother considered, for no sensible reason, her bitter rival. I nodded in the right places and looked through the menu and managed to order some wine from a passing waiter, all without breaking the flow of

Miriam's talk, her numbers and percentages, the careful regurgitations of the various "brilliant" things my mother had said to so-and-so at this or that vital moment and how so-and-so had responded, poorly, to whatever brilliant thing it was my mother had said.

"But you're going to win," I said, with an intonation I realized, too late, was posed awkwardly between statement and question.

My mother looked stern, unfolded her napkin and lay it on her lap, like a queen who has been asked, impertinently, if her people still love her.

"If there's any justice," she said.

Our food arrived, my mother had ordered for me. Miriam set about squirreling hers away—she reminded me of a small mammal who expects to hibernate soon—but my mother let her knife and fork rest where they were and instead reached down to the empty chair beside her to bring up a copy of the **Evening Standard**, already open to a large picture of Aimee, on stage, juxtaposed with a stock photo of some destitute African children, from where exactly I couldn't tell. I hadn't seen the piece and it was held too far from me to read the text but I guessed the source: a recent press release, announcing Aimee's commitment to "global poverty reduction." My mother tapped a finger on Aimee's abdomen.

"Is she serious about it?"

I considered the question. "She's very passionate about it."

My mother frowned and picked up her cutlery.

"'Poverty reduction.' Well, fine, but what's the policy, specifically?"

"She's not a politician, Mum. She doesn't have policies. She has a foundation."

"Well, what is it she wants to **do**?"

I poured some wine for my mother and made her pause for a moment and clink a glass with me.

"I think it's really a school she wants to build. A girls' school."

"Because if she's serious," said my mother, over my reply, "you should advise her that she needs to talk to us, to be in partnership with government in one way or another . . . Obviously she has the financial means and the public's attention—that's all good—but without understanding the mechanics, it's just a lot of good intention that goes nowhere. She needs to meet with the relevant authorities."

I smiled to hear my mother referring to herself, already, as "government."

The next thing I said so irritated her she turned and gave her answer to Miriam instead.

"Oh, **please**—I really wish you wouldn't behave as if I'm asking for some great favor. I've no interest AT ALL in meeting that woman, none at all. Never have had. I was offering some advice. I thought it would be welcome."

"And it's welcome, Mum, thank you. I just—"

"I mean, really, you'd think this woman would **want** to talk to us! We gave her a British passport, after all. Well, never mind. It just seemed, from this"—she held up the paper again—"that she had serious intentions, but maybe that's not right, maybe she just wants to embarrass herself, I wouldn't know. 'White woman saves Africa.' Is that the idea? Very old idea. Well, it's your world, not mine, thank God. But she should really speak with Miriam, at least, the fact is Miriam has a lot of useful contacts, rural contacts, educational contacts—she's too modest to tell you. She was at Oxfam for a decade, for God's sake. Poverty is not just a headline, my love, it's a lived reality, on the ground—and education is at the heart of it."

"I know what poverty is, Mum."

My mother smiled sadly, and bit down on a forkful of food.

"No, dear, you don't."

My phone, which I had been trying, with all the will available to me, not to look at, buzzed again—it had buzzed a dozen times since I'd sat down—and now I took it out and tried to move quickly through the backlog, eating with my phone in one hand. Miriam brought up a dull administrative matter with my mother, often her way when she found herself caught up in some argument of ours, but in the middle of dealing with it my mother became visibly bored.

"You're addicted to that phone. You do know that?"

I didn't stop typing but made my face as calm as I could manage.

"It's work, Mum. This is how people work now."

"You mean: like slaves?"

She ripped a piece of bread in half and offered the smaller section to Miriam, something I'd seen her do before, it was her version of a diet.

"No, not like slaves. Mum, I have a nice life!"

She thought about this with her mouth full. She shook her head.

"No, that's not right—you don't have a life. **She** has a life. She has her men and her children and her career—**she** has the life. We read about it in the papers. You **service** her life. She's a giant sucking thing, sucking your youth, taking up all your—"

To stop her talking I pushed my chair back and went to the bathroom, lingering at the mirrors for longer than I needed, sending more e-mails, but when I got back, the conversation continued un-interrupted, as if no time at all had passed. My mother was still complaining, but to Miriam: "—all your time. She distorts everything. She's the reason I won't be having any grandchildren."

"Mum, my reproductive situation's really got nothing—"

"You're too close, you can't see it. She's made you suspicious of **everybody**."

I denied it, but the arrow hit the target. Wasn't I

suspicious—always on guard? Primed for any sign of what Aimee and I called, between ourselves, "customers"? A customer: someone we judged to be using me in the hope of getting close to her. Sometimes, in the early years, if a relationship of mine did manage—despite all the obstacles of time and geography—to putter along for a few months, I would build up a bit of confidence and courage, and would introduce whoever it was to Aimee, and this was usually a bad idea. The moment he went to the bathroom or out for a cigarette, I'd ask Aimee the question: customer? And the answer would come: Oh, honey, I'm sorry, **definitely** a customer.

"Look at the way you treat old friends. Tracey. You two were practically sisters, grew up together—now you don't even speak to her!"

"Mum, you always **hated** Tracey."

"That's not the point. People come from somewhere, they have roots—you've let this woman pull yours right out of the ground. You don't live anywhere, you don't have anything, you're constantly on a plane. How long can you live like that? I don't think she even **wants** you to be happy. Because then you might leave her. And **then** where would she be?"

I laughed, but the sound I made was ugly, even to me.

"She'd be fine! She's Aimee! I'm only assistant number one, you know—there're three others!"

"I see. So she can have any amount of people in her life but you can only have her."

"No, you don't see." I looked up from my phone. "I'm actually going out with someone tonight? Who Aimee set me up with, so."

"Well, that's nice," said Miriam. Her favorite thing in life was to see a conflict resolved, any conflict, and so my mother was a great resource for her: everywhere she went she made conflict, which Miriam then had to resolve.

My mother perked up: "Who is he?"

"You wouldn't know him. He's from New York."

"Can't I know his name? Is it a state secret?"

"Daniel Kramer. His name is Daniel Kramer."

"Ah," said my mother, smiling inscrutably at Miriam. An infuriating look of complicity passed between them. "Another nice Jewish boy."

As the waiter came to clear our plates the sun appeared in the gunmetal sky. Rainbows passed through the wine glasses on to the wet silverware, through the backs of the Perspex chairs, spreading from Miriam's commitment ring to a linen napkin that sat between the three of us. I refused dessert, said I had to get going, but as I moved to take my raincoat off the back of the chair my mother nodded at Miriam and Miriam passed me a folder, official-looking, ring-bound, with chapters and photographs, lists of contacts, architectural suggestions, a brief history of education in the region, an analysis of the likely "media impact," plans for government partnership, and so on: a "viability study." The sun crept through the gray, a mental fog cleared, I saw that the whole lunch had been for this purpose, really, and I was just a channel through which information was meant to pass, to Aimee. My mother, too, was a customer.

I thanked her for the folder and sat looking at its cover, closed in my lap.

"And how are you feeling," asked Miriam, blinking anxiously behind her glasses, "about your father? The anniversary's Tuesday, isn't it?"

It was so unusual to be asked a personal question during a lunch with my mother—never mind having a date significant to me remembered—that at first I wasn't sure it was addressed to me. My mother, too, looked alarmed. It was painful for us both to be reminded that the last time we'd seen each other had in fact been at the funeral, a full year earlier. Bizarre afternoon: the coffin met the flames, I sat next to my father's children—now adults in their late thirties and forties—and experienced a replay of the only other time I'd met them: the daughter wept, the son sat back in his chair with his arms folded across his chest, skeptical of death itself. And I, who couldn't cry, once again found them both to be far more convincing children of my father than I had ever been. And yet, in our family, we had never wanted to admit this unlikelihood, we always batted away what we considered to be the banal and prurient curiosity of strangers—"But won't she grow up confused?" "How will she choose between your cultures?"—to the point that sometimes I felt the whole purpose of my childhood was to demonstrate to the less enlightened that I was not confused and had no trouble choosing. "**Life** is confusing!"—my mother's imperious rebuff. But isn't there also a deep expectation of sameness between parent and child? I think I was strange to my mother and to my father, a changeling belonging to neither one of them, and although this is of course true of all children, in the end—we are not our parents and they are not us—my father's children would have come to this knowledge with a certain slowness, over years, were perhaps only learning it fully at this very moment, as the flames ate the pinewood, whereas I was born knowing it, I have always known it, it is a truth stamped all over my face. But this was all my private drama: afterward, at the reception, I realized something larger than my loss had been going on the whole time, yes, wherever I walked in that crematorium I heard it, an ambient buzz, Aimee, Aimee, Aimee, louder than my father's name and more frequent, as people tried to figure out if she was really in attendance, and then, later—when they decided she must have already come and gone—you could hear it again, in mournful echo, Aimee, Aimee, Aimee . . . I even heard my sister ask my brother if he'd seen her. She was there

throughout, hiding in plain sight. A discreet, sur-
prisingly short woman, make-up free, so pale as to
be almost translucent, in a prim-tweed suit with
blue veins running up her legs, wearing her own
natural, straight, brown hair.

"I think I'm going to lay flowers," I said, pointing vaguely across the river, toward North London. "Thanks for asking."

"One day off work!" said my mother, turning
back, joining the train of the conversation at an
earlier stop. "The day of his funeral. One day!"

"Mum, one day was all I asked for."

My mother affected a face of maternal wound-
edness.

"You used to be so close to your father. I know
that I always encouraged you to be. I really don't
know what happened."

For a moment I wanted to tell her. Instead I
watched a pleasure boat churn up the Thames. A
few people sat dotted among the rows of empty
seats, looking out at the gray water. I went back to
my e-mail.

"Those poor boys," I heard my mother say, and
when I raised my head from my phone I found her
nodding at Hungerford Bridge as the boat passed
under it. At once the same image that I knew was
in her mind floated up in my own: two young
men, thrown over the railing, into the water. The
one who lived and the one who died. I shivered and
pulled my cardigan more tightly across my chest.

"And there was a girl, too," added my mother, tipping a fourth sugar into a frothy cappuccino. "I don't think she was even sixteen. Practically children, all of them. Such a tragedy. They must still be in prison."

"Of **course** they're still in prison—they killed a man." I drew a breadstick from a thin china vase and broke it into quarters. "He's also still dead. Also a tragedy."

"I understand that," snapped my mother. "I was in the public gallery almost every day for that case, if you remember."

I remembered. I was not long out of the flat and it had been my mother's habit to call me each evening when she got home from the High Court, to tell me the stories—though I didn't ask to hear them—each with its own grotesque sadness, but all somehow the same: children abandoned by mothers or fathers or both, raised by grandparents, or not raised at all, whole childhoods spent caring for sick relatives, in crumbling prison-like estates, all south of the river, teenagers kicked out of school, or home, or both, drug abuse, sexual abuse, on the rob, sleeping rough—the thousand and one ways a life can be sunk in misery almost before it's begun. I remember one of them was a college drop-out. Another had a five-year-old daughter, killed in a car accident the day before. They were all already petty criminals. And my mother was fascinated by them, she had a vague idea to write something about the case, for what was, by that point, her Ph.D. She never did.

"Have I annoyed you?" she asked, placing a hand over mine.

"Two innocent boys walking across a fucking bridge!"

As I spoke I rapped my free fist on the table, without meaning to—an old habit of my mother's. She looked concernedly at me and righted the toppled salt-cellar.

"But darling, who's **arguing** with that?"

"We can't all be innocent." Out of a corner of my eye I saw a waiter, who'd just come out to check on the bill, tactfully withdraw. "Somebody has to be guilty!"

"Agreed," murmured Miriam, twisting a napkin fretfully in her hands. "I don't think anybody's disagreeing, are they?"

"They didn't have a chance," said my mother quietly, but firmly, and only later, walking back across the bridge, when my bad temper had passed, did I see that it was a sentence moving in two directions.

PART FOUR
Middle Passage

One

The greatest dancer I ever saw was the kankurang. But in the moment I didn't know who or what it was: a wildly swaying orange shape, of a man's height but without a man's face, covered in many swishing, overlapping leaves. Like a tree in the blaze of a New York fall that uproots itself and now dances down the street. A large gang of boys trailed behind it in the red dust, and a phalanx of women, with palm leaves in their hands—their mothers, I assumed. The women sang and stepped heavily, beating the air with the palms, walking and dancing both. I was squeezed into a taxi, a beat-up yellow Mercedes with a green stripe running down its middle. Lamin was next to me, in the backseat, alongside somebody's grandfather, a woman feeding a squalling baby, two teenage girls in their uniforms, and one of the Koranic teachers from the school. It was a scene of chaos that Lamin met calmly, ever conscious of his status, as a trainee teacher, his hands folded priest-like on his lap, looking as always—with his long, flat nose and broad nostrils, and sad, slightly yellowed eyes—like a big cat in repose. The car stereo played reggae from my mother's island, turned up to a crazy volume. But whatever was coming toward us was dancing to rhythms reggae never approaches. Beats so fast, so complex, that you had to think about them—or see them expressed through the body of a dancer—to understand what you were hearing. Otherwise you might mistake it for one rumbling bass note. You might think it was the sound of thunder overhead.

Who was drumming? I looked out of my window and spotted three men, their instruments gripped between their knees, walking like crabs, and when they scuttled in front of our car the whole travel-ing dance party paused in its forward momentum, took root in the middle of the road, forcing us to stop. It made a change from the checkpoints, the sullen, baby-faced soldiers, their machine guns held loosely at the hip. When we stopped for soldiers— often a dozen times in a single day—we would fall silent. But now the cab exploded in talk and whistles and laughter and the schoolgirls reached out of the window and jimmied the broken handle until the passenger door opened and everyone ex-cept the breastfeeding woman tumbled out.

"What is it? What's happening?"

I was asking Lamin, he was supposed to be my guide, but he seemed barely to remember I existed, much less that we were meant to be heading for the ferry, to cross the river into the city, and on to the airport, to greet Aimee. None of that mattered now. There was only the present moment, only the dance. And Lamin, as it turned out, was a dancer. I spotted it in him that day, before Aimee had even met him, long before she saw the dancer in him. I saw it in every hip swivel, each nod of his head. But I couldn't see the orange apparition any more, there was such a crowd between me and it that I could only hear it: what must have been its feet pounding the ground, and the raw clang of metal on metal, and a piercing shriek, otherworldly, to which the women replied in song, as they, too, danced. I was dancing involuntarily myself, pressed up close to so many moving bodies. I kept asking my questions—"What is it? What's happening?"—but English, the "official language," that heavy formal coat people only put on in my presence, and even then with obvious boredom and difficulty, had been thrown to the ground, everyone was dancing on it, and I thought, not for the first time in that first week, of the adjustment Aimee would have to make when she finally arrived and discovered, as I already had, the chasm between a "viability study" and life as it appears before you on the road and the ferry, in the village and the city, within the people and in a half-dozen languages, in the food and the faces and the sea and the moon and the stars.

People were clambering on to the car for a better view. I looked for Lamin and found him, too, scrambling up, on to the front bonnet. The crowd was dispersing—laughing, screaming, running— and I thought at first that a firecracker must have gone off. A group of the women fled leftwards, and now I saw why: the kankurang wielded two machetes, long as arms. "Come!" cried Lamin, reaching a hand down for me, and I pulled myself up to him, clinging to his white shirt as he danced, trying to keep my balance. I looked down at the frenzy below. I thought: here is the joy I've been looking for all my life.

Directly above me an old woman sat decorously on the roof of our car, eating a bag of peanuts, looking like a Jamaican lady at Lord's, following a day's cricket. She spotted me and waved: "Good morning, how is your morning?" The same cour- teous, automatic greeting that followed me round the village—no matter what I wore, no matter who I was with—and which by now I understood as a nod to my foreignness, which was obvious to every- one everywhere. She smiled mildly at the machetes as they spun, at the boys who kept daring each other to approach the dancing tree and match its frenetic moves—while steering clear of its circling knives—imitating in their own narrow bodies the convulsive stamps and twists and crouches and high kicks and general rhythmic euphoria that ra- diated from the figure to all points on the horizon, through the women, through Lamin, through me, through everyone I could see, as beneath us the car shook and rolled. She pointed at the kankurang. "It is a dancer," she explained.

A dancer who comes for the boys. Taking them to the bush, where they are circumcised, initiated into their culture, told the rules and the limits, the sacred traditions of the world in which they will live, the names of the plants to help with this or that illness and how to use them. Who acts as threshold, between youth and maturity, wards off evil spirits and is the guarantor of order and justice and continuity between and within his people. He is a guide who leads the young through their difficult middle passage, from childhood to adolescence, and he is also, simply, a young man himself, anonymous, chosen in great secrecy by the elders, covered in the leaves of the fara tree and stained with vegetable dyes. But I learned all this on my phone, back in New York. I did try to ask my guide about it, at the time, what it all meant, how it fitted into or diverged from local Islamic practice, but he couldn't hear me over the music. Or did not want to hear me. I tried again, a little later, after the kankurang had moved on elsewhere, and we were all squeezed back into the cab, along with two of the young dancing boys, they lay across our laps, sticky with the sweat of their efforts. But I could see my questions were annoying to everybody and by then the euphoria was over. Lamin's depressing formality, which he brought to all his dealings with me, had returned.

"A Mandinka tradition," he said and then turned back to the driver and the rest of the passengers to laugh and argue and discuss things I couldn't guess in a language I didn't know. We drove on. I wondered about the girls. Who comes for the girls? If not the kankurang, who? Their mothers? Their grandmothers? A friend?

Two

When Tracey's time came there was no one to guide her over the threshold, to advise her or even tell her that this was a threshold she was crossing. But her body was developing quicker than anybody else's and so she had to improvise, to make her own arrangements. Her first idea was to dress wildly. Her mother was blamed—mothers usually are—but I'm sure her mother barely saw or knew the half of it. She was still asleep when Tracey left for school and not home when she got back. She'd found some work finally, I think she was cleaning an office block somewhere, but my mother and the other mothers disapproved of her employment almost as much as they had disapproved of her unemployment. Before she had been a "bad influence," now she was "never home." Both her presence and her lack of presence were no good somehow, and the way they began to speak of Tracey took on a tragic dimension, for isn't it only tragic heroes who have no choices before them, no alternative routes, only unavoidable fates? In a few years Tracey would be pregnant, according to my mother, and so would drop out of school, and the "cycle of poverty" would complete itself, ending, most probably, in prison. Prison ran in the family. Of course, prison ran in my family, too, but somehow I was linked to a different star: I would be and do none of these things. My mother's certainty about all this worried me. If she was right it meant her dominion over other people's lives extended far beyond anything I had up till now imagined. And yet if anyone might defy fate—as presented in the form of my mother—surely Tracey could manage it?

But the signs were bad. Now when Tracey was asked to take her coat off in class she no longer refused, instead performing the action with terrible relish, unzipping slowly and in such a way that her breasts were presented to the rest of us with as much impact as possible, barely contained by an unsuitable top that showed off her abundance where the rest of us still had only nipples and bone. Everybody "knew" it cost 50p to "touch Tracey's tits." I had no idea whether this was true or not, but all the girls united in shunning her, black, white and brown. We were nice girls. We did not let people touch our non-existent tits, we were no longer the crazed things we'd been back in Year Three. Now we had "boyfriends," chosen for us by other girls, in notes passed from desk to desk, or in long, tortuous phone calls ("Want to know who fancies you and told everyone he fan-

cies you?"), and once these boyfriends had been
formally assigned we stood solemnly with them
in the playground in the thin winter sun, hand
in hand—more often than not a head taller than
them—until the inevitable moment came for us
to break up (the timing of this, too, was decided
by our friends) and the round of notes and calls
would begin again. You could not take part in this
process without belonging to a clique of willing females and Tracey had no girlfriends left, only me,
and only then when she chose to be friendly. She
took to spending her break-times in the boys' football cage, sometimes cursing them, even picking
up the ball and stopping play, but more often than
not acting as their accomplice, laughing with them
as they teased us, never attached to any boy in particular and yet, in the school's imagination, freely
handled by all. If she saw me through the bars,
playing with Lily or doing Double Dutch with
the other black and brown girls, she would make
a show of turning and talking with her male circle,
whispering with them, laughing, as if she, too, had
an opinion on whether or not we wore bras or had
started our periods. Once when I was walking past
the football cage in a very dignified way, hand in
hand with my new "boyfriend"—Paul Barron, the
policeman's son—she stopped what she was doing,
gripped the bars of the cage and smiled out at me.
Not a nice smile, a deeply sarcastic smile, as if to
say: Oh, is that who you're pretending to be now?

Three

By the time we'd escaped the kankurang, and passed through all intervening checkpoints, and after our taxi had made it through the clogged, pot-holed streets of the market town and on to the ferry port, by then it was too late, we were out of time, we ran down the gangway but found ourselves stranded with at least a hundred others, watching the rusty, hulking prow push forward into the water. The river split this finger of land in half throughout its length, and the airport was on the other side. I looked up at the ferry's chaotic three-story cargo: mothers and their babies, schoolchildren, farmers and workers, animals, cars, trucks, bags of grain, tourist tat, oil drums, suitcases, furniture. The children waved at us. Nobody seemed sure if it was the last ferry. We waited. Time passed, the sky turned pink. I thought of Aimee, at the airport, having to make small talk with the Minister of Education—and of Judy in a rage, hunched over her phone, calling me over and over and getting nowhere—but these thoughts did not have their expected effect. I felt quite calm as

I waited, resigned, alongside all these other people who seemed likewise to betray no impatience, or at least did not express impatience in any form I recognized. I had no network, there was nothing I could do. I was completely unreachable, for the first time in years. It gave me an unexpected but not unpleasant sense of stillness, of being outside of time: it reminded me somehow of childhood. I waited, leaning on the bonnet of the taxi. Others sat on their own luggage, or hitched themselves up on to the lids of oil drums. An old man rested on half of a giant bedstead. Two little girls straddled a cage of chickens. Periodically, articulated lorries inched their way along the gangway, shunting black diesel smoke down all our throats, honking to alert whoever might be sitting or sleeping in their path, but finding nowhere to go and nothing to do soon joined us in this wait that seemed to have no beginning and no end: we had always been looking out across the water for the ferry and always would be. At sunset our driver threw in the towel. Turned his taxi round, inched back through the crowd, and was away. To avoid a woman determined to sell me a watch I moved, too, toward the edge of the water, and sat down. But Lamin was concerned for me, he was always concerned for me, a person like me should be in the waiting room, which cost two of the filthy, crumpled notes I had balled up in my pocket, and for that reason naturally he would not go with me, but still he was insistent that **I** must go there, yes, the waiting room was certainly the place for a person like me.

"But why can't we just wait where we are?"

He gave me his agonized smile, the only kind he had.

"For me it's OK . . . but for you?"

It was still forty degrees outside: the idea of being in a room was nauseating. Instead I made him sit with me, our feet dangling over the water, kicking our heels against the heaps of dead oysters cemented to the struts of the pier. All the other young men in the village had dance music on their phones, precisely to listen to at times like these, but Lamin, a serious young man, preferred the World Service, and so taking one earbud each we listened to a story about the cost of university tuition in Ghana. Below us, at the shoreline, topless, broad-backed boys carried determined travelers on their shoulders, through the choppy shallows, to some brightly painted, perilous-looking narrowboats. I pointed to a very fat woman with a baby strapped to her back being hoisted on to the shoulders of one of them. Her thighs crushed his sweating head.

"Why can't **we** do that? We'd be across in twenty minutes!"

"For me it's OK," Lamin whispered—it was as if every conversation we had were somehow shameful to him and must not be overheard—"not for you. You should go to the waiting room. It will be a long time."

I watched the beach boy, soaking wet now up to his thighs, lower his passenger on to her seat. He looked less pained, shifting this cargo, than Lamin looked simply talking to me.

As it began to get dark, Lamin entered the crowd to ask questions, becoming another Lamin altogether, not the monosyllabic whisperer he was with me but what must have been the real Lamin, serious and respected by everyone, funny and loquacious, seeming to know everybody, greeted with warm, fraternal affection by beautiful young people wherever we went. His "age mates," he called them, and this could mean either that he had grown up in the village with them, or that they had been in the same class in school, or else in his year at the teachers' college. It was a tiny country: age mates were everywhere. The girl who sold us cashews in the market was his age mate, also a security guard in the airport. Sometimes age mates turned out to be one of the young police or army cadets who stopped us at the checkpoints, and that always felt like a piece of luck, the tension dissipated, they took their hands off their guns, leaned in through the passenger window and happily indulged in nostalgia. Age mates gave you a better price, issued tickets more quickly, waved you through. And now here was another one, a bosomy girl in the ferry office, wearing a confounding combination of items I had seen on many local

girls and looked forward to showing Aimee, with
the superior knowledge of the traveler who has arrived a whole week earlier. Skin-tight, low-riding,
studded jeans, the skimpiest of vests—revealing
the neon edges of a lacy bra—and a scarlet-red
hijab, wrapped modestly round the face and secured with a glittering pink pin. I watched Lamin
and this girl talk for a long time, in one of the
several local languages Lamin spoke, and I tried to
imagine how the simple answers we were seeking
to the questions "Is there another ferry? When will
it come?" could possibly be turned into as involved
a debate as the two of them seemed to be having.
Across the bay I heard a honking sound and saw
a great shadowy shape moving toward us in the
water. I ran over to Lamin and gripped his elbow.

"Is that it? Lamin, is that it?"

The girl stopped her chattering and turned
to look at me. She could tell I was no age mate.
She examined the drab, utilitarian clothes I had
bought especially for wearing in her country: olive
cargo pants, long-sleeved wrinkled linen shirt, an
ex-boyfriend's battered old pair of Converse and
a black scarf I'd felt silly and self-conscious wearing and so had slipped off my head and now wore
round my neck.

"That is a container ship," she said, with undisguised pity. "You miss the last ferry."

We paid what Lamin considered an exorbitant

amount for our narrowboat passage, despite fierce negotiations, and the moment my giant boy lowered me on to my seat a dozen young men appeared from nowhere and joined us, sitting on every viable piece of the boat's frame and transforming us from private water taxi into public boat. But on the other side of the water, my network reappeared and we learned that Aimee had decided to stay in one of the beach hotels and set out for the village tomorrow. The giant boy was delighted: we paid him again and thus subsidized another trip for some local kids, sailing back the way we'd come. Once on shore, we made our way finally to the village, in a beat-up minibus. The idea of two boats and two cabs in a single day was excruciating to Lamin, even if I paid for the second ride, even if the price quoted—which made him wince—would not buy me a bottle of water on Broadway. He sat on the roof of the vehicle, with another boy who could not be squeezed in, and as my fellow passengers talked and slept and prayed and ate and fed babies and shouted at the driver to let them off at what appeared to me to be completely deserted intersections, I could hear Lamin beating out a rhythm on the roof, over my head, and for two hours it was the only language I understood. We reached the village after ten. I was staying with a local family, and had never been outside their compound at that hour, or realized the total darkness that surrounded us, through which Lamin walked now with complete confidence, as if it were floodlit. I scurried behind him through the many narrow, sandy, trash-strewn paths I could not see, past the corrugated-iron sheets that marked each breeze-block single-story compound from the next, until we reached the Al Kalo's compound, no grander or taller than the rest, but with a large open wasteground in front of it, in which at least a hundred children, in the uniform of their school—the school we were here ultimately to replace—huddled under the canopy of a single mango tree. They'd waited six hours to do their dance for a woman called Aimee: now it fell to Lamin to explain why this lady would not be arriving today. But when Lamin had finished speaking the chief appeared to want it explained to him all over again. I waited as the two men discussed the matter, their hands moving in an animated way, while the children grew ever more bored and agitated, until the women lay aside the drums they would not now play and told the children finally to stand, and in dribs and drabs sent them running back to their homes. I held up my phone. It cast its artificial light over the Al Kalo. He was not, I thought, the great African chief Aimee had in her mind. Small, ashy, wrinkled and toothless, in a threadbare Man U T-shirt, tracksuit bottoms and plastic Nike house slippers held together with gaffer tape. And how surprised the Al Kalo would be, in turn, to hear what a figure he had become for us all, in New York! It had started with an e-mail from Miriam—subject heading: **Protocol**—which outlined, in Miriam's view, what any visitor to the village must present to its Al Kalo upon arrival, as a mark of respect. Scrolling through it, Judy released her seal-bark and put her phone in my face: "This a joke?"

I read the list:

Reading glasses
Paracetamol
Aspirin
Batteries
Body wash
Toothpaste
Antiseptic cream

"Don't think so . . . Miriam doesn't make jokes."

Judy smiled fondly at her screen: "Well, I think we can swing that."

Not many things charmed Judy, but that list did. It charmed Aimee even more, and for a few weeks afterward, whenever any good people of means visited us, in the Hudson Valley house, or in Washington Square, Aimee would repeat this list with mock-solemnity and then ask everybody present if they could even imagine, and everybody would confess they could hardly even imagine and seemed very moved and comforted by this failure to imagine, it was taken as a sign of purity, both in the Al Kalo and in themselves.

"But it's just so challenging to make that translation," commented a young man from Silicon Valley, on one of these nights—he was leaning over the dining table into a candle centerpiece and his face seemed lit from below with his own insight—"I mean, between one reality and the other. Like passing through the matrix." Everybody at the table nodded and agreed that it was, and later I caught Aimee seamlessly adding this dinner-party line to her recitations of the Al Kalo's now famous list, as if it were her own.

"What's he **saying**?" I whispered to Lamin. I was tired of waiting. I lowered my phone.

Lamin put a hand gently on the chief's shoulder, but the old man continued to make his endless, agitated address to the darkness.

"The Al Kalo is saying," Lamin whispered, "that things are very difficult here."

The next morning I went with Lamin to the school and charged my phone in the headmaster's office, through the sole outlet in the village, run on a solar-powered generator and paid for by an Italian charity years earlier. Around midday network mysteriously reappeared. I read through my fifty texts and established I had two more days alone here before I would have to go back to the ferry and collect Aimee: she was "resting" in a city hotel. At first I was excited by this unexpected solitude, and surprised myself with all kinds of plans. I told Lamin I wished to go to the famous compound of the rebel slave, two hours away, and that I wanted to see at last, with my own eyes, the shore from which the ships had left, carrying their cargo of humans, destined for my mother's island, and then on to the Americas and Britain, bearing the sugar and the cotton, before turning back again, a triangle that had produced—among its numberless consequences—my own existence. Yet two weeks earlier, in front of my mother and Miriam, I had called all of this, contemptuously, "diaspora tourism." Now I told Lamin I would ride a minibus unaccompanied to the old slave forts that once held my ancestors. Lamin smiled and seemed to agree but in practice stepped between all such plans and me. Between me and all attempted interactions, personal or economic, between me and the incomprehensible village, between me and the elders and me and the children, meeting any questions or requests with his anxious smile and his favored— whispered—explanation: "Things are difficult here." I was not allowed to walk into the bush, pick my own cashews, help cook any meals or wash my own clothes. It dawned on me that he saw me as a sort of child, someone to be treated with kid gloves and presented with reality by degrees. Then I realized everyone in the village thought of me that same way. Where grandmothers crouched to eat from the communal bowl, resting on their powerful haunches, gathering up rice and scraps of ladyfish or garden egg in their fingers, I was brought a plastic chair and a knife and fork, because it was assumed, correctly, that I would be too weak to assume the position. As I poured a full liter of water down the drop toilet, to flush out a cockroach that disturbed me, not one of the dozen young girls I lived with ever let me know exactly how far she'd walked that day for that liter. When I snuck off by myself, to the market, to buy a red-and-purple wrapper for my mother, Lamin smiled his anxious smile but spared me the knowledge of what proportion of his yearly teacher's salary I'd just spent on a single piece of cloth.

Toward the end of that first week I worked out that the preparations for my dinner began moments after my breakfast had been served. But when I tried to approach the corner of the yard where all those women and girls were hunkering in the dust to peel and cut and pound and salt, they laughed at me and sent me back to my leisure, to sit on a plastic chair in my dark room and read the American newspapers I'd brought with me—now crumpled and comically irrelevant—so that I never did discover how, exactly, with no oven and no electricity, they made the oven fries I did not want, or the great bowls of more appetizing rice they cooked for themselves. Food preparation was not for me, nor was washing, or fetching water or pulling up onions or even feeding the goats and chickens. I was, in the strictest sense of the term, good-for-nothing. Even babies were handed to me ironically, and people laughed when they saw me holding one. Yes, great care was taken at all times to protect me from reality. They'd met people like me before. They knew how little reality we can take.

The night before we were to pick up Aimee I was woken very early, by the call to prayer and the hysterical roosters, and finding that it was not yet insanely hot I got dressed in the darkness and left my compound, alone, without any of the small army of women and children I lived with—as Lamin had insisted I must never do—and went looking for Lamin. I wanted to tell him I was going to the old slave fort today, whether he liked it or not, I was going. As morning broke I found myself followed by many barefoot, curious children— "Good morning, how is your morning?"—like so many shadows, as here and there I paused to say Lamin's name to the dozens of women I passed, already heading off to work on the communal farm. They nodded and pointed me on, through the scrub, down this path and that, round the bright green concrete mosque half eaten on each side by twelve-foot orange termite hills, past all those dusty front yards that were swept, at this hour, by sullen, half-dressed teenage girls, who rested on their brooms to watch me pass. Everywhere I looked women were working: mothering, digging, carrying, feeding, cleaning, dragging, scrubbing, building, fixing. I didn't see a man until I found Lamin's compound, finally, at the outskirts of the village, before the farmland. It was very dark and dank, even by local standards: no front door, only a bed sheet, no huge wooden couch, only a single plastic chair, no floor covering, only earth, and a tin bucket of water with which he must have only recently finished washing himself, for he was on his knees beside it, soaking wet in a pair of football shorts. On the breeze-block wall behind him I could make out the crudely drawn logo of Man United, daubed in red paint. Topless, slender, made only of muscle, skin incandescent with its own youth—flawless. How pale, practically colorless, I looked beside him! It made me think of Tracey, of the many times, as a child, she'd placed her arm next to mine, to check once again that she was still a little paler than me—as she proudly maintained that she was—just in case summer or winter had changed this state of affairs since last she'd checked. I didn't dare tell her that I lay out on our balcony on any hot day, aiming at exactly the quality she seemed to dread: more color, darkness, for all my freckles to join and merge and leave me with the same deep dark brown of my mother. But Lamin, like most people in the village, was as many times dark as my mother was to me, and looking at him now I found the contrast between his beauty and these surroundings to be—among many other things—surreal. He turned and saw me standing over him. His face was full of hurt—I had broken some unspoken contract. He excused himself. Stood the other side of a rag-curtain that notionally separated one part of the dismal space from the other. But I could still see him, pulling on his pristine white Calvin Klein shirt with the monogram, and his white chinos and white sandals, all of it kept white by a means I couldn't imagine, covered as I was every day in red dust. His fathers and uncles mostly wore jellabas, his many young cousins and siblings ran around in the ubiquitous threadbare soccer shirts and crumbling denim, barefoot, but Lamin wore his Western whites, almost every time I saw him, and a big silver wristwatch, studded with zirconia, whose hands were perpetually stuck at 10:04. On Sunday, when the whole village gathered for a meeting, he wore a tan, bishop-collared suit, and sat close to me, whispering in my ear like a UN delegate, translating only whatever he chose to translate of whatever was being discussed. All the young male teachers in the village dressed in this way, in traditional bishop-collars or sharp chinos and shirts, with big watches and thin black bags, their flip-phones and huge-screened androids always in hand, even if they didn't work. It was an attitude I remembered from the old neighborhood, a way of representing, which in the village meant dressing for a certain part: **I am one of the serious, modern young men. I am the future of my country.** I always felt absurd next to them. Compared to their sense of personal destiny, I looked like I was in the world by mere accident, having given no thought at all to what I represented, dressed in my wrinkled olive cargo pants and my filthy Converse, dragging a battered rucksack around.

Lamin got back on his knees and quietly restarted his first prayer of the day—I had interrupted that, too. Listening to his whispered Arabic, I wondered exactly what form his prayer took. I waited. I looked around me at the poverty Aimee hoped to "reduce." It was all I could see, and the kinds of questions children ask were the only kind that came to me. **What is this? What's happening?** The same mindset had led me, on the very first day I'd arrived, to the headmaster's office, where I sat sweating under his molten tin roof, frantically trying to get online, although I could, of course, have googled what I wanted to know in New York, far more quickly, with infinitely more ease, at any time in the previous six months. Here it was a laborious process. A page would half load, then crash, the energy from the solar rose and fell and sometimes cut off completely. It took more than an hour. And when the two sums of money I was looking for finally appeared in their adjacent windows all I did was sit and stare at them for a long time. In the comparison, as it turned out, Aimee came out a little ahead. And just like that the GDP of an entire country could fit into a single person, like one Russian doll into another.

Four

That last June of primary school Tracey's father got out and we met for the first time. He stood on the communal grass, looking up at us, smiling. Suave, modern, full of a kind of kinetic joy, but also somehow classic, elegant, Bojangles himself. He stood in fifth position, legs apart, in an electric-blue bomber jacket with a Chinese dragon on the back and tight white jeans. A thick, rakish mustache, and an Afro in the old style, with no fades or lines cut into it and no high-top. Tracey's happiness was intense, she reached over the balcony, as if to pull her father up to her, yelling at him to come, come up here, Dad, come up, but he winked at us and said: "I've got a better idea, let's go down the high road." We ran down and each took a hand.

The first thing I noticed was that he had the body of a dancer, and moved like a dancer, rhythmically, with force but also with lightness, so that we three didn't just walk along the high road, we promenaded. Everybody looked at us, we strutted in the sunshine, and several people stopped what they were doing and came to hail us—to hail Louie—from across the street, from a grotty window above a hairdresser's, from the doorways of the pubs. As we approached the betting shop, an old Caribbean gentleman, in a flat cap and thick woolen vest, despite the heat, stepped in front of us, blocking our way, and asked: "Dem your daughters?" Louie held up our hands like we were two prizefighters. "No," he said, letting my hand drop, "just this one." Tracey lit up with the glory of it all. "I hear dem say tirteen months all you do," said the old man, chuckling. "Lucky, lucky Louie." He nudged Louie in his neat waist, it was cinched by a thin gold belt, like a superhero. But Louie was insulted, he stepped back from the old man—a deep sliding plié—and loudly sucked his teeth. He corrected the record: didn't even do seven.

The old man drew out a newspaper he'd had tucked into his armpit, unrolled it and showed Louie a certain page, which he studied before bending down to show it to us. We were told to close our eyes and stick our fingers wherever the mood took us, and when we opened our eyes we each had a horse under a finger, I can still remember the name of mine, Theory Test, because five minutes later Louie ran back out through the bookie's doors, scooped me up off the floor and threw me into the air. A hundred and fifty quid won on a five-pound stake. We were diverted to Woolworths, and each told to choose whatever we wanted. I left Tracey at the videos intended for kids like us—the suburban comedies, action films, space sagas—walking on and bending over the big wire bin, the "bargain bin," set aside for those who had little money or choice. There were always a lot of musicals in there, nobody wanted them, not even the old ladies, and I was scavenging through, happily enough, when I heard Tracey, who had not moved on from the modern section, asking Louie: "So how many can we have?" The answer was four, though we were to hurry up about it, he was hungry. I snatched four musicals in a blissful panic:

Ali Baba Goes to Town
Broadway Melody of 1936
Swing Time
It's Always Fair Weather

The only one of Tracey's purchases I remember is **Back to the Future**, more expensive than all mine put together. She pressed it to her chest, giving it up only for a moment so that it might be passed to the cashier, and snatching it back again afterward, like an animal snapping at its food.

When we got to the restaurant we sat at the best table, just by the window. Louie showed us a funny way to eat a Big Mac, dismantling its layers and placing fries above and below each burger and then putting it all together again.

"You coming to live with us, then?" Tracey asked.

"Hmmm. Don't know about that. What she say?"

Tracey stuck her piggy nose in the air: "Don't care what she says."

Both her little hands were screwed into tight fists.

"Don't disrespect your mum. Your mum's got her own problems."

He went back up to the counter to get milkshakes. When he returned he looked burdened, and without introducing the topic in any formal way, he began to talk to us about the inside, about how you found, when you were inside, that it wasn't like the neighborhood, no, not at all, it was very different, because when you were inside everybody understood that people had better keep to their own kind, and that's how it was, "like stayed with like," there was hardly any mixing, not like up at the flats, and it wasn't the guards or anyone telling you to do it, that's just the way it was, tribes stick together, and it even goes by shade, he explained, pulling up his sleeve and pointing at his arm, so all of us that was dark like me, well, we're over here, tight with each other, always—he drew a line on the Formica tabletop—and brown like you two is somewhere over here, and Paki is somewhere else, and Indian is somewhere else. White is split, too: Irish, Scottish, English. And in the English some of them are BNP and some are all right. Everybody goes with their own is the point, and it's natural. Makes you think.

We sat slurping our milkshakes, thinking.

And you learn all kinds of things, he continued, you learn who the **real** God of the black man is! Not this blue-eyed, long-haired Jesus individual—no! And let me arks you: how comes I never even really heard of him or his name before I get up in there? Look it up. You learn a lot that you can't learn in school, because these people won't tell you nothing, nothing about African kings, nothing about Egyptian queens, nothing about Mohammed, they hide it all, they hide the whole of our history so we feel like we're nothing, we feel like we're at the bottom of the pyramid, that's the whole plan, but the truth is we built the fucking Pyramids! Oh, there's a devilishness in them, but one day, one day, God willing, this white day will be done. Louie lifted Tracey on to his lap and jiggled her as if she were a much younger child, and then worked her arms from below, like a puppet, so she seemed to be dancing to the music that was playing through the speakers that nestled between the security camera. You still dancing? It was a casual question, I could tell he wasn't particularly interested in the answer, but Tracey always took her opportunities, no matter how small, and now she told her father, in a great, happy rush of detail, about all her dance medals from that year, and from the previous year, and of what Miss Isabel had said about her pointe work, of what all kinds of people said about her talent, and about her upcoming audition for stage school, on which subject I had already heard about as much as I could stand. My own mother would not allow stage school, not even if I won a full scholarship, of the kind Tracey was betting on. We had been battling over it, my mother and I, ever since I heard that Tracey would be allowed to audition. The thought of having to go to a normal school while Tracey spent her days dancing!

Now see, with me, said Louie, tiring suddenly of his daughter's talk, with me I didn't need dance school, matter of fact I used to rule the dance floor! This girl got it all from her daddy. Believe me: I can do all the moves! Arks your mum! Used to even make some money off it, back in the day. You look doubtful!

To prove it, to allay our doubts, he slipped off his stool and kicked his leg up, jerked his head, shifted the line of his shoulders, spun, stopped on a dime and ended on the points of his toes. A group of girls who sat across from us in a booth whistled and cheered, and watching him I felt I understood now what Tracey had meant by placing her father and Michael Jackson in one reality, and I didn't find that she was a liar, exactly, or at least I felt that within the lie there was a deeper truth. They were touched by the same inheritance. And if Louie's dancing happened not to be famous like Michael's, well, this was, to Tracey, only a kind of technicality—an accident of time and place—and now, thinking back on his dancing, writing it all down, I think she was exactly right.

Afterward we decided to walk with our huge milkshakes back up the high road, stopping again to speak to a few friends of Louie's—or perhaps they were simply people who knew enough about him to fear him—including a young Irish builder hanging one-handed off the scaffolding outside the Tricycle Theater, his face burned red from too much work in the sun. He reached down to shake Louie's hand: "Now, if it isn't the Playboy of the West Indies!" He was rebuilding the Tricycle's roof, and Louie was very struck by this, it was the first time he'd heard about the terrible fire of a few months before. He asked the boy how much it would cost to rebuild, how much he and the rest of Moran's men were getting paid an hour, what cement they were using and who were the wholesalers, and I looked over at Tracey as she filled up with pride at this glimpse of another possible Louie: respectable young entrepreneur, quick with numbers, good with his staff, taking his daughter round his place of work, holding her hand so tightly. I wished it could be like that for her every day.

It didn't occur to me that there would be any consequences to our little outing but even before I'd got back on to Willesden Lane somebody had told my mother where I'd been and with whom. She caught hold of me as I walked through the door and slapped the milkshake out of my hand, it struck the opposite wall, very pink and thick—unexpectedly dramatic—and for the rest of the time we lived in that place we coexisted with a faint strawberry stain. She started in yelling. What did I think I was doing? Who did I think I was with? I ignored all her rhetorical questions and asked her again why I couldn't audition like Tracey. "Only a fool gives up an education," said my mother, and I said, "Well, then, maybe I'm a fool." I tried to get by her, into my room, my haul of videos behind my back, but she blocked my way and so I told her bluntly that I was not her and did not ever want to be her, that I didn't care about her books or her clothes or her ideas or any of it, I wanted to dance and live my own life. My father emerged from wherever he'd been hiding. Gesturing at him, I tried to make the point that if it were up to my father I'd be allowed to audition, because my father was a man who believed in me, as Tracey's father believed in her. My mother sighed. "Of course he'd let you do it," she said. "He's not worried—he knows you'll never get in."

"For God's sake," muttered my father, but he couldn't look at me and I understood with a stab of pain that what my mother was saying must be true.

"All that matters in this world," she explained, "is what's written down. But what happens with this"—she gestured at my body— "that will never matter, not in this culture, not for these people, so all you're doing is playing their game by their rules, and if you play that game, I promise you, you'll end up a shade of yourself. Catch a load of babies, never leave these streets, and be another one of these sisters who might as well not exist."

"**You** don't exist," I said.

I grabbed at this line as a child grabs at the first thing to hand. The effect on my mother was beyond anything I could have hoped for. Her mouth turned slack and all her self-possession and beauty drained from her. She began to cry. We stood at the threshold to my room, my mother with her head bowed. My father had retreated, it was just we two. It took a minute before she found her voice again. She told me—in a fierce whisper—not to take another step. But as soon as she'd said it she saw her own mistake: it was an admission, this was exactly the time of my life when I **could** finally take a step away from her, many steps, I was almost twelve, I was already as tall as her—I could dance right out of her life—and so a shift in her authority was inevitable, was happening precisely as we stood there. I said nothing, stepped around her, went into my room and slammed the door.

Five

Ali Baba Goes to Town is a strange film. It's a variation of **A Connecticut Yankee in King Arthur's Court** in which Eddie Cantor plays Al Babson, an everyday schmuck who finds himself working as an extra on an **Arabian Night**s–type picture, out in Hollywood. On set he falls asleep and dreams he's back in ninth-century Arabia. One scene made a very strong impression on me, I wanted to show it to Tracey, but she'd become hard to pin down, she didn't call, and when I tried to call her flat there was always a pause on the line before her mother told me she was out. I knew she had her legitimate reasons, she was busy preparing for her stage-school audition—which Mr. Booth had kindly agreed to assist her with—she rehearsed most weekday afternoons in the church hall. But I wasn't ready to release her into her new life. I made many attempts to ambush her: the doors to the church would be open, sun streaming through the stained glass, Mr. Booth accompanying her on the piano, and if she spotted me spying on her, she'd wave—the adult, distracted greeting of a busy woman—but never once did she come out to talk to me. By some obscure pre-teen logic, I decided my body was to blame. I was still a lanky, flat-chested child, lurking in the doorway, while Tracey, dancing in the light, was already a little woman. How could she have any interest in the things that still interested me?

"Nah, don't know it. What's it called again?"

"I just told you. **Ali Baba Goes to Town.**"

I'd been bold and walked into the church at the end of one of her rehearsals. She was sitting in a plastic chair taking off her tap shoes, while Mr. Booth was still in his corner, messing around with the piece—"Can't Help Loving That Man of Mine"—speeding it up and slowing it down, playing it now as jazz, now as ragtime.

"I'm busy."

"You could come now."

"I'm busy now."

Mr. Booth packed his music into his bag and wandered over. Tracey's nose shot in the air, sniffing out praise.

"Well, that was smashing," he said.

"Was it good, really?"

"Smashing. You dance like a dream."

He smiled and patted her on the shoulder, and a flush of happiness passed over her face. It was the kind of praise I got from my own father daily, no matter what I did, but for Tracey it must have been very rare, for hearing it seemed to change everything, including how she felt about me, in that moment. As Mr. Booth made his way slowly out of the church, she smiled, slung her dance bag over her shoulder and said: "Let's go."

The scene comes early in the film. A group of men sits on the sandy ground, they seem apathetic, depressed. These, the sultan tells Al, are the musicians, the Africans, whom nobody can understand, for they speak an unknown language. But Al wants to talk to them and he tries everything: English, French, Spanish, Italian, even Yiddish. Nothing doing. Then a brainwave. **Hi dee hi dee hi dee hi!** The call of Cab Calloway, and the Africans, recognizing it, leap to their feet and cry out the response: **Ho dee ho dee ho dee ho!** Excited, Cantor starts blacking up, right then and there, painting his face with a burned piece of cork, leaving only those rolling eyes, the elastic mouth.

"What **is** this? I don't want to watch this!"

"Not this bit. Just wait, Trace, please. Wait."

I took the remote control from her and asked that she sit back on the settee. Now Al was singing to the Africans, a verse that seemed to swing time itself, flashing far ahead, to a moment when these Africans would no longer be as they were presently, a time a thousand years in the future when they would set the tempo the world wants to dance to, in a place called Harlem. Hearing this news, the

delighted musicians stood up and started dancing and singing, on a raised platform, in the town
square. The sultana and her advisers look down
from a balcony, the Arabians look up from the
street. The Arabs are Hollywood Arabs, white, in
Aladdin costumes. The Africans are black Americans dressed up—loincloths and feathers, outland-
ish head-dresses—and they play primitive musical
instruments, in a parody of their future Cotton
Club incarnations: trombones made of actual
bone, clarinets formed from hollowed-out sticks,
that sort of thing. And Cantor, true to the origins
of his name, is the bandleader, with a whistle round
his neck, which he blows to end a solo or usher
a performer off stage. The song reached its chorus, he told them that swing was here to stay, that
there was no avoiding it, and so they must choose
their partner—and dance. Then Cantor blew his
whistle and the wonderful thing happened. It was
a girl—a girl arrived. I made Tracey sit as close
to the screen as she could, I didn't want there to
be any doubt about it. I looked across: I saw her
lips part in surprise, as mine had done the first
time I watched it, and then I knew that she could
see what I saw. Oh, the nose was different—this
girl's nose was normal and flat—and there was, in
her eyes, no hint of Tracey's brand of cruelty. But
the heart-shaped face, the adorable puffy cheeks,
the compact body and yet the long limbs, these
were all Tracey. The physical resemblance was so

strong and yet she didn't dance like Tracey. Her arms wheelbarrowed as she moved, her legs flew back and forth, she was a hoofer, not an obsessed technician. And she was funny: walking on her toes or freeze-framing for a second in an absurd comic attitude, on one leg, arms in the air, like the hood ornament of an expensive car. Dressed like the rest—grass skirt, feathers—but nothing could diminish her.

For the big finish the girl came back out on stage and joined all those Americans dressed like Africans, and Cantor himself, and they all stood still in a line and leaned forward at a forty-five-degree angle to the floor. It was a move back from the future: a year later we were all trying it ourselves in the playground, having just seen Michael Jackson in a music video doing the exact same thing. And for weeks after that video first aired Tracey and me and many other kids in the playground tried our best to imitate the move, but it was impossible, no one could do it, we all fell flat on our faces. At the time I didn't know how it was done. Now I know. In the video, Michael used wires and, a few years later—when he wanted to achieve the effect live on stage—he wore a pair of "anti-gravity" shoes, they had a slot in the heel that engaged with a peg in the stage, and he was their co-inventor, the patent is in his name.

The Africans of **Ali Baba** nailed their own shoes to the floor.

Six

At Aimee's hotel we got into a series of SUVs. It was the full circus on that first trip: her children were with us, and their nanny, Estelle, and Judy of course, plus the three other PAs, a PR girl, Granger, a French architect I'd never seen before in my life, a star-struck woman from the Department for International Development, a journalist and photographer from **Rolling Stone**, and a man called Fernando Carrapichano, our project manager. I watched the sweating bellboys in their white linen uniforms heaving bags into trunks, helping everyone to their seats, and wondered what village they came from. I'd expected to ride with Aimee, in her car, to debrief her—for what it was worth—on my week's reconnaissance, but when Aimee saw Lamin her eyes widened and the first thing she said to him after "Hello" was "You should ride with me." I was directed to the second car, with Carrapichano. He and I were to pass the time together, so we were told, "ironing out the details."

The drive back to the village was uncanny. All

the difficulties I had come to expect from that journey were now absent, as when in a dream the dreamer is lucid and able to manipulate everything around her. No checkpoints, not any longer, and no pot-holed roads bringing us to a standstill, and instead of the enervating, stifling heat, a perfectly air-conditioned twenty-one-degree environment and an ice-cold bottle of water in my hand. Our convoy, which included a pair of jeeps filled with government officials and a police motorcade, moved swiftly along streets that seemed at times to have been artificially cleared, at others artificially populated—lined with flag-waving children, like a stage set—and we took an odd, elongated route, weaving through the electrified tourist strip and then on through a series of suburban enclaves I had not realized existed, where huge, unfinished houses, blighted with rebar, struggled to rise up from behind their fortress walls. Under the influence of this state of unreality, I kept seeing versions of my mother's face everywhere, in young girls running down the street, in old women selling fish in the markets, and once in a young man hanging off the side of a minibus. When we got to the ferry it was empty but for us and our cars. I wondered what Lamin made of it all.

Carrapichano I didn't know very well and the only time we'd spoken before I'd made a fool of myself. It was on the plane to Togo, six months earlier, back when Togo was still on the shortlist, before Aimee had offended that tiny nation by suggesting, in an interview, that its government did "nothing for their people." "What's it like?" I'd asked, leaning over him, looking out of the porthole window, and meaning, I must admit, "Africa."

"I have not been," he said coldly, without turning round.

"But you practically live here—I read your résumé."

"No. Senegal, Liberia, Côte d'Ivoire, Sudan, Ethiopia, yes—Togo, never."

"Oh, well, you know what I mean."

He'd turned to me, red-faced, and asked: "If we were flying to Europe and you wanted to know what France was like, would it help if I described Germany?"

Now I tried to make amends, small talk, but he was busy with a huge sheaf of papers, on which I spotted graphs I couldn't follow, sets of statistics from the IMF. I felt a little sorry for him, stuck with us and our ignorance, he was so far outside his natural milieu. I knew he was forty-six, had a Ph.D., was an economist by training, with a background in international development, and that like Miriam he'd worked at Oxfam for many years: she was the one who'd recommended him to us in the first place. He'd spent most of the nineties managing aid projects in East and West Africa, in remote villages without television, and one interesting consequence of this—for me, anyway—was that he really did not have a very clear idea who Aimee was, beyond having registered her name, vaguely, as a phenomenon of his youth. Now he was having to spend all of his time with her, and therefore with people like Mary-Beth, Aimee's ditzy second assistant, whose job consisted entirely of sending e-mails, dictated by Aimee, to other people, and then reading out the replies. Or grim Laura, assistant number three, who reigned over Aimee's muscle aches, toiletries and nutrition, and happened to believe that the moon landings were staged. He had to listen to Judy read the star signs out each morning and plan her day accordingly. Amid the insanity of Aimee's world, I should have been the closest thing he had to an ally, but every conversation we attempted went awry somehow, the way he understood the world was so genuinely alien to me that it felt as if he occupied a parallel reality, which I didn't doubt was the real one, but which I couldn't "speak to," to use a favorite phrase of his. Aimee, equally helpless before a graph, liked him because he was Brazilian and handsome, with rich, curly, black hair and lovely gold glasses that made him look like an actor playing an economist in a movie. But it was obvious from the start there would be trouble for them ahead. Aimee's way of communicating her ideas relied on a shared understanding—of Aimee herself, of her "legend"—and "Fern," as she called him, had no context for any of that. He was excellent at ironing out the details: architectural plans, government negotiations, land contracts—all the various practical considerations. But when it came to speaking directly with Aimee about the project itself—which for her was primarily a personal and emotional undertaking—he was out of his depth.

"But what does it **mean** when she is saying to me: 'Let's make it kind of an illuminated ethos'?"

He pushed his glasses up his handsome nose and examined his many notes, the result, I presumed, of having dutifully transcribed every little piece of nonsense that had fallen from Aimee's mouth during their eight-hour flight together. He held the paper up as if it might resolve itself into sense if only he stared at it long enough.

"Maybe I misunderstand? In what way can a school be 'illuminated'?"

"No, no, it's a reference to an album of hers: **Illuminated.** From '97? She thinks of it as her most "positive" album, so the lyrics are, well, they're sort of like: **Hey, girls, go get your dreams, blah blah, you're strong, blah blah, never give up**. That sort of thing? So she's basically saying: I want this to be an empowering school for girls."

He looked bewildered.

"But why not just say this?"

I patted him gently on his shoulder: "Fernando, don't worry—it's going to be fine."

"I should listen to this album?"
"Honestly, I don't think that would help."

Up ahead, in the next car, I could see Aimee leaning out of the passenger seat with her arm over the
door, happily engaged with every wave or whistle
or scream of delight from the street, which were,
I felt pretty certain, not responses to Aimee herself but to this shiny cavalcade of SUVs rolling
through rural areas in which not one in two hundred owned a car. In the village, out of curiosity,
I often commandeered the phones of the young
teachers, put my earphones in and listened to the
thirty or so songs they tended to play on rota-
tion, some of which came free with their minutes,
others—especially beloved—they had spent precious credit to download. Hip-hop, R&B, soca,
reggae, ragga, grime, dub-step, hi-life—ringtone
scraps of the whole glorious musical diaspora
could be heard, but rarely any white artists, and
never Aimee. Now I watched her smile and wink
at the many soldiers, who, relieved of their usual
activity, stood aimlessly at the sides of the road,
guns by their side, watching us pass. And wherever there was music, wherever kids were dancing,
Aimee would clap her hands to get their attention
and imitate their moves as best she could while
still sitting down. This element of roadside rolling chaos that so affected and disturbed me, like

a zoetrope unfurled and filled with every form of human drama—women feeding children, carrying them, talking to them, kissing them, hitting them, men talking, fighting, eating, working, praying, animals living and dying, wandering down the street bleeding from their necks, boys running, walking, dancing, pissing, shitting, girls whispering, laughing, frowning, sitting, sleeping—all of this delighted Aimee, she leaned so far out of that window I thought she might fall right through her beloved matrix and into it. But then she was always happiest in ungovernable crowds. Until her insurance company stopped her doing it she often crowd-surfed, and it never frightened her, as it did me, to be suddenly swarmed by people in an airport or the lobby of a hotel. Meanwhile the only thing I could see through my tinted window did not appear to surprise or alarm her, and when I made some reference to it in the few minutes we were together, standing on the gangway, watching our cars roll on to the spookily empty ferry and her children run delightedly up the cast-iron steps, to the upper deck, she turned to me and snapped: "Jesus Christ, if you're gonna be shocked by every fucking sign of poverty you see here, this is going to be a mighty long trip. You're in Africa!"

Just as if I'd asked why it was light outside and been told: "It's daytime!"

Seven

All we had was her name, we found it in the credits. Jeni LeGon. We had no idea where she'd come from, if she was alive or dead, if she'd made any other films, we had only these four minutes from **Ali Baba**—well, I had them. If Tracey wanted to watch them she had to come round, which she began to do, every now and then, like Narcissus bending over a pool of water. I understood it wouldn't take her long to learn the whole routine— excepting the impossible lean—but I wasn't going to give her the video to take home, I knew better than that, I knew when I had collateral. And I had begun to spot LeGon here and there, bit parts in movies I'd seen many times. There she was as a maid to Ann Miller, wrestling with a baby pug, and as a tragic mulatto, dying in the arms of Cab Calloway, and once more a maid, helping Betty Hutton get dressed. These discoveries, widely spaced, sometimes many months apart, became a reason to call Tracey, and even if her mother answered Tracey would come round right away, with no hesitation or excuses. She sat inches from the television screen, ready to point out this or that moment of action or expression, an emotion passing over Jeni's face, a variation in one step or another, and interpreting everything she saw with that sharpness of insight I felt I lacked, that I considered, at this point, Tracey's possession alone. A gift for seeing that seemed to have its only outlet and expression here, in my living room, in front of my television, and which no teacher ever saw, and no exam ever managed to successfully register or even note, and of which, perhaps, these memories are the only true witness and record.

One thing she failed to notice, and I didn't want to tell her: my parents had broken up. I only knew it myself because my mother told me it was so. They still lived in the same flat and slept in the same room. Where else could they go? Real divorces were for people who had lawyers and new places to live. There was also the question of my mother's capabilities. We all three knew that in divorces the father left, but my father could not leave, there was no question of that. Who, in his absence, would tape up my knee when I fell, or remember when my medicine was to be taken, or calmly comb the nits out of my hair? Who would come to me when I had my night terrors? Who would wash my stinking, yellow sheets the next morning? I don't mean that my mother didn't love me but she was not a domestic person: her life was in her mind. The fundamental skill of all mothers—the management of time—was beyond her. She measured time in pages. Half an hour, to her, meant ten pages read, or fourteen, depending on the size of the type, and when you think of time in this way there isn't time left for anything else, there's no time to go to the park or get ice cream, no time to put a child to bed, no time to listen to the teary recounting of a nightmare. No, my father could not leave.

One morning when I was brushing my teeth my mother walked into the bathroom, sat on the rim of our avocado bathtub and euphemistically outlined the new arrangement. At first I could hardly understand her, she seemed be taking a very long time to get to the point of whatever she really wanted to say, speaking of child-psychology theories, and "places in Africa" where children were raised not by their parents but "by a village," and other matters I either didn't understand or didn't care about, but finally she pulled me to her, hugged me very tightly and said, "Your dad and me—we're going to live as brother and sister." I can remember thinking this was the most perverse thing I'd ever heard: I was to be left an only child, while my parents became siblings to each other. My father's initial reaction must have been similar, because for several days after that it was warfare in the flat, all-out warfare, and I had to sleep with two pillows pressed to my ears. But when he at last understood that she was not joking, that she would not change her mind, he fell into a depression. He began to spend whole weekends on the sofa, watching television, while my mother kept to the kitchen and to her high stool, busy with the homework for her degree. I went to dance class alone. I ate my tea with one or the other of them, no longer with both.

A little while after my mother's announcement my father made a baffling decision: he went back to delivering the post. It had taken him ten years to become a Delivery Office Manager but in his sadness he read Orwell's **Coming Up for Air** and this novel had convinced him that he'd be better off doing "honest labor," as he put it—and have the rest of his days free to "get the education he never had"—than work at a soulless desk job that used up all his time. It was the kind of impractical, high-principled action that my mother usually appreciated, and the timing of the announcement did not seem, to me, accidental. But if winning her back was his plan it didn't work: he rose once again each morning at three and returned at one in the afternoon, often ostentatiously reading some sociological textbook nicked from my mother's shelves, but although my mother respectfully asked after his morning's work and occasionally after his reading, she did not fall back in love with him. After a while they stopped talking to each other altogether. The weather in the flat changed. In the past I had always had to wait for one of the rare gaps in my parents' decade-long argument, into which I would then try to insert myself. Now I could speak without interruption, if I wanted, to either of them, but it was already too late. In the fast-forward style of city childhoods, they were no longer the most important people in my life. No, I really didn't care what my parents thought of me any longer. Only my friend's judgment counted, now more than ever, and sensing this, I suspect, more and more she chose to withhold it.

Eight

It was said later that I was a bad friend to Aimee, always had been, that I was only waiting for the right moment to hurt her, even to ruin her. Maybe she believes that. But it's a good friend who wakes a friend from her dream. At first I thought that it wouldn't have to be me at all, that the village itself would wake her up, because it didn't seem possible to stay dreaming in that place or to think of yourself as in any way an exception. I was wrong about that. On the northern outskirts of the village, beside the road that led to Senegal, there stood a large pink brick house of two stories—the only one of its kind for miles around—abandoned, but basically finished except for the windows and doors. It had been built on remittances, Lamin told me, sent back by a local young man who had been doing well, driving a cab in Amsterdam, until his luck changed and the money abruptly stopped. Now the house, empty for a year, would have a new life as our "base of operations." By the time we reached it the sun was going down, and the Minister for Tourism was pleased to show us the bare bulbs burning from the ceiling of each room. "And every time you visit," we were told, "it will be only better and better." The village had been waiting for light a long time—since the coup, over twenty years earlier—yet in a couple of days Aimee had managed to convince the relevant authorities to attach a generator to this shell of a house, and there were sockets to charge all our phones and a team of workmen had affixed Perspex windows and put in serviceable MDF doors, beds for everybody and even a stove. The children were thrilled—it was like camping—and for Aimee the two nights she was scheduled to spend here took the form of an ethical adventure. I heard her tell the **Rolling Stone** reporter how important it was to stay "in the real world, among the people," and the next morning, alongside the formal photographed events—soil-breaking, schoolgirls dancing—many images were taken of Aimee in this real world, eating from the communal bowls, crouching down with ease alongside the women—using the muscles she had developed indoor-cycling—or showing off her agility, climbing the cashew trees with a group of young boys. After lunch, she put on her olive cargo pants and together we toured the village with the woman from DfID, whose task it was to point out "areas of particular deprivation." We saw drop toilets crawling with hookworm, a forgotten, half-constructed clinic, many airless rooms with corrugated-iron roofs in which children slept ten to a bed. Afterward we toured the communal gardens—to witness the "limits of subsistence farming"—but as we entered the field the sun happened to be casting long, captivating shadows and the potato plants were hugely bushy and green and the trees looped with vines, the lushness of everything creating an effect of extraordinary beauty. The women, young and old, had a utopian look to them, in their colorful wrappers, pulling weeds from the ground, chatting to each other as they worked, shouting across the rows of peas or peppers, laughing at each other's jokes. Spotting us approaching, they straightened up and wiped the sweat from their faces, with their own headscarves, if they wore them, with their hands if not.

"Good day to you. How is the day?"

"Oh, I see what's happening here," said Aimee to an ancient old woman who had been so bold as to put her arm around Aimee's tiny waist. "You gals get to really talk to each other out here. No men in sight. Yeah, I can just imagine what goes on."

The woman from DfID laughed too much. I thought of how little I could imagine of what went on. Even the simplest ideas I'd brought with me did not seem to work here when I tried to apply them. I was not, for example, standing at this moment in a field with my extended tribe, with my fellow black women. Here there was no such category. There were only the Sere women, the Wolof, and the Mandinka, the Serahuli, the Fula and the

Jola, the last of whom, I was told once, grudgingly, I resembled, if only in basic facial architecture: same long nose, same cheekbones. From where I stood now I could hear the call to prayer coming from the square concrete minaret of the green mosque, rising above the trees and over this village where women covered and uncovered were sisters and cousins and friends to each other, were each other's mothers and daughters, or were covered in the morning and uncovered in the afternoon, simply because some age mates had come visiting, boys and girls, and one of them had offered to plait their hair. Here where Christmas was celebrated with a startling fervor, and all the people of the book were considered "brothers, sisters," while I, representing the utterly godless, was nobody's enemy, no, just someone who should properly be pitied and protected—so one of the girls I shared a room with explained to me—as you would a calf whose mother died in the having of her.

Now I watched girls lining up at the well, filling their huge plastic tubs with water and then lifting these tubs on to their heads to begin the long walk back to the village. A few of them I recognized from the compound I had been staying in this past week. The twin cousins of my host, Hawa, as well as three of her sisters. I waved at them all, smiling. They acknowledged me with a nod.

"Yes, we're always struck by how much the women and girls do here," said the woman from DfID, sotto voce, following my line of sight. "They do the housework, you see, but then also all the field work, and as you'll see it's largely women running both the school and the market. Girl Power indeed."

She bent down to feel the stem of a garden egg and Aimee took the opportunity to turn to me, cross her eyes and stick her tongue out. The DfID woman straightened up and glanced over at the growing queue of girls.

"Many of them should be in school, of course, but unfortunately their mothers need them here. Then you think of those young boys we just saw, lounging about in a hammock among the cashews . . ."

"Education is the answer to development for our girls and women," Lamin piped up, with the slightly wounded and weary air, I thought, of someone who had endured a great many lectures from representatives of DfID. "Education, education, education."

Aimee gave him a dazzling smile.

"That's what we're here for," she said.

During all the activities of the day Aimee kept Lamin close, mistaking his tendency to whisper for a special intimacy between them, and after a while she began whispering back at him, flirting like a schoolgirl. Dangerous, I thought, in front of the ever-present journalist, but there was not a moment when we were alone that I could firmly tell her so. Instead I watched her struggling to restrain her impatience whenever poor Carrapichano had no choice but to draw her away from Lamin and back toward all the necessary mundane tasks of the day: signing papers, meeting ministers, discussing school fees, sustainability, curriculum, teachers' pay. Half a dozen times he made Aimee and the rest of us stop where we were so that we might listen to yet another government functionary give yet another speech—about partnership and mutual respect, and in particular the respect the President-for-Life wanted passed on to Aimee in his absence, which itself was only the correct response owed for the respect Aimee "clearly does possess for our beloved President"—as we all stood suffering in the sun. Each speech was near-identical to the one before it, as if there were some ur-text back in the city from which all these ministers had been instructed to quote. As we approached the school, slowly, so as not to outpace the photographer—who scuttled backward before us—one of these ministers once more pressed Carrapichano's hand, and when Carrapichano tried, quietly and out of Aimee's sightline, to dissuade him, the minister refused to be dissuaded, standing his ground at the school gate, blocking the entrance and beginning his speech, upon which Aimee abruptly turned her back.

"Look, Fern, I don't mean to be an asshole about it but I'm really trying to be present in this moment? And you're making that very hard for me right now. It's hot, we're all hot, and I'm really mindful that we haven't got a lot of time this time round. So I think we can put a hold on the speeches. I think we all know where we stand, we all feel welcomed, we all feel mutually respected or whatever. Right now I'm here to be present. No more speeches today—OK?"

Carrapichano looked down, half defeated, at his clipboard, and for a moment I thought he was about to lose his temper. Beside him the minister stood unperturbed, not having followed what Aimee had said, simply waiting for his cue to begin again.

"It is time to visit the school," said Carrapichano, without looking up, reaching round the minister and pushing open the gate.

The nanny, Estelle, was there to meet us, with the children, and they ran through the mammoth sandy schoolyard—empty except for two bent and netless goal mouths—high-fiving any child who came near, delighted to be let loose among so many of their kind. Jay was eight at the time, and Kara six, they'd been home-tutored all their lives. As we passed through our whistle-stop tour of six large, hot, cheerily painted classrooms, their many childish questions came tumbling out, questions not unlike my own, but in their case unedited and unconsidered, and which their nanny kept trying, unsuccessfully, to hush and silence. I wished I could add to them. Why does the headmaster have two wives, why do some girls wear scarves and some not, why are all the books torn and dirty, why are they being taught in English if they don't speak English at home, why do the teachers spell the words wrong on the board, if the new school is for girls what will happen to the boys?

Nine

Most Saturdays, as my own middle passage approached, I accompanied my mother to a protest march of one kind or another, against South Africa, against the government, against nuclear bombs, against racism, against cuts, against the deregulation of the banks or in support of the teachers' union, the GLC or the IRA. The purpose of all this was hard for me to grasp, given the nature of our enemy. I saw her on television most days—rigid handbag, rigid hair, unturned, unturnable—and always unmoved by however many people my mother and her cronies had managed to gather to march, the previous Saturday morning, through Trafalgar Square and right up to her shiny black front door. I remember marching for the preservation of the Greater London Council, a year earlier, walking for what felt like days—half a mile behind my mother, who was up at the front, deep in conversation with Red Ken—carrying a placard above my head, and then, after that got too heavy, carrying it over my shoulder, like Jesus at the Crucifixion, lugging it down Whitehall, until finally, we got the bus home, collapsed in the lounge, switched on the TV and learned that the GLC had been abolished earlier that same day. Still I was told there was "no time for dancing" or, in a variation, that "this was not the time for dancing," as if the historical moment itself forbade it. I had "responsibilities," they were tied to my "intelligence," which had been recently confirmed by a young supply teacher up at the school who had thought to ask our class to bring in "whatever we were reading at home." It was one of those moments—there were many—when we, the students, were reminded of the fundamental innocence of our teachers. They gave us seeds in the spring to "plant in our gardens," or asked us, after the summer break, to write a page about "where you went on holiday." It wasn't something that hurt me: I'd been to Brighton, many times, and once on a booze cruise to France, and was a keen window-box gardener. But what about the gypsy girl who smelled, who had weeping sores around her mouth and a weekly black eye? Or the twins, too old and dark for adoption, who bounced around the local foster homes? What about the boy with the eczema, whom Tracey and I spotted through the bars of Queen's Park one summer night, alone, fast asleep, on a bench? Supply teachers were the most innocent of them all. I remember the surprise of this one at the not small number of children who brought in either the **Radio** or **TV Times**.

I brought in my biographies of dancers, thick books with soft-focus seventies portraits on the cover, of the great stars in their old age—in their silk dressing gowns and cravats, in their pink ostrich-feather capes—and on page count alone it was decided that my future should be "discussed." My mother came in for a meeting, early, before school, where she was told that the same books she sometimes teased me for reading were evidence of my intelligence, and that there was a test such "gifted" children could take, which, if they passed, would enable them to attend the kind of good schools that give scholarships—no, no, no—no fees, don't worry, I meant "grammars," which are a different thing altogether, no money involved at all, no, no, please don't worry. I glanced at my mother, whose face gave nothing away. It's because of the reading age, explained the teacher, passing over our silence, you see her reading age is really quite advanced. The teacher looked my mother over—her bra-less vest and jeans, the kente-cloth head-wrap, a pair of huge earrings shaped like Africa—and asked if the father would be joining us. The father's at work, said my mother. Oh, said the teacher, turning to me, and what does your father do, dear, is he the reader of the house, or . . .? The father's a postman, said my mother. The mother's the reader. Now, normally, said the teacher, blushing, consulting her notes, normally, we don't suggest the entrance exam for the independent schools really.

I mean, there are some scholarships available but there's no point setting these kids up for disappointment . . . But this young Miss Bradwell we've had in recently thought perhaps, well, she thought that, in your daughter's situation, it might just be the case that . . .

We walked home in silence, there was nothing more to discuss. We had already been to visit the huge and raucous comp I'd be attending in the autumn, it had been sold to me on the promise it had a "dance studio" somewhere in that warren of scuffed corridors, Portakabin classrooms and temporary toilets. Everyone that I knew—excepting Tracey—was heading there, and this was one comfort: safety in numbers. But my mother surprised me. In the grounds of the estate she stopped at the base of the stairwell and told me that I'd take that test, and work hard to pass it. No dancing at the weekend, no distractions of any kind, I was being given the kind of opportunity, she said, that she had never had herself, having been advised, at the same age I was now—and by her own teachers—to work on mastering forty words a minute, like all the other black girls.

It felt to me as if I were on a certain train, heading wherever it was people like me usually went in adolescence, except now suddenly something was different. I'd been informed that I would be getting off at an unexpected stop, further down the line. I thought of my father, pushed off the train before he'd barely left the station. And of Tracey, so determined to jump off, exactly **because** she'd rather walk than be told which stop was hers or how far she was allowed to go. Well, wasn't there something noble in that? Wasn't there some fight in it, at least—some defiance? And then there were all the outrageous historical cases I heard of at my mother's knee, tales of the furiously talented women—and these were all women, in my mother's telling—women who might have run faster than a speeding train, if they had been free to do so, but for whom, born in the wrong time, in the wrong place, all stops were closed, who were never even permitted to enter the station. And wasn't I so much freer than any of them—born in England, in modern times—not to mention so much lighter, so much straighter of nose, so much less likely to be mistaken for the very essence of Blackness itself? What could possibly stop me traveling on? Yet when I sat down in my own school hall, on a stifling July day, outside of normal school hours—an unnatural time to be at school—and opened those test papers, to read through the opportunity my mother wished I would "grab with both hands," a great, sullen fury came over me, I didn't feel like traveling on their train, wrote a few words here and there, ignored the pages of maths and science, flagrantly failed.

Ten

A few weeks later, Tracey got into her stage school. Her mother had no choice but to ring my mother's doorbell, enter our flat and tell us all about it. She stuck Tracey in front of her like a shield, shuffled into the hall, wouldn't sit down or have tea. She'd never been over the threshold before. "The judges said they'd not seen anything like her original"— Tracey's mother stopped dead and looked angrily at her daughter, who then provided the unfamiliar word—"original **choreography**, not like that. That's how new it was. Never! I always told her that she'd have to be twice as good as the next girl to get anywhere," she said, hugging her Tracey into her mammoth bosom, "and now she is." She had a video of the audition to give us, which my mother took graciously enough. I found it under a pile of books in her bedroom and watched it alone one night. The song was "Swing Is Here to Stay" and every movement, every blink, every nod, was Jeni LeGon's.

That autumn, in my first term at my new school, I found out what I was without my friend: a body without a distinct outline. The kind of girl who moved from group to group, neither welcomed nor despised, tolerated, and always eager to avoid confrontation. I felt I made no impression. There were, for a while, a couple of girls in the year above who believed I prided myself on my high color, on my long nose, on my freckles, and they bullied me, stole money from me, harassed me on the bus, but bullies need resistance of some kind, even if it's only tears, and I gave them none and they soon got bored and left me alone. Most of my years in that school I don't remember. Even as I was living them a stubborn part of me never accepted it as anything more than a place I had to survive each day until I was free again. I was more engaged with what I imagined of Tracey's schooling than with the reality of my own. I remember her telling me, for example, not long after she arrived in the place, that when Fred Astaire died, her school held a memorial assembly, and some of the students were asked to dance in tribute. Tracey, dressed as Bojangles, in a white top hat and tails, brought the house down. I know I never saw her do this but even now I feel I have a memory of it.

Thirteen, fourteen, fifteen, the difficult middle passage—in those years I really didn't see much of her. Her new life swallowed her up. She was not there when my father finally moved out or when I got my period. I don't know when she lost her virginity or if and by whom she first got her heart broken. Whenever I saw her in the streets it seemed to me that she was doing well. She would be wrapped around a very handsome, mature-looking young man, often tall and with a sharp fade cut into his hair, and I think of her on these occasions as not so much walking as bouncing by—fresh-faced, hair pulled up tight in a dancer's bun, wearing neon leggings and a crop top—but also red-eyed, clearly stoned. Electric, charismatic, outrageously sexual, filled with the summer's energy at all times, even in freezing February. And to come across her like this, as she really was—that is, outside of my own envious ideas about her— was always a form of existential shock, like seeing someone from a storybook in real life, and I would do everything I could to make the encounter as brief as possible, sometimes crossing the street before she reached me, or jumping on a bus, or claiming to be heading for somewhere urgently. Even when I heard, a little later on, from my mother and others in the neighborhood, that she was having difficulties, more and more frequently in trouble, I couldn't imagine why that would be, her life was perfect as far as I was concerned, and this is one side-effect of envy, maybe, this failure of imagination. In my mind, her struggles were over. She was a dancer: she'd found her tribe. I, meanwhile, was caught completely unawares by adolescence, still humming Gershwin songs at the back of the classroom as the friendship rings began to form and harden around me, defined by color, class, money, postcode, nation, music, drugs, politics, sports, aspirations, languages, sexualities . . . In that huge game of musical chairs I turned round one day and found I had no place to sit. At a loss, I became a Goth—it was where people who had nowhere else to go ended up. Goths were already a minority, and I joined the oddest chapter, a small group of only five kids. One was from Romania and had a club foot, another was Japanese. Black Goths were rare but not unprecedented: I'd seen a few of them hanging around Camden and now copied them as best I could, dusting my face ghost-white and painting my lips blood red, letting my hair half-dread and spraying some parts of it purple. I bought a pair of Dr. Martens and covered them in Tipp-Exed anarchy symbols. I was fourteen: the world was pain. I was in love with my Japanese friend, he was in love with the fragile blonde in our circle who had scars all up her arms and looked like a broken cat left out in the rain—she couldn't love anybody. For almost two years we spent all our time together. I hated the music, and there was no dancing allowed—just pogoing up and down, or else swaying drunkenly into each other—but I liked that the political apathy disgusted my mother and that the brutality of my new look brought out the keenly maternal side of my father, who now worried about me endlessly and tried to feed me up as I gothically lost weight. I bunked off for the greater part of each week: the bus that went to school also went to Camden Lock. We sat on the towpaths, drinking cider and smoking, DMs hanging over the canal, discussing the phoniness of everyone we knew, free-form conversations that could eat up whole days. Violently I denounced my mother, the old neighborhood, everything from my childhood, above all Tracey. My new friends were made to listen to every detail of our mutual history, all of it retold in a bitter spirit, stretching back to the very first day we met, walking across a churchyard. After an afternoon of that I'd get back on the bus, pass by the grammar school I'd failed to get into and get off at a stop outside— but precisely outside—my father's new bachelor flat, where I could happily go back in time, eat his comfort food, indulge in the old secret pleasures. Judy Garland pretending to be a Zulu, dancing the cakewalk, in **Meet Me in St. Louis.**

Eleven

Our second visit came four months later, in the rainy season. We arrived in darkness, after a delayed flight, and when we reached the pink house, I couldn't get over the oddness of that place, the sadness and emptiness of it, the feeling I had of moving into somebody else's broken ambition. Rain pelted the cab roof. I asked Fernando if he wouldn't mind if I went back to Hawa's compound.

"For me it's very fine. I have a lot of work to do."

"You'll be all right? I mean, by yourself?"

He laughed: "I have been alone in much worse places."

We parted at the huge, peeling billboard that marked the beginning of the village. I got soaked walking twenty yards, pushed open the aluminum door of Hawa's family compound, weighted by an oil-can half filled with sand but unlocked as always. Inside was almost unrecognizable to me. In the yard, where there had been, four months earlier, neatly raked red earth, and grandmothers, cousins, nephews, nieces, sisters and many babies, sitting all around, late into the night, now there was nobody, only a churned mud-pit into which I immediately sank and lost a shoe. When I reached down for it I heard laughter. I looked up and realized I was being watched from the concrete verandah. Hawa and a few of her girlfriends, carrying the tin plates from dinner back to wherever they were kept.

"Oh-oh," cried Hawa, laughing at the sight of me, bedraggled, and now carrying in my arms a large suitcase that refused to roll through the sludge. "Look what the rain brings!"

I had not expected to stay with Hawa again, hadn't warned her, but neither she nor anybody else in the compound seemed very surprised by my arrival, and though I hadn't been a particularly successful or well-loved house guest the first time round, I was welcomed like family. I shook hands with the various grandmothers, and we hugged, Hawa and I, and said how much we'd missed each other. I explained that on this trip there was only Fernando and me—Aimee was recording in New York—and that we were here to observe in further detail what was being done in the old school and what might be improved in the new one. I was invited to join Hawa and her visitors in the small living room, dimly lit with white solar, more keenly illuminated by the screens of each girl's phone. We smiled at each other, the girls, Hawa, me. My mother's and father's health were politely asked after—it was again considered astonishing that I had no siblings—and then Aimee's and her children's health were asked after, and Carrapichano's and Judy's, but none more solicitously than Granger's. Granger's health was what they were really interested in, for Granger had been the real hit of the first visit, far more than Aimee or any of the rest of us. We were curiosities—he was loved. Granger knew all the cheesy R&B tracks that Hawa adored, Aimee disdained and I'd never heard of, he wore the kinds of sneakers she most admired, and during a celebratory drum circle, put on by the mothers at the school, without hesitation had entered the ring, brushed his shoulders, body-popped, vogued and performed the moonwalk, while I cringed in my seat and busied myself taking pictures. "That Granger!" said Hawa now, shaking her head happily at the thrilling memory of Granger, compared to the dull reality of me. "Such a crazy dancer! All the boys were saying: 'Are these the new moves?' And remember, your Aimee said to us: 'No, these are the old ones!' You remember? But he's not with you this time? It's a shame. Oh, Granger is such a fun guy!" The young women in the room laughed and shook their heads and sighed, and then a silence fell again, and it began to dawn on me that I had interrupted a get-together, a gossipy good time, which now, after a minute of awkward silence, resumed in Wolof. Not wanting to go to the complete darkness of the bedroom, I sat back in the sofa, let the talk wash

over me and my clothes air-dry on my body. Next
to me Hawa held court, two hours' worth of stories which—from what I could tell—ranged from
the hilarious to the mournful to the righteously offended but never stretched as far as anger. Laughter
and sighs were my guide, and the photos from her
phone which she flashed in the middle of certain
anecdotes and cursorily explained in English if I
made a point of asking. I gathered she had a love
problem—a young policeman in Banjul whom she
rarely saw—and a big plan, already anticipated, to
go to the beach when the rains ended, for a family gathering, to which the policeman would be
invited. She showed me the picture from this event
the previous year: a panoramic shot that took in at
least a hundred people. I spotted her in the front
row and noticed the absence of scarf, instead she
had a silky weave on her head, parted in the center
and falling to her shoulders.

"Different hair," I said, and Hawa laughed, put
her hands to her hijab and removed it, revealing four inches of her own hair twisted into little
dreads.

"But it grows so **slow**, oh!"

It took me a while to figure out that Hawa was
that relative rarity in the village, a middle-class girl.
The daughter of two university teachers, neither of
whom I ever met, her father was working in Milan
now, as a traffic warden, and her mother lived in

the city and still worked at the university. Her father had taken what people in the village called "the back way," along with Hawa's elder brother, traveling through the Sahara to Libya and then finally making the dangerous crossing to Lampedusa. Two years later, by then married to an Italian, he sent for the other brother, but that was six years ago, and if Hawa was still waiting for her call she was far too proud to tell me. The money the father sent home had brought certain luxuries to the compound, rare in the village: a tractor, a large lot of private land, a toilet, though it was not connected to anything, and a television, though it did not work. The compound itself housed the four wives of Hawa's dead grandfather and many of the children, grandchildren and great-grandchildren his unions had produced, in ever-changing combinations. It was never possible to locate all the parents to these children: only the grandmothers remained constant, passing babies and toddlers back and forth between themselves and to Hawa, who, despite her youth, often seemed to me to be the head of the household, or at least the heart of it. She was one of those people who attract everybody. Emphatically cute, with a perfectly circular, blue-black face, Disney-bright features, very pretty long eyelashes and something adorably duck-like in her full and forward upper lip. Anybody seeking lightness, silliness, or simply to be playfully teased for an hour or two knew to come to Hawa, and she took an equal interest in everybody, wanted to hear all news, no matter how apparently quotidian or banal ("You were just in the market? Oh, so tell me! Who was there? And was the fish man there?"). She would have been the jewel in the crown of any small village anywhere. She had, unlike me, no contempt whatsoever for village life: she loved the smallness, the gossip, the repetition and the closeness of family. She liked that everybody's business was her business and vice versa. A neighbor of Hawa's, with a more difficult love problem than her own, came by to visit us daily—she'd fallen for a boy her parents wouldn't let her marry—and held Hawa's hands as she spoke and wept, often not leaving till one in the morning, and yet, I noticed, she always left smiling. I tried to think of ever performing a similar service for a friend. I wanted to know more about this love problem, but translation bored Hawa, and in her impatient version two hours of talk was easily boiled down to a couple of sentences ("Well, she is saying he is very beautiful and kind and they will never marry. I'm so sad! I tell you I won't sleep tonight! But come on: haven't you learned even a **little** bit of Wolof yet?"). Sometimes, when Hawa's guests arrived and found me sitting in my dark corner they would look wary and turn back, for just as Hawa was known everywhere as the bearer of lightness, someone whose very presence brought relief from woe, it was very soon clear to everyone that the visitor from England had brought with her only weight and sorrow. All the morbid questions I felt I must ask with a pen in my hand, concerning poverty reduction, or the lack of supplies at the school, or the apparent hardships of Hawa's own life—to which were now added the difficulties of the rainy season, the mosquitoes, the threat of untreated malaria—all of this repelled our guests and severely tested Hawa's patience. Political talk didn't interest her—unless it was conspiratorial, intensely local and directly concerned people she knew—and she also disliked any too strenuous conversation on the topics of religion or culture. Like everybody, she prayed and went to the mosque, but as far as I could see she had no serious religious interest. She was the kind of girl who wants only one thing from this life: to have fun. I remembered the type very well from my own school days, girls like that have always mystified me—they still do—and I felt I mystified Hawa equally. I lay on the floor next to her each night, on our neighboring mattresses, grateful for the blue aura that came off her Samsung as she scrolled through her messages and photographs, sometimes well into the wee hours, laughing or sighing at pictures that amused her, breaking up the dark and relieving the need for conversation. But nothing ever seemed to outrage or seriously depress her, and perhaps because I saw so many things that elicited exactly these emotions in me, every day, I found myself consumed by a perverse desire to rouse the same feelings in her. One night as we lay side by side, as she again reflected on how much fun Granger had been, how cool and fun, I asked her what she made of the President's promise to personally decapitate any homosexual he found in the country. She sucked her teeth and continued scrolling: "That man is always talking up some nonsense. Anyway, we have none of those people here." She did not connect my question with Granger but I went to sleep that night burning with shame, that I should be so willing to casually destroy the possibility of Granger ever returning here, and for the sake of—what? Principle? I knew how much Granger had loved it here, even more than Paris—and much more than London—and that he felt this way despite the existential threat the visit had surely represented for him. We'd spoken about it often, it broke up the boredom of recording sessions—sitting in the booth together, smiling at Aimee through the glass, never listening to her sing—and these were the most substantial conversations I'd ever had with Granger, as if the village had unlocked in us a relation we did not know we had. Not that we agreed or made the same connections. Where I saw deprivation, injustice, poverty, Granger saw simplicity, a lack of materialism, communal beauty—the opposite of the America in which he'd been raised. Where I saw polygamy, misogyny, motherless children (my mother's island childhood, only writ large, enshrined in custom), he remembered a sixth-floor walk-up, a tiny studio apartment shared with a depressed single mother, the loneliness, the food stamps, the lack of meaning, the threat of the streets right outside his front door, and spoke to me with genuine tears in his eyes of how happier he might have been raised by not one woman but fifteen.

Once, when it happened to be just Hawa and me in the yard, and she was plaiting my hair, I tried again to speak of difficult things, exploiting the intimacy of the moment to ask her about a rumor I'd heard, about a vanished village woman, apparently seized by the police, the mother of a young man who'd participated in a recent attempted coup. No one knew where she was, or what had happened to her. "There was a girl who came here last year, her name was Lindsay," said Hawa, as if I had not spoken at all. "It was before Aimee and you all came, she was from the Peace Corps—she was American and she was really fun! We played Twenty-one and we played Blackjack. You play cards? I tell you, she was really fun, man!" She sighed, laughed and pulled my hair tight. I gave up. Hawa's own preferred topic was the R&B star Chris Brown, but I had almost nothing to say about Chris Brown and only one song of his on my phone ("That is a very, very, very old song," she informed me) whereas she knew everything there was to know about the man, including all his moves. One morning, just before she left for school, I spotted her in the yard, dancing with her earphones in. She was dressed in her technically modest yet intensely form-hugging trainee-schoolteacher outfit: a white blouse, long black Lycra skirt, yellow hijab, yellow sandals, yellow watch, and a snug pinstripe waistcoat, which she made sure was pulled especially tight at the back to make a feature of a tiny waist and spectacular bosom. She looked up from where she was admiring the quick steps of her own feet, saw me and laughed: "Don't you tell my students!"

Each day of that visit, Carrapichano and I went into the school, visiting Hawa's and Lamin's classrooms, making notes. Carrapichano focused on every aspect of the school's functioning, while my remit was narrower: I went first to Lamin's class and then Hawa's, looking for the "best and the brightest," as I had been instructed by Aimee to do. In Lamin's class, a maths class, this was easy: I only had to put down the names of the girls who got the right answers. And that's what I did, waiting each time for Lamin to confirm, on the board, that the answers of the children were correct. For anything beyond basic addition and subtraction was, in truth, beyond my ability, and I watched Lamin's ten-year-olds multiply more quickly than me and reach long-division answers I could not even stumble toward. I would grip my pen and feel my hands sweating. It was like time travel. I was right back in my own maths classes, I had the

same old, familiar feelings of shame, and still re-
tained, as it turned out, my childhood habit of self-
deception, covering my workings with my hand
as Lamin passed by and always managing to half
convince myself, once the answer was up on the
board, that I had been very close to getting it all
along, but for this or that small error, the terrible
heat in the room, my own irrational anxiety in the
face of numbers . . .

I was relieved to leave Lamin and head to Hawa's session, a general class. There I had decided
to look for the Traceys, that is, for the brightest,
the quickest, the most willful, the lethally bored,
the troublesome, the girls whose eyes burned like
lasers straight through the government-issued English sentences—dead sentences, sentences devoid
of content or meaning—that were being laboriously transcribed in chalk up on to the board by
Hawa before being equally laboriously translated
back into Wolof and thus explained. I had expected to find only a few Traceys in each class,
but it soon became clear that there were more of
Tracey's tribe in those hot rooms than anyone else.
Some of these girls' uniforms were so worn they
were now little more than rags, others had open
sores on their feet or eyes weeping pus, and when I
watched the school fees being paid into the teachers' hands each morning in coins, many did not
have their coin to give. And yet they had not given
up, these many Traceys. They were not satisfied

with singing their lines back to Hawa, who herself, only a few years earlier, must have sat in these seats, singing these same lines, clinging to her textbook then as she did now. Watching all that fire with so little kindling, it was of course easy to despair. But each time the conversation was freed from its pointless English shackles and allowed to fall back into the local tongues I would see it again, the clear sparks of intelligence—like flames licking through a grille meant to smother them—and taking the same form natural intelligence takes in classrooms around the world: backchat, humor, argument. It was Hawa's unfortunate duty to silence all of this, all natural inquiry and curiosity, and drag the class back to the government textbook in hand, to write **The pot is on the fire** or **The spoon is in the bowl** with a piece of broken chalk on the board, and have them repeat it, and then to have them write this down, copying it exactly, including Hawa's own frequent errors. After watching this painful process for a few days I realized that she never once tested them on these written lines without the answer being already front of them, or having just been repeated, and one especially hot afternoon I felt I had to resolve the question for myself. I asked Hawa to sit where I sat, on a broken stool, so I could stand up before the class and ask them to write in their books: **The pot is on the fire**. They looked up at the empty board, and then expectantly at Hawa, awaiting the translation. I wouldn't let her speak. Two long minutes followed, as children stared blankly at their half-ruined exercise books, re-covered many times over in old wrapping paper. Then I went around the room, collecting the books to show to Hawa. Some part of me enjoyed doing this. Three girls in forty had written the sentence correctly in English. The rest had one word or two, almost all of the boys had no written letters at all, just vague markings reminiscent of English vowels and consonants, the shadows of letters but not letters themselves. Hawa nodded at each book, betraying no emotion, and then, when I had finished, stood up and continued her class.

When the bell rang for lunch I ran across the yard to find Carrapichano, who was sitting under the mango tree, making notes in a pad, and told him in an excitable hurry all the events of the morning, and the implications as I saw them, imagining how slow my own progress might have been if my teachers had taught our curriculum in, say, Mandarin, though I spoke Mandarin nowhere else, heard no Mandarin, had parents who spoke no Mandarin . . .

Carrapichano put his pen down and stared at me.

"I see. And what is it you think you just achieved?"

At first I thought he hadn't understood me, so

restated my case from the top, but he cut me off, stamping a foot in the sand.

"All you did was humiliate a teacher. In front of her class."

His voice was quiet but his face very red. He took off his glasses and glared at me, and looked so gravely handsome it lent a certain weight to his position, as if those who are right are always more beautiful.

"But—it's—I mean, I'm not saying it's a question of ability, it's a 'structural issue'—you always say that yourself—and I'm just saying maybe we could have an English lesson, OK, of course, but let's teach them in their own languages in their own country, and then they can—they could, I mean, you know, take English tests home, as homework or something."

Fernando laughed bitterly and swore in Portuguese.

"Homework! Have you been to their homes? Do you see books on their shelves? Or shelves? Desks?" He stood up and started shouting: "What do you think these children do when they get home? Study? Do you think they have time to study?"

He had not moved toward me but I found myself backing away from him, until I was up against the trunk of the mango tree.

"What are you doing here? What experience do you have in this work? This is adult work! You behave like a teenager. But you're not a teenager any more, are you? Isn't it time you grew up?"

I burst into tears. Somewhere a bell rang. I heard Fernando sigh with what sounded like sympathy, and I had a wild hope, for a moment, that he was about to put his arm around me. With my head in my hands I heard hundreds of kids burst from their classrooms and run through the yard, laughing and shouting, on their way to their next lessons, or out of the gates to help their mothers on the farm, and then Carrapichano kicking the leg of his chair, toppling it and walking back across the yard to class.

Twelve

The end of my own middle passage came in mid-winter, the perfect time to be a Goth: you're in tune with the misery all around you, like that clock that's right twice a day. I was on the way to my father's, the bus doors wouldn't open for the height of snow already in front of them, I had to force them apart with my black leather gloves and step down into a drift, protected from the intense cold by steel-capped black DMs and layerings of black jersey and black denim, by the heat of bird's-nest Afro hair, the fug of hardly ever washing. I had become an animal perfectly adapted to its environment. I rang my father's doorbell: a young girl answered the door. Perhaps she was twenty. Her hair was in very basic twists, she had a sweet teardrop of a face and flawless skin that shone like the peel of an aubergine. She looked fearful, smiled nervously, turned around, and called my father's name, but with such a thick accent it was hardly his name at all. She disappeared and was replaced by my father and after that she didn't come out of his bedroom for the rest of my visit. As we walked through the dilapidated communal hallway, past the curling wallpaper, rusted mail boxes, filthy carpet, he quietly explained to me, as if he were a missionary and a little bashful to reveal the true extent of his charity, that he had found this girl in King's Cross station. "She was barefoot! She'd nowhere to go, nowhere at all. You see, she's from Senegal. Her name is Mercy. You should have rung to say you were coming."

I ate dinner as usual, watched an old movie— **The Green Pastures**—and when it came time to go, and still nothing more about Mercy had been said by either of us, I saw him look back over his shoulder at his bedroom door, but Mercy did not reappear, and after a while I left. I didn't tell my mother or anyone at school. The only person I felt would understand was Tracey, and I hadn't seen her in months.

I'd noticed that other people had this adolescent gift for "spiraling out of control," of "going off the rails," but whatever catch inside of themselves they managed to release in times of sadness or trauma I wasn't able to find in myself. Instead, self-consciously, like an athlete deciding on a new training regime, I decided to go off the rails. But no one took me very seriously, least of all my mother, for she considered me a fundamentally reliable teenager. When other local mothers stopped her in the street, as they often did, to ask advice about their wayward sons and daughters, she would listen to them sympathetically but without any concern on her part, sometimes bringing the conversation to a close by putting a hand to my shoulder and saying something like: "Well, we're very lucky, we don't have those sorts of problems, not yet." This narrative was so cemented in her mind that any attempt I made to stray from it she simply couldn't see: she was attached to a shadow-me and followed this instead. And wasn't she right? I was not really like my new friends, not especially self-destructive or reckless. I hoarded (unnecessary) condoms, was terrified of needles, too afraid of blood generally to contemplate cutting myself, always stopped drinking before truly incapacitated, had a very healthy appetite, and when I went clubbing would sneak away from my crew—or conspire to lose them—at around a quarter past midnight, so that I could meet my mother, whose rule it was to pick me up at exactly half past the hour every Friday night, outside the stage door of the Camden Palace. I'd get into her car and bitch spectacularly about this arrangement while always, secretly, feeling grateful it existed. The night we rescued Tracey was like that, a Camden Palace night. Normally, my circle went to an indie night there, which I could just about tolerate, but this time we had gone for some reason to a hardcore show, shredded guitars distorting the huge speakers, a raging noise, and at a certain point I realized I wasn't going to make it till midnight—even though I'd battled with my mother for exactly this dispensation. Around eleven thirty I said I was heading to the bathroom and stumbled through that old theater, once a vaudeville place, found a spot in one of the empty booths on the first floor and set about getting drunk on the little bottle of cheap vodka I carried around in a pocket of my black trench coat. I knelt on the threadbare velvet where the chairs had been ripped out and looked down into the mosh pit. I got a sad sort of satisfaction from the thought that I was very likely the only soul in the place at that moment who knew that Chaplin had played here, and Gracie Fields, not to mention all the long-forgotten dog acts, family acts, lady hoofers, acrobats, minstrels. I looked down at all those disaffected suburban white kids dressed in black, hurling themselves at each other, and imagined in their place G. H. Elliott, "The Chocolate-Colored Coon," dressed head to toe in white, singing of the silvery moon. Behind me I heard the curtain swish: a boy walked into my booth. He was a white boy, very skinny, no older than me, and clearly high on something, with deep-pitted acne and a lot of dyed black hair falling over his cratered forehead. But his eyes were a beautiful blue. And we were of the same ersatz tribe: we wore the same uniform, the black denim, black cotton, black jersey, black leather. I don't think we even spoke to each other. He just came forward and I faced him, already on my knees, and reached up for his fly. We undressed as minimally as possible, lay back on that ashtray of a carpet and became attached at the groin for a minute or so, while the rest of our bodies remained apart, each swaddled in its layers of black. It was the only time in my life that sex occurred without its shadow, without the shadow of ideas about sex or fantasies regarding it of the kind that can only accumulate over time. On that balcony all was still exploratory, experimental, and technical in the sense of figuring out exactly what went where. I'd never seen any pornography. That was still possible then.

It seemed wrong for Goths to kiss so we bit gently at each other's necks like little vampires. Afterward he sat up and said in a much posher voice than I'd expected: "But we didn't use anything." Was it his first time, too? I told him it didn't matter, in a voice which probably surprised him just as much, and then asked him for a cigarette, which he gave me in the form of a pinch of tobacco, a Rizla and a square of cardboard. We agreed to go down to the bar and get a snakebite together, but on the staircase I lost him in a crowd surging upward, and suddenly desperate for air and space I made my way instead to the exit and out into Camden at the witching hour. Everyone was barrelling around half-lit, falling out of the pubs, in their torn denim and check or black-on-black, some sitting on the floor in circles, singing, playing guitars, others being told by a man to see another man, further down the road, who had the drugs that the first man was meant to have. I felt at once brutally sober, lonely, and wished my mother would appear. I joined a ring of strangers on the ground, who looked to be from my tribe, and rolled that fag.

From where I sat I could see up the side street to the Jazz Café and was struck by what a different crowd was gathered at its doors, not on their way out but on the way in, and not at all drunk, as these were people who loved dancing, who did not need to be drunk to convince their bodies to move. Nothing they wore was torn, or shredded or defaced with Tipp-Ex, everything was flash as flash could be, the women shone and dazzled, and no one sat on the ground, on the contrary all effort had been made to separate the clientele from the ground: the men's trainers had two inches of air built into them, and the women's shoes had double that in heel. I wondered what they were queuing for. Maybe a brown girl with a flower in her hair was going to sing for them. I thought of walking up there and seeing for myself but just then I became aware of a commotion, outside the entrance to the Mornington Crescent tube stop, some sort of problem between a man and a woman, they were yelling at each other, and the man had the woman up against the wall, he was shouting at her and had his hand around her throat. The boys I was sitting with did not move, or seem very concerned, they kept playing the guitar or else rolling up their joints. It was two girls who took action—a tough-looking bald girl and perhaps her girlfriend—and I stood up with them both, not shouting like them but following quickly behind. As we got closer, though, the situation became confused, it became less clear whether the "victim" was being hurt or helped—we saw her legs had gone floppy beneath her and that the man was in some sense holding her up—and we all slowed down a little in our approach. The bald girl became less aggressive, more solicitous, and in the same moment I realized the woman was not a woman but a girl and that I knew her: Tracey. I ran up to her. She recognized me but couldn't speak, she only reached out and smiled sadly. Her nose was bleeding, both nostrils. I smelled something awful and looked down and saw vomit, all over her front and in a pool at the floor. The man let go of her and stepped back. I stepped in, held her and said her name—Tracey, Tracey, Tracey—but her eyes rolled back in her head and I felt her full weight in my arms. This being Camden, every passing pisshead and stoner had a theory: bad E, dehydration, alcohol poisoning, probably done a speedball. You had to keep her standing, or lie her down, or give her some water, or move back and give her some air, and I was beginning to panic when, cutting through this noise, from across the road, came a much louder voice, one with real authority, calling Tracey's name and mine together. My mother, pulling up in front of the Palace as previously agreed, at twelve thirty a.m, in her little 2CV. I waved at her and she lurched forward again and parked beside us. Confronted with such a fierce-looking and capable adult, everyone else dispersed, and my mother did not even pause to ask what seemed to me to be necessary questions. She separated the two of us, lay Tracey out on the backseat, elevated her head with a couple of the serious books she had with her at all times, even in the middle of the night, and drove us straight to St. Mary's. I wanted so much to tell Tracey of my balcony adventure, of how, for once, I had been truly reckless. We emerged onto the Edgware Road: she snapped out of it and sat up. But when my mother tried gently to explain what was happening and where we were going, Tracey accused us both of kidnapping her, of trying to control her, we who had always been trying to control her, ever since she was a child, who always thought we knew what was best for her, what was best for everybody, we had even tried to steal her from her own mother, her own father! Her anger grew in proportion to my mother's icy calm, until, when we pulled into the A&E car park, she was leaning right forward in her seat, spitting on the back of our necks in her fury. My mother would not be baited or diverted. She told me to take the left side of my friend as she took the right and we half dragged, half compelled Tracey into the waiting room, where she became, to our surprise, utterly compliant, whispering "speedball" to the nurse, and then waiting with a handful of tissues pressed to her nostrils until she was seen. My mother went in with her. About fifteen minutes later she came out—I mean, my mother did—and said Tracey would be staying overnight, that her stomach would have to be pumped, and that she'd said—Tracey had—a number of sexually explicit things, in her delirium, to a stressed Indian doctor on his night shift. She was still only fifteen years old. "Something serious happened to that girl!" my mother murmured, kissed her teeth and bent over a desk to sign some papers **in loco parentis**.

In this context my own mild drunkenness wasn't worth troubling over. Spotting the vodka bottle in my coat, my mother removed it, without discussion, and dropped it into a hospital bin meant for medical waste. On the way out I caught a reflection of myself in the long mirror on the wall of a disabled toilet that happened to have, at that moment, its door flung wide open. I saw my drab black uniform and absurd dusted face—of course, I'd seen it all before, but not under that stark hospital lighting, and now it was no longer the face of a girl, now a woman stared back. The effect was very different from anything I had seen before by the light of the dim purple bulb in my black-walled room. I was over the threshold: I gave up the gothic life.

PART FIVE
Night and Day

One

They sat opposite each other, it felt very intimate, if you could put out of mind the millions of people looking on. Earlier they had wandered through his peculiar home together, looking at his treasures, his gaudy art, his terrible gilt furniture, talking of this and that, and at one point he sang for her and performed a few of his signature moves. But there was only one thing we wanted to know and finally she seemed to be preparing to ask it, and even my mother, who was pottering around the flat and claimed not to be interested, paused and sat down next to me in front of the television and waited to see what would happen. I reached for the remote control and turned it up. OK, Michael, she said, then let's go to the thing that is most discussed about you, I think, is the fact that the color of your skin is obviously different than when you were younger, and so I think it has caused a great deal of speculation and controversy as to what you have done or are doing . . . ?

He looked down, began his defense. My mother didn't believe a word of it, and for the next few minutes I couldn't hear a thing either of them said, there was only my mother, arguing with the television. So I'm a slave to the rhythm, he said, and smiled, though he looked bewildered, desperate to change the subject, and Oprah let him change it and the conversation moved on. My mother walked out of the room. After a while I got bored myself and switched it off.

I was eighteen. My mother and I never lived together again after that year, and already we were unsure how to relate to each other in our new incarnations: two adult women occupying, for the moment, the same space. Were we mother and daughter still? Friends? Sisters? Flatmates? We had different schedules, didn't see much of each other, but I worried I'd outstayed my welcome, like a show that goes on too long. Most days I went to the library, tried to revise, while she worked each morning as a volunteer, at a center for troubled youth, and, in the evenings, at a Black and Asian women's refuge. I don't say she was not sincere in this work, and good at it too, but it's also the case that both commitments look impressive on your CV if you happen to be standing for election as a local councilor. I'd never seen her so busy. She seemed to be all over the neighborhood at once, involved in everything, and everybody agreed that divorce suited her, she looked younger than ever: I sometimes had fears that at some point, not many years in the future, we would converge upon the exact same age. I didn't often get down the street in her ward now without someone coming up to thank me "for all your mother is doing for us" or to ask me to ask her if she had any idea about how to start an after-school club for the newly arrived Somali children or what local space might be appropriate for a cycling-proficiency class. She hadn't been elected to anything, not yet, but round our way the people had already crowned her.

One important aspect of her campaign was the idea to turn the old bike shed on the estate into a "community meeting space," which brought her into conflict with Louie and his crew, who used the shed for their own activities. My mother told me later that he sent two young men round to the flat to intimidate her, but she "knew their mothers," and was not afraid, and they left without winning the argument. I can believe it. I helped her paint the place a vivid yellow and went with her around the local businesses, looking for unwanted stackable chairs. Entry was set at a quid and covered some basic refreshments, Kilburn Books sold relevant literature from a trestle table in the corner. It opened in April. Every Friday at six o'clock speakers appeared, at my mother's invitation, all kinds of eccentric local people: spoken-word poets, political activists, drug counselors, an unaccredited academic who wrote self-published books about suppressed historical conspiracies;

a brash Nigerian businessman who lectured us about "black aspirations"; a quiet Guyanese nurse, evangelical about shea butter. Many Irish speakers were invited, too—as a mark of respect toward that original, fast-fading local population—but my mother could be tin-eared about the struggles of other tribes and did not hesitate to give lofty introductions ("Wherever we fight for freedom, the fight is the same!") to shifty-looking gangsters who pinned tricolors to the back wall and passed round IRA collection buckets at the end of their speeches. Subjects that seemed to me historically obscure and distant from our situation—the twelve tribes of Israel, the story of Kunta Kinte, anything to do with ancient Egypt—were the most popular, and I was often sent over to the church on these occasions to beg the deacon for extra chairs. But when speakers were concerned with the more prosaic aspects of our everyday lives—local crime, drugs, teenage pregnancy, academic failure—then they could count only on the few old Jamaican ladies who came whatever the subject, who came really for the tea and biscuits. But there was no way for me to get out of any of it, I had to go to it all, even the schizophrenic who walked into the room carrying foot-high piles of notes—held together with elastic bands and organized according to some system known only to him—and spoke to us with great passion about the racist fallacy of evolution that dared connect Sacred African Man to the base and earthly monkey when in fact he, Sacred African Man, was descended from pure light, that is, from the angels themselves, whose existence was somehow proved—I forget exactly how—by the pyramids. Sometimes my mother spoke: on those nights the room was packed. Her subject was pride, in all its forms. We were to remember that we were beautiful, intelligent, capable, kings and queens, in possession of a history, in possession of a culture, in possession of ourselves, and yet the more she filled the room with this effortful light, the clearer the sense I got of the shape and proportions of the huge shadow that must, after all, hang over us.

One day she suggested that I speak. Maybe a young person could reach the young people more easily. I think she was genuinely confused that her own speeches, though popular, had not yet stopped the girls getting pregnant or the boys smoking weed or dropping out of school or going on the rob. She gave me a number of possible topics, none of which I knew anything about, and when I said as much she got exasperated with me: "The problem with you is you've never known struggle!" We settled into a long row. She attacked the "soft" subjects I'd chosen to study, the "inferior" colleges I'd applied to, the "lack of ambition," as she saw it, that I had inherited from the other side of my family. I walked out. Tramped up and down the high road for a bit, smoking fags, before submitting to

the inevitable and heading to my father's. Mercy
was long gone, there had been no one since, he was
living alone once more and seemed to me stricken,
sadder than I'd ever known him. His working
hours—which still began each morning before
dawn—were a new kind of problem for him: he
didn't know what to do with his afternoons. A
family man by instinct, he was completely lost
without one, and I wondered if his other children,
his white children, ever came to see him. I didn't
ask—I was embarrassed to ask. The thing I feared
was no longer my parents' authority over me but
that they might haul out into the open their own
intimate fears, their melancholy and regrets. I saw
enough of all this in my father already. He'd become one of those people he'd once liked to tell me
about, that he met on his route and had always pitied, old boys in their house slippers watching the
afternoon shows until the evening shows began,
seeing hardly anyone, doing nothing. Once I came
round and Lambert turned up, but after a brief
flurry of cheeriness between them, they fell into
the dark and paranoid moods of middle-aged men
abandoned by their women, made worse by the
fact that Lambert had neglected to bring any relief
in the form of weed. The TV went on and they sat
before it in silence for the rest of the afternoon, like
two drowning men clinging to the same piece of
driftwood, while I tidied up around them.

Sometimes I had the idea that complaining to

my father about my mother might be a form of entertainment for us both, something we could share, but this never went well, because I severely underestimated how much he continued to love and admire her. When I told him about the meeting space, and of being forced to speak there, he said: "Ah, well, that sounds like a very interesting project. Something for the whole community." He looked wistful. How happy it would have made him, even now, to be schlepping chairs across the road, adjusting the microphone, shushing the audience in preparation for my mother to come on stage!

Two

A stack of posters, not photocopied but drawn, each one, by hand, announcing a talk—"The History of Dance"—were placed around the estate, where, like all public notices, they were soon defaced in creative and obscene ways, one piece of graffiti spawning a response, and then a response to the response. I was tacking one up in a walkway on Tracey's estate when I felt a pair of hands on my shoulders—a short, hard squeeze—turned around and there she was. She looked at the poster but didn't mention it. She reached for my new glasses, put them on her own face and laughed at her reflection in a warped piece of sheet mirror stuck up next to the noticeboard. Laughed again when she offered me a fag and I dropped it, and then again at the ratty espadrilles I was wearing, stolen from my mother's wardrobe. I felt like some old diary she'd found in a drawer: a reminder of a more innocent and foolish time in her life. We walked together across the yard and sat on the grass verge at the back of her estate, facing St. Christopher's. She nodded at the door and said: "That weren't real dancing, though. I'm on a whole other level now." I didn't doubt it. I asked how her revision was going and learned that at her kind of school there were no exams, all of that had finished at fifteen. Where I was in chains, she was free! Now everything depended on an "end of school revue" that "most of the big agents come to," and to which I was also grudgingly invited ("I could try and ask for you"), and this was where the best of the dancers got picked up, found representation and began auditioning for the autumn run of West End shows or the regional traveling troupes. She preened about it. I thought she had become more boastful generally, especially on the subject of her father. He was building a huge family home for her, so she claimed, in Kingston, and soon she'd move there with him, and from there it was just a hop, skip and a jump to New York, where she'd have the chance to perform on Broadway, where they really appreciated dancers, not like here. Yes, she'd work in New York but live in Jamaica, in the sun with Louie, and finally be rid of what I remember she called "this miserable fucking country"—as if it were only an accident that she had ever lived here in the first place.

But a few days later I saw Louie, in a completely different context, it was in Kentish Town. I was on a bus, on the top deck, I spotted him in the street, with his arm around a very pregnant woman, the kind we used to call a "home girl," with big gold earrings in the shape of pyramids, wearing a lot of chains and with her hair greased and frozen in a pattern of kiss-curls and spikes. They were laughing and joking together, and kissing every now and then. She was pushing a buggy with a child in it, of about two years old, and holding the hand of a seven- or eight-year-old. My first thought was not "Who are these children?" But: "What's Louie doing in Kentish Town? Why's he walking down Kentish Town High Street like he lives there?" I really couldn't think beyond a one-mile radius. Only when they were out of sight did I consider all the occasions Tracey had lied or bluffed about his absence—she stopped crying about it when she was very young—without ever guessing how close by he likely was the whole time. Not at the school concert or the birthday or the show or the sports day or even simply in the house, for dinner, because he was tending, supposedly, to an eternally sick mother in south Kilburn, or dancing with Michael Jackson, or thousands of miles away in Jamaica, building Tracey's dream home. But that one-sided conversation on the grassy verge had confirmed for me that we could no longer speak of intimate things. Instead, when I got home, I told my mother what I'd seen. She was in the middle of trying to cook dinner, always a stressful moment of the day, and she became annoyed with me, with a speed and heat out of all proportion. I couldn't understand it, I knew she hated Louie—so why defend him? Slamming pots about, speaking passionately of Jamaica, and not present-day Jamaica but Jamaica in the 1800s, the 1700s, and beyond—present-day Kentish Town was pushed aside as an irrelevance—telling me about breeders and bucks, of children torn from their mother's arms, of repetition and return, through the centuries, and the many missing men in her bloodline, including her own father, all of them ghost men, never seen close up or clearly. I drew back from her as she ranted, until I was pressed up against the warmth of the oven door. I didn't know what to do with all the sadness. A hundred and fifty years! Do you have any idea how long a hundred and fifty years is in the family of man? She clicked her fingers, and I thought of Miss Isabel, counting children in for the beats of a dance. That long, she said.

A week later somebody set a fire in the old bike shed, the night before I was due to speak, reducing it to a black box of carbon. We toured it with the firemen. It smelled terribly of all the plastic chairs that had been piled up against the walls and were now melted and melded together. I was relieved, it felt like an act of God, although all signs pointed closer to home, and soon enough Louie's boys reclaimed their space. The day after the fire, when my mother and I were out and about together, a few well-meaning people crossed the street to offer their sympathies or try to engage her on the subject, but she pursed her lips and stared at them as if they had said something coarse or personal. Brute force outraged her, I think, because it was outside her beloved realm of language, and in response to it she really had nothing to say. Despite her revolutionary stylings I don't think my mother would have been very useful in a real revolution, not once the talking and the meetings were over and the actual violence began. There was a sense in which she couldn't quite believe in violence, as if it were, in her view, too stupid to be real. I knew—from Lambert only—that her own childhood had been full of violence, emotional and physical, but she rarely referred to it other than calling it "that nonsense," or sometimes "those ridiculous people," because when she ascended to the life of the mind everything that was not the life of the mind stopped existing for her. Louie as a sociological phenomenon or a political symptom or a historical example or simply a person raised in the same grinding rural poverty she'd known herself—a person whom she recognized, and I believe intimately understood—**that** Louie my mother could deal with. But the look of utter forsakenness on her face as the firemen led her to a far corner of the shed to show her the spot where the fire had been started, by someone she knew personally, had tried to reason with, but who, despite this, had chosen to violently destroy what she'd lovingly created—this look is something I've never forgotten. Louie did not even need to do it personally, and equally did not have to hide that he had ordered it done. On the contrary he wanted it known: it was a show of power. At first I thought this fire had destroyed something essential in my mother. But a few weeks later she regrouped, convincing the vicar to let her move her community meetings to the back room of the church. The incident even turned out to be useful, in a way, for her campaign: it was the visual, literal confirmation of the "urban nihilism" of which she had often spoken and partly built her campaign around. Not long after, she became our local councilor. And here the second act of her life, the political act—which I'm sure she considered the true act of her life—began.

Three

The build finished with the rainy season, in October. To celebrate, an event was planned in the new yard, half a football pitch of cleared ground. We weren't involved in the planning—the village action committee did that—and Aimee didn't arrive till the morning of the same day. But I'd been on the ground for a fortnight, and had grown worried about the logistics, the sound system, the size of the crowd, and the conviction, shared by everybody—children and adults, the Al Kalo, Lamin, Hawa, all her friends—that the President himself was going to make an appearance. The source of this rumor was hard to determine. Everybody had heard it from someone else, it wasn't possible to get any further information, only winks and smiles, as the assumption was that we, "the Americans," were behind the visit anyway. "You ask **me** if he is coming?" said Hawa, laughing, "but don't you know yourself?" The rumor and the scale of the event quickly fed upon each other: first three local nursery schools would participate in the parade, then five, then fifteen. First it was the President coming, then also the leaders of Senegal, Togo and Benin, and so to the mothers' drumming circle were added half a dozen griots playing their long-necked **kora** and a police marching band. We started to hear that communities from several other villages were being bussed in and that a famous Senegalese DJ would play after the formal events. Running underneath all this noisy planning there was something else, a low rumble of suspicion and resentment, which I couldn't hear at first but which Fernando recognized at once. For no one knew exactly how much money Aimee's people had wired to the bank in Serrekunda, and so no one could be sure how much Lamin personally had received, nor was anybody able to say precisely how much of that money he had placed in the envelope which later arrived at the Al Kalo's house, and how much he had left at that house with Fatu, our Lady Treasurer, before the remainder finally landed in the coffers of the village committee itself. No one accused anybody, not directly. But all conversations, no matter where they began, seemed to end up circling the question, usually coiled up inside proverb-like constructions such as "It is a long way from Serrekunda to here" or "This pair of hands, then this pair, then another. So many hands! Who will keep clean what so many hands have touched?" Fern—as I also called him now—was disgusted by the general ineptitude: he'd never worked with such idiots as these idiots in New York, they made only problems and had no conception of procedure or local realities. He too became a proverb-producing machine: "In a flood the water goes everywhere, you don't have to think about it. In a drought, if you want water, you have to direct it carefully along each inch of its path." But his obsessive worrying, what he called "detail-orientation," didn't annoy me any more: I made too many mistakes, every day, not to understand by now that he knew better. It was not possible any longer to ignore the real difference between us, which went far beyond his superior education, his Ph.D., or even his professional experience. It was about a quality of attention. He listened and noticed. He was more open. Whenever I spotted him in my reluctant daily walk around the village—something I did purely for exercise and to escape the claustrophobia of Hawa's compound—Fern would be locked in intense discussion with men and women of every age and circumstance, crouching by them as they ate, jogging next to donkey-drawn carts, sitting drinking **ataya** with the old men by the market stalls, and always listening, learning, asking for more detail, assuming nothing until he was told it. I compared all of this to my own way of being. Keeping to my dank room as much as possible, talking to no one if I could help it, reading books about the region by the light of a headtorch, and feeling a homicidal fury, adolescent in nature, toward the IMF and the World Bank, the Dutch who'd bought the slaves, the local chiefs who'd sold them, and many other distant mental abstractions to which I could do no practical damage.

My favorite part of each day became the early evenings, when I would walk over to Fern's and have a simple dinner with him in the pink house, cooked for us by the same ladies who fed the school. A single tin bowl, full of rice, sometimes with just a green tomato or garden egg buried in it somewhere, other times with an abundance of fresh vegetables and a very skinny but delicious fish laid on top which Fern graciously let me tear at first. "We are kin now," he told me, the first time we ate like this, two hands in the same bowl. "They seem to have decided we're family." Since our last visit the generator had broken down, but as we were the only ones to use it Fern considered this a "low priority"—for the same reason I considered it a high priority—and refused to lose a day traveling to the city in search of a replacement. So now, once the sun went down, we strapped on our little head-torches, making sure to wear them at an angle so as not to blind each other, and talked late into the night. He was good company. He had a subtle, compassionate, intricate mind. Like Hawa, he didn't get depressed, but he managed this not by looking away but by looking closely, attending to each logical step in any particular problem, so that the problem itself filled all available mental space. A few nights before the party, while we sat considering the imminent arrival of Granger and Judy and the rest—and the end of a certain peaceful version of our life here—he began to tell me of a new problem, at the school: six children missing for two weeks from their classes. They were unrelated to each other. But their absences had all begun, the headmaster told him, on the day Fern and I arrived back in the village.

"Since **we** arrived?"

"Yes! And I thought: but this is odd, why is it? First, I ask around. Everybody says: 'Oh, we don't know. It's probably nothing. Sometimes the children have to work at home.' I go back to the headmaster and get the list of names. Then I go through the village to their compounds, one by one. Not easy. There's no address, you have to follow your nose. But I find everybody. 'Oh, she is sick,' or, 'Oh, he is visiting his cousin in town.' I have the feeling no one tells me the truth. Then I am looking at the list today and I think: these names are familiar. I go back to my papers and I find this microfinance list—you remember?—this thing Granger did, independently. He is a sweet man, he reads a book on microfinance . . . Anyway, I look at this list and I find it is the same six families exactly! The mothers are all the same women Granger gave these thirty-dollar stakes, for their market stalls. Exactly the same. So I think: what is the connection between the thirty-dollar stake and these missing children? Now it's obvious: their mothers, who could not repay their debt on whatever schedule Granger has arranged with them, they assume the money will be taken coin by coin, from their children's school fees, and the children will be shamed! They see us back in the village, 'the Americans,' and they think: better keep these kids at home! It's smart, it makes sense."

"Poor Granger. He'll be disappointed. He meant well."

"No, no, no . . . it's easily resolved. It's just for me an interesting example of follow-through. Or of not following through. The financing is a good idea, I think, or not a bad idea. But we may have to change the repayment schedule."

Through one of the blown-out windows I saw a bush taxi rumble down the one good road in the moonlight. Kids hung from it even at this hour, and three young men lay on their bellies on its roof, holding down a mattress with the weight of their own bodies. I felt that wave of absurdity, of pointlessness, that usually caught me in the earliest hours, laying wide awake next to a deep-sleeping Hawa as the roosters went berserk on the other side of the wall.

"I don't know . . . Thirty dollars here, thirty dollars there . . ."

"Yes?" said Fern brightly—he often failed to pick up on tone—and when I looked up I saw in his face so much optimism and interest in this small, new problem that it irritated me. I wanted to crush it.

"No, I mean—look, you go into the city, to every other village around here, you see these Peace Corps kids, the missionaries, the NGOs, all these well-meaning white people busy worrying about a few trees—as if none of you see the forest!"

"Now you are the one speaking in proverbs."

I stood up and began urgently burrowing through the pile of supplies in the corner, looking for the Calor gas stove and the teapot.

"You wouldn't accept these . . . **microscopic** solutions in **your** homes, in **your** countries—why should we accept them here?"

" 'We'?" queried Fern and then began to smile. "Wait, wait." He came over to where I was wrestling with the gas canister and bent down to help me attach it to the ring which in my bad temper I was managing badly. Our faces came very close to each other. " 'These well-meaning white people.' You think far too much about race—did anyone ever tell you this? But wait: to you I am white?" I was so startled by the question I started to laugh. Fern drew back: "Well, it's interesting for me. In Brazil we don't understand ourselves as white, you understand. At least my family does not. But you're laughing—this signifies yes, you think I am?"

"Oh, Fern . . ." Who did we have out here except each other? I directed my torch away from where it had lit up the sweet concern in his face, which after all was not much paler than mine. "I don't think it matters what I think, does it?"

"Oh, no, it matters," he said, returning to his chair, and despite the dead bulb above our heads I thought I saw him blush. I concentrated on looking for a small and exquisite pair of Moroccan glass tumblers with a green stain. He told me once that he carried them everywhere with him on his travels, and this admission was one of the few concessions I ever heard Fern make to personal pleasure, to comfort.

"But I am not offended, no, all of this it is interesting to me," he said, sitting back in his chair and stretching out his legs like a professor in his study. "What are we doing here, what is our effect, what will be left behind as legacy, and so on. It all has to be thought about, of course. Step by step. This house is a good example." He reached to his left and patted a patch of exposed wiring in the wall. "Maybe they paid off the owner or maybe he has no idea we are in it. Who knows? But now we are in it and all of the village sees we are in it, and so now they know that it belongs, in essence, to nobody, or to anybody the state on a whim decides to give it to. So what will happen when we leave, when the new school is up and running and we don't visit here much any more—or at all? Maybe several families will move in, maybe it will become a community place. Maybe. My guess is it will be taken apart, brick by brick." He took off his glasses and massaged them with the hem of his T-shirt. "Yes, first someone will take the wires, then the sheeting, then the tiles, but eventually every stone will be repurposed. This is my bet . . . I may be wrong, we will have to wait and see. I am not as ingenious as these people. No one is more ingenious than the poor, wherever you find them. When you are poor every stage has to be thought through. Wealth is the opposite. With wealth you get to be thoughtless."

"I don't see anything ingenious about poverty like this. I don't see anything ingenious about having ten children when you can't afford one."

Fern put his glasses back on and smiled at me sadly.

"Children can be a kind of wealth," he said.

We were silent for a while. I thought—though I really didn't want to—of a shiny red remote-control car, bought from New York for a young boy in the compound of whom I was especially fond, but it had come with the unforeseen problem of batteries—unforeseen by me—batteries for which there was sometimes money, most of the time not, and so the car was destined for a shelf I had noticed Hawa kept in the living room, filled with decorative but fundamentally useless objects, brought by clueless visitors, to keep company with several dead radios, a Bible from a library in Wisconsin and the picture of the President in a broken frame.

"I see my job this way," said Fern firmly, as the kettle began to whistle. "I am not of her world, that's clear. But I am here so that if she gets bored—"

"**When** she gets bored—"

"My job is to make sure something of use is left here, on the ground, whatever happens, whenever she leaves."

"I don't know how you do it."

"Do what?"

"Deal with the drops when you can see the ocean."

"Another proverb! You said you hated them, but see how you've caught the local habit!"

"Are we having tea or what?"

"Actually, it's easier," he said, pouring the dark liquid into my glass. "I respect the person who can think of the ocean. My mind no longer works that way. When I was young like you, maybe, not now."

I couldn't tell any more if we were talking of the whole world, of the continent in general, of the village in particular, or simply of Aimee, who, for all our good intentions, all our proverbs, neither of us seemed able to think of very clearly.

Woken at five most days by the roosters and the call to prayer, I got into the habit of going back to sleep till ten or later, getting to the school in time for the second period or the third. The morning of Aimee's arrival, though, I felt a fresh determination to see the whole day while it was still mine to enjoy. I surprised myself—and Hawa, Lamin and Fern—by appearing at eight o'clock, outside the mosque, where I knew they met each morning without me and walked together to school. The beauty of the morning was another surprise: it reminded me of my earliest experiences of America. New York was my first introduction to the possibilities of light, crashing through gaps in curtains, transforming people and sidewalks and buildings into golden icons, or black shadows, depending on where they stood in relation to the sun. But the light in front of the mosque—the light I stood in as I was greeted like a local hero, simply for rising from my bed three hours after most of the women and children I lived with—this light was something else again. It buzzed and held you in its heat, it was thick, alive with pollen and insects and birds, and because nothing higher than one story interrupted its path, it gave all its gifts at once, blessing everything equally, an explosion of simultaneous illumination.

"What do you call those birds?" I asked Lamin. "The little white ones with the blood-red beaks? They're beautiful."

Lamin tipped his head back and frowned.

"Those? They are just birds, not special. You

think they're beautiful? We have much more beautiful birds than that in Senegal."

Hawa laughed: "Lamin, you begin to sound like a Nigerian! 'You like that river? We have a much more beautiful river in Lagos.'"

Lamin's face creased into an irresistible, shamefaced smile—"I am only telling the truth when I say we have a similar bird but bigger. It is more impressive"—and Hawa put her hands either side of her tiny waist and gave Lamin the flirtatious side-eye: I saw how it delighted him. I should have seen it before. Of course he was in love with her. Who wouldn't be? I liked the idea, and felt vindicated. I looked forward to telling Aimee she was barking up the wrong tree.

"Well, now you sound like an American," announced Hawa. She looked out over her village. "I think every place has its share of beauty, thanks be to God. And right here is as beautiful as any place I know." A beat later, though, a new emotion passed over her pretty face, and when I looked over to where she seemed to be looking I saw a young man standing by the UN fresh well-water project, washing his arms up to the elbow, and glancing over at us with an equally pensive look. It was clear that these two represented a kind of provocation to each other. As we got closer I recognized that he belonged to a type I'd seen before here and there, on the ferry, walking along the highways, often in the city but rarely in the village. He had a bushy beard and a white turban tied loosely round his head, he carried a raffia pack on his back and his trousers were oddly cut, several inches above the ankle. As Hawa ran ahead of us to greet him I asked Lamin who he was.

"It is her cousin Musa," said Lamin, returning to his usual whisper, now laced with acid disapproval. "It is unfortunate we meet him here. You must not bother with him. He was a bumster and now he is a **mashala**, he is a trouble to his family, and you must not bother with him." But when we reached Hawa and her cousin, Lamin greeted him with respect and even a little awkwardness, and I noticed Hawa, too, seemed shy of him—as if he were an elder rather than not much more than a boy—and remembering that her scarf had slipped to her neck she now lifted it back till it covered all of her hair. Hawa introduced me to Musa politely in English. We nodded at each other. He seemed to be struggling to stabilize a certain look on his face, of benign serenity, like a visiting king from a more enlightened nation. "How are you, Hawa?" he mumbled, and she, who always had a lot to say on that question, outdid herself in a nervous tumble of description: she was well, her grandmothers were well, various nephews and nieces were well, the Americans were here, and well, for the school was opening tomorrow afternoon, and there was to be a big celebration, DJ Khali was playing—

did he remember that time on the beach dancing to Khali? Oh, man, that was fun!—and people were coming from upriver, from Senegal, from everywhere, because it was a wonderful thing that was happening, a new school for the girls, because education is a very important thing, especially for girls. This last part was for me and I smiled to approve it. Musa nodded, a little anxiously I thought, through all of it, but now that Hawa had at last stopped he turned a little, more toward me than his cousin, and said in English: "Unfortunately I will not be there. Music and dancing is Shaytan. Like many things done around here it is **aadoo**, custom, not religion. In this country we dance our lives away. Everything is an excuse for dancing. Anyway, I am leaving on **khuruj** today to Senegal." He looked down at the simple leather sandals he wore on his feet as if to check they were prepared for the journey ahead. "I go there for **Da'wah**, to invite and to call."

At this Lamin laughed, heavily sarcastic, and Hawa's cousin replied sharply to Lamin in Wolof—or perhaps it was Mandinka—and Lamin back to Musa, and back again, while I stood there, smiling the awkward idiot grimace of the untranslated.

"Musa, we miss you at home!" cried Hawa suddenly in English, with real feeling, hugging her cousin's skinny left arm as if this were as much of him as she dared hug, and he nodded many times again but did not answer. I thought he might leave us here—his and Lamin's exchange had seemed to me of the kind where someone really should leave afterward—but instead we all walked on together toward the school. Musa put his hands behind his back and began talking, in a low, quiet, pleasant stream, it sounded to me like a lecture, to which Hawa listened respectfully but which Lamin kept interrupting, with increasing energy and volume, in a style I couldn't recognize as his. With me he would wait till I finished each sentence, and leave long gaps of silence before he replied, silences I came to think of as conversational graveyards, where anything awkward or unpleasant I might have presented to him was sent to be buried. This angry, confrontational Lamin was so alien to me that I felt as if he, Lamin, would not want me to see him in action. I picked up my pace a little, and when I was several yards ahead of them all I turned round to see what was going on and saw that they, too, had stopped. Musa had Lamin's wrist in his hand: he was pointing to his big broken watch and saying something very solemn. Lamin snatched his arm back, and seemed to sulk, and Musa smiled as if all this had been very pleasant, or at least necessary, shook Lamin's hand despite their apparent dispute, accepted another hug of his arm from Hawa, nodded at me across the way, and turned back the way he had come.

"Musa, Musa, Musa . . ." said Hawa, shaking her head as she approached me. "Everything is **nafs** with Musa now—everything is a temptation—**we** are a temptation. It's so strange, we were age mates, we played together always, he was like my brother. We loved him at home, and he loved us, but he couldn't stay. We are too old-fashioned for him now. He wants to be modern. He wants to live in the city: just him, one wife, two babies and God. He is right anyway: when you are a young man, living all crazy with your family, it's hard to be very pure. I like to live crazy—oh, I can't help it, but maybe when I am older," she said, looking down at her own body as her cousin had looked at his sandals, with curiosity, as if they belonged to someone else: "Maybe when I am older I will be wiser. We'll see."

She seemed half amused, considering the Hawa she was now and the Hawa she might become, but Lamin was worked up.

"That crazy boy is telling everyone, 'Don't pray like this, pray like that, cross your arms across your body, don't put them by your sides!' In his own family home he is calling people **Sila keeba**—he is **criticizing** his own grandmother! But what does it mean, 'old Muslim,' 'new Muslim'? We are one people! He tells her: 'No, you should not have a big naming ceremony, have a modest one, with no music, no dancing—but Musa's grandmother is from Senegal, like me—when a baby comes, we dance!"

"Last month," began Hawa, and I prepared myself for the long haul, "my cousin Fatu had her first baby, Mamadu, and you should have seen this place that day, we had five musicians, dancing everywhere, the food was so much—Oh! I could not eat everything, actually, I was in pain from all this food, and all the dancing, and my cousin Fatu was watching her brother dancing like—"

"And Musa is married now," Lamin broke in. "And how did he marry? With hardly nobody there, no food—your grandmother was crying, crying for days!"

"It's true . . . Our grandmothers love to cook."

" 'Don't wear charms, don't go to the—' we call them **marabouts**—and in fact **I** don't go to them," he said, showing me, for some reason, his right hand and turning it round. "I am probably in some ways different than my father, than his father, but do I tell my elders what to do? And Musa told **his own grandmother she cannot go?!**"

Lamin was addressing me, and though I had no idea what a **marabout** was or why you would go to one I feigned outrage.

"They go all the time—" confided Hawa, "our grandmothers. My grandmother got me this." She held up her wrist and I admired a beautiful silver bracelet with a small charm hanging from it.

"Please show me where it says that to respect your elders is a sin?" demanded Lamin. "You cannot show it to me. Now he wants to take his new son to the 'modern' hospital instead of to the bush.

That is his choice. But why can't the boy have a coming-out ceremony? Musa will break his grandmother's heart again with this, I promise you. But am I going to be told this and that by a ghetto boy who knows no Arabic? **Aadoo**, Shaytan—this is the only Arabic he knows! He went to a Catholic mission school! I can recite every hadith, every hadith. No, no."

It was the longest, most sustained, most impassioned speech I had ever heard from Lamin, and even he seemed surprised by it, stopping for a second and wiping the sweat from his forehead with a white, folded handkerchief he kept for the purpose in his back pocket.

"I say people will always have their differences—" began Hawa, but Lamin interrupted her again: "And then he says to me"—Lamin pointed to his broken watch—"'This life is nothing compared to eternity—this life you are in is only the half-second before midnight. I am not living for this half-second but for what comes after.' But he thinks because he prays with his arms folded across his chest he is better than me? No. I said to him: 'I read Arabic, Musa, do you?' Believe me, Musa is a man in confusion."

"Lamin . . ." said Hawa, "I think you are a bit unfair, Musa only wants to perform jihad, and there is nothing wrong with—"

My face must have done something startling: Hawa pointed at my nose and burst out laughing.

"Look at her! Oh, man! She thinks my cousin wants to go shoot up people—oh no, that's funny—a **mashala** doesn't even have a toothbrush, forget a gun—ha ha ha!"

Lamin, less amused, pointed to his own chest, and returned to whispers: "No more reggae, no more hanging out in the ghetto, no more smoking of marijuana. She means this. Musa used to have dreadlocks—you know what are these? OK, so dreadlocks down to here! But now he is in this spiritual jihad, inside. She means this."

"I wish I was so pure!" announced Hawa, sighing sweetly. "Oh, oh . . . it's good to be pure—probably!"

"Well, of **course** it is," said Lamin, frowning. "We all try to perform jihad, every day in our own way, as much as we are able. But you don't need to cut your trousers and insult your grandmother. Musa dresses like an Indian. We don't need this foreign imam here—we have our own!"

We had come to the school gate. Hawa twisted her long skirt, dislodged by the walk, until it sat straight again on her hips.

"Why **are** his trousers like that?"

"Oh, you mean short?" said Hawa dully, with that gift she had for always making me feel I'd asked the most obvious question of all. "So his feet don't burn in hell!"

* * *

That night, under an exquisitely clear sky, I helped Fern and a team of local volunteers lay out three hundred chairs and erect white canopies to go over them, to send flags up poles and paint "WELCOME, AIMEE" on a wall. Aimee herself, Judy, Granger and the PR girl were all asleep in the hotel in Banjul, exhausted from their journey, or at the thought of the pink house, who knew. All around us the talk was of the President. We endured the same jokes over and over: how much we knew, or were claiming not to know, or who between the two of us knew more. No one mentioned Aimee. What I couldn't work out among all this frenetic rumor and counter-rumor was whether a visit from the President was longed for or dreaded. It's the same when you hear of a storm that's coming to town, explained Fern, as we drove the tin legs of the folding chairs into the sand. Even if you fear it you're curious to see it.

Four

I was at King's Cross station with my father in the early morning, on one of our last-minute trips to view a university. We'd just missed our train, not because we were late but because the price of a ticket was twice what I'd warned my father it might be, and during the argument about what to do next—one of us go now, the other later, or both not go or both go another afternoon, outside the peak-fare period—the train had pulled away from the platform without us. We were still snapping testily at each other in front of the announcement board when we spotted Tracey coming up the escalator from the tube. What a vision! Spotless white jeans and little high-heeled ankle boots and a black leather jacket cut close to her body and zipped up right to her chin: it looked like a kind of body armor. My father's mood transformed. He lifted both his arms like an air-traffic controller signaling in a plane. I watched Tracey walk toward us in a weirdly formal way, a formality my father missed altogether, hugging her as he had done in the old days, without noting the rigidity of her body next to his or the ram-rod stillness of her arms. He pulled back and asked after her parents, how her summer was going. Tracey gave a series of bloodless replies that contained, to my ear, no real information. I saw his face cloud over. Not at what she was saying, exactly, but at the manner in which it was being said, a brand-new style of hers that seemed to have nothing to do with the wild, funny, courageous girl he thought he had known. It belonged to a different girl altogether, from a different neighborhood, a different world. "What they giving you in that crazy place," he asked, "elocution lessons?" "Yes," said Tracey primly and stuck her nose in the air, and it was clear she wanted to end the subject here, but my father, never very good at hints, wouldn't let it go. He kept teasing her, and to defend herself against his ridicule Tracey now began listing the many skills she was developing in her summer singing and fencing lessons, her ballroom dancing and drama lessons, skills not necessary in the neighborhood but which a person needed to perform on what she was now calling the "West End stage." I wondered, but did not ask, how she was paying for it all. As she rambled on to me, my father stood staring at her and then suddenly interrupted. "But you're not serious, are you, Trace? Stop it with all that—it's just us here! No need to talk fancy with us. We know you, we've known you since you were this high, you don't have to pretend to be Lady

Muck with us!" But Tracey became agitated, she spoke faster and faster, in this funny new voice of hers that perhaps she had thought would impress my father instead of repel him, and which did not quite have control over itself and veered unnaturally every other sentence back to our shared past and jaggedly forward into her mysterious present, until my father lost control of himself entirely and giggled at her, in the middle of King's Cross station, in front of all those rush-hour commuters. He meant no harm—he was only bemused—but I saw how it hurt her. To her credit, though, Tracey didn't lose her famous temper, not at that moment. At eighteen she was already expert at the older woman's art of fermenting rage, conserving it, for later use. She excused herself politely and said she had to get to a class.

In July, Miss Isabel called my mother to ask if Tracey and I would be volunteers at her end-of-summer show. I was flattered: when we were kids ex-students had seemed like gods to us, long-legged and independent, giggling with each other and speaking their whispered adolescent currency as they took our tickets, ran the tombola, served snacks, handed out prizes. But that painful morning in King's Cross was still fresh in my mind. I knew that Miss Isabel's vision of our friendship was stuck in time, but I couldn't stand to break her image of it. I said yes via my mother and waited to hear about Tracey. The next day Miss Isabel called again: Tracey had agreed. But neither of us phoned the other or made any attempt at contact. I didn't see her till the morning of the concert itself, when I decided I'd be the bigger person and go over to her place. I pressed the doorbell twice. After a strangely long pause Louie answered. I was surprised: we seemed to have surprised each other. He wiped some sweat from above his mustache and asked me gruffly what I wanted. Before I could answer I heard Tracey, in a funny sort of voice—I almost didn't recognize it—shouting at her father to let me in, and Louie nodded and let me pass, but walked the other way, straight out of the door and along the corridor. I watched him hurry down the stairs, across the lawn and away. I turned back into the flat, but Tracey was not in the hall, and then not in the living room and then not in the kitchen: I had the feeling she was leaving each room a moment before I reached it. I found her in the bathroom. I would have said she had been recently crying, but I can't be sure. I said hello. At the same moment she looked quickly down at herself, at the same spot I was looking at, straightening her crop top until it once again fully covered her bra.

We walked back out and down the stairs. I couldn't speak but Tracey was never tongue-tied, not even in extreme situations, and chatted now in a bright, comical style, about all the "skinny bitches" she was up against in her auditions, the new moves she had to learn, the problem of projecting your voice beyond the footlights. She spoke quickly and constantly, to ensure no gap or pause in which I might ask a question, and in this way she got us both safely out of the estate and to the church door, where we met Miss Isabel. We were given matching keys, shown how to lock the cash-box and where to store it, how to close and open up the church before and after, and other small, practical things. As we walked around the space Miss Isabel asked a lot of questions about Tracey's new life, about the small roles she was already getting within her school and the big roles outside of it she hoped one day to get. There was something beautiful and innocent in these questions. I could see Tracey wanted to be the girl Miss Isabel had in her mind, the kind whose life is uncluttered and straightforward, who has nothing but goals in front of her, bright and clear and nothing standing in her way. Taking on the role of this girl, she walked through this familiar space of our girlhood, reminiscing, remembering to shorten her vowels, her hands behind her back, like a tourist wandering through a museum, looking over the exhibits of a painful history, the kind of tourist who has no personal attachment to what she sees.

When we came to the back of a church, where the children were queuing up for their juice and biscuits, they all looked up at Tracey with a wild admiration. She had her hair in a dancer's bun and a Pineapple Studios bag slung over her shoulder, she turned her feet out as she walked, she was the dream we'd both had, a decade before, when we'd queued up for juice here, little girls ourselves. No one paid much attention to me—even the children could see I wasn't a dancer any longer—and Tracey seemed happy to be surrounded by all these little admirers. To them she was beautiful and grown-up, enviably talented, free. And by looking at her this way, too, it was easy to tell myself I'd been imagining things.

I made my way across the room, and back in time, until I got to Mr. Booth. He was still sitting on his battered piano seat, a little older, but to me unchanged, and playing an unseasonable tune: "Have Yourself a Merry Little Christmas." And here that seamless thing happened, which, in its very unreality, makes people hate musicals, or so people tell me when I say I like them: we began making music together, without discussion or rehearsal. He knew the music, I knew the words. I sang about faithful friends. Tracey turned my way, and smiled, a melancholy but affectionate smile, or maybe it only carried the memory of affection. I saw the seven-, eight-, nine- and ten-year-old in her, the teenager, the little woman. All of these versions of Tracey were reaching across the years of the church hall to ask me a question: **What are you going to do?** To which we both already knew the answer. Nothing.

Five

It looked less like the opening of a school than the announcement of the end of an old regime. A troop of young soldiers dressed in dark blue uniforms stood in the middle, holding their brass instruments, brutally sweating. There was no shade out there and they'd been in position for an hour already. I was sitting a hundred yards from them, under the canopy, with the great and good of the whole upper-river region, some local and international press, Granger and Judy, but not the President, and not Aimee, not yet. Fern was to bring her over, when everything was set and all were in place: a long process. Lamin and Hawa, who were neither great nor good, had been relegated to some far-off spot, distant from us, for the hierarchy of the seating was absolute. Every fifteen minutes or so Judy, or sometimes Granger, or sometimes me, would suggest that someone should really get those poor musical soldiers some water, but none of us did, and no one else did either. Meanwhile the nursery schools trooped in, each school in its distinctive uniform, pinafores, shirts and shorts in striking combinations of colors—orange and gray, or purple and yellow—led by small groups of women, their teachers, who had pulled out all the stops in terms of glamour. The teachers of Kunkujang Keitaya Nursery School wore tight red T-shirts and black jeans with rhinestone pockets and their hair in elaborate braids. The teachers of Tujereng Nursery School wore wrappers and headscarves of matching red-and-orange design and identical white platform sandals. Each team took a different approach from the next but like the Supremes maintained a perfect uniformity within their group. They entered through the main gate, sashayed across the yard, trailing children, poker-faced—as if they didn't hear us all cheering—and when they reached their assigned spot two of the women would then unsmilingly unfurl a home-made banner with the name of the school upon it and stand holding it, shifting their weight from hip to hip as the wait continued. I don't think I ever saw so many outrageously beautiful women in one place. I'd been dressed up too—Hawa told me firmly that my usual khakis and crumpled linen would not do—borrowing a white-and-yellow wrapper and top from my host, which, being far too narrow for me, I could not close at the back and so had to disguise the open seam with a wide red scarf casually thrown over my shoulders, although it was at least 102 degrees.

Finally, almost two hours after we'd sat down,

all who were to be in the yard were in the yard, and Aimee, surrounded by a jostling crowd of well-wishers, was led by Fern to her central seat. Camera bulbs flared. And the first thing she turned to ask me was: "Where's Lamin?" I didn't have a chance to tell her: horns blew, the main event was upon us, and sitting back in my chair, I wondered if I might in fact have misunderstood everything I'd been so sure I'd understood in the previous two weeks. For now a parade of children walked into the square in costume, all of about seven or eight years old, dressed as the leaders of African nations. They came in kente-cloth and dashikis and Nehru collars and safari suits, and each had their own entourage, made up of other children who'd been done up as security guards: dark suits and dark glasses, speaking into fake walkie-talkies. Many of the little leaders had little wives by their side, dangling little handbags, though Lady Liberia walked alone, and South Africa came with three wives, who linked arms with each other as they walked behind him. To look at the crowd you would think nothing funnier had been seen by anyone in their lives, and Aimee, who also found it hilarious, wiped tears from her eyes as she reached out to hug the President of Senegal or squeeze the cheek of the President of Côte d'Ivoire. The leaders paraded past the desperate, sweating soldiers, and then in front of our seats, where they waved and posed for pictures but would not smile or speak. Then the band stopped blaring welcome horns and began a very loud brass rendition of the national anthem. Our chairs vibrated. I turned and saw two massive vehicles rumbling into the yard over the sandy ground: the first an SUV like the one in which we'd traveled four months before, and the second a real police jeep, so heavily armored it looked like a tank. Maybe a hundred children and teenagers from the village ran alongside these vehicles, behind, sometimes in front, but always dangerously close to the wheels, cheering and whooping. In the first car, standing up through the sun-roof, was an eight-year-old version of the President himself, in his white grand boubou and white kufi cap, holding his cane. A real stab at verisimilitude had been attempted: he was as dark as the President and had the same frog face. Next to him stood an eight-year-old glamour-girl, of about my shade, in a wig and a slinky red dress, throwing handfuls of Monopoly money into the crowd. Clinging to the sides of the car were more of these little security guards, with little sunglasses and little guns, which they pointed at the children, some of whom opened their arms in delight to expose their little chests to the aim of their peers. Two adult versions of these security types, in the same outfit, but with no gun, or not as far as I could see, ran beside the car, filming all this on the latest video cameras. In the police jeep bringing up the rear the little policemen with their toy guns shared space with real policemen with real Kalashnikovs. Both the little and big policemen held their guns in the air, to the delight of the children, who ran behind and tried to clamber into the back of the jeep themselves, to get to where the power was. The adults I sat among seemed torn between smiling cheers—whenever the cameras swung round to catch them—and crying out in terror as the vehicles threatened every moment to collide with their running children. "Move on over," I heard a real policeman shout, to a persistent boy at his right axel, who was pleading for sweets. "Or we'll move on over you!"

At last, the vehicles parked, the miniature President alighted and walked to the podium and gave a short speech I couldn't hear a word of due to the feedback from the speakers. No one else could hear it either but we all laughed and applauded once it was done. I had the thought that if the President himself had come the effect would not have been so very different. A show of power is a show of power. Then Aimee went up, said a few words, kissed the little man, took his cane off him and waved it in the air to great cheering. The school was declared open.

We did not move from this formal ceremony on to a separate party as much as the formal ceremony instantly dissolved and a party replaced it. All those who had not been invited to the ceremony now invaded the pitch, the neat colonial line-up of chairs broke apart, everyone took whatever seating they needed. The glamorous lady teachers ushered their classes to areas of shade and laid out their lunches, which emerged hot and sealed in big pots from those large tartan-checked shopping bags they also sell in Kilburn market, international symbol of the thrifty and far-traveled. In the northernmost corner of the grounds the promised sound system started up. Any child who could get away from an adult or had no adult in the first place was over there, dancing. It sounded Jamaican to me, a form of dancehall, and as I seemed to have lost everybody in the sudden transition, I wandered over and watched the dancing. There were two modes. The dominant dance was an ironic imitation of their mothers: bent at the knees, hunched backs, backside out, watching their own feet as they stomped the rhythm into the ground. But every now and then—especially if they spotted me watching them—the moves jumped to other times and places, more familiar to me, through hip-hop and ragga, through Atlanta and Kingston, and I saw jerking, popping, sliding, grinding. A smirking, handsome boy of no more than ten knew some especially obscene moves and would do them in little bursts so that the girls around him could be periodically scandalized, scream, run to hide behind a tree, before creeping back to watch him do some more. He had his eye on me. He kept pointing at me, shouting something over the music, I couldn't quite make it out: "Dance? Too bad! Dance? Dance! Too bad!" I took a step closer, smiled and shook my head no, though he knew I was considering it. "Ah, there you are," said Hawa, from behind me, linked her arm with mine and led me back to our party.

Under a tree Lamin, Granger, Judy, our teachers and some of the children were gathered, all sucking from little saran-wrapped pyramids of either orange ice or ice-cold water. I took a water from the little girl selling them and Hawa showed me how to tear a corner with my teeth to suck the liquid out. When I finished I looked at the little twisted wrapper in my hand, like a deflated condom, and realized there was nowhere to put it but the ground, and that these pyramid drinks must be the source of all those plastic twists I saw piled up in every street, in the branches of trees, littering compounds, in every bush like blossom. I put it in my pocket to delay the inevitable and went to take a seat between Granger and Judy, who were in the middle of an argument.

"I didn't **say** that," Judy hissed. "What I said was: 'I've never seen anything like it.'" She paused to take a loud suck of her ice pop. "And I bloody haven't!"

"Yeah, well, maybe they've never seen some of the crazy shit we do. St. Patrick's Day. I mean, what the **fuck** is St. Patrick's Day?"

"Granger, I'm an Aussie—and basically a Buddhist. You can't pin St. Patrick's Day on me."

"My point is: we love **our** President—"

"Ha! Speak for yourself!"

"—why shouldn't these people respect and love their own damn leaders? What business is it of yours? You can't just walk up in here with no context and judge—"

"Nobody loves him," said a sharp-eyed young woman who was sitting opposite Granger with her wrapper pulled down to her waist and a baby at her right breast, which she now shifted, applying the child to the left. She had a handsome, intelligent face and was at least a decade younger than me, but her eyes had that same look of experience I'd begun to see in certain old college friends during long, awkward afternoons visiting with their dull babies and duller husbands. Some girlish layer of illusion gone.

"All these young women," she said, lowering her voice, taking a hand from underneath her baby's head and waving it dismissively at the crowd. "But where are the men? Boys, yes—but young men? No. Nobody here loves him or what he has done here. Everybody who can leaves. Back way, back way, back way, back way." As she spoke she pointed to some boys dancing near us, on the verge of adolescence, picking them out as if she had the power to disappear them herself. She sucked her teeth, exactly as my mother would. "Believe me, I'd go too if I could!"

Granger, who I'm sure, like me, had assumed this woman did not speak English—or at least could not follow his and Judy's variations on it—nodded now to every word she said, almost before she said it. Everyone else in earshot—Lamin, Hawa, some of the young teachers from our school, others I didn't know—murmured and whistled, but without adding anything else. The handsome young woman pulled up straight in her seat, acknowledging herself as someone suddenly invested with the power of the group.

"**If** they loved him," she said, not whispering at all now, but neither, I noticed, ever using his proper name, "wouldn't they be here, with us, instead of throwing their life away in the water?" She looked down and readjusted her nipple and I wondered if "they," in her case, was not an abstraction, but had a name, a voice, a relation to the hungry baby in her arms.

"Back way is craziness," whispered Hawa.

"Every country's got its struggle," said Granger—I heard an inverted echo of what Hawa had told me that morning—"**Serious** struggles in America. For our people, black people. That's why it does our soul good to be here, with you." He spoke slowly, with deliberation, and touched his soul, which turned out to be dead center between his pectorals. He looked like he might cry. It was my instinct to turn away, to give him his privacy, but Hawa stared into his face and, taking his hand, said, "See how Granger really feels us"—he squeezed her hand back—"not just with his brain, but with his heart!" A not so subtle rebuke intended for me. The fierce young lady nodded, we waited for more, it seemed only she could bring a final meaning to the episode, but her baby had finished feeding and her speech was done. She pulled up her yellow wrapper and stood to burp him.

"It is an amazing thing to have our sister Aimee here with us," said one of Hawa's friends, a lively young woman called Esther, who I'd noticed disliked any hint of silence. "Her name is known all over the world! But she is one of us now. We will have to give her a village name."

"Yes," I said. I was watching the woman in the yellow wrapper who had spoken. Now she was wandering toward the dancing, her back so straight. I wanted to follow her and talk some more.

"Is she here now? Our sister Aimee?"

"What? Oh, no . . . I think she had to go and do some interviews or something."

"Oh, it is amazing. She knows Jay-Z, she knows Rihanna and Beyoncé."

"Yes."

"And she knows Michael Jackson?"

"Yes."

"Do you think she is Illuminati, too? Or she just is acquaintances with Illuminati?"

I could still make out the woman in yellow, distinctive among so many others, until she passed behind a tree and the toilet block and I couldn't find her again.

"I wouldn't . . . Honestly, Esther, I don't think any of that stuff is real."

"Oh, well," said Esther equably, as if she'd said she liked chocolate and I'd said I didn't. "Here for us it is real, because there is a lot of power there for sure. We hear a lot about this."

"It is real," confirmed Hawa, "but on this internet, believe me, you can't trust everything! For example, my cousin showed me photos of this white man, in America, he was as big as four men, so fat! I said, 'Are you so foolish, this is not a real photograph, come on! It's not possible, no one could be like this.' These kids are crazy. They believe everything they see."

By the time we made our way back to the compound it was black outside, starlit. I linked arms with Lamin and Hawa and tried teasing them a little.

"No, no, no, even although I call her Little Wife," protested Lamin, "and she calls me Mr. Husband, it is the truth that we are just age mates."

"Flirt, flirt, flirt," said Hawa, flirting, "and that's it!"

"And that's it?" I asked, kicking the door wide with my foot.

"That is certainly it," said Lamin.

In the compound many of the younger children were still awake and ran to Hawa, delighted, as she was delighted to receive them. I shook hands with all four grandmothers, which always had to be done as if it were the first time, and each woman leaned in to try to tell me something important—or, more accurately, did tell me something important, which I happened not to understand—and then, when words failed, as they always did, pulled me slightly by my wrapper toward the far end of the porch.

"Oh!" said Hawa, walking over with a nephew in her arms, "but there is my brother!"

He was a half-brother in fact and did not look much like Hawa to me, was not beautiful like her and had none of her flair. He had a kind, serious face, which was round like hers but double-chinned with it, a smart pair of glasses and an utterly neutral way of dressing that told me, before he did, that he must have spent time in America. He was standing on the verandah, drinking a large mug of Lipton's, his elbows resting on the lip of the concrete wall. I came round the pillar to shake hands with him. He took my hand warmly but with his head drawn back, and a half-smirk, as if bracketing the gesture in irony. It reminded me of someone—my mother.

"And you're staying here in the compound, I

see," he said, and nodded at the quiet industry all round us, the shrieking nephew in Hawa's arms, whom she now released to the yard. "But how does rural village life treat you? You have to first habituate yourself to the circumstances to appreciate it fully, I think."

Instead of answering him I asked him where he had learned his perfect English. He smiled formally but his eyes hardened briefly behind his glasses.

"Here. This is an English-speaking country."

Hawa, unsure what to do with this awkwardness, giggled into her hand.

"I'm enjoying it very much," I said, blushing. "Hawa has been very kind."

"You like the food?"

"It's really delicious."

"It's simple." He patted his well-rounded belly and handed his empty bowl to a passing girl. "But sometimes the simple is more flavorsome than the complicated."

"Yes, exactly."

"So: in conclusion, everything is good?"

"Everything is good."

"It takes a while to acclimatize to this rural village life, as I say. Even for me, it takes a minute, and I was born here."

Somebody now passed me a bowl of food, though I had already eaten, but as I felt that everything I did in front of Hawa's brother was being presented as a kind of test I took it.

"But you can't eat like that," he fussed, and when I tried to rest the bowl on the wall, said: "Let's sit."

Lamin and Hawa stayed resting against the wall, while we lowered ourselves on to a pair of slightly wonky homemade stools. No longer under the eyes of every soul in the yard, Hawa's brother relaxed. He told me he had gone to a good school in the city, near the university his father had taught in, and from that school had applied for a place at a private Quaker college in Kansas which gave ten scholarships a year to African students, and he had been one of them. Thousands apply, but he got in, they liked his essay, though it was so long ago now he barely remembered what it was about. He did graduate work in Boston, in economics, later he lived in Minneapolis, Rochester and Boulder, all places I had visited at one time or another with Aimee, and none of which had ever meant a thing to me, yet now I found I wanted to hear about them, perhaps because a day spent in the village felt, to me, like a year—time radically slowed there—so much so that now even Hawa's brother's tan slacks and red golf T-shirt could apparently inspire an exile's nostalgic fondness in me. I asked him a lot of very specific questions about his time spent in my not-quite home, while Lamin and Hawa stood next to us, frozen out of the conversational picture.

"But why did you have to leave?" I asked him,

more plaintively than I'd intended. He looked at me shrewdly.

"Nothing compelled me at all. I could have stayed. I came back to serve my country. I wanted to return. I work for the Treasury."

"Oh, for the government."

"Yes. But to him our Treasury is like a personal money-box . . . You are a bright young woman. I'm sure you probably heard about that." He took a strip of gum from his pocket and was a long time removing the silver foil. "You understand, when I say 'serve my country,' I mean all of the people, not one man. You'll understand, too, that at the moment our hands are tied. But they won't always be. I love my country. And when things change, at least I will be here to see it."

"Babu, right now you are here one day!" protested Hawa, throwing her arms around her brother's neck. "And I want to talk to you about the drama in **this yard**—never mind the city!"

Brother and sister inclined their heads affectionately toward each other.

"Sister, I don't doubt the situation here is more complicated—wait, I would like to finish this point for our concerned guest. You see, my last stop was New York. Am I correct in understanding that you're from New York?"

I said yes: it was easier.

"Then you will know how it is, and how class

works, in America. Frankly it was too much for me.
I'd really had enough of it by the time I reached
New York. Of course we have a system of class
here, too—but not the contempt."

"The contempt?"

"Now, let's see . . . This compound you are in?
This is our family you are among. Well, actually,
a very, very small portion of it, but it will do in
this example. Maybe to you they live very simply,
they are rural village people. But we are **foros**,
originally, nobles, through my grandmother's line.
Some people you will meet—the headmaster, for
example, is a **nyamalos**, which means his people were artisans—they come in different varieties, blacksmiths, leather workers, etcetera . . . Or,
Lamin, your family are **jali**, aren't they?"

An extremely strained look passed over Lamin's
face. He nodded in a minimal way and then looked
up and away, at the huge full moon threatening to
slot itself into the mango tree.

"Musicians, storytellers, griots," said Hawa's
brother, miming the strumming of an instrument.
"While some people, on the other hand, are **jongo**.
Many in our village are descended from **jongos**."

"I don't know what that is."

"The descendants of slaves." He smiled as he
looked me up and down. "But my point is, the
people here are still able to say: 'Of course, a **jongo**
is different from me but I do not have contempt for
him.' Under God's eye we have our difference but

also our basic equality. In New York I saw low-class people treated in a way I never imagined was possible. With total contempt. They are serving food and people are not making even eye contact with them. Believe it or not, I was sometimes treated that way myself."

"There are so many different ways to be poor," murmured Hawa, in a sudden leap of inspiration. She was in the middle of collecting a pile of fishbones from the floor.

"And rich," I said, and Hawa's brother, smiling faintly, conceded the point.

Six

The morning after the show the doorbell rang, too early, earlier than a postman. It was Miss Isabel, distraught. The cashboxes were gone, with almost three hundred pounds in them, and no sign of a break-in. Someone had let themselves in, overnight. My mother sat on the edge of the sofa in her dressing gown, rubbing her eyes against the morning light. I listened in from the doorway, my innocence presumed from the start. The discussion was what to do about Tracey. After a while I was brought in and questioned and I told the truth: we locked up at eleven-thirty, stacking all the chairs, after which Tracey went her way and I went mine. I thought she'd posted the key back through the door, but of course it's possible she pocketed it. My mother and Miss Isabel turned to me as I spoke, but they listened without much interest, their faces blank, and the moment I had finished they turned away and returned to their discussion. The more I listened, the more alarmed I became. There was something obscenely complacent to me in their certainty, both of Tracey's guilt and my innocence, even though I understood, rationally, that Tracey must have been involved in some way. I listened to their theories. Miss Isabel believed Louie must have stolen the key. My mother was equally sure he'd been given it. It didn't seem unusual, at the time, that neither of them considered calling the police. "With a family like that . . ." said Miss Isabel, and accepted a tissue to dab at her eyes. "When she comes into the center," my mother assured her, "I'll have a talk." It was the first I'd heard of Tracey going to the youth center, the one at which my mother volunteered, and now she looked up at me, startled. It took her a moment to regain her cool, but without looking me in the eye she began to smoothly explain that "after the incident with the drugs" she had naturally arranged for Tracey to get some free counseling, and if she hadn't told me that was because of "confidentiality." She hadn't even told Tracey's mother. Now I see that none of this was especially unreasonable, but at the time I saw maternal conspiracies everywhere, manipulations, attempts to control my life and the lives of my friends. I made a fuss and fled to my room.

Everything happened quickly after that. Miss Isabel, in her innocence, went to talk to Tracey's mother and was more or less chased out of their flat, returning to ours looking shaken, her face pinker than ever. My mother sat her down again and went to make tea, but a moment later we heard the sound of the open front door banging in its frame: Tracey's mother, propelled by her own unfinished fury across the road, up the stairs and into our lounge, where she stayed long enough to make a counter-accusation, a terrible one, about Mr. Booth. It was loud enough that I heard it through the ceiling. I ran down the stairs and right into her, she was filling the doorway, defiant, full of contempt—for me. "You and your fucking mother," she said. "You've always thought you were better than us, always thought you were some kind of bloody golden child, but turns out it ain't you at all, is it? It's my Tracey, and all of you are just fucking jealous, and I'll be dead before I let you people get in her way, she's got her whole life in front of her and you can't stop her with lies, none of you can."

No adult had ever spoken to me like that before, as if they despised me. According to her, I was trying to ruin Tracey's life, and so was my mother, and so were Miss Isabel and Mr. Booth, and miscellaneous others on the estate, and all the jealous mothers from dance class. I ran, crying, back up the stairs, and she screamed: "You can cry as much as you bloody want, love!" Upstairs I heard the front door slam and for several hours everything went quiet. Just before supper my mother came up to my room and asked a series of delicate questions—the only time the subject of sex ever came up explicitly between us—and I made it as clear as I could that Mr. Booth had never laid a hand on me or on Tracey, nor anyone else, as far as I knew.

It didn't help: by the end of the week, he was forced to give up playing the piano in Miss Isabel's dance class. I don't know what happened to him after that, whether he carried on living in the neighborhood, or moved away, or died, or was simply broken by the rumors. I thought of my mother's intuition—"Something serious happened to that girl!"—and I felt now that she was right as usual, and that if we had only asked Tracey the proper questions at the right moment and in a more delicate way we might have got the truth. Instead our timing was bad, we backed her and her mother into a corner, to which they both reacted predictably, with wildfire, tearing through whatever was in its path—in this case poor old Mr. Booth. And so we got something like the truth, quite like it, but not exactly.

PART SIX
Day and Night

One

That autumn, after clearing, I got into my second-choice university, to study media, half a mile from the flat gray English Channel, a scene I remembered from childhood holidays. The sea was fringed by a pebble beach of many sad brown stones, every now and then a large, pale blue one, pieces of white shell, knuckles of coral, bright shards easy to mistake for something precious that turned out to be only glass or broken crockery. My parochial city attitude I took with me, along with a pot plant and several pairs of trainers, sure that every soul on the street would be astounded to see the likes of me. But the likes of me were not so uncommon. From London and Manchester, from Liverpool and Bristol, in our big jeans and bomber jackets, with our little twists or shaved heads or tight-pulled buns slick with Dax, with our proud collection of caps. Those first weeks we gravitated toward each other, walking in a defensive gang together along the seafront, readied for insults, but the locals were never as interested in us as we were in ourselves. The salty air cracked our lips, there was never anywhere

to get your hair done, but "You up at the college?"
was a genuine polite inquiry, not an attack on
our right to be there. And there were other, unexpected advantages. Here I had a "maintenance
grant," covering food and rent, and weekends were
cheap—there was nowhere to go and nothing to
do. We spent our spare time together, in each other's rooms, asking after each other's pasts, with a
delicacy that felt right to people whose family trees
could be traced back only a branch or two before
being sunk in obscurity. There was one exception,
a boy, a Ghanaian: he came from a long line of
doctors and lawyers and was daily agonized not to
find himself at Oxford. But for the rest of us, who
were only ever one remove, or occasionally two,
distant from father machinists and mother clean-
ers, from grandmother orderlies and grandfather
bus drivers, we still felt we had done the miracu-
lous thing, that we were the "first in our line to
go," and this in itself was enough. If the institution
was almost as fresh as we were, that, too, came to
feel like an advantage. There was no grand academic past here, we didn't have to doff our caps to
anyone. Our subjects were relatively new—Media
Studies, Gender Studies—and so were our rooms,
and the young faculty. It was our place to invent.
I thought of Tracey escaping early into that community of dancers, of how jealous I'd been, but
now on the contrary I felt a little sorry for her, her
world seemed childish to me, just a way of playing

with the body, whereas I could walk down the hall and attend a lecture called something like "Thinking the Black Body: A Dialectic," or dance happily in my new friends' rooms, late into the night, and not to the old show tunes but to the new music, to Gang Starr or Nas. When I danced now I didn't have to obey any ancient rules of position or style: I moved as I pleased, as the beats themselves compelled me to move. Poor Tracey: the early-morning starts, anxiety on the scales, her aching insteps, the offering up of her young body to the judgment of other people! I was very free compared to her. Here we stayed up late, ate as we pleased, smoked weed. We listened to the golden age of hip-hop, unaware at the time that we were living through a golden age. I got schooled on lyrics by those who knew more than me and took these informal lessons as seriously as anything I heard in the lecture halls. It was the spirit of the times: we applied high theory to shampoo ads, philosophy to NWA videos. In our little circle to be "conscious" was the thing, and after years of forcing my hair straight with the hot-comb I now let it frizz and curl, and took to wearing a small map of Africa around my neck, the larger countries made out in a patchwork leather of black and red, green and gold. I wrote long, emotional essays on the phenomenon of the "Uncle Tom."

When my mother came down to stay for three nights, near the end of that first term, I thought she'd be very impressed by all this. But I'd forgotten that I was not quite like the others, not really the "first in our line to go." In this steeplechase my mother was one leap ahead of me and I'd forgotten that what was enough for others was never enough for her. Walking along the beach together on that final morning of her stay, she started a sentence which I could see myself somehow escaped her, going far beyond whatever she had intended, but still she said it, she compared her just-completed degree to the one I was starting, called my college a "trumped-up hotel," not a university at all, nothing but a student-loan trap for kids who didn't know any better, whose parents were uneducated themselves, and I became infuriated, we argued horribly. I told her not to bother visiting again, and she didn't.

I expected to feel desolate—as if I had cut through the only cord that connected me to the world—but this feeling didn't arrive. I had, for the first time in my life, a lover, and was so completely occupied with him that I found I could bear the loss of anything and everything else. He was a conscious young man called Rakim—he had renamed himself after the rapper—and his face, long like mine, was of a deeper honey-brown shade, with two very fierce, very dark eyes dropped into it, a prominent nose, and a gently feminine, unexpected overbite, like Huey P. Newton himself. He wore skinny dreadlocks to his shoulders, Converse All Stars in all weather, little round Lennon glasses. I thought he was the most beautiful man in the world. He thought so, too. He considered himself a "Five Percenter," that is, a God in himself—as all the male sons of Africa were Gods—and when he first explained this concept to me my initial thought was how nice it must be to think of yourself as a living God, how relaxing! But no, as it turned out, it was a heavy duty: it was not easy to be burdened with truth while so many people lived in ignorance, eighty-five percent of people, to be exact. But worse than the ignorant were the malicious, the ten percent who knew all that Rakim claimed to know but who worked to actively disguise and subvert the truth, the better to keep the eighty-five in ignorance and wield advantage over them. (In this group of perverse deceivers Rakim included all the churches, the Nation of Islam itself, the media, the "establishment.") He had a cool vintage Panthers poster on his wall, in which the big cat looked about to leap out at you, and he spoke often of the violent life of the big American cities, of the sufferings of our people in New York and Chicago, in Baltimore and LA, places I had never visited and could barely imagine. Sometimes I had the impression that this ghetto life—though it was three thousand miles away—was more real to him than the quiet, pleasant seascape in which we actually lived.

There were times when the stress of being a Poor Righteous Teacher could overwhelm. He pulled down the shades in his room, waked and baked, missed lectures, begged me not to leave him alone, spent hours studying the Supreme Alphabet and the Supreme Mathematics, which to me looked like only note book after note book filled with letters and numbers in incomprehensible combinations. At other times he appeared well suited to the task of global enlightenment. Serene and knowledgeable, sitting cross-legged like a guru upon the floor, pouring out hibiscus tea for our little circle, "dropping science," bopping his head gently to his namesake on the stereo. I had never before met a boy like this. The boys I'd known had had no passions, not really, they couldn't afford them: it was the act of not caring that was important to them. They were in a lifelong contest with each other— and with the world—exactly to demonstrate who cared less, who among them gave less of a fuck. It was a form of defense against loss, which seemed to them inevitable anyway. Rakim was different: all his passions were on the surface, he couldn't hide them, he didn't try to—that's what I loved about him. I didn't notice at first how hard it was for him to laugh. Laughter did not feel appropriate for a God in human form—much less for the girlfriend of a God—and I should probably have read a warning in that. Instead I followed him devotedly, to the strangest places. Numerology! He was besotted with numerology. He showed me how to render my name in numbers, and then how to manipulate these numbers in a particular way, in accordance with the Supreme Mathematics, until they meant: "The struggle to triumph over the division within." I didn't understand all of what he said—we were most often stoned during these conversations—but the division he claimed he could see inside of me I understood very well, nothing was easier for me to grasp than the idea that I was born half right and half wrong, yes, as long as I did not think of my actual father and the love I bore him I could tap this feeling in myself very easily.

Such ideas had nothing to do with, and no place in, Rakim's actual schoolwork: his degree was in Business Studies and Hospitality. But they dominated our time together and little by little I began to feel myself under a cloud of constant correction. Nothing I did was right. He was repelled by the media that I was supposed to be studying—the minstrels and the dancing mammies, the hoofers and the chorus girls—he saw no worth in any of it, even if my purpose was critique, the whole subject for him was empty, a product of "Jewish Hollywood," whom he included, en masse, in that deceitful ten percent. If I tried to talk to him about something I was writing—especially in front of our friends—he would make a point of diminishing or ridiculing it. Too stoned in company once,

I made the mistake of trying to explain what I found beautiful about the origins of tap dancing— the Irish crew and the African slaves, beating out time with their feet on the wooden decks of those ships, exchanging steps, creating a hybrid form— but Rakim, also stoned and in a cruel mood, stood up, rolled his eyes, stuck his lips out, shook his hands like a minstrel, and said: **Oh massa, I's so happy on this here slave ship I be dancing for joy.** Cut his eyes at me, sat back down. Our friends looked at the floor. The mortification was intense: for months afterward just the thought of it could bring the heat back to my cheeks. But at the time I didn't blame him for behaving in this way, or feel I loved him any less: my instinct was always to find the fault in myself. My biggest flaw at the time, in his view and my own, was my femininity, which was of the wrong kind. Woman, in Rakim's schema, was intended to be the "earth," she grounded man, who was himself pure idea, who "dropped science," and I was, in his judgment, far from where I should be, at the roots of things. I did not grow plants or cook food, never spoke of babies or domestic matters, and competed with Rakim when and where I should have been supportive. Romance was beyond me: it required a form of personal mystery I couldn't manufacture and disliked in others. I couldn't pretend that my legs do not grow hair or that my body does not excrete a variety of foul substances or that my feet

aren't flat as pancakes. I could not flirt and saw
no purpose in flirting. I did not mind dressing
up for strangers—when out at college parties or if
we went up to London for the clubs—but in our
rooms, within our intimacy, I could not be a girl,
nor could I be anybody's baby, I could only be a
female human, and the sex I understood was of the
kind that occurs between friends and equals, bracketing conversation, like a shelf of books between
bookends. These deep faults Rakim traced back to
the blood of my father, running through me like
a poison. But it was also my own doing, my own
mind, too busy in itself. A city mind, he called it,
the kind that can never know peace, because it has
nothing natural to meditate upon, only concrete
and images, and images of images—"simulacra,"
as we said back then. The cities had corrupted me,
making me mannish. Didn't I know that the cities had been built by the ten percent? That they
were a deliberate tool of oppression? An unnatural habitat for the African soul? His evidence for
this theory was sometimes complex—suppressed
government conspiracies, scrawled diagrams of architectural plans, obscure quotations ascribed to
presidents and civic leaders which I had to take
on faith—and at other times simple and damning.
Did I know the names of the trees? The names
of the flowers? No? But how could an African
live this way? Whereas he knew them all, though
this was due to the fact—which he didn't care to

broadcast—that he was a son of rural England, raised first in Yorkshire and then in Dorset, in remote villages, and always the only one of his kind on his street, the only one of his kind in his school, a fact I found more exotic than all his radicalism, all his mysticism. I loved that he knew the names of the counties and how they connected to each other, the names of rivers and where and how exactly they ran into the sea, could tell a mulberry from a blackberry, a copse from a coppice. Never in my life had I gone walking with no purpose, but now I did, accompanying him on his walks, along the stark seafront, down abandoned piers, and sometimes deep into the town, down its little cobbled lanes, crossing parkland, weaving through cemeteries and along A-roads, so far along that we would come upon fields finally and lie down in them. On these long walks he did not forget his preoccupations. He used them to frame what we saw, in ways that could surprise me. The Georgian grandeur of a crescent of houses facing the sea, their façades white as sugar—these were, he explained, also paid for by sugar, built by a plantation owner from our own ancestral island, the island neither of us had ever visited. And the little churchyard in which we sometimes gathered at night, to smoke and drink and lie on the grass, this was where Sarah Forbes Bonetta was married, a story he retold with such verve you'd have thought he'd married the woman himself. I lay down with him on the scrubby grass of the cemetery and listened. A little seven-year-old West African girl, high born but caught up in intertribal war, kidnapped by Dahomey raiders. She witnessed the murder of her family, but was later "rescued"—a word Rakim placed in finger quotes—by an English captain who convinced the King of Dahomey to give her as a present to Queen Victoria. "A present from the King of the Blacks to the Queen of the Whites." This captain named her Bonetta, after his own ship, and by the time they'd reached England he'd realized how smart a little girl she was, how unusually quick and alert, as bright as any white girl, and when the Queen met her she could see all of this, too, deciding to raise Sarah as her god-daughter, marrying her off, many years later, when she came of age, to a rich Yoruba merchant. In this church, said Rakim, it happened in this church right here. I got up on my elbows in the grass and looked over at the church, so unassuming, its simple crenellations and solid red door. "And there were eight black bridesmaids in a procession," he said, tracing their journey from the gate to the church door with the tip of a glowing joint. "Imagine it! Eight black and eight white, and the African men walked with the white girls and the white men with the African girls." Even in the darkness I could see it all. The twelve gray horses pulling the carriage, and the magnificent ivory lace of the gown, and the great crowd gathered to see the spectacle, spilling out of the church, on to the lawn, and back all the way to the lych-gate, standing on the low stone walls and hanging in the trees, just to catch a look at her.

I think of how Rakim gathered his information back then: in the public libraries, in the college archive, doggedly reading old newspapers, examining microfiche, following footnotes. And then I think of him now, in the age of the internet, and how perfectly happy he must be, or else how consumed, to the point of raving madness. Now I can find out myself in a moment the name of that captain and can learn in the same click what he thought of the girl he gifted to a queen. **Since her arrival in the country, she has made considerable progress in the study of the English language and manifests great musical talent and intelligence of no common order. Her hair is short, black, and curling, strongly indicative of her African birth; while her features are pleasing and handsome, and her manners and conduct most mild and affectionate to all about her.** I know now that her Yoruba name was Aina, meaning "difficult birth," a name you give to a child who is born with her umbilical cord tied round her neck. I can see a photo of Aina in her high-necked Victorian corsetry, with her face closed, her body perfectly still. I remember that Rakim had a refrain, always proudly declaimed, with his overbite pulled back over his teeth: "We have our own kings! We have our own queens!" I would nod along for the sake of peace but in truth some part of me always rebelled. Why did he think it so important for me to know that Beethoven dedicated a sonata to a mulatto violinist, or that Shakespeare's dark lady really was dark, or that Queen Victoria had deigned to raise a child of Africa, "bright as any white girl?" I did not want to rely on each European fact having its African shadow, as if without the scaffolding of the European fact everything African might turn to dust in my hands. It gave me no pleasure to see that sweet-faced girl dressed like one of Victoria's own children, frozen in a formal photograph, with a new kind of cord round her neck. I always wanted life—movement.

One slow Sunday Rakim blew some smoke out of his mouth and started talking about going to see a "real film." It was French, playing at the college film society that same day, and over the course of the morning we had steadily torn apart a flyer for it, using the glossy card to make many little roaches for our joints. But you could still make out the face of a brown girl in a blue headscarf who, Rakim now claimed, had something of my features, or I had hers. She was staring directly at me with what was left of her right eye. We dragged ourselves across campus to the media room and sat in the uncomfortable fold-up chairs. The film started. But with the fog in my head it was quite hard to understand what I was watching, it seemed to be made out of many little pieces, like a stained-glass window, and I did not know which parts were important or on what scenes Rakim felt I should focus, although maybe everyone in the room felt the same, maybe it's part of the effect of that film that each viewer should see something different in it. I can't say what Rakim saw. I saw tribes. Many different tribes, from every corner of the world, operating under the internal rules of their groups and then edited together in a complex pattern that appeared to have, in the moment, its own weird logic. I saw Japanese girls in traditional costume, dancing in formation, making strangely hip-hop movements on their elevated **geta**. Cape Verdeans waiting with perfect, timeless patience for a boat that may or may not come. I saw white-blond children walking down an otherwise deserted Icelandic road, in a town painted black by volcanic ash. I heard a dubbed and disembodied woman's voice speak over these images, she was contrasting African time to the time of Europe and time as it is experienced in Asia. She said that a hundred years ago mankind was confronted with the question of space, but that the problem of the twentieth century was the simultaneous existence of different notions of time. I looked over at Rakim: he was making notes in the darkness, hopelessly stoned. It got to the point where the images themselves were too much for him, he could only listen to the woman's voice and make his notes, faster and faster as the film went on, until he'd written half the script out in his pad.

For me the film had no beginning or end, and this was not an unpleasant sensation, just a mysterious one, as if time itself had expanded to make space for this infinite parade of tribes. On and on it went, refusing to end, there were parts I admit I slept through, only to awaken sharply when my chin hit my chest, at which point I would look up and find myself confronted with a bizarre image—a temple consecrated to cats, Jimmy Stewart chasing Kim Novak up a spiral staircase—images made all the more alien because I hadn't followed what came before and would not see what came after. And in one of these lucid gaps between waking up and falling asleep I heard once more that same disembodied voice speak of the essential indestructibility of women, and of men's relation to it. For it is the job of men, she said, to stop women from realizing their own indestructibility, and for as long as possible. Each time I woke with a start I could feel Rakim's impatience with me, his need to correct me, and I began to fear the closing credits, I could imagine the exact intensity and length of the argument that would follow them, in that dangerous moment when we were out of the cinema, back in his room and far from witnesses. I never wanted that film to end.

*   *   *

A few days later I dumped Rakim, in a cowardly way, in the form of a letter, slipped under his door. In it I blamed myself and said I hoped we could be friends, but he sent me one back, in livid red ink, informing me he knew that I was in the ten percent, and that from now on he would be on his guard against me. He was as good as his word. For the rest of my college life he would turn on his heel if he saw me coming, cross the street if he spotted me in town, leave any lecture room I entered. Two years later, at graduation, a white woman hurried across the hall and grabbed my mother's sleeve, and said, "I **thought** it was you—you're an inspiration to our young people, you really are—but I'm so glad to meet you! And this is my son." My mother turned around with her face already fixed in an expression I knew rather well by then—gentle condescension mixed with pride, the same face she often had now when on television, whenever she was called upon to "speak for those who had no voice." She put out her hand to greet this white woman's son, who would not at first come out from behind his mother and when he did looked at the ground, his skinny dreads obscuring his face, though I knew him at once by his Converse All Stars, poking out from beneath his graduation gown.

Two

On my fifth visit, I went alone. Strode straight through the airport, out into the heat, feeling a glorious competency. To my left, to my right, were the lost and the wary: beach-bound tourists, evangelicals in their oversized T-shirts and all the serious young German anthropologists. No representative led me to my vehicle. I was not waiting for "the rest of my party." I had my coins ready for the cripples in the car park, my cab fare already tucked in the back of my jeans, my half a dozen phrases. **Nakam! Jamun gam? Jama rek!** Khakis and crumpled white linen long gone. Black jeans, a black silk shirt and big gold swinging hoops in my ears. I believed I'd mastered local time. I knew now how long it took to get to the ferry and at what time of day, so that when my cab pulled up to the gangway hundreds of other people had already done my waiting for me, all I had to do was get out of the car and walk right on board. The ship lurched from the shore. On the top deck the sway pitched me forward, through two layers of people up to the barrier, and happy to be there, like someone just then pushed into their lover's arms. I looked down at all the life and movement below: jostling people, squawking chickens, dolphins leaping in the foam, narrowboats reeling in our wake, half-starved dogs running along the shore-line. Here and there I spotted what I knew now to be the Tablighi, their short trousers flapping around their ankles, because if they were longer they would get dirty, and the prayers of the dirty don't get answered, so you end up burning your feet in hell. But beyond their dress it was really their stillness that marked them out. Amid all that activity they looked paused, either reading from their prayer books or sitting in silence, often with their kohl-rimmed eyes closed and a blissful smile nestled in their henna-stained beards, so peace-ful compared to the rest of us. Dreaming of their pure and modern **iman** maybe: of small, nuclear families worshipping Allah in discreet apartments, of praise without magic, of direct access to God without local intermediaries, of sterilized hospital circumcisions, babies born without any celebra-tory dancing, women who did not think to pair a hot-pink hijab with a lime-green Lycra minidress. I wondered how hard it must be to maintain this dream, right now, on this ferry, as the unruly ev-eryday faith unfolded all around them.

I settled on to a bench. On my left sat one of these spiritual young men, his eyes closed, clutch-ing a folded prayer mat to his chest. On my other

side, a glamorous girl with two sets of eyebrows—
one pair painted strangely above her own—who
sat joggling a small bag of cashews in her hands. I
considered all the months that separated my first
ferry trip from this one. The Illuminated Academy
for Girls—which, for convenience's sake, and to
save everyone the shame of saying it, we abbrevi-
ated, behind Aimee's back, to IAG—had survived
its first year. Thrived, if you counted success in column inches. For the rest of us it had been a periodic
ordeal, intense whenever the visits rolled round
or some crisis brought the embattled headmaster
into our meeting rooms in London or New York,
via fraught video-conference. Oddly distant at all
other times. I often had cause to recall Granger, in
Heathrow, the night of our first return, hugging
me round my shoulders as we queued for Customs:
"None of this looks real to me now! Something's
changed. Can't be the same after seeing what I've
seen!" But in a few days he was exactly the same,
we all were: we left taps running, abandoned plastic bottles after a few sips, bought a single pair of
jeans for the same sum as a trainee teacher's yearly
wage. If London was unreal, if New York was unreal, they were powerful stage shows: as soon as we
were back inside them they not only seemed real
but **the only possible reality**, and decisions made
about the village from these locations always appeared to have a certain plausibility while we were
making them, and only later, when one or other

of us arrived back here, and crossed this river, did the potential absurdity of whatever it was become clear. Four months ago, for example, it had seemed important, in New York, to teach the theory of evolution to these children—and their teachers— many of whom had never so much as heard of the name Darwin. It seemed far less of a priority in the village itself, when we reached it in the middle of the rainy season to find a third of the kids off with malaria, half a classroom ceiling fallen in, the toilet contract unfulfilled and the solar-panel-powered electricity circuits rusted and corrupted. But our biggest problem, as Fern had predicted, was not our pedagogical illusions, exactly, but the wavering nature of Aimee's attention. Her new thing was technology. She had begun to spend a lot of social time with the brilliant young people of Silicon Valley, and liked to consider herself one of their tribe, "basically a nerd." She'd become very responsive to their vision of a world transformed—saved—by technology. In the first flush of this new interest she did not abandon IAG or poverty reduction as much as patch the fresh preoccupation on to the old ones, with sometimes alarming results ("We're going to give each one of these damn girls a laptop: **that's** going to be their exercise book, **that's** their library, their teacher, their everything!"). Which Fern then had to massage back into some semblance of reality. He stayed "on the ground" not for mere weeks but for whole seasons, partly out of

affection for the village and his own commitment
to his role there but also, I knew, to avoid working any more closely with Aimee than his preferred
distance of four thousand miles. He saw what no
one else saw. He noted the growing resentment of
the boys, who had been left to fester in the old
school, which—though Aimee sporadically rained
a little money on it—was now little more than a
ghost town, in which children sat around waiting
for teachers unpaid so long they'd stopped coming
to work. The government seemed to have with-
drawn from the village generally: many other previously well-running, or reasonably well-running,
services now languished cruelly. The clinic had not
reopened, a huge pot-hole in the road just outside
the village had been left to crater and spread. An
Italian environmental scientist's reports of dangerous levels of pesticides in the groundwater well
were ignored no matter how many times Fern tried
to alert the relevant ministries. Perhaps this kind
of thing would have happened anyway. But it was
hard to avoid the suspicion that the village was
being punished for its connection with Aimee, or
deliberately neglected in the expectation that Aimee's money would flow into the gap.

One problem you could not find written down in
any of the reports but Fern and I were both acutely
aware of it, although we experienced it from opposite ends. Neither of us bothered discussing it
with Aimee any more. ("But what if I love him?"

was her only response, when we combined forces, by way of conference call, in an attempted intervention.) Instead we worked around her, swapping information like two PIs on the same case. I probably was the one who noticed it first, in London. I kept walking in on sweet nothings being passed back and forth, at her desktop, on her phone, always closed up or shut down the moment I entered whichever room. Then she stopped being shy. When he passed the AIDS test she'd made him take she was so glad she told me about it. I got used to seeing Lamin's disembodied head in a corner, smiling at me, streaming at us live from, I presumed, the only internet café in Barra. He was there at breakfast with the kids in the mornings, and waved good-bye to them when their tutors arrived. He'd appear for dinner, like another guest at the table. He began to be included in meetings, the ridiculous "creative" kind ("Lam, what do you think about this corset?") but also in serious meetings with accountants, the business manager, the PRs. From Fern's end the situation was less queasily romantic, more concrete: Lamin's compound got a new front door, then a toilet, then interior dividing walls, then a new roof of tile. This did not go unnoticed. A flat-screen TV had caused the latest trouble. "The Al Kalo called a meeting about it on Tuesday," Fern informed me, when I called him to tell him the jet was taking off. "Lamin was away in Dakar, visiting family. Mostly the young people came. Everybody was very upset. It came down to a long discussion about how and when Lamin joined the Illuminati . . ."

I was in the process of texting Fern, to give him my latest location, when I heard a commotion the other side of the engine room, and looked up and saw bodies parting, moving toward the stairs, to avoid a skinny, flailing man who now came into view, shouting, waving his bony arms, in some form of severe distress. I turned to the man to my left: his face remained placid, eyes closed. The lady to my right raised both pairs of her brows and said: "Drunk man, oh my." Two soldiers appeared and were on top of him in a moment, they took him by each of his wild arms and tried to force him down on to a spot on the bench a little way along from us, but each time his narrow buttocks connected with the seat he sprang up as if the wood were on fire, and so the plan changed, now they dragged him toward the entrance of the engine room, directly opposite me, and tried to force him through the little door and down the dark steps to where he could no longer be seen. I knew by then he was epileptic—I could see the foam gathering at the corners of his mouth—and at first I thought this was what they didn't understand. As they twisted him out of his T-shirt I kept shouting, "Epileptic! He's epileptic!" Until four eyebrows explained: "Sister, they know this." They knew this but had no gentle arsenal of movements. They were the kind of soldiers instructed in brutality only. The more the man convulsed, the more he foamed, the more he infuriated them, and after a brief struggle in the doorway, where he momentarily convulsed in such a way that his limbs locked rigid like a toddler who refuses to be moved, they kicked him down the stairs, reached behind themselves and closed the door. We heard struggle, and terrible screams, dull connecting punches. Then silence. "What are you doing to that poor man?" cried four eyebrows, beside me, but when the door reopened, she lowered her eyes and returned to her cashews, and I didn't say any of the things I thought I was going to say, and the crowd parted and the soldiers walked down the stairs unmolested. We were the weak and they were the strong, and whatever force is meant to mediate between the weak and the strong was not present, not on the ferry, not in the country. Only when the soldiers were out of sight did the Tablighi who was sitting next to me—with two other nearby men—enter the engine room and retrieve the epileptic and bring him out into the light. The Tablighi lay him tenderly across his lap: it looked like the pietà. He had two bleeding split eyes but was alive and calm. A portion of bench was cleared for him, and for the rest of the crossing he lay there, shirtless, gently moaning, until we docked, when he stood up like any other commuter, climbed down the stairs and merged into the hordes heading for Barra.

How happy I was to see Hawa, genuinely happy! It was lunch time when I kicked open the door, and also cashew season: everyone was arranged in circles of five or six, crouched around large bowls of the fire-blackened nuts that had to now be removed from their burned shells and placed in a series of luridly tie-dyed buckets. Even very small children could do this so it was all hands on deck, even for incompetents, like Fern, who was being laughed at by Hawa for his relatively tiny mound of shells.

"Look at you! You look like Miss Beyoncé herself! Well, I hope your nails are not too fancy, my lady, because now you have to come and show this poor Fern man how it's done. Even Mohammed has a bigger pile—and he's three!" I abandoned my single rucksack at the door—I had also learned to pack—and went to hug Hawa around her strong, narrow back. "Still no baby?" she whispered in my ear, and I whispered the same back, and we hugged yet more tightly and laughed into each other's necks. It was very surprising to me that Hawa and I should have found a bond in this, across continents and cultures, but that's how it was. For just as, in London and New York, Aimee's world—and therefore mine—had erupted into babies, her own and the babies of her friends, dealing with them and talking about them, so that nothing seemed to exist except birth, and not just in the private realm, but also all newspapers, the television, stray songs on the radio seemed, to me, obsessed with the subject of fertility in general and of the fertility of women like me in particular, just so Hawa was coming under pressure in the village, as the time passed and people cottoned on to the fact that the policeman in Banjul was only a decoy, and Hawa herself a new kind of girl, perhaps uncircumcised, certainly unmarried, with no children, and no immediate plans for having any. "Still no baby?" had become our shorthand and catchphrase for all this, our mutual situation, and it seemed the funniest thing in the world whenever we exchanged the phrase with each other, we giggled and groaned over it, and only occasionally did it occur to me—and only when I was back in my own world—that I was thirty-two and Hawa ten years younger.

Fern stood up from his cashew disaster and wiped the ash off his hands on to his trousers: "She returns!"

Lunch was brought to us right away. We ate in a corner of the yard, our plates on our knees, both hungry enough to ignore the fact that nobody else got a lunch break from cashew-crushing.

"You look very well," said Fern, beaming at me. "Very happy."

The tin door at the back of the compound was

wide open, giving on to a view of Hawa's family's land. Several acres of purple-tinged cashew trees, pale yellow bush and scorched black hillocks of ash that marked where Hawa and her grandmothers burned, once a month, huge pyres of household waste and plastic. It was somehow lush and barren simultaneously, and beautiful to me in this mix. I saw that Fern was right: this was a place in which I was happy. Aged thirty-two and one quarter I was finally having my year off.

"But what is a 'year off'?"

"Oh, it's when you're young and you spend a year in some distant country, learning its ways, communing with the . . . community. We could never afford one."

"Your family?"

"Well, yes, but—I was thinking specifically of me and my mate Tracey. We just used to watch people go on them and then slag them off when they got back."

I laughed to myself at the memory.

"'Slag off'? What is this?"

"Oh, we used to call them 'poverty tourists' . . . You know, those kinds of students who'd come back with their stupid year-off ethnic trousers and African 'hand-carved' overpriced statuary made in some factory in Kenya . . . We used to think they were so idiotic."

But maybe Fern himself had been one of these

optimistic young hippy travelers. He sighed and lifted his finished bowl from the floor to rescue it from a curious goat.

"What cynical young people you were . . . you and your mate Tracey."

The cashew-shelling was going to continue into the night. To avoid helping, I suggested a walk to the well, on the thin excuse of collecting water for a morning shower, and Fern, usually so conscientious, surprised me by saying he would come. Along the way, he told a story about visiting Musa, Hawa's cousin, to check on the health of a new baby. When he had reached the place, a small, very basic dwelling Musa had built himself on the edge of the village, he found Musa alone. His wife and children had gone to see her mother.

"He invited me in, he was a little lonely, I think. I noticed he had a small old TV with VHS attached. I was surprised, he is always so frugal, like all **mashala**, but he said a Peace Corps woman who was going back to the States had left it to him. He was very keen to let me know he never watched Nollywood movies on it or any of the telenovelas or anything like that, not any more. Only 'pure films.' Did I want to see one? I said sure. We sit down, and in a minute I realize it's one of these training videos from Afghanistan, boys dressed all in black doing backflips with Kalashnikovs . . . I said to him, 'Musa? Do you understand what is being said in this video?' Because a speech in Ara-

bic was droning on and on—you can imagine—
and I could tell he didn't understand a word. And
he says to me, so dreamy: 'I love the way they leap!'
I think to him it was like a beautiful dance video.
A radical Islamic dance video! He told me: 'The
way they move, it makes me want to be more pure
inside.' Poor Musa. Anyway, I thought you would
find this funny. Because I know you are interested
in dance,' he added, when I didn't laugh.

Three

The first e-mail I ever received came from my mother. She sent it from a computer lab in the basement of University College London, where she had just taken part in a public debate, and I received it on a computer in my own college library. The content was a single Langston Hughes poem: she made me recite it in full when I called her later that evening, to prove it had arrived. **While night comes on gently, Dark like me**—Ours was the first graduating class to receive e-mail addresses, and my mother, always curious about new things, acquired a battered old Compaq, to which she attached a doddering modem. Together we entered this new space that now opened up between people, a connection with no precise beginning or end, that was always potentially open, and my mother was one of the first people I knew to understand this and exploit it fully. Most e-mails sent in the mid-nineties tended to be long and letter-like: they began and ended with traditional greetings—the ones we'd all previously used on paper—and they were keen to describe the surrounding scene, as if the new medium had made of everybody a writer. ("I'm typing this just by the window, looking out to blue-gray sea, where three gulls are diving into the water.") But my mother never e-mailed that way, she got the hang of it at once, and when I was only a few weeks out of college, but still by that blue-gray sea, she began sending me multiple two- or three-line messages a day, mostly unpunctuated, and always with the sense of something written at great speed. They all had the same subject: when was I planning on coming back? She didn't mean to the old estate, she had moved on from there the year before. Now she lived in a pretty ground-floor flat in Hampstead with the man my father and I had taken to calling "the Noted Activist," after my mother's habitual parenthetical ("I'm writing a paper with him, he's a noted activist, you've probably heard of him?" "He's just a wonderful, wonderful man, we're very close, and of course he's a noted activist"). The Noted Activist was a handsome Tobagonian, of Indian heritage, with a little Prussian beard, and a lot of sweeping black hair dramatically arranged on top of his head the better to highlight a single gray streak. My mother had met him at an anti-nuclear conference two years before. She had gone on marches with him, written papers on him—and then with him—before moving on to drinking with him, dining with him, sleeping with him and now moving in with him. Together they were often photographed, standing between the lions in Trafalgar Square, giving speeches one after the other—like Sartre and de Beauvoir, only far better-looking—and now, whenever the Noted Activist was called upon to speak for those who have no voice, while on demonstrations, or at conferences, my mother was more often than not by his side, in her new role as "local councilor and grass-roots activist." They'd been together a year. In that time my mother had become somewhat well known. One of the people a line producer on a radio show might call and ask to weigh in on whatever left-leaning debate was happening that day. Not the first name on that list, perhaps, but if the President of the Students' Union, the editor of the **New Left Review** and the spokesperson for the Anti-Racist Alliance happened all to be busy, my mother and the Noted Activist could be counted on for their near-constant availability.

I did try to be happy for her. I knew it was what she'd always wanted. But it's hard, when you're at a loose end yourself, to be happy for others, and besides I felt bad for my father, and sorrier for myself. The thought of moving back in with my mother seemed to cancel out what little I had achieved in the previous three years. But I couldn't survive on my student loan much longer. Despondent, packing up my room, flicking through my now pointless essays, I looked out to sea and felt I was waking from a dream, that this was all that college had been for me, a dream, placed at too far a distance from reality, or at least from my reality. My rented mortar board was barely returned before kids who had seemed not so different from me began announcing that they were leaving for London, right away, sometimes heading to my neighborhood, or others like it, which they discussed in derring-do terms, as if these were wild frontiers to be conquered. They left with deposits in hand, to lay down for flats or even houses, they took unpaid internships, or applied for jobs where the interviewer happened to be their own father's old university pal. I had no plans, no deposit and no one who might die and leave me money: what relatives we had were all poorer than us. Hadn't **we** been the middle-class ones, in aspiration and practice? And perhaps for my mother this dream was the truth, and just by dreaming it she felt she had brought it to pass. But I was awake now, and clear-eyed: some facts were immutable, unavoidable. Whichever way I looked at it, for example, the eighty-nine pounds currently in my current account was all the money I had on this earth. I made meals of baked beans on toast, sent out two dozen application letters, waited.

Alone in a town that everyone else had already left, I had too much time to brood. I began to look at my mother from a new, sour angle. A feminist who had always been supported by men—first my father and now the Noted Activist—and who, though she continually harangued me about the "nobility of labor," had never, as far as I knew, actually been gainfully employed. She worked "for the people"—there was no wage. I worried that the same was true, more or less, for the Noted Activist, who seemed to have written many pamphlets but no books, and had no official university position. To put all her eggs in the basket of such a man, to give up our flat—the only security we'd ever known—to go and live with him up in Hampstead, in exactly the kind of bourgeois fantasy she'd always bad-mouthed, struck me as being both in bad faith and extremely reckless. I went down to the seafront each night to use a dodgy phone box that thought two-pence coins were tens and had many ill-tempered conversations with her about it. But I was the only one in an ill temper, my mother was in love and happy, full of affection for me, although this only made her more difficult to pin down on practical details. Any attempt to delve into the precise financial situation of the Noted Activist, for example, got me fudged answers or a change of subject. The only thing she was always happy to discuss was his three-bedroom flat, the one she wanted me to move into, bought for twenty thousand pounds in 1969 with the money from a dead uncle's will and now worth "well over a million." This was a fact which, despite her Marxist tendencies, evidently gave her a huge sense of pleasure and well-being.

"But Mum: he's not going to sell it, is he? So it's irrelevant. It's not worth anything with you two lovebirds living in it."

"Look, why don't you just get on the train and come for dinner? When you meet him you'll love him—everybody loves this man. You'll have a lot to talk about. He met Malcolm X! He's a noted activist . . ."

But like a lot of people whose vocation it is to change the world he proved to be, in person, outrageously petty. Our first meeting was dominated not by political or philosophical discussion but by a long rant against his next-door neighbor, a fellow Caribbean who, unlike our host, was wealthy, multiply published, tenured in an American university, owned the whole building and was presently constructing "some kind of fucking pergola" at the end of his garden. This would slightly obscure the Noted Activist's vista of the Heath, and after dinner, as the June sun finally went down, we took a bottle of Wray & Nephew and, in an act of solidarity, stepped into the garden to glare at the half-built thing. My mother and the Noted Activist sat at their little cast-iron table and slowly rolled and smoked a very poorly constructed spliff. I drank too much rum. At a certain point the mood turned meditative and we all gazed over at the ponds, and beyond the ponds to the Heath itself, as the Victorian lamplights came on and the scene emptied of all but ducks and adventurous men. The lights turned the grass a purgatorial orange.

"Imagine two island kids like us, two barefoot kids from nothing, ending up here . . ." murmured my mother, and they held each other's hands and pressed their foreheads together, and I felt, looking at them, that even if they were absurd, how much more absurd was I, a grown woman resentful of another grown woman who had done, after all, so much for me, so much for herself and yes, for her people, and all, as she rightly said, from nothing at all. Was I feeling sorry for myself because I had no dowry? And when I looked up from the joint I was rolling it seemed my mother had read my mind. But don't you realize how incredibly lucky you are, she said, to be alive, at this moment? People like us, we can't be nostalgic. We've no home in the past. Nostalgia is a luxury. For our people, the time is now!

I lit my joint, poured myself another finger of rum and listened with my head bowed while the ducks quacked and my mother speechified, until it got late and her lover put a hand softly to her cheek and I saw it was time to get the last train.

In late July I moved back to London, not to my mother's, but to my father's. I offered to sleep in the living room, but he wouldn't have it, he said if I slept there the noise of him leaving for his rounds each morning would wake me, and I quickly ac-

cepted this logic and let him fold himself into the
sofa. In return I felt I'd really better find a job:
my father truly **did** believe in the nobility of labor,
he'd staked his life on it, and he made me ashamed
to be idle. Sometimes, unable to go back to sleep
after hearing him creep out of the door, I would
sit up in bed and think about all this work, both
my father's and his people's, going back many generations. Labor without education, labor usually
without craft or skill, some of it honest and some
of it crooked, but all of it leading somehow to my
own present state of laziness. When I was quite
young, eight or nine, my father had showed me his
father's birth certificate, and the professions of his
grandparents stated upon it—rag boiler and rag
cutter—and this, I was meant to understand, was
the proof that his tribe had always been defined by
their labor, whether they wanted to be or not. The
importance of labor was a view he held as strongly
as my mother held her belief that the definitions
that really mattered were culture and color. Our
people, our people. I thought of how readily we'd
all used the phrase, a few weeks earlier, on that
beautiful June night at the Noted Activist's, sitting drinking rum, admiring families of fat ducks,
their heads turned inwards, their bills nestled into
the feathers of their own bodies, roosting along the
bank of the pond. Our people! Our people! And
now, lying in the funk of my father's bed, turning
the phrase over in my mind—for lack of anything

better to do—it reminded me of the overlapping quack and babble of those birds, repeating over and over the same curious message, delivered from their own bills into their own feathers: "I am a duck!" "I am a duck!"

Four

Stepping out of a bush taxi—after several months' absence—I spotted Fern standing by the side of the road, apparently waiting for me, right on time, as if there were a bus stop and a timetable. I was happy to see him. But he proved to be not in the mood for greetings or pleasantries, falling in step with me and immediately launching into a low-voiced debriefing, so that before I'd even reached Hawa's door I, too, was burdened with the rumor presently gripping the village: that Aimee was in the process of organizing a visa, that Lamin would soon move permanently to New York. "Well, is it the case?" I told him the truth: I didn't know, and didn't want to know. I'd had an exhausting time in London, holding Aimee's hand through a difficult winter, personally and professionally, and I was feeling as a consequence particularly averse to her brand of personal drama. The album she'd spent a grim British January and February recording—which should have been released about now—had instead been abandoned, the consequence of a brief, ugly affair with her young producer, who then took his songs with him. Only a few years earlier a break-up like this would have been only a minor setback to Aimee, hardly worth half a day in bed watching old episodes of long-forgotten Aussie soaps—**The Flying Doctors**, **The Sullivans**—something she did in moments of extreme vulnerability. But I had noticed a change in her, her personal armor was no longer what it once was. Leaving, and being left—these operations now affected her far more deeply, they were no longer water off a duck's back to her, she was actually wounded, and took no meetings with anyone except Judy for almost a month, barely leaving the house and asking me several times to sleep in her room, just by her bed, on the floor, as she did not want to be alone. During this period of purdah I had assumed, for better or worse, that nobody was closer to her than me. Listening to Fern, my first feeling was that I had been betrayed, but the more I considered it I saw that this was not quite right: it was not deceit but a form of mental separation. I was comfort and company for her in a stalled moment, while, in another compartment of her heart, she was busily planning for the future, with Lamin—and Judy was her co-conspirator in that. Instead of being annoyed at Aimee I found myself frustrated by Fern: he was trying to get me involved, but I didn't want any part of it, it was inconvenient for me, I had my trip already all planned out, and the more Fern spoke the further I saw the itinerary plotted in my head

slipping away from me. A visit to Kunta Kinteh
Island, a few afternoons at the beach, two nights
in one of the fancy hotels in town. Aimee gave me
almost no annual leave, I had to be resourceful,
stealing holidays where I could.

"OK, but why not take Lamin with you? He'll
talk to you. With me he is like a clam."

"To the hotel? Fern—no. Terrible idea."

"On your trip then. You cannot go out there by
yourself anyway, you'll never find it."

I gave in. When I told Lamin he was happy, not
about visiting the island itself, I suspected, but because of the opportunity to escape the classroom
and spend an afternoon negotiating with his friend
Lolu, a cab driver, over the round-trip price. Lolu's
Afro had been cut into a Mohican, tinged orange,
and he wore a thick belt with a big silver buckle
that read BOY TOY. They appeared to negotiate
all the way there, a two-hour journey filled with
laughter and debate in the front seat, Lolu's deaf-
ening reggae music, many phone calls. I sat in the
back, with little more Wolof than I'd had before,
watching the bush go by, spotting the odd silver-
gray monkey and ever more isolated settlements of
people, you couldn't even call them villages, just
two or three huts together, and then nothing again
for another ten miles. I remember in particular two
barefoot girl children walking by the road, hand in
hand, they looked like best friends. They waved at
me and I waved back. There was nothing and no

one around them, they were out on the edge of the world, or of the world I knew, and watching them I realized it was very hard, almost impossible, for me to imagine what time felt like for them, out here. I could remember being their age, of course, holding hands with Tracey, and how we had considered ourselves "eighties kids," more savvy than our parents, far more modern. We thought we were products of a particular moment, because as well as our old musicals we liked things like **Ghostbusters** and **Dallas** and lollipop flutes. We felt we had our place in time. What person on the earth doesn't feel this way? Yet when I waved at those two girls I noticed I couldn't rid myself of the idea that they were timeless symbols of girlhood, or of childish friendship. I knew it couldn't possibly be the case but I had no other way to think of them.

The road ended finally at the river. We got out and walked up to a thirty-foot concrete statue of a stick man who stood facing the river. He had the whole of planet Earth for a head and was yanking his stick arms free from slavery's chains. A lone nineteenth-century cannon, the red-brick shell of an original trading post, a small "slavery museum built in 1992" and a desolate café completed what a desperate guide with few teeth described as "the Welcome Center." Behind us a village of broken-down shacks, poorer by many orders of magnitude than the one we had come from, stubbornly faced the old trading post, as if hoping it might reopen. A crowd of children sat watching our arrival but when I waved to them our guide told me off: "They are not allowed to come any closer. They beg for money. They bother you tourists. The government has chosen us as official guides so that you are not bothered by them." About a mile across the river I could see the island itself, a small, rocky outcrop with the picturesque ruins of barracks upon it. All I wanted was a minute's quiet to contemplate where I was and what, if anything, it meant. Here and there, between the triangle of café, slave statue and watching children, I could see and hear groups of tourists—a solemn Black-British family, some enthusiastic African-American teenagers, a couple of white Dutch women, both already freely weeping—who were all trying to do the same, and likewise enduring a recited lecture from one of the official government guides in their ragged blue T-shirts, or having menus thrust into their hands from the café, or haggling with boatmen eager to take them across to see the prison cells of their ancestors. I saw I was lucky to have Lamin: while he engaged in his favorite activity—intense, whispered financial negotiation, with several parties at once—I was free to wander over to the cannon, to sit astride it and look out over the water. I tried to put myself in a meditative frame of mind. To picture the ships in the water, the human property walking up the gangplanks, the brave few who took their chances and leaped into the water, in a doomed attempt to swim to shore. But every image had a cartoon thinness to it, and felt no closer to reality than the mural on the side of the museum that showed a strapping, naked Mandinka family in neck chains being chased out of the bush by an evil Dutchman, as if they'd been trapped like prey by a hunter rather than sold like grain by their chief. All paths lead back there, my mother had always told me, but now that I was here, in this storied corner of the continent, I experienced it not as an exceptional place but as an example of a general rule. Power had preyed on weakness here: all kinds of power—local, racial, tribal, royal, national, global, economic—on all kinds of weakness, stopping at nothing, not even at the smallest girl child. But power does that everywhere. The world is saturated in blood. Every tribe has their blood-soaked legacy: here was mine. I waited for whatever cathartic feeling people hope to experience in such places, but I couldn't make myself believe the pain of my tribe was uniquely gathered here, in this place, the pain was too obviously everywhere, this just happened to be where they'd placed the monument. I gave up and went in search of Lamin. He was leaning against the statue, on his new phone, a fancy-looking Black-Berry, with a dozy look on his face, a big, foolish smile, and when he saw me coming he shut it off without saying good-bye.

"Who was that?"

"And so if you are ready," whispered Lamin, wedging the huge thing into his back pocket, "this man will now take us across."

We shared a narrowboat with the Black-British family. They tried to strike up a conversation with the guide concerning how far it was from the island to the mainland and whether any man, never mind one in chains, could conceivably swim through these fast-moving currents. The guide listened to them talk but looked so tired, the whites of his eyes obscured by the sheer number of broken blood vessels, and did not seem overly interested in hypotheticals. He repeated his mantra: "If a man reached the shore, he was given his freedom." On the island we shuffled around the ruin and then queued to enter the "last resort," a small underground room, ten by four, where "the most rebellious men, like Kunta, were held." **Imagine!** Everybody kept saying this to each other, and I did try to imagine being brought down here but knew instinctively I was not the rebellious type, not likely to be one of Kunta's tribe. Few people are. My mother I could certainly imagine down here, and Tracey, too. And Aimee—she was in her way another of the breed. But not me. Unsure what to do with myself I reached out to grasp an iron hoop in the wall to which these "most rebellious" had been chained at the neck. "Makes you want to cry, dunnit?" said the mother of the British family, and I felt it really should, but when I looked away from her in preparation, upward to the tiny window, I found the government guide laid out on his belly, his three-toothed mouth blocking almost all of the available light.

"You will now feel the pain," he explained through the bars, "and you will need a minute alone. I will meet you outside after you have felt the pain."

On the boat back I asked Lamin what it was he and Aimee had to talk about so often. He was sitting on the thwart of the boat and straightened his back, lifted his chin.

"She thinks I am a good dancer."

"Does she?"

"I have taught her many moves she didn't know. On the computer. I demonstrate our local steps. She says she will use them in her performances."

"I see. And does she ever talk about you coming to America? Or England?"

"It is all in the hands of God," he said, casting an anxious eye over the other passengers.

"Yes. And the Foreign Office."

Lolu, who had been waiting patiently in his cab, drove up to the shoreline as we approached, and opened the car door, apparently intending to take me straight from the water to the car, another two-hour ride, without lunch.

"But Lamin, I have to eat!"

I noticed he'd been clutching the café's laminated menu throughout our visit to the island and now he showed it to me, the vital, clinching piece of evidence in a courtroom drama.

"This is too much money for lunch! Hawa will make us lunch back home."

"**I'll** pay for lunch. It's, like, three pounds a head. I promise you, Lamin, it's not too much for me."

An argument ensued between Lamin and Lolu which, I was pleased to see, Lamin appeared to lose. Lolu put his hands on his buckle like a triumphant cowboy, closed the door of his car and rolled it back up the hill.

"It's too much," said Lamin again, sighing hugely, but I followed Lolu and Lamin followed me.

We sat at one of the picnic tables and ate fish in foil with rice. I listened to the talk at the neighboring tables, strange, uneven conversations that could not decide what they were: the heavy reflections of visitors to a historical trauma or the light cocktail chatter of people on their beach holiday. A tall, sun-ravaged white woman, in her seventies at least, sat alone at a table at the back, surrounded by piles of folded printed cloth, drums and statues, T-shirts that said NEVER AGAIN, other local merchandise. No one came near her stall or looked likely to buy anything, and after a while she stood up and began passing from table to table, welcoming guests, asking them where they were staying, where they were from. I was hoping we would have finished eating before she reached our table, but Lamin was a painfully slow eater and she caught us, and when she heard that I was not from any hotel, and not an aid worker and not a missionary, she took a special interest and sat down with us, too close to Lolu, who hunched over his fish and wouldn't look at her.

"Which village did you say?" she asked, although I hadn't, but now Lamin told her before I had an opportunity to be vague. The penny dropped. "Oh, but you're involved with the school! Of course. Well, I know people say the most awful things about that woman but I really love her, I admire her, honestly. I'm actually an American, too, originally," she said, and I wondered how she thought anyone could be uncertain on this point. "Normally I don't care for Americans, in general, but she's the kind with a passport, if you know what I mean. I really find her so curious and passionate, and it's a great thing for the country, all the publicity she brings. Oh, Australian? Well, either way she's a woman after my own heart! An adventuress! Although of course I came here for love, not charity. The charity came afterward, in my case."

She touched her heart, which was half exposed, in a multicolored spaghetti-strap dress with a frighteningly deep décolletage. Her breasts were long, red and crêpy. I was absolutely determined not to ask her whose love she had come here for, nor to what good deeds this act had ultimately led, but sensing my resistance, she decided, with an old woman's prerogative, to tell me anyway.

"I was just like these people, just here on holiday. I didn't mean to fall in love! With a boy half my age." She winked at me. "And that was twenty years ago! But it was much, much more than a holiday romance, you see: together we built all this." She looked around proudly at this great monument to love: a tin-roofed café with four tables and three items on the menu. "I'm not a rich woman, I was really just a humble yoga teacher. But these people in Berkeley, you only have to say to them: 'Look, this is the situation, these people are in desperate need,' and I can tell you, you'd be surprised, these people really just go for it, they really do. Just about **everybody** wanted to pitch in. When you explain what a dollar does here? When you explain how far that dollar's gonna go? Oh, people can't believe it! Now, sadly, my own children, from my first marriage? They have not been so supportive. Yes, sometimes it's the strangers that sustain you. But I always say to the people here, "Don't believe everything you hear, please! Because not all Americans are bad news, not at all." There's a big difference between the folks in Berkeley and the folks in Fort Worth, if you catch my meaning. I was born in Texas, to Christian folks, and when I was young

America was a pretty hard place for me, because I was a free spirit and I just couldn't find my place. But I guess it suits me a little more now."

"But you live here, with your husband?" asked Lamin.

She smiled but did not seem overly enthralled by the question.

"In the summers. The winters I spend in Berkeley."

"And he goes then with you?" asked Lamin. I had the sense he was conducting subtle research.

"No, no. He stays here. He has a lot to do here, all year round. He's the big man round here and I guess you could say I'm the big woman back there! So it works very well. For us."

I thought of that layer of girlish illusion Aimee's new-mother friends all appeared to have lost, a kind of light in their eyes that had gone out, notwithstanding even their own celebrity and wealth, and then I looked into the wide, blue, half-crazed eyes of this woman and saw a total excavation. It hardly seemed possible someone could have had so many layers stripped from her and still be able to play her part.

Five

After graduation, from the base of my father's flat, I applied for every entry-level media job I could think of, leaving my begging letters on the kitchen counter each night for him to post in the morning, but a month passed, and nothing. I knew my father's relationship to these letters was complicated—good news for me meant bad news for him, meant me moving out—and sometimes I had paranoid fantasies that he never posted them at all, just deposited them in the bin at the end of our street. I considered what my mother had always said about his lack of ambition—against which accusation I had always angrily defended him—and was forced to admit that I could see now what she was getting at. Nothing made him jollier than my Uncle Lambert's occasional Sunday visits, when we would all three plant ourselves in deckchairs on the ivy-covered flat roof of my father's downstairs neighbors and smoke weed, eat the homemade fish dumplings that were Lambert's excuse for being two to three hours late, listen to the World Service and watch the Jubilee Line trains rise up, every eight to ten minutes, from the bowels of the earth.

"Now this is the life, love, wouldn't you say? No more: **do this, don't do that.** Just us all friends together—equals. Eh, Lambert? When you get to be friends with your own kid? This is the life, isn't it?"

Was it? I didn't remember him ever taking on the parental power dynamic he claimed now to be sloughing off, he'd never said, "Do this, don't do that." Love and latitude—that was all he'd ever offered me. And where did it lead? Was I going to enter early stoned retirement with Lambert? Not knowing what else to do, I went back to a terrible job, one I'd had the first summer of college, in a pizza place in Kensal Rise. It was run by a ridiculous Iranian called Bahram, very tall and thin, who considered himself, despite his surroundings, to be a man of quality. He liked to wear a long, chic, camel-colored coat, no matter the weather, often hanging it from his shoulders like an Italian baron, and he called his dump a "restaurant," though the premises were the size of a small family bathroom, occupying a corner plot of scrubland wedged between the bus terminal and the railway. No one ever came in to eat, they ordered delivery or took their food home. I used to stand at the counter and watch the mice dart across the linoleum. There was a single table at which theoretically a customer was free to dine, but in reality Bahram occupied

this table all day long and half the night: he had
troubles at home, a wife and three difficult, unmarried daughters, and we suspected he preferred
our company to this family, or at least preferred
shouting at us to arguing with them. At work his
day was not strenuous. He passed it commenting
on whatever was on the TV in the top-left corner
of the place, or else verbally abusing us, his staff,
from this sitting position. He was in a rage all the
time about everything. A flamboyant, comic rage
that expressed itself in a constant obscene teasing
of everyone around him—racial, sexual, political,
religious teasing—and which almost every day re-
sulted in a lost customer or employee or friend, and
so came to seem to me not so much offensive as
poignantly self-defeating. Anyway it was the only
entertainment on offer. But the first time I walked
in there, aged nineteen, I was not abused, no, I was
greeted in what I later understood to be Farsi, and
so effusively that I really felt I got a sense of what
he was saying. How young I was, and lovely, and
clearly smart—was it true I was in college? But how
proud my mother must be! He stood up and held
me by the chin, turning my face one way and then
the other, smiling. But when I replied in English
he frowned and looked closely, critically, at the red
bandanna covering my hair—I'd thought it would
be welcome in a place of food production—and a
few moments later, after we had established that
despite my Persian nose I was not Persian, not even

a little bit, nor Egyptian, nor Moroccan, nor an Arab of any kind, I made the mistake of speaking the name of my mother's island, and all friendliness vanished: I was directed to the counter, where my job was to answer the phone, take orders to the kitchen and organize the delivery boys. My most important task was attending to a beloved project of his: the Banned Customers List. He had taken the trouble to write this list out on a long roll of paper and stuck it up on the wall behind my counter, sometimes with Polaroids attached. "Mostly your people," he pointed out to me casually, on my second day.

"They don't pay, or they fight, or they drug dealers. Don't give me face! How you be offended? You know! Is truth!" I couldn't afford to be offended. I was determined to last those three summer months, long enough to put something toward a deposit so I could start renting the moment I graduated. But the tennis was on, and this made everything impossible. A Somali delivery boy and I were following it avidly, and Bahram, who would normally also follow the tennis—he considered sport the purest manifestation of his sociological theories—was this year in a fury about it, and in a fury with us for enjoying it, and each time he caught us watching it he became more enraged, his sense of order having been deeply disturbed by the failure of Bryan Shelton to drop out in the first round.

"Why you follow him? Huh? Huh? 'Cos he's one of you?"

He was jabbing his finger into the narrow chest of the Somali delivery boy, Anwar, who had a great luminosity of spirit, a notable capacity for joy—despite nothing in his life seeming to provide just cause for it—and whose response now was to clap his hands and grin from ear to ear.

"**Yeah**, man! We for Bryan!"

"You are idiot, this we know," said Bahram, and then turned to me, behind the counter: "But you are smart, and this makes you more idiot." When I said nothing he came right up to me and slammed his fists on the counter: "This man Shelton—he won't win. He can't."

"He win! He win!" cried Anwar.

Bahram picked up the remote and turned down the TV so he could get himself heard all the way to the back, even as far as the Congolese woman scrubbing the sides of the pizza oven.

"Tennis not black game. You must understand: every people have their game."

"What's your game?" I asked, genuinely curious, and Bahram pulled himself up very tall and proud in his seat: "Polo." The kitchen exploded in laughter.

"Fuck all of you sons of bitches!" Hysteria.

As it happened, I hadn't been following Shelton, had never heard of him really before Anwar pointed him out, but now I did follow him, along with

Anwar I became his number-one fan. I bought little American flags to work on the days of his games and made sure to send out, on these occasions, all the other delivery boys except Anwar. Together we cheered Shelton, danced around the place at each successful point, and as he won one match and then another, we began to feel like we, with our dancing and whooping, were the ones propelling him forward, and that without us he'd be done for. At times Bahram behaved as if he believed this, too, as if we were performing some ancient African voodoo rite. Yes, somehow we put a spell on Bahram just as much as Shelton, and as the days of the tournament passed and Shelton still refused to be knocked out I saw Bahram's many other pressing worries—the business, his difficult wife, the stressful search for suitors for his daughters—all slip away, until his sole preoccupation was ensuring we did not cheer for Bryan Shelton, and that Shelton himself did not get to the Wimbledon final.

One morning, halfway through the tournament, I was standing, bored, at the counter when I saw Anwar on his bike, riding up the pavement toward us at great speed, then break haphazardly, leap off and rush up to my counter with his fist in his mouth and a smile he could barely control. He slapped a copy of the **Daily Mirror** in front of me, pointed to a column in the sports pages, and said: "Arab!" We couldn't believe it. His name was Karim Alami. He was from Morocco, and he was

seeded even lower than Shelton. Their match was
to start at two. Bahram arrived at one. There was
a great feeling of anxiety and anticipation in the
place, delivery boys who were not meant to come
till five came early, and the Congolese cleaner
began working through the back of the kitchen at
unprecedented speed in the hope she would reach
front-of-house—and therefore the television—by
the time the game began. That match went five
rounds. Shelton started strong and at various points
in the first set Bahram was reduced to standing on
a chair and screaming. When the first set ended
six–three to Shelton, Bahram jumped off his chair
and walked straight out of the building. We looked
at each other: was this victory? Five minutes later
he sloped back in with a packet of Gauloises in
hand, retrieved from his car, and began chain-
smoking with his head down. But in the second set
things began to look a little better for Karim, and
Bahram sat up straight as straight, then stood, and
began pacing in a circular way around the small
space, offering his own commentary, which had as
much to do with eugenics as backhands and lobs
and double faults, and as we reached a tiebreak, he
became increasingly fluent in his lecture, waving
his cigarette around in his hand, ever more confi-
dent in his English. The black man, he informed
us, he is instinct, he is moving body, he is strong,
and he is music, yes, of course, and he is rhythm,
everybody know this, and he is speed, and this is

beautiful, maybe, yes, but let me tell you tennis is game of the mind—the mind! The black man can be good strength, good muscle, he can hit ball hard, but Karim he is like me: he think one, two step in front. He have Arab mind. Arab mind is complicated machine, delicate. We invent mathematics. We invent astronomy. Subtle people. Two steps ahead. Your Bryan now he is lost.

But he was not lost: he took the set seven–five, and Anwar took the broom away from the Congolese cleaner—whose name I did not know, whose name no one ever thought to ask—and made her dance with him, to some hi-life he had going on the transistor radio he carried everywhere. In the next set Shelton collapsed, one–six. Bahram was exultant. Wherever you go in world, he told Anwar, you people at bottom! Sometimes at top White man, Jew, Arab, Chinese, Japan—depends. But your people always they lose. By the time the fourth set started we had stopped pretending to be a pizza place. The phone rang and no one answered, the oven was empty, and everybody was crammed into the small space at the front. I sat on the counter with Anwar, our nervous legs kicking the cheap MDF panels until they rattled. We watched these two players—in truth, almost perfectly matched—battling toward an elongated, excruciating tiebreak that Shelton then lost, six–seven. Anwar burst into bitter tears.

"But Anwar, little friend: he have one more set,"

explained the kindly Bosnian chef, and Anwar
was as grateful as the man sitting in an electric
chair who's just spotted the governor through the
Plexiglas, running down the hall. The final set
was quick: six–two. Game, set, match—Shelton.
Anwar turned his radio up full blast and every kind
of dance burst forth from me, winding, stomping,
shuffling—I even did the shim-sham. Bahram accused us all of having sex with our mothers and
stormed out. About an hour later he returned. It
was the early-evening rush when mothers decide
they can't face cooking dinner and all-day tokers
suddenly realize they haven't eaten since breakfast. I was harried on the phone, trying as usual
to parse many different kinds of pidgin English,
both on the phones and among our own delivery
crew, when Bahram walked up to me and put the
evening paper in my face. He pointed to a picture
of Shelton, his arm swung high in preparation for
one of his forceful serves, ball in the air before him,
paused at the moment of connection. I cupped the
phone receiver with a hand.

"What? I'm working."

"Look close. Not black. Brown. Like you."

"I'm working."

"Probably he is half-half, like you. So: this ex-
plains."

I looked not at Shelton but at Bahram, very
closely. He smiled.

"Half-winner," he said.

I put the phone down, took my apron off and walked out.

I don't know how Tracey found out I was back working at Bahram's. I didn't want anyone to know, I could hardly face the truth of it myself. Probably she simply spotted me through the glass. When she walked in, one steamy afternoon in late August, she caused a sensation, in her skin-tight leggings and navel-skimming crop top. I noticed her clothes had not changed with the times, that they had no need of change. She did not struggle, as I did—as most women I knew did—to find ways to dress her body in the symbols, shapes and signs of the age. It was as if she were above all of that, timeless. She was always dressed for a dance rehearsal and always looked wonderful that way. Anwar and the rest of the boys, waiting outside on their bikes, took a good long time over the front view and then repositioned themselves to get what Italians call the B-side. When she leaned over the counter to speak to me I saw one of them cover his eyes, as if in physical pain.

"Good to see you. How was the seaside?"

She smirked, confirming the sense I already had that my college life had been some kind of local joke, a poor attempt at playing a role outside of my range, one that had not come off.

"See your mum about. She's everywhere these days."

"Yes. I'm glad to be back, I think. You look great. Are you working?"

"Oh, I'm doing all sorts. Got big news. When do you get off?"

"I just started."

"So what about tomorrow?"

Bahram sidled up to us and in his most courtly manner inquired whether Tracey happened to be Persian.

We met up the following evening, in a local pub that we had always known as Irish but which was now neither Irish nor anything else. The old booths had gone and been replaced by a great many sofas and wingback chairs, from different historical eras, covered in clashing prints, and scattered around the place, like a stage set recently dismantled. Purple flock wallpaper was plastered above the chimney breast and many poorly stuffed woodland creatures, arrested in the act of leaping or crouching, were encased in glass bell jars and had been placed on high shelves, looking over mine and Tracey's reunion with their wonky glass eyes. I broke the gaze of a petrified squirrel to greet Tracey, who was returning from the bar with two white wines in her hands and a powerful look of disgust on her face.

"Seven quid? What fuckery is this?"

"We could go somewhere else."

She screwed up her nose: "No. That's what they want. We were born here. Drink slowly."

We never could drink slowly. We kept going, on Tracey's credit card, reminiscing and laughing— laughing harder than I had in all three years of college—taking each other back to Miss Isabel's yellow shoes, to my mother's clay pit, to **The History of Dance**, through all of it, even things I never thought we would ever be able to laugh at together. Louie dancing with Michael Jackson, my own Royal Ballet delusion. Feeling bold, I asked after her father.

She stopped laughing.

"Still over there. Got a whole bunch of 'out the house' children now, so I'm told . . ."

Her ever-expressive face turned pensive and then took on that look of utter icy coldness I remembered so well from childhood. I considered telling her about what I had seen, years before, in Kentish Town, but that coldness stopped up the sentence in my mouth.

"What about your old man? Haven't seen him for time."

"Believe it or not, I think he's still in love with my mother."

"That's nice," she said, but that look stayed on her face. She was staring past me, at the squirrel. "That's nice," she said once again.

I could see we had got to the end of reminiscence, that it was properly time to venture into the present day. I could guess how easily Tracey's news would outstrip whatever I had to offer. And so it

did: she had a part on the West End stage. It was
in a revival of one of our favorite shows, **Guys and
Dolls**, and she was playing "Hot Box Girl Number One," which I remembered was not a huge
role—in the film she had no name of her own
and spoke only four or five lines—but all the same
she was present a lot, singing and dancing in the
Hot Box club, or else trailing Adelaide, whose best
friend she's meant to be. Tracey would get to do
"Take Back Your Mink"—a song we did as children, brandishing a mangy-looking pair of feather
boas—and she'd wear lace corsets and real satin
gowns and have her hair set and curled. "We're in
proper dress rehearsal now. They use flat irons on
me every night, it's killing me." She touched her
hairline and underneath the wax that had been
used to slick it down I saw that indeed it was already frayed and patchy.

She'd got her boast out of the way. In its after-
math, though, she struck me as vulnerable and defensive and I had the sense that I had not reacted
quite as she'd wanted. Perhaps she had really imagined that a twenty-one-year-old college graduate
would hear her good news and collapse weeping
on the floor. She picked up her wine and drained
it. She asked, at last, about my life. I took a deep
breath and repeated the sorts of things I said to my
mother: only a stopgap, waiting to hear of other
opportunities, staying at my dad's temporarily,
rent being high, no relationship, but then relation-

ships were so complicated, not what I needed right now, and I wanted time to work on my own—

"Right, right, right, but you can't keep working for pizza cunt, can you? You need a plan."

I nodded and waited. Relief came over me, familiar, though I had not felt it for a long time, and I connected it to being taken in hand by Tracey, to having decisions removed from me and replaced instead by her will, her intentions. Hadn't Tracey always known what games to play, what stories to tell, what beat to choose, what move to make to it?

"Look, I know you're a big woman now," she said, confidingly, leaning back in her chair, with her feet pointed below, creating a beautiful vertical line from her knees to her toes. "It's none of my business. But if you need something, they're looking for stagehands right now. You could try for it. I could put a good word in. It's just four months but it's better than fuck all."

"I don't know anything about theater. I've got no experience."

"Oh my gosh," said Tracey, shaking her head at me, standing up to get another round in. "Just lie!"

Six

I assumed my questioning of Lamin had got back to Aimee, because on the day of my departure from the Coco Ocean hotel the front desk called up to my room to tell me they had a message for me, and when I opened the white envelope I found this note: Jet unavailable. You'll have to fly commercial. Save receipts. Judy.

I was being punished. At first I thought it was funny that Aimee's idea of punishment was flying commercial, but when I got to the airport I was surprised by how much I had in fact forgotten: the waiting, the queuing, the submitting to irrational instructions. Every aspect of it, the presence of so many other people, the brusqueness of the staff, even the immutable flight time on the screens in the waiting room—it all felt like an affront. My seat was next to two truck drivers from Huddersfield, they were in their sixties and had traveled together. They loved it here, they'd come "every year, if they could afford it." After lunch they started in on some little bottles of Baileys and compared notes on their "girls." They both wore wedding rings, half embedded in their fat, hairy fingers. I had my earphones in by then: they probably thought I couldn't hear them. "My one said to me she were twenty, but her cousin—he's a waiter there, too—he told me she were seventeen. Wise beyond her years, though." He had hardened egg yolk down his T-shirt. His friend had yellowed teeth and bloody gums. They had seven days of holiday in any calendar year. The man with the yellow teeth had worked double shifts for three months simply to afford this long weekend with his girl in Banjul. I had murderous fantasies—of taking my serrated plastic knife, drawing it across each of their throats—but the longer I listened, the sadder the whole thing seemed. "I said to her, don't you want to come to England? And she basically says to me: 'No fear, love.' She wants us to build a house in Wassu, wherever the fuck that is. They're no fools, these girls. Realistic. Pound goes a lot bloody further out there than it does back home. It's like the missus moaning about she wants to go to Spain. I said to her, 'You're living in the past, love. You know how much Spain is these days?'" One kind of weakness feeding on another.

A few days later I was back at work. I kept waiting for a formal meeting or a debrief but it was as if I hadn't made the visit at all. Nobody mentioned my trip and in itself that was not so unusual, many other things were going on at the time—a new album, a new tour—but in the subtle way of the best bullies Judy and Aimee strove to freeze me out of all important decisions while simultaneously ensuring that nothing they said or did could be explicitly interpreted as punishment or retribution. We were preparing for our autumn transition to New York—a period in which Aimee and I were usually glued to each other—but now I hardly saw her, and for two weeks I was given the kind of grunt-work more appropriate to the housekeepers. I was on the phone to freight companies. I was cataloging shoes. I accompanied the children to their yoga class. I cornered Judy about it early one Saturday morning. Aimee was in the basement, working out, the children were watching their one hour of weekly television. I trawled the house and found Judy sitting in the library with her feet up on the baize desk, painting her toenails a terrible fuchsia, a white foam wedge stuck between each long toe. She didn't look up until I'd finished speaking.

"Yeah, well, hate to break it to you, love, but Aimee doesn't give a flying fuck what you think of her private life."

"I'm trying to look out for her interests. That's my job as a friend."

"No, love, not accurate. Your job is: personal assistant."

"I've been here nine years."

"And I've been here twenty-nine." She swung her feet round and placed them in a black box on the floor that glowed purple. "I've seen a lot of these assistants come and go. But Christ, none of them has been as delusional as you."

"Isn't it true? Isn't she trying to get him a visa?"

"I'm not discussing that with you."

"Judy, I spent today mainly working for the dog. I have a degree. Don't tell me I'm not being punished."

Judy pulled her fringe back with both hands.

"First of all, don't be so bloody melodramatic. What you are doing is **working.** Whatever you may think, chook, your job is not **and has never been** 'best mate.' You're her assistant. You always have been. But recently you seem to have forgotten that—and it's about time you were reminded. So that's our first issue. Number two: if she wants to bring him over here, if she wants to marry him, or dance with him on top of Big fucking Ben, that is no concern of yours. You're very far out of your area." Judy sighed and looked down at her toes. "And the funny part of it is, she's not even pissed off with you about the boy. It's not even **about** the bloody boy."

"What, then?"

"You spoken to your mum recently?"

This question made me violently blush. How long had it been? A month? Two? Parliament was in session, she was busy, and if she wanted me she knew where I was. I was going through these justifications in my head for a long moment before it occurred to me to wonder why Judy was interested.

"Well, maybe you should. She's making life difficult for us right now and I don't really know why. Would help if you could find out."

"My **mother**?"

"I mean, there's a million issues in this little shithole of an island you call a country—literally a million. She wants to talk about 'Dictatorships in West Africa'?" said Judy, using finger quotes. "British complicity with dictatorships in West Africa. She's on the TV, she's writing the op-eds, she's standing up in bloody Prime Minister's Question Tea Hour or whatever the fuck it is you people call it. She's got a bee in her bonnet about it. Fine. Well, that's not my problem—what DfID does, what the IMF does—that's out of **my** area. Aimee, however, **is** my area—and yours. We're in partnership with this crazy bloody President, and if you go and ask your beloved Fern he'll tell you what a tightrope we're walking right now. Believe me, love, if his Highness-for-life the all-mighty King of Kings doesn't want us in his country? We are out of there in two shakes of a lamb's tail. The school gets fucked, everybody gets fucked. Now, I **know** you have a degree. You've told me, many, many times. Is it in International Development? No, I didn't think so. And I'm sure your big-mouth mother out there on the back benches probably thinks she's being helpful, too, God knows, but you know what she's **actually** doing? Hurting the people she claims to want to help, and pissing on those of us who are trying to make some kind of difference out there. Biting the hand. Seems to run in the family."

I sat down on the chaise longue.

"Jesus, don't you ever read the papers?" asked Judy.

Three days after that conversation we flew to New York. I left messages with my mother, texted her, e-mailed her, but she didn't call me till the end of the following week, and with the extraordinary timing of mothers chose two thirty p.m. on a Sunday, just as Jay's cake came out of the kitchens and streamers fell from the ceiling of the Rainbow Room, and two hundred guests sang "Happy Birthday," accompanied by violinists from the string section of the New York Philharmonic.

"What's all that noise? Where **are** you?"

I opened the sliding doors to the terrace and shut them behind me.

"It's Jay's birthday. He's nine today. I'm at the top of the Rockefeller."

"Look, I don't want to have an argument with you on the phone," said my mother, sounding very much like she wanted to have an argument on the phone. "I've read your e-mails, I understand your position. But I hope you understand that I don't work for that woman—or for you, actually. I work for the British people, and if I've developed an interest in that region, if I've become increasingly concerned—"

"Yes, but Mum, can't you become increasingly concerned about something else?"

"Doesn't it matter to you **who** your partners are in this project? I know you, darling, and I know you're not a mercenary, I know you have ideals—I raised you, for God's sake, so I know. I've been into it very deeply, Miriam, too, and we've come to the conclusion that at this point the human-rights issue is really becoming untenable—I wish it wasn't, for your sake, but there it is. Darling, don't you want to know—"

"Mum, sorry—I'll call you back—I have to go."

Fern, in an ill-fitting, clearly rented suit, a little too short at the ankles, was walking toward me, waving goofily, and I don't think I realized how far out of the loop I had fallen until that moment. To me he was a cut-out figure pasted in the wrong photograph, in the wrong moment. He smiled, pulled open the sliding doors, his head cocked to the side like a terrier: "Ah, but you look really beautiful."

"Why didn't anyone tell me you were coming? Why didn't you?"

He drew a hand through curls half tamed by cheap hair gel, and looked sheepish, a schoolboy caught out in a minor misdemeanor.

"Well, I was on confidential business. It's ridiculous, but all the same I couldn't tell you, I'm sorry. They wanted it kept quiet."

I looked over to where he was pointing and saw Lamin. He sat at the central table in a white suit, like the groom at a wedding, with Judy and Aimee either side of him.

"Jesus Christ."

"No, no, I don't think it was him. Not unless he works for the State Department." He took a step forward and put his hands on the barrier wall. "But what a view this is!"

The whole city lay before us. I set my back to it, turning to study Fern instead, to check on his reality, and then to watch Lamin accept a slice of cake from a passing waiter. I tried to account for the panic I felt. It was more than simply being kept in the dark, it was a rejection of the way I ordered my own reality. For in my mind, at that time—as perhaps it is for most young people—I was at the center of things, the only person in the world with true freedom. I moved from here to there, observing life as it presented itself to me, but everybody else in these scenes, all the subsidiary characters, belonged only in the compartments in which I had placed them: Fern eternally in the pink house, Lamin confined to the dusty paths of the village. What were they doing here, now, in my New York? I didn't know how to talk to either of them in the Rainbow Room, wasn't sure what our rela-

tion should be, or what, in this context, I owed or
was due. I tried to imagine how Lamin was feeling
right now, on the other side of the matrix at last,
and if he had someone to guide him through this
bewildering new world, someone to help explain
to him the obscene amounts of money that had
here been expended on things like helium balloons
and steamed squid buns and four hundred peonies. But it was Aimee at his side, not me, and she
had no such concerns, I could see that from here,
this was her world and he had simply been invited
into it as she would have invited anyone else, as
a privilege and a gift, the same way queens once
unself-consciously offered their patronage. In her
mind it was all fate, always meant to be, and therefore fundamentally uncomplicated. That's what I
and Judy and Fern and all of us were being paid
for really: to keep life uncomplicated—for her. We
waded through the tangled weeds so she might
float over the surface.

"Anyway, I was glad to come. I wanted to see you."
Fern reached over and brushed my right shoulder
with his hand, and in the moment I thought he
was only removing some dust, my mind was elsewhere, I was stuck on this image of me caught in
the weeds and Aimee floating serenely over my
head. Then his other hand went to my other shoulder: still I did not understand. Like everybody else
at that party, except perhaps Fern himself, I could
not take my eyes off Lamin and Aimee.

"My God, look at this!"

Fern glanced over briefly to where I was pointing and caught Lamin and Aimee as they exchanged a brief kiss. He nodded: "Ah, so they do not hide any more!"

"Jesus Christ. Is she going to marry him? Is she going to adopt him?"

"Who cares? I don't want to talk about her."

Suddenly Fern grabbed both my hands in his hands, and when I turned back I found that he was staring at me with comic intensity.

"Fern, what are you doing?"

"You pretend to be cynical"—he kept seeking my eyes as I tried equally hard to avoid his—"but I think you are just afraid."

In his accent it sounded like a line from one of the Mexican telenovelas we used to watch with half the village, each Friday afternoon, in the school's TV room. I couldn't help it—I laughed. His eyebrows came together in a sad line.

"Please don't laugh at me." He looked down at himself, and I looked, too: I think it was the first time I'd ever seen him out of cargo shorts. "The truth is I don't know how to dress in New York."

I eased my hands from his.

"Fern, I don't know what you think this is. You really don't know me."

"Well, you are hard to know well. But I want to know you. That is what it's like, being in love. You want to know someone, better."

It seemed to me that the situation was so awkward that he should just disappear at this point—just as such scenes in the telenovelas cut to a commercial—because otherwise I didn't see how we were going to get through the next two minutes. He didn't move. Instead he grabbed two passing flutes of champagne from a waiter's tray and drank his down in one go.

"You have nothing to say to me? I am offering you my heart!"

"Oh my God—Fern—please! Stop talking like that! I don't want your heart! I don't want to be responsible for anybody else's heart. For anybody else's anything!"

He looked confused: "A peculiar idea. Once you're alive in this world, you're responsible."

"For myself." Now I drank down a whole flute. "I just want to be responsible for myself."

"Sometimes in this life you have to take risks on other people. Look at Aimee."

"Look at **Aimee**?"

"Why not? You have to admire her. She's not ashamed. She loves this young man. It will probably mean a lot of trouble for her."

"You mean: for us. It'll mean a lot of trouble for us."

"But she doesn't care what people think."

"That's because as usual she has no idea what she's getting into. The whole thing is absurd."

They were leaning on each other, watching the

magician, an engaging gentleman in a Savile Row suit and a bow-tie who'd been at Jay's eighth birthday, too. He was doing the trick of the Chinese rings. Light poured into the Rainbow Room and the rings slipped in and out of each other despite their apparent solidity. Lamin looked mesmerized—everybody did. I could hear, very faintly, Chinese prayer music, and understood, in the abstract, that this must be part of the effect. I could see what everyone was feeling, but I was not with them and could not feel it.

"You are jealous?"

"I wish I could fool myself the way she can. I'm jealous of anyone that oblivious. A little ignorance never stopped her. Nothing stops her."

Fern emptied his glass and placed it awkwardly on the ground.

"I should not have spoken. I believe I have misinterpreted the situation."

His love language had been very silly but now that he returned to his more usual administrative language I felt sorry. He turned and went back indoors. The magician finished. I watched Aimee get up and approach the little, rounded stage. Jay was called up, or at least arrived at her side, and then Kara, and then Lamin. The whole party surrounded them in an adoring crescent shape. I seemed to be the only person still outside, looking in. With one arm she was hugging Jay and Kara, with the other she held up Lamin's left hand in triumphal pose. Everybody clapped and cheered, a muffled roar through the double-glazed glass. She held this position: a room full of cameras flashed. From where I stood it was a pose that collapsed many periods in her life into one: mother and lover, big sister, best friend, superstar and diplomat, billionaire and street kid, foolish girl and woman of substance. But why should she get to take everything, have everything, do everything, be everyone, in all places, at all times?

Seven

The thing I remember most vividly is the warmth of her body as she ran off stage and into the wings, into my arms, where I stood ready with a pencil skirt to replace her satin dress, or a black cat's tail to be pinned on her behind—once she had shimmied out of the pencil skirt—and clean tissues to wipe the sweat that always sprung from the bridge of her freckled nose. There were of course many other guys and dolls to whom I had to hand guns or canes, or fix a tiepin, straighten a seam or set a brooch just so, but it's Tracey I remember, holding on to my elbow for balance with one hand and stepping lightly into a pair of bright green capri pants which I then zipped up the side, taking care not to catch her skin, before kneeling down to tie the bows on her stack-heeled white taps. She was always serious and silent during these quick changes. She never giggled or fidgeted like the other Hot Box Girls, nor was she in any way self-doubting or in need of reassurance, as I soon learned was typical of chorus girls but alien to Tracey's nature. As I dressed or undressed her she remained fixated upon whatever was happening on stage. If she could watch the show, she would. If she was stuck backstage in a changing room and listening to it over the monitors, she was so focused on what she was hearing that you couldn't engage her in conversation. It didn't matter how many times she saw that show, she never tired of it, she was always impatient to get back inside it. Everything backstage bored her. Her real life was out there, in that fiction, under the lights, and this confused me because I knew, as no one else in the cast did, that she was having a secret affair with one of the stars, a married man. He played Brother Arvide Abernathy, the kindly older gentleman who carries a bass drum in the Salvation Army band. They didn't need to spray any gray in his hair, he was almost three times Tracey's age and had plenty already, a salt-and-pepper Afro that contributed to that air theatrical critics like to call "distinguished." In real life he was Kenyan-born and raised, followed by a stint at RADA, followed by another at the Royal Shakespeare Company: he had a very plummy Shakespearean speaking voice, which most people laughed at, behind his back, but that I liked to hear, especially on stage, it was so luxuriant, verbal velvet. Theirs was an affair conducted in little pockets of time, with no freedom to expand. On stage they had almost no scenes together—their characters came from two different worlds, a house of prayer and a den of sin—while off stage everything was clandestine and harried. But I was glad to take on the role of intermediary, scouting out empty dressing rooms, keeping watch, lying for them when lying was required—it gave me something concrete to do with my time instead of wondering, as I did most nights, what on earth I was doing there.

Observing their affair was interesting to me too for it was curiously constructed. Every time the poor man caught sight of Tracey he looked as if he might die of love for her, and yet she was never very kindly to him, as far as I could see, and I often heard her call him an old fool, or tease him about his white wife, or make cruel jokes about his aging libido. Once, I interrupted them by mistake, walking into a dressing room I didn't realize they were in, and found a singular scene: he was on his knees on the floor, fully dressed but head bowed and frankly weeping, and she was sitting on a stool, her back to him, facing the mirror, applying some lipstick. "Please don't," I heard her say as I slammed the door shut. "And get up. Get up off your fucking knees . . ." Later she told me he was offering to leave his wife. What was strangest to me about her ambivalence toward him was how severely it disturbed the hierarchies of the theatrical world she occupied, in which every soul in the production had a precise value and a corresponding power, and all relations conformed strictly to a certain schema. Socially, practically, sexually, a female star was worth all twenty chorus girls, for example, and Hot Box Girl Number One was worth about three chorus girls and all the understudies, while a male speaking part of any kind was equal to all the women on stage put together—except perhaps the female lead—and a male star could print his own currency, when he entered a room it re-formed around him, when he chose a chorus girl she submitted to him at once, when he suggested a change the director sat up in his seat and listened. This system was so solid it was unaffected by revolutions elsewhere. Directors had begun, for example, to cast across and against the old class and color lines—there were black King Henrys and cockney Richard IIIs and Kenyan Arvide Abernathys sounding just like Larry Olivier—but the old onstage hierarchics of rank remained firm as ever. In my first week, lost backstage and confused about the location of the prop cupboard, I stopped a pretty Indian girl in a corset who happened to be running by and tried to ask her for directions. "Don't ask me," she said, without slowing down, "I'm nobody . . ." Tracey's affair struck me as a form of revenge upon all that: like watching a house cat capture a lion, tame him, treat him like a dog.

I was the only person the two lovers could socialize with after hours. They couldn't go to the Coach and Horses with the rest of the crew, but they had the same urge to drown a post-show adrenalin high in alcohol, so they went instead to the Colony Room, where nobody else from the show went, but where he had been a member for years. Often I was invited to go with them. Here everyone called him "Chalky," and they knew his drink—whisky and ginger ale—and it was always sitting on the bar waiting for him when he arrived on the dot of ten forty-five. He loved that, and the stupid nickname, because it was a posh English habit to give stupid nicknames, and he was devoted to all things posh and English. I noticed he hardly ever talked of Kenya or Africa. One night I tried to ask him about his home but he became irritable: "Look, you kids, you grow up here, you think where I come from it's all starving children and Live Aid or whatever the hell you think it is. Well, my father was a professor of economics, my mother is a government minister, I grew up in a very beautiful compound, thank you very much, with servants, a cook, a gardener . . ." He went on like this for a while and then returned to his preferred subject, the glory days of Soho. I felt embarrassed but also that he had deliberately misunderstood me: of course I knew his world existed—that kind of world exists everywhere. That wasn't what I'd wanted to know.

His real allegiance was to the bar itself, which affection he struggled to translate to two girls who had barely heard of Francis Bacon and saw only a narrow, smoke-stained room, the lurid green walls and the crazed clutter—"Art shit," Tracey called it—that took over every surface. To annoy her lover, Tracey liked to make a show of her ignorance, but though she tried to disguise it I suspected she was often interested in the long, digressive, drunken stories he told, about artists, actors and writers he had known, their lives and works, who they'd fucked and what they'd drunk or taken and how they'd died. When he went to the toilet or out to buy fags I sometimes caught her deep in contemplation of one nearby painting or another, following the movement, I thought, of the brush, looking intently, with that sharpness she brought to all things. And when Chalky staggered back in and resumed his subject, she'd roll her eyes but she was listening, I could tell. Chalky had known Bacon only a little, enough to raise a drink with, and they'd had a good friend in common, a young actor called Paul, a man of "great beauty, great personal charm," the son of Ghanaians, who'd lived with his boyfriend, and Bacon, for a while, in a platonic triangle, down in Battersea. "And the thing you have to understand," said Chalky (after a certain number of whiskies there were always these things we had to understand), "the thing you have to understand is that here, in Soho, at that time, there was no black, there was no white. Nothing so banal. It wasn't like Brixton, no, here we were brothers, in art, in love"—he gave Tracey a squeeze—"in everything. Then Paul got that part in **A Taste of Honey**—we came here to celebrate it—and everyone was talking about it, and we felt like we were the center of the whole thing, swinging London, bohemian London, literary London, theatrical London, that this was our country, too, now. It was beautiful! I tell you, if London began and ended on Dean Street, all would be . . . happiness."

Tracey wriggled off his lap back on to her own stool. "You're a fucking pisshead," she muttered, and the barman, overhearing what she'd said, laughed and told her: "'Fraid that's a condition of membership round here, love . . ." Chalky turned to Tracey and kissed her sloppily: "**Come, come, you wasp; i' faith, you are too angry** . . ." "Look what I'm dealing with!" cried Tracey, pulling him off her. Chalky had a fondness for dirge-like Shakespearean ballads, it drove Tracey up the green walls, in part because she was jealous of his beautiful voice but also because when Chalky started singing of willow trees and faithless shrews it was a reliable sign that he'd soon have to be half carried down that steep and rickety staircase, heaved into a cab and sent back to his white wife, his fare prepaid with money Tracey had lifted from his wallet, usually taking a bit more than was strictly required. But she was pragmatic, she only ended the night when she'd learned something. I believe she was trying to pick up what she'd missed this past three years and I'd gained: a free education.

* * *

The show was very well reviewed and in November, backstage, five minutes before curtain, we were gathered together and told, by the producers, that our run was to be extended, past its Christmas deadline and into the spring. The cast was delighted, and that night they took their delight out with them on stage. I stood in the wings, happy for them, too, but with my own secret news tucked up inside me, which I hadn't yet told the management or Tracey. One of my applications had come through, finally: a production-assistant position, a paid internship, at the newly launched British version of YTV. The previous week I'd gone for an interview, hit it off with my interviewer, who told me, a little unprofessionally, I thought, given the queue of girls outside, that I had the job, there and then. It was only thirteen grand, but if I stayed at my father's it was more than enough. I was happy and yet hesitant to tell Tracey, without really asking myself what was at the root of my hesitancy. The Hot Box Girls dashed past me, fresh from Make-up, and on to the stage, dressed as cats, with Adelaide front and center and Hot Box Girl Number One just to her left. They puffed up their chests provocatively, licked their paws, got a hold of their tails—one of which I had pinned on Tracey ten minutes before—crouched like kittens about to pounce, and started to sing, of mean "poppas" who, holding you too tightly, make you want to roam, and other, gentle strangers, who make you feel at home . . . It was always a riotous number, but that night it was a real sensation. From where I stood, with a clear view of the front row, I could see the undisguised lust in the eyes of the men, and how many of those eyes were drawn specifically to Tracey when they should have rightfully been on the woman playing Adelaide. Everyone else was eclipsed by the litheness of Tracey's legs in that leotard, the pure vitality of her movements, truly cat-like, ultra-feminine in a mode I envied and could not hope to create in my own body no matter how many tails you stuck on me. There were thirteen women dancing in that number but only Tracey's movements really mattered, and when she ran off stage with the rest and I told her how wonderfully she'd danced, she did not, like the other girls, second-guess me or ask for any repetition of the praise, she only said, "Yes, I know," bent over, stripped and handed me her balled-up tights.

That night the cast celebrated at the Coach and Horses. Tracey and Chalky went with them and so did I, but we were used to the drunken and intimate intensity of the Colony Room—also to our own seats, and to hearing ourselves speak—and after about ten minutes of standing, screaming at the top of our voices and not getting served, Tracey wanted to leave. I thought she meant back to the Colony Room, with Chalky, to do as we usually did, so she and her lover could drink too much and go over their impossible situation: his wish to tell his wife, her determination that he would not, the complication of his children—who were around our age—and the possibility, dreaded by Chalky but unlikely I thought, that the papers might find out and make some kind of story of it. But when he went to the bathroom Tracey pulled me outside and said, "I don't want to do him tonight"—I remember that "do"— "Let's just go back to yours and get caned."

It was about eleven thirty when we got to Kilburn. Tracey had rolled one on the train and now we smoked walking down the street, remembering the times we'd performed this same action down the same road aged twenty, fifteen, thirteen, twelve . . .

As we walked I told her my news. It sounded very glamorous, YTV, three letters from a world that had preoccupied us as teenagers, and I felt almost embarrassed to bring it up, obscenely lucky, as if I were about to **be** on the channel rather than filing its British post and brewing its British tea. Tracey stopped walking and took the joint from me.

"But you're not going to leave right now? In the middle of a run?"

I shrugged and confessed: "Tuesday. Are you really fucked off?"

She didn't reply. We walked in silence for a bit and then she said: "You planning on moving out as well or what?"

I wasn't. I'd found I liked living with my father, and being near—but not in the same space as—my mother. To my own surprise I was in no hurry to leave. And I remember making a lot of this to Tracey, of how much I "loved" the old neighborhood, wanting to impress her, I suppose, prove how firmly my feet were still on the local ground, notwithstanding any change in my fortunes, I still lived with my father as she lived with her mother. She listened, smiled in a tight sort of way, lifted her nose into the air and kept her counsel. A few minutes later we reached my father's and I realized I didn't have my key. I often forgot it, but didn't like to ring the bell—in case he was already asleep, knowing he had to be up early—so would go down the side return and let myself in the back kitchen, which was usually open. But at that moment I was finishing the joint and didn't want to risk my father seeing me—we had recently promised each other we'd stop smoking. So I sent Tracey. A minute later she came back and said the kitchen was locked and we'd better go to hers.

The next day was a Saturday. Tracey left early for the matinee, but I didn't work Saturdays. I went back to my father's flat and spent the afternoon with him. I didn't see the letter that day though it might already have been on the mat. I found it on Sunday morning: it had been pushed through my door and was addressed to me, handwritten, with a little food stain on the corner of one page, and I think of it as the last truly personal written letter I ever received, for even though Tracey had no computer, not yet, the revolution was happening all around us and soon enough the only paper addressed to me would come from banks, utilities or the government, with a little plastic window to warn me of the contents. This letter came with no warning—I hadn't seen Tracey's handwriting in years—and I opened it as I sat at my father's table with my father sitting opposite me. "Who's that from then?" he asked, and for a few lines I still didn't know myself. Two minutes later the only question remaining was whether it was fact or fiction. It had to be fiction: to believe otherwise was to make everything in my present life impossible as well as destroying much of the life I had led up to this point. It was to allow Tracey to place a bomb under me and blow me to smithereens. I read it again, to make sure I had understood. She began by speaking of her duty, and of it being a horrible duty, and that she had asked and asked herself ("asked" spelled wrong) what to do and had felt she had no choice ("choice" spelled wrong.) She described Friday night as I, too, remembered it: walking up the street to my father's, smoking a joint, up to the point where she went down the side return to let herself in via the kitchen, unsuccessfully. But here the timeline broke in two, into her reality and mine, or her fiction—as far as I was concerned—and my fact. In her version she walked round the back of my father's flat, stood in the small gravel courtyard, and then, because the kitchen seemed to be locked, took two steps to the left and brought her nose right up to the back window, to my father's bedroom window, the one in which I slept, cupped her hands upon the glass and looked in. There she saw my father, naked, on top of something, moving up and down, and at first she had naturally thought it was a woman, and if it had been a woman, or so she assured me, then she never would have mentioned it, it was none of her business or mine, but the fact was it was not a woman at all, it was a doll, human-sized, but inflated, and of very dark complexion—"like a golliwog," she wrote—with a crescent of synthetic lamb's-wool hair and a huge pair of bright red lips, red as blood. "You all right, love?" asked my father, across the table, as I held that comic, tragic, absurd, heartbreaking, hideous letter shaking in my hand. I said I was fine, took Tracey's letter to the back courtyard, took out a lighter and set it on fire.

PART SEVEN
Late Days

One

I didn't set eyes on Tracey again for eight years. It was an unseasonably warm May evening, the night I went out with Daniel Kramer, a first date. He came to the city quarterly, and was one of Aimee's favorites in the sense that he did not, by virtue of being handsome, meld entirely with all the other accountants and financial advisers and copyright lawyers she regularly consulted, and so in her mind had been granted things like a name, qualities like a "good aura" and a "New York sense of humor" and a few biographical details she had managed to recall. Originally from Queens. Attended Stuyvesant. Plays tennis. Trying to keep the arrangements as loose as possible, I had suggested to him that we go to Soho and "play it by ear," but Aimee wanted us to come first to the house for a drink. It wasn't common at all, this kind of casual, intimate invitation, but Kramer didn't seem surprised or alarmed to receive it. The twenty minutes we were granted passed with no customer-like behavior. He admired the art—without overdoing it—listening politely as Aimee repeated all the things the dealer who sold the art to her had told her about the art when she bought it, and soon enough we were free, of Aimee, of the oppressive grandeur of that house, skipping down the back stairs, both a little giddy on good champagne, emerging on to the Brompton Road and into a warm, close night, muggy, threatening a storm. He wanted to take the long walk into town—we had vague plans to see what was on at the Curzon—but I was not a tourist and those were my salad days of impossible heels. I was about to look for a taxi when, for "fun," he stepped off the curb and waved down a passing pedicab.

"She collects a lot of African art," he said, as we climbed into the leopard-print seats—he was only making conversation, but primed against any hint of a customer, I cut him down: "Well, I don't really know what you can mean by 'African art.'"

He looked surprised by my tone but managed a neutral smile. He relied on Aimee's business and I was an extension of Aimee.

"Most of what you saw," I began in a tone better suited for a lecture hall, "is actually Augusta Savage. So Harlem. It's where she lived when she first came to New York—I mean, Aimee. Of course, she's a great supporter of the arts generally."

Now Kramer looked bored. I was boring myself. We didn't speak again until the bike stopped at the corner of Shaftesbury Avenue and Greek Street. As we pulled up at the curb we were surprised by the existence of a Bangladeshi boy, whose independent reality we had, up to that point, entirely forgotten, but who had undeniably brought us this far, and now turned round on his bike seat, his face soaked with sweat, hardly able to explain, through gasps, how much this form of human toil cost per minute. There was nothing we wanted to see at the cinema. In a slightly tense mood, our clothes sticking to us in the heat, we wandered toward Piccadilly Circus, without knowing which bar we were heading for, or whether we should eat instead, both already considering the evening a failure, looking straight ahead and confronted, every few steps, with the giant playbills of the theaters. It was in front of one of these, a little way down, that I stopped dead. A performance of the musical **Showboat**, a shot of the "Negro chorus": head-handkerchiefs, rolled-up trousers, aprons and work skirts, but all done tastefully, carefully, "authentically," with no hint of Mammy or Uncle Ben about it. And the girl closest to the camera, her mouth open wide in song, with one arm stretched high above her head, clutching a broom—the very picture of kinetic joy—was Tracey. Kramer came up behind me to peer over my shoulder. I pointed a finger at Tracey's upturned nose, as Tracey herself used to point at a dancer's face as it passed across our TV screens.

"I know her!"

"Oh, yeah?"

"I know her really well."

He tapped a cigarette out of a packet, lit it and looked the theater up and down.

"Well . . . you wanna go see it?"

"But you don't like musicals, do you? Nobody serious does."

He shrugged. "I'm in London, it's a show. That's what you're meant to do in London, isn't it? Go see a show?"

He passed me his cigarette, pushed open the heavy doors and headed to the box office. It all of a sudden seemed very romantic and coincidental and well timed and I had a ridiculous girlish narrative running in my head, of a future moment in which I would be explaining to Tracey—backstage somewhere in some sad regional theater, as she pulled on a pair of tired old fishnets—that the very moment I realized I'd met my love, the moment I came into my true happiness, was the same moment I happened to spot her, quite by chance, in that very small role she'd had, back in the day, in the chorus of **Showboat**, all those years and years ago . . .

Kramer came back out with two tickets, great seats in the second row. In lieu of dinner I bought myself a huge bag of chocolates, of the kind I rarely got to eat, Aimee considering such things not only nutritionally fatal but clear evidence of moral weakness. Kramer bought two large plas-

tic tumblers of bad red wine and the program. I
searched through it but couldn't find Tracey. She
wasn't where she should be in the alphabetical list
of the cast, and I started to worry that I was suffering from some kind of delusion, or had made an
embarrassing error. I flicked the pages back and
forth, sweat breaking out on my forehead—I must
have looked crazy. "You OK?" asked Kramer. I
was almost at the end of the program again when
Kramer pressed a finger to a page to stop me turning it.

"But isn't that your girl?"

I looked again: it was. She'd changed her
common-sounding, barbarous last name—the
name by which I'd always known her—to the
Frenchified and, to me, absurd Le Roy. Her first
name, too, had been adapted: now it was Tracee.
And in the picture her hair was straight and glossy.
I laughed out loud.

Kramer looked at me curiously.

"And you're good friends?"

"I know her very well. I mean, I haven't seen her
in about eight years."

Kramer frowned: "See, in guy world we'd call
that an 'ex-friend,' or better still: 'a stranger.'"

The orchestra started up. I was reading Tracey's
bio, parsing it furiously, in a race against time
before the house lights dimmed, as if the visible
words were hiding another set, with a far deeper

meaning that required decoding and would reveal something essential about Tracey and the way her life was now:

TRACEE LE ROY
CHORUS/DAHOMEY DANCER
Theater Includes:
Guys and Dolls (Wellington Theater);
Easter Parade (UK tour); **Grease**
(UK tour); **Fame!** (Scottish National
Theater); Anita, **West Side Story** (workshop)

If it was the story of her life it was disappointing. It lacked the ubiquitous accomplishments of all the other bios: no TV, no film, and no mention of where she'd been "trained," which I took to mean she'd never graduated. Apart from **Guys and Dolls**, there was no other West End work, only those bleak-sounding "tours." I imagined small church halls and rowdy schools, empty matinees on the stages of abandoned cinemas, minor local drama festivals. But if some part of all this pleased me, another part, equally large, was incensed at the idea that this bio of Tracee Le Roy could be fairly compared—by any of the people in the theater presently reading it, or by any of the actors in the cast—with any of these other stories. What did Tracee Le Roy have to do with these people? With this girl right next to her in the program, the girl with the endless biography, Emily Wolff-Pratt, who had studied at RADA, and who couldn't know, as I did, the huge statistical unlikelihood of my friend standing on this stage, or any stage at all—in any role, in any context—and who perhaps had the temerity to think that **she**, Emily Wolff-Pratt, was a true friend of Tracey's, just because she saw her every night, just because they danced together, when in fact she hadn't the slightest idea of who Tracey was or where she had come from, or how much it had cost her to get here. I turned my attention to Tracey's headshot. Well, I had to admit it: she'd turned out rather well. Her nose didn't seem so much of an outrage any more, she'd grown into it, and the cruelty I'd always detected in her face was obscured by the megawatt Broadway smile she had in common with every other actor on the page. The surprise wasn't that she was pretty, or sexy—she had already been in possession of these attributes as a very young teenager. The surprise was how elegant she had become. Her Shirley Temple dimples were gone, along with any hint of the provocative fleshiness she'd carried around as a child. It was almost impossible for me to imagine her voice, as I'd known it, as I remembered it, coming out of this pert-nosed, slick-haired, delicately freckled creature. I smiled down at her. Tracee Le Roy, who are you pretending to be now?

"Here we go!" said Kramer, as the curtain parted. He placed his elbows on his knees, his hands in two childish fists under his chin and made a facetious face: **I am agog.**

Stage left, a Southern oak, draped in Spanish moss, beautifully rendered. Stage right, the suggestion of a Mississippi town. Center stage, a showboat in harbor, the **Cotton Blossom.** Tracey—along with four other women—was first on stage, appearing from behind the oak, holding her broom, and behind her came the men with their various hoes and spades. The orchestra played the opening bars of a song. I recognized it as soon as I heard it, the big chorus number, and at once felt a panic, without knowing why, it took a moment, until the music itself prompted the memory. I saw the whole song laid out on the old sheet music, and remembered, too, how I'd felt the first time I saw it. And now the lyrics, shocking to me as a child, formed in my mouth, in perfect time with the orchestra's preamble, I remembered the Mississippi, where the "niggers" all work, where the white people don't, and I gripped the armrest and felt an urge to rise up out of my seat—it was like a scene in a dream— with the idea of stopping Tracey before she even started, but as soon as I'd had the thought it was already too late, and over the lyrics I'd thought I knew some new words had been substituted, but of course they had—no one had sung the original words for years and years. "**Here we all work . . . Here we all work . . .**"

I sank back into the seat. I watched Tracey expertly maneuver her broom this way and that, giving it life, so that it seemed almost another human presence on the stage, like the trick Astaire pulls, with that hat rack, in **Royal Wedding**. At one point she was perfectly aligned with the image from the poster, broom in the air, arm outstretched, kinetic joy. I wanted to pause her there in that position for ever.

The real stars arrived on stage, to begin the drama. In the background Tracey swept the front step of a general store. She was stage left from the main characters, Julie LaVerne and her devoted husband, Steve, two cabaret actors who work together on the **Cotton Blossom** and are in love. But Julie LaVerne is soon revealed, just before the interval, to be Julie Dozier, that is, not a white woman, as she has always pretended, but really a tragic mulatto, who "passes," who convinces everybody, including her own husband, until the day she's found out. At which point the couple are threatened with prison, for their marriage is illegal under the miscegenation laws. Steve cuts Julie's palm and drinks a little of her blood: the "one drop rule"—they're both Negroes now. In the dim light, in the middle of this ridiculous melodrama, I checked the bio of the actress playing Julie. She had a Greek last name and was no darker than Kramer.

During the interval I drank a lot, and too quickly, and talked at Kramer relentlessly. I was leaning against the bar, blocking other people's route to the bar staff, waving my hands around and ranting about the injustice of the casting, of how few roles there were for actors like me and even when such roles did exist you couldn't get them, somebody always gave them to a white girl, for even a tragic mulatto apparently wasn't quite fit to play a tragic mulatto, even in this day and—

"Actors like you?"

"What?"

"You said: **actors like me**."

"No, I didn't."

"Yeah, you did."

"My point is: that role should be Tracey's."

"You just said she can't sing. From what I've seen, it's pretty much a singing role."

"She sings fine!"

"Jesus, why are you shouting at me?"

We sat through the second half as silent as we had been in the first but this time the silence had a new texture, chilled with the iciness of mutual contempt. I longed to get out of there. Long stretches of the show passed without any sign of Tracey and held no interest for me. Only toward the end did the chorus reappear, this time as the "Dahomey Dancers," that is, as Africans, from the Kingdom of Dahomey, they were supposedly performing at the 1893 Chicago World's Fair. I watched Tracey in the circle of women—the men danced opposite, in their own circle—swinging her arms, crouching low and singing in a fictional African tongue, while the men stamped their feet and banged their spears in reply: **gunga, hungo, bunga, gooba!** I thought unavoidably of my mother, and of her line in Dahomey stories: the proud history of the kings; the shape and feel of the cowrie shells, used as money, the Amazon battalion, made up solely of women, taking prisoners of war as slaves for the kingdom, or else simply severing their enemies' heads and holding them up in their hands. The way other children hear tell of Red Riding Hood and Goldilocks, I heard of this "Black Sparta," the noble kingdom of Dahomey, fighting to hold off the French to the very end. But it was almost impossible to reconcile these memories with the farce presently happening, both on stage and off, for most of the people I sat among did not know what came next in the show and consequently, I realized, they felt they were watching some kind of shameful minstrel show and were willing the scene to end. On stage, too, the "audience" at the world's fair backed away from the Dahomey Dancers, though not out of shame but their own sense of fear, that these dancers were perhaps vicious, no different from the rest of their tribe, their spears not props but weapons. I looked over at Kramer; he was squirming. I turned back and watched Tracey. What great fun she was having with the general discomfort, just as she had always enjoyed such moments as a child. She waved her spear and roared, marching with the rest, toward the fearful audience at the fair, and then laughed with the others as their audience ran off stage. Left to their own devices, the Dahomey Dancers cut loose: they sang of how glad and tired they were, glad to see the back of the white folks, and tired, so tired, of being in a "Dahomey show."

And now the audience—the real audience—understood. They saw that what they were watching was intended to be funny, ironic, that these were American dancers, not Africans—yes, finally they grasped that a trick had been played on them. These folks weren't from Dahomey at all! They were just good old Negroes, after all, straight from Avenue A, in New York City itself! Kramer chuckled, the music turned to ragtime, and I felt my feet moving beneath me, trying to echo on the plush red carpet the complicated soft-shoe shuffle Tracey was performing right above me on the hard-wood stage. The steps were familiar to me—they would have been to any dancer—and I wished I was up there with her. I was stuck in London, in the year 2005, but Tracey was in Chicago in 1893, and Dahomey a hundred years before that, and anywhere and any time that people have moved their feet like that. I was so jealous I cried.

Show over, I came out of the long queue for the ladies and spotted Kramer before he saw me, he was standing in the lobby, bored and angry, holding my coat over his arm. Outside it had started to lash with rain.

"So, I'm gonna go," he said, passing me my coat, barely able to look at me. 'I'm sure you'll want to go say hello to your 'friend.'"

He turned his collar up and walked into that horrible evening, umbrella-less, still angry. Nothing offends a man so much as being ignored. But I was impressed: his dislike of me was so clearly stronger than any fear of my influence over his employer. Once he was out of sight I walked around to the side of the theater and found it was just as you always see it in the old movies: the door said "Stage Door" and there was a reasonable crowd of people waiting for the cast to emerge, despite the rain, clutching their little notepads and pens.

With no umbrella, I pressed against the side of the wall, facing out, just covered by a narrow awning. I didn't know what I planned to say or how I was going to approach her, but I was just beginning to think about it when a car pulled up in the alleyway, driven by Tracey's mother. She was hardly changed: through the rain-streaked windscreen I could see the same tin hoops in her ears, the triple chin, hair scraped back tight, a cigarette hanging from her mouth. I turned at once to the wall and, as she parked, made my escape. I ran down Shaftesbury Avenue, getting soaked, thinking about what I'd seen in the back of that car: two sleeping young children, strapped in their seats. I wondered whether this, and nothing else, was the true reason the story of Tracey's life took so little time to read.

Two

You want to believe there are limits to what money can make happen, lines it can't cross. Lamin in that white suit in the Rainbow Room felt like an example of the opposite lesson. But in fact he didn't have a visa, not yet. He had a new passport and a date of return. And when it was time to leave I would accompany him back to the village, along with Fern, staying on a week to complete the yearly report for the board of the foundation. After which Fern would remain, and I'd fly to London, to meet the children and supervise their quarterly visit to their fathers. So we were informed by Judy. Until then, a month together in New York.

For the past decade, whenever we were in the city, my base had been the maid's room, on the ground floor off the kitchen, although occasionally a half-hearted discussion would take place about the possibility of a separate space—a hotel, a rental somewhere—which never led to anything and was soon forgotten. But this time an apartment had been rented for me before I even arrived, a two-bedroom on West 10th Street, high ceilings, fireplaces, the whole second floor of a beautiful brownstone. Emma Lazarus had once lived here: a blue plaque under my window memorialized her huddled masses, yearning to breathe free. My view was of a pink-blush dogwood in full bloom. I mistook all this for an upgrade. Then Lamin appeared and I understood I'd been moved out so he could move in.

"What exactly is going on with you?" Judy asked me, the morning after Jay's birthday party. No preliminaries, just her strident yell coming at me through my phone as I tried to tell the bodega guy on Mercer to skip the apple in my green juice. "Have you had some kind of argument with Fernando? Because we just can't have him in the house right now—there's no room for him at the inn. We've got a full inn, as you probably noticed. Our lovebirds want their privacy. The plan was meant to be he'd stay with you for a few weeks, in the apartment, it was all settled—now suddenly he's resistant."

"Well, I wouldn't know anything about that. Because nobody told me. Judy, you didn't even mention to me that Fern was coming to New York!"

Judy made a sound of impatience: "Look, it was something Aimee wanted me to handle. It had to do with accompanying Lamin over here, she didn't want it out in the world . . . It was delicate, and I handled it."

"Do you handle who I live with too now?"

"Oh, love, I'm **sorry**—are you paying rent?"

I managed to get her off the phone and called Fern. He was in a taxi somewhere on the West Side Highway. I could hear the foghorn of a cruise ship docking.

"Better I find somewhere else. Yes, it's better. This afternoon I look at a place in . . ." I heard papers being sadly shuffled. "Well, it doesn't matter. Midtown somewhere."

"Fern, you don't know this city—and you don't want to pay rent here, believe me. Take the room. I'll feel shitty about it if you don't. I'll be at Aimee's day and night—she's got that show in two weeks, we'll be up to our ears. I promise you—you'll hardly see me."

He closed a window, the river winds stopped rushing in. The quiet was unhelpfully intimate.

"I **like** to see you."

"Oh, Fern . . . Please just take the room!"

That evening the only sign of him was an empty coffee cup in the kitchen and a tall canvas rucksack—the kind a student packs for a year off—leaning in the doorframe of his empty room. As he'd climbed the steps of the ferry with this single bag on his back, Fern's simplicity, his frugality, had seemed to have something noble in it, I'd aspired to it, but here in Greenwich Village the idea of a forty-five-year-old man with a single rucksack to his name struck me as merely sad and eccentric.

I knew he'd crossed Liberia, alone and on foot, aged only twenty-four—it was some kind of homage to Graham Greene—but now all I could think was: **Brother, this city will eat you alive**. I wrote a pleasant and neutral note of welcome, tucked it under the straps of his bag and went to bed.

I was right about barely seeing him: I had to be at Aimee's for eight each morning (she woke daily at five, to exercise for two hours in the basement followed by an hour of meditation) and Fern always slept in—or pretended that he did. In Aimee's townhouse all was frantic planning, rehearsal, anxiety: the new show was in a mid-size venue, she'd be singing live, with a live band, things she hadn't done in years. To keep out of the line of fire, the meltdowns, the arguments, I stayed as much as I could in the office and avoided rehearsals whenever possible. But I gathered some kind of West African theme was afoot. A set of **atumpan** drums were delivered to the house, and a long-necked **kora**, swathes of kente, and—one fine Tuesday morning—a twelve-person dance troupe, African-by-way-of-Brooklyn, who were taken to the basement studio and didn't emerge till after dinner. They were young, mostly second-generation Senegalese, and Lamin was fascinated by them: he wanted to know their last names and the villages of their parents, chasing down any possible connection of family or location. And Aimee was glued to Lamin: you couldn't talk to her alone any more, he was there at all times. But which Lamin was it? She thought it very provocative and funny to tell me he still prayed five times a day, in her walk-in closet, which apparently faced Mecca. Personally I wanted to believe in this continuity, in this part of him still beyond her reach, but there were days I barely recognized him. One afternoon I brought a tray of coconut waters down to the studio and found him, in his white shirt and white slacks, demonstrating a move I recognized from the kankurang, a combination of side-stamp, shuffle and dip. Aimee and the other girls watched him carefully and repeated the movements. They were sweating, dressed in crop tops and ripped unitards, and were pressed so closely to him and each other that each movement he made looked like a single wave passing through five bodies. But the truly unrecognizable gesture was the one that swept a bottle of coconut water from my tray, without a thank-you, without the vaguest acknowledgment—you'd have thought he'd been taking drinks from the wobbling trays of serving girls every day of his life. Maybe luxury is the easiest matrix to pass through. Maybe nothing is easier to get used to than money. Though there were times when I saw a haunted quality in him, like he was being stalked by something. Wandering into the dining room toward the end of his visit, I found him still at the breakfast table, talking at Granger, who looked very weary, as if he'd been there a long time. I sat down with them. Lamin's eyes were fixed somewhere between Granger's shaved head and the opposite wall. He was whispering again, a perplexing, uninflected speech that ran on like an incantation: ". . . and right now, our women are sowing the onions in the right-hand beds and then the peas in the left-hand beds, and if the peas are not irrigated in the correct way then when they will come to rake the ground, about two weeks from now, they will have a problem, there will be an orange curl to the leaf, and if it has this curl, then it has the blight and then they will dig up what has been sown and re-sow the beds, making sure I hope to put a layer of this rich soil we get from upriver, you see, when the men go upriver, about a week from now, when we travel up there we get the rich soil . . ."

"Uh-huh," Granger was saying, every other sentence. "Uh-huh, Uh-huh."

Fern made sporadic appearances in our lives, at board meetings or when Aimee required his presence to deal with practical problems related to the school. He looked pained at all times—physically winced whenever we made eye contact—and advertised his misery wherever he went, like a man in a comic with a black cloud above his head. In front of Aimee and the rest of the board he gave a pessimistic update, focused on recent aggressive statements of the President's, concerning foreign presence in the country. I'd never heard him talk like that before, so fatalistically, it was not really in his character, and I knew I was the true, oblique target of his critique.

That afternoon in the apartment, instead of hiding in my room as usual, I confronted him in the hall. He'd just come back from a run, sweating, bent over, with his hands on his knees, breathing hard, looking up at me from under thick brows. I was very reasonable. He didn't speak but seemed to take it all in. Without his glasses his eyes looked enormous, like a cartoon baby's. When I finished he straightened up and bent the other way, pushing the small of his back forward with both hands.

"Well, I apologize if I embarrassed you. You are right: it was unprofessional."

"Fern—can't we be friends?"

"Of course. But you also want me to say: 'I am happy we are friends'?"

"I don't want you to be unhappy."

"But this is not one of your musicals. The truth is I am very sad. I wanted something—I wanted you—and I didn't get at all what I wanted or hoped and now I am sad. I will get over it, I suppose, but for now I am sad. Is it OK for me to be sad? Yes? Well. Now I shower."

It was very difficult for me, at the time, to understand a person who spoke like that. It was alien to me, as an idea—I hadn't been raised that way. What response could such a man—the type who gives up all power—possibly expect from a woman like me?

I didn't go to the show, couldn't face it. I did not want to stand in the bleachers with Fern, feeling his resentment while watching funhouse versions of the dances we had both seen at their source. I told Aimee I was going and I intended to go but when eight o'clock rolled around I was still in my house sweats, lying half propped up on my bed with my laptop over my groin, and then it was nine o'clock, and then it was ten. I absolutely had to go—my mind kept repeating this fact to me and I was in agreement with it—but my body freeze-framed, felt heavy and immovable. Yes, I must go, that was clear, and just as clear was the fact I was not going anywhere. I got on YouTube, skipped from dancer to dancer: Bojangles up the stairs, Harold and Fayard on a piano, Jeni LeGon in her swishing grass skirt, Michael Jackson at **Motown 25**. I often ended up at this clip of Jackson, although this time as he moonwalked across the stage, the thing that really interested me was not the crowd's ecstatic screams or even the surreal fluidity of his movements but the shortness of his trousers. And still the option of going did not seem lost or completely closed until I looked up from my aimless surfing and found eleven forty-five had happened, which signified we were now in the undeniable past tense: I hadn't gone. Search Aimee, search venue, search Brooklyn dance troupe, image search, AP wire search, blog search. At first simply out of a sense of guilt, but soon enough with the realization that I could reconstruct—140 characters at a time, image by image, blog post by blog post—the experience of having been there, until, by one a.m., nobody could have been there more than me. I was far more there than any of the people who had actually been there, they were restricted to one location and one perspective—to one stream of time—whereas I was everywhere in that room at all moments, viewing the thing from all angles, in a mighty act of collation. I could have stopped there—I had more than enough to give a detailed account of my evening to Aimee in the morning—but I didn't stop. I was compelled by the process. To observe, in real time, the debates as they form and coalesce, to watch the developing consensus, the highlights or embarrassments identified, their meanings and subtexts accepted or denied. The insults and the jokes, the gossip and rumor, the memes, the Photoshop, the filters, and all the many varieties of critique given free rein here, far from Aimee's reach or control. Earlier in the week, watching a costume fitting—in which Aimee, Jay and Kara were being dressed up to resemble Asante nobles—I'd hesitantly brought up the matter of appropriation. Judy groaned, Aimee looked at me and then down at her own ghost-pale pixie frame wrapped in so much vibrantly colored cloth, and told me that she was an artist, and artists have to be allowed to love things, to touch them and to use them, because art is not appropriation, that was not the aim of art—the aim of art was love. And when I asked her whether it was possible both to love something and leave it alone, she regarded me strangely, pulled her children into her body and asked: Have you ever been in love?

But now I felt defended, virtually surrounded. No, I didn't feel like stopping. I kept refreshing and refreshing, waiting for new countries to wake up and see the images and form their own opinions or feed off opinions already voiced. In the wee hours I heard the front door squeak and Fern stumbling into the apartment, surely straight from the after-party. I didn't move. And it must have been at about four in the morning, while scrolling through the fresh opinions and listening to the birds chirp in the dogwood, that I saw the handle "Tracey LeGon," the subtitle "Truthteller." My contact lenses were brittle in my eyes, it hurt to blink, but I wasn't seeing things. I clicked. She'd posted the same photo I'd seen hundreds of times by then—Aimee, the dancers, Lamin, the children—all lined up at the front of the stage, wearing the **adinkra** cloth for which I'd seen them fitted: a rich cerulean blue printed with a pattern of black triangles, and in each triangle there was an eye. Tracey had taken this image, expanded it many times, cropped it, so only the triangle and the eye were still visible, and underneath this image she asked the question: LOOK FAMILIAR?

Three

Returning with Lamin, we took the jet, but without Aimee—who was in Paris, being awarded a medal by the French government—and so had to process through the main airport, just like everybody, into an arrival hall packed with returning sons and daughters. The men wore fancy jeans of heavy denim, stiff, patterned shirts with stockbroker collars, branded hooded tops, leather jackets, the latest sneakers. And the women were likewise determined to wear all of their best things at the same time. Hair beautifully done, nails freshly painted. Unlike us, they were all familiar with this hall, and quickly secured the services of the porters, to whom they handed their mammoth suitcases, instructing them to take care—though each bag was wrapped in layers of plastic—before leading these hot and harassed young baggage carriers through the crowds toward the exit, turning back every now and then to bark instructions like mountain climbers with their Sherpas. This way, this way! Smartphones held up above their heads, indicating the route. Looking at Lamin in this context,

I realized his traveling outfit must be a deliberate choice: despite all the clothes and rings and chains and shoes Aimee had given him this past month, he was dressed exactly as he had been when he left. Same old white shirt, the chinos and a simple pair of leather sandals, black and worn thin at the heel. It made me think there were things about him I had not understood—maybe many things.

We took a taxi and I sat with Lamin in the backseat. The car had three broken windows and a hole in the lower carriage through which I could see the road rolling beneath. Fern sat in the front, next to the driver: his new policy was to keep a cool distance from me at all times. On the jet he read his books and journals, in the airport he restricted himself to practical matters, get that trolley, join that queue. He was never mean, never said anything cruel, but the effect was isolating.

"Want to stop to eat?" he asked me now, by way of the rearview mirror. "Or you can wait?"

I wanted to be the kind of person who didn't mind skipping lunch, who could power through, like Fern often did, replicating the practice of the poorest families in the village by eating only once, in the late afternoon. But I was not that kind of person: I couldn't miss a meal without getting aggravated. We drove for forty minutes and stopped at a roadside café opposite something called the American College Academy. It had bars on its windows and half the letters missing from the

sign. Inside the café the menus depicted glisten-
ing American-style meals "with fries," the prices of
which Lamin read aloud, shaking his head gravely,
as if encountering something deeply sacrilegious or
offensive, and after a long conversation with the
waitress three plates of chicken yassa arrived for a
negotiated "local" rate.

We were bent over our food, eating in silence,
when we heard a booming voice coming from
the very back of the café: "My boy Lamin! Little
brother! It's Bachir! Over here!"

Fern waved. Lamin did not move: he had spotted this Bachir long ago and had been praying not
to be spotted in return. I turned and saw a man
sitting alone at the last table near the counter, in
the shadows, the only other customer in the place.
He was broad and muscular like a rugby player,
and wore a dark blue suit with stripes, a tie, a tiepin, loafers without socks and a thick gold chain
around his wrist. The suit was straining against his
muscles and his face was running with sweat.

"He is not my brother. He is my age mate. He is
from the village."

"But aren't you going to—"

Bachir was already upon us. Up close, I saw he
was wearing a headset, consisting of earpiece and
microphone, not unlike the kind Aimee wore on
stage, and in his arms carried a laptop, a tablet and
a very large phone.

"Gotta find a place to put all this stuff!" But he

sat down with us still clasping it all to his chest. "Lamin! Little brother! Long time!"

Lamin nodded at his lunch. Fern and I introduced ourselves and received firm, painful, damp handshakes.

"Me and him grew up together, man! Village life!" Bachir grabbed Lamin's head and put him in a sweaty headlock. "But then I had to go to the city, baby, know what I'm saying? I was chasing the money, baby! Working with the big banks. Show me the money! Babylon for real! But I'm still a village boy at heart." He kissed Lamin and released him.

"You sound American," I said, but that was only one thread of the rich tapestry of his voice. Many different movies and adverts were in there, and a lot of hip-hop, **Esmeralda** and **As the World Turns**, the BBC news, CNN, Al Jazeera and something of the reggae that you heard all over the city, from every taxi, market stall, hairdresser. An old Yellowman tune was playing right now, from the tinny speakers above our heads.

"For real, for real . . ." He rested his very large, square head on his fist in a thoughtful pose. "You know, I've not actually been to the US as yet, not as yet. Got a lot going on. It's all happening. Talking, talking, gotta keep up with technology, gotta keep relevant. Look at this girl: she is ringing my number, baby, night and day, day and night!" He flashed me an image on his tablet, of a beautiful woman with a glossy weave and dramatic lips painted a deep purple. It looked to me to be a commercial image. "These big-city girls, they're too crazy! Oh, little brother, I need an upriver girl, I want to start a nice family. But these girls don't even want a family any more! They're crazy! How old are you, though?"

I told him.

"And no babies? Not even married? No? OK! OK, OK . . . I feel you, sister, I feel you: Miss Independent, is it? That's your way, OK. But for us, a woman without children is like a tree without fruit. Like a tree"—he raised his muscular backside half out of his chair in a squat, stretched his arms like branches and his fingers like twigs—"without fruit." He sat back down and closed his hands back into fists. "Without fruit," he repeated.

For the first time in many weeks Fern managed a half-smile in my direction.

"I think what he is saying is that you are like a tree—"

"Yes, Fern, I got it, thank you."

Bachir spotted my flip-phone, my personal phone. He picked it up and turned it over in his palm with exaggerated wonder. His hands were so big it looked a child's toy.

"This is **not** yours. Serious? This is yours?! This is what they are using in London? HA HA HA. Oh man, we more fresh over here! Oh, man! Funny,

funny. I would not have expected this. Globalization, right? Strange times, strange times!"

"Which bank did you say you work for?" asked Fern.

"Oh, I got a lot going on, man. Development, development. Land here, land there. Building. But I work for the bank here, yes, trading, trading. You know how it is, brother! Government makes life **hard** sometimes. But show me the money, right? You like Rihanna? You know her? She got **her** money! Illuminati, right? Living the dream, baby."

"We must go now to the ferry," whispered Lamin.

"Yeah, I guess I got a lot of trades these days— complicated business, man—gotta make those moves, moves, moves." He demonstrated by moving his fingers over his three devices as if primed to use any one of them at any moment for something terrifically urgent. I noticed the screen on the laptop was black and cracked in several places. "See, some people gotta get to that farm life every day, shell those groundnuts, right? But I gotta make my moves. This is the new work–life balance right here. You know about that? Yes, man! That's the latest thing! But in this country we have our old-world mindset, right? A lot of people around here are behind the damn times. It takes these people a little while, OK? To get it into their minds." With his fingers he drew a rectangle in the air: "The Future. Gotta get it into your mind. But listen: for you? Any time! I like your face, man, it's beautiful, so clear and light. And I could come to London, we could talk business for real! Oh, you're not in business? Charity? NGO? Missionary? I like the missionaries, man! I had a good friend, he was from South Bend, Indiana—Mikey. We spent a lot of time together. Mikey was cool, man, he was really cool, he was a Seventh-Day Adventist, but we're all God's children for sure, for sure . . ."

"They are here doing some educational work, with our girls," said Lamin, turning his back on us, trying to get the waitress's attention.

"Oh, sure, I hear about the changes up there. Big times, big times. Good for the village, right? Development."

"We hope so," said Fern.

"But little brother: are you getting a piece of that? Did you guys know little brother here is too good for money? He's all about the next life. Me, no: I want this life! HA HA HA HA. Money, money, rolling. Ain't that the truth. Oh man, oh man . . ."

Lamin stood up: "Good-bye, Bachir."

"So serious, this one. But he loves me. You would love me, too. My oh my, you're gonna be thirty-three, girl! We should talk! Time flies. Gotta live your life, right? Next time, in London, girl, in Babylon—let's talk!"

Walking back to the car, I heard Fern chuckling to himself, cheered by the episode.

"This is what people call 'a character,'" he said,

and when we reached our waiting taxi and turned to get in we found Bachir the character standing in the doorway, still with his earpiece on, holding all his various technologies and waving at us. Seen standing up, his suit looked especially peculiar, the trousers too short at the ankles, like a **mashala** in pinstripes.

"Bachir lost his job three months ago," said Lamin quietly, as we got back into the car. "He is in that café every day."

Yes, everything about that trip felt wrong from the start. Instead of my previous glorious competency, I couldn't rid myself of a nagging sense of error, of having misread everything, beginning with Hawa, who opened the door of her compound wearing a new scarf, black, that covered her head and stopped halfway down her torso, and a long, shapeless shirt, the kind she had always ridiculed when we saw them in the market. She hugged me as firmly as ever, would only nod at Fern, and seemed annoyed by his presence. We all stood in the yard for a while, Hawa making polite, grating small talk—none of it addressed to Fern—and me hoping for some mention of dinner, which, I soon understood, would not come until Fern left. Finally he got the message: he was tired and would head back to the pink house. And as soon as the door closed behind him the old Hawa returned, grabbed my hand, kissed my face and cried: "Oh, sister—good news—I'm getting married!" I hugged her but felt the familiar smile fasten itself on my face, the same one I wore in London and New York in the face of similar news, and I experienced the same acute sense of betrayal. I was ashamed to feel that way but couldn't help it, a piece of my heart closed against her. She took my hand and led me into the house.

So much to tell. His name was Bakary, he was a Tablighi, a friend of Musa's, and she would not lie and say he was handsome, because in fact he was quite the opposite, she wanted me to understand that right away, pulling out her phone as evidence.

"See? He looks like a bullfrog! Honestly I wish he would not wear the black stuff on his eyes or use henna that way, in the beard . . . and sometimes he even wears the lungi! My grandmothers think he looks like a woman in make-up! But they must be wrong because the Prophet himself wore kohl, it is good for eye infections, and there's really so much I don't know that I have to learn. Oh, my grandmothers are weeping day and night, night and day! But Bakary is kind and patient. He says nobody cries for ever—and don't you think that's true?"

Hawa's twin nieces brought in our dinner: rice for Hawa, oven fries for me. I listened in a kind of daze as Hawa told me funny stories about her recent **masturat** to Mauritania, the furthest she had ever traveled, where she had often fallen asleep in the lecture sessions ("The man who is talking, you can't see him, because he is not allowed to look at us, so he speaks from behind a curtain, and all us women are sitting on the floor and the lecture is very long, so sometimes we just want to sleep") and had thought to sew a pocket into the inside of her waistcoat so as to hide her phone and surreptitiously text her Bakary during the duller recitations. But she always concluded these stories with some pious-sounding phrase: "The important thing is the love I bear for my new sisters." "It is not for me to ask." "It is in the hands of God."

"In the end," she said, as two more young girls brought us our tin mugs of Lipton's, heavily sweetened, "all that matters is praising God and leaving **dunya** things behind. I tell you in this compound **dunya** business is all you ever hear. Who went to market, who has a new watch, who is going 'back way,' who has money, who has not, I want this, I want that! But when you are traveling, bringing people the truth of the Prophet, there is no time for any of these **dunya** things at all."

I wondered why she was still in the compound if life here now annoyed her so much.

"Well, Bakary is good but he is very poor. As soon as we can we will marry and move, but for now he sleeps in the **markaz**, close to God, while I am here, close to the chickens and the goats. But we will save a lot of money because my wedding will be very, very small, like the wedding of a mouse, and only Musa and his wife will be there and there will no music or dancing or feasts and I will not even need to get a new dress," she said with practiced brightness, and I felt so sad suddenly, for if I knew anything at all about Hawa it was how much she loved weddings and wedding dresses and wedding feasts and wedding parties.

"So, you see, a lot of money will be saved there, for sure," she said, and folded her hands in her lap to formally mark the end of this thought, and I did not contest her. But I could see she wanted to talk, that her pat phrases were like lids dancing on top of bubbling cooking pots, and all I had to do was sit patiently and wait for her to boil over. Without me asking another question she began to speak, first tentatively and then with increasing energy, of her fiancé. What seemed to impress her most about this Bakary was his sensitivity. He was boring and ugly but he was sensitive.

"Boring how?"

"Oh, I should not say 'boring,' but I mean, you should see him and Musa together, they listen to these holy tapes all day long, they are very holy tapes, Musa is trying now to learn more Arabic, and I am also learning to appreciate them fully, at the moment they are still very boring for me—but when Bakary listens to them he weeps! He weeps and holds Musa in his arms! Sometimes I go to the market and come back and they are still hugging each other and crying! I never saw a bumster weep!

Unless somebody stole his drugs! No, no, Bakary is very sensitive. It is really a heart matter. At first I thought: my mother is a learned woman, she taught me a lot of Arabic, I will be ahead of Bakary in my **iman**, but that is so wrong! Because it's not what you read, it's what you feel. And I have a long way to go before my heart is as full of **iman** as Bakary's. I think a sensitive man makes a good husband, don't you? And our **mashala** men—I should not call them that, Tablighi is the proper word—but they are so kind to their women! I didn't know that. My grandmother always said: they are half big, they are crazy, don't talk to these girly-men, they don't even have jobs. Oh boy, she's weeping **every day.** But she doesn't understand, she's so old-fashioned. Bakary is always saying, 'There is a hadith that goes: "The best man is the one who helps his wife and children and has mercy on them."' And that's how it is. So, if we go on these tours, on **masturat**, well, to avoid other men seeing us in the market, **our men go themselves** and do the shopping for us, **they** buy the vegetables. I laughed when I heard this, I thought: it can't be true—but it's true! My grandfather did not even **know** where the market was! This is what I try to explain to my grandmothers, but they are old-fashioned. They are weeping every day because he is a **mashala**—I mean, Tablighi. According to me, they are jealous in secret. Oh, I wish I could leave this place right now. When I went to be with my sisters I was so happy! We prayed together. We walked together. After lunch, one of us had to lead the prayer, you know, and one of the sisters said to me: 'You do it!' And so I was the Imam for the day, you know? But I wasn't shy. Many of my sisters are shy, they say, 'It is not for me to speak,' but I really found out on this tour that I am not at all a shy person. And everybody listened to me—oh! People even asked **me** questions afterward. Can you believe it?"

"It doesn't surprise me at all."

"My topic was the six fundamentals. This is about how a person should eat? In fact, I am not observing them right now, because you are here, but they are certainly in my mind for the next time."

This guilty thought led to another: she leaned forward to whisper something to me, her irresistible face set in a half-smile.

"Yesterday I went to the school TV room and we watched **Esmeralda**. I shouldn't smile," she said, and abruptly stopped, "but you especially know how I **love Esmeralda**, and I'm sure you would agree that nobody can rid themselves of all **dunya** things all in one go." She looked down at her shapeless skirt. "Also my clothes will have to change, in the end, not just the skirt, everything from head to toe. But my sisters all agree it is hard at first because you get so hot and people stare, they call you ninja or Osama in the street. But I remembered what you said to me once when you first came here: "Who cares what other people think?" And this is a strong thought that I keep with me, because my reward will be in Heaven, where nobody will call me ninja because certainly those people will be on fire. I still love my Chris Brown, I can't help it, and even Bakary still loves his Marley songs, I know because I heard him sing one the other day. But we will learn together, we are young. As I told you already, when we were on tour Bakary did all my chores for me, he went to the market for me, even when people laughed at him, he did this. He did my washing. I said to my grandmothers: did my grandfather ever wash **even a sock** for any of you in forty years?"

"But Hawa, **why** can't the men see you in the market?"

She looked bored: I had asked the dullest question once again.

"When men look at women who are not their wife that is the moment Shaytan is waiting to rush in, to fill them with sin. Shaytan is everywhere! But don't you even know that?"

I couldn't listen to any more of it and made my excuses. But the only place I could go or knew how to get to in the darkness was the pink house. From some way down the road I could see all the lights were dead, and when I reached the door I found it hanging at an angle from a broken hinge.

"You in there? Can I come in?"

"My door is always open," replied Fern from the

shadows, in a sonorous voice, and we laughed at the same time. I came in, he made me tea, I regurgitated all the news from Hawa.

Fern listened to me rant, his head cast further and further back until his head-torch shone on the ceiling.

"I have to say it does not seem strange to me," he said when I finished. "She works like a dog in that compound. She hardly leaves it. I imagine she is desperate, like any bright young person, to have her own life. Didn't you want to get out of your parents' house, at that age?"

"When I was her age I wanted freedom!"

"And you would consider her less free, I mean, touring Mauritania, preaching, than she is now, shut up at home?" He drew his sandal through the covering of red dust that had accumulated on the plastic flooring. "That's interesting. It's an interesting point of view."

"Oh, you're just trying to annoy me."

"No, I never mean to do that." He looked down at the pattern he had made on the floor. "Sometimes I wonder if people don't want freedom as much as they want meaning," he said, speaking slowly. "This is what I mean to say. At least, this has been my experience."

We would argue if we carried on so I changed the subject and offered him one of the biscuits I had swiped from Hawa's room. I remembered I had some podcasts saved on my iPod and, with one earbud each, we sat peaceably side by side, nibbling our biscuits and listening to accounts of these American lives, their minor dramas and satisfactions, their pleasures and irritations and tragicomic epiphanies, until it was time for me to go.

The next morning when I woke my first thought was Hawa, Hawa soon married, the babies that would surely follow, and I wanted to speak to someone who shared my sense of disappointment. I got dressed and went looking for Lamin. I found him in the schoolyard, going over a lesson plan under the mango tree. But disappointment was not his reaction to Hawa's news, or not his first reaction—that was heartbreak. It wasn't even nine in the morning and I had managed to break someone's heart.

"But where did you hear this?"

"Hawa!"

He struggled to gain control of his face.

"Sometimes girls say they will marry someone and they do not. It's common. There was a policeman . . ." He trailed off.

"I'm sorry, Lamin. I know how you feel about her."

Lamin laughed stiffly and returned to his lesson plan.

"Oh no, you are mistaken, we are brother and sister. We have always been. I said this to our friend Aimee: this is my little sister. She will remember me saying this, if you ask her. No, I am just sorry for Hawa's family. They will be very sad."

The school bell rang. I visited classrooms all morning and for the first time got a feeling for what Fern had achieved here, in our absence, despite Aimee's interference, and by working, in a sense, around her. The school office had all the new computers she had sent, and more reliable internet, which I could see, from their search histories, had been so far used exclusively by the teachers for two purposes: trawling Facebook and entering the President's name into Google. Each classroom was scattered with mysterious—to me—3D logic puzzles and small handheld devices on which you could play chess. But these were not the innovations that impressed me. Just behind the main building, Fern had used some of Aimee's money to create a garden in the yard, which I don't remember him ever mentioning in our board meetings, and here all kinds of produce were growing, which belonged, he explained, to the parent body collectively, which—along with many other consequences—meant that when first period ended, half the school did not disappear to help their mothers on the farm, instead staying on site and tending to their seedlings. I learned that Fern, at the suggestion of the mothers in the PTA, had invited several teachers from the local **majlis** into our school, where they were given a room to teach Arabic and Koranic studies, for which they

were paid a small fee directly, and this stopped another large portion of the school population disappearing at midday or spending a part of every
afternoon doing domestic chores for these **majli**
teachers, as they once had, in lieu of payment.
I spent an hour in the new art room, where the
youngest girls sat at their tables mixing colors and
making hand prints—playing—while the laptops
that Aimee had envisioned for them all had, Fern
now confessed, disappeared en route to the village,
no surprise, given that each one was worth twice
any teacher's yearly wage. All in all the Illuminated
Academy for Girls was not that shining, radically
new, unprecedented incubator-of-the-future I had
heard so much about around Aimee's dinner tables in New York and London. It was the "Loomy
Academy," as people called it locally, where many
small but interesting things were happening, every
day, which were then argued over and debated
at the end of each week, in the village meetings,
which led to further adaptations and changes,
few of which I sensed Aimee ever knew or heard
about, but to which Fern closely attended, listening to everyone in that strikingly open way of his,
making his reams of notes. It was a functioning
school, built by Aimee's money but not contained
by it, and whatever small part I had played in its
creation, I now felt, like any minor member of the
village, my own portion of pride in it. I was enjoying this warm feeling of achievement, walking

back from the school garden to the headmaster's office, when I spotted Lamin and Hawa under the mango tree, standing too close together, arguing.

"I don't listen to lectures from you," I heard her say, as I approached, and when she spotted me, she turned and repeated the point: "I don't take lectures from him. He wants me to be the last person remaining in this place. No."

Over by the headmaster's office, thirty yards from us, a circle of curious teachers who had just finished lunch stood in the shade of the doorway, washing their hands from a tin kettle filled with water and watching the debate.

"We won't speak now," whispered Lamin, conscious of this audience, but Hawa in full flow was hard to stop.

"You have been gone one month, is it? Do you know how many others have gone from here in this month? Look for Abdulaye. You won't see him. Ahmed and Hakim? My nephew Joseph? He is seventeen. Gone! My Uncle Godfrey—no one has seen him. I have his children now. He is gone! He didn't want to stay and rot here. Back way—all of them."

"Back way is crazy," murmured Lamin, but then attempted to be bold: "**Mashala** are crazy, too."

Hawa took a step toward him: he shrank back into himself. As well as being in love with her, I thought, he is a little afraid of her. I understood that—I was a little afraid of her myself.

"And when I go to teachers' college in September," she said, jabbing a finger into his chest, "will you still be here, Lamin? Or do you have somewhere else to be? Will you still be here?" Lamin looked over at me, a panicked, guilty glance, which Hawa took as confirmation: "No, I did not think so."

A wheedling tone entered Lamin's whisper.

"Why not just go to your father? He got your brother the visa. He could get you the same, if you asked. It is not impossible."

I'd had this thought myself, many times, but had never asked Hawa about it directly—she never seemed to want to speak of her father—and now, seeing her face alive with righteous fury, I was very glad I'd never asked. The circle of teachers burst into chatter like the crowd at a boxing match when a hard punch lands.

"There's no love between me and him, you should know that. He has his new wife, his new life. Some people can be bought, some people can smile in the face of other people they do not love, just to gain advantage. But I am not like you," she said, the pronoun landing somewhere between Lamin and me, as she turned and walked away from us both, her long skirt swishing in the sand.

That afternoon I asked Lamin to come with me to Barra. He said yes but seemed overcome with humiliation. Our cab ride was silent, as was our ferry trip. I needed to change some money, but when we got to the little holes in the wall—where the men sat on high stools behind shutters, counting out huge towers of grubby notes held together by elastic bands—he left me. Lamin had never left me alone anywhere before, not even when I had most wanted him to, and now I discovered how panicked I was by the idea.

"But where will I meet you? Where are you going?"

"I have some errands to run myself, but I will be around, close by, near the ferry. It is fine, just call me. I will be forty minutes."

Before I had a chance to argue he was gone. I didn't believe in his errands: he only wanted to be rid of me for a while. But my money-changing took all of two minutes. I wandered around the market, and then, to avoid people calling out to me, I walked beyond the ferry to an old military fort, once a museum, now abandoned, but you could still climb up its fortifications and see the river and the infuriating way the whole of this town had been built with its back to the water, ignoring the river, in a defensive crouch against it, as if the beautiful view of the opposite bank, of the sea and the leaping dolphins, was offensive somehow or surplus to requirements or simply carried the memory of too much pain. I climbed back down and lingered by the ferry, but I still had twenty minutes so I went to the internet café. It was the usual scene: boy

after boy with his headset on, saying, "I love you"
or "Yes, my baby girl," while on the screens white
women of a certain age waved and blew kisses, almost always British women—judging from their
household interiors—and as I stood at the desk,
about to pay my twenty-five dalasi for fifteen minutes, I could watch them all simultaneously coming out of their glass-brick showers, or eating at
their breakfast bars, or walking around their rock-
eries or lounging in a swing chair in the conserva-
tory, or just sitting on a sofa, watching telly, their
phones or laptops in hand. There was nothing unusual in any of this, I'd seen it many times before,
but this particular afternoon, as I put my money
on the desk, a crazed, babbling man ran into the
place and began weaving in and out of the computers, brandishing a long, carved stick, and the
owner of the café abandoned our transaction to
chase him round the terminals. The lunatic was incredibly beautiful and tall, like a Masai, and barefoot, wearing a traditional dashiki embroidered
with gold thread, though it was torn and dirty,
and on top of his dreaded hair perched a baseball
cap from a Minnesota golf course. He tapped the
young men on their shoulders, once on each side,
like a king performing many knighthoods, until
the owner managed to grab his cane from him and
started beating him with it. And as he was being
beaten, he kept talking, in a comically refined En-

glish accent, it reminded me of Chalky's, from all those years ago. "Good sir, do you not know who I am? Do any of you fools know who I am? You poor, poor fools? Do you not even recognize me?"

I left my money on the counter and headed back out to wait in the sun.

Four

When I got back to London I had dinner with my mother, she'd booked a table at Andrew Edmunds, downstairs—"my treat"—but I felt oppressed by the dark green walls and confused by the surreptitious glances of the other diners, and then she unclenched my right hand from its death grip on a phone and said: "Look at this. Look what she's doing to you. No nails and bleeding fingers." I wondered when my mother started eating in Soho, and why she looked so thin, and where Miriam was. Maybe I would have thought a little more deeply about all of these questions if there had been any space in which to seriously consider them, but that evening my mother was on a talking tear, and most of the meal was taken up with a monologue about London gentrification—addressed as much to the nearby tables as to me—stretching from the usual contemporary complaints back through the years until it became an impromptu history lesson. By the time the main course turned up we'd arrived at the early eighteenth century. The very row of townhouses in which we sat—a backbench

MP and a pop star's personal assistant, eating oysters together—was once the accommodation of joiners and sash makers, bricklayers and carpenters, all of whom had paid a monthly rent which, even when adjusted for inflation, would not presently cover the single oyster I was putting in my mouth. "Working people," she explained, tipping a Loch Ryan down her throat. "Also radicals, Indians, Jews, runaway Caribbean slaves. Pamphleteers and agitators. Robert Wedderburn! The 'Blackbirds.' This was their spot too, right under Westminster's nose . . . Nothing like that happens round here now—sometimes I wish it would. Give us all something to work with! Or toward! Or even against . . ." She reached out to the three-hundred-year-old wood paneling beside her head and gave it a wistful stroke. "The truth is most of my colleagues don't even remember what the real Left **is**, and believe me they don't **want** to remember. Oh, but once upon a time it was a real hotbed around here . . ." She went on in this vein, for a bit too long, as usual, but in thrilling full flow—nearby diners leaned in to catch the scraps of it—and none of it was barbed or directed at me, all her sharp corners had been filed off. The empty oyster shells were taken away. Out of habit I started in on the skin around my cuticles. As long as she is talking about the past, I thought, well then she isn't asking me about the present or the future, when I'll stop working for Aimee or have a baby, and avoiding this two-pronged attack had become my first priority whenever I saw her. But she didn't ask me about Aimee, she didn't ask me about anything. I thought: she's reached the center at last, she's "in power." Yes, even if she likes to characterize herself as a "thorn in the party's side," the fact is she's at the center of things, finally, and this must be the difference. She had now what she'd wanted and most needed all of her life: respect. Maybe it didn't even matter to her any more what I did with my life. She didn't have to take it as a judgment upon her any longer, or on the way she raised me. And though I noticed she wasn't drinking, I chalked this up, too, to my new version of my mother: mature, sober, self-confident, no longer on the back foot, a success on her own terms.

It was this train of thought that left me unprepared for what came next. She stopped talking, rested her head in a hand, and said: "Love, I have to ask for your help with something."

She winced as she said it. I steeled myself against some form of self-dramatization. Terrible to think back now and realize this grimace was most likely a real, involuntary reaction to a genuine physical pain.

"And I wanted to deal with it myself," she was saying, "not to bother you with it, I know you're very busy, but I don't know who else to turn to at this point."

"Yes—well, what is it?"

I was very involved in trimming the fat off a pork chop. When I at last raised my eyes to my mother's face she looked as tired as I'd ever seen her.

"It's your friend—Tracey."

I put down my cutlery.

"Oh, it's ridiculous, really, but I got this e-mail, friendly . . . it came to my surgery. I hadn't seen her in years . . . but I thought: Oh, Tracey! It was about one of her children, the eldest boy—he'd been expelled from school, she felt unfairly, and she wanted my help, you see, and so I replied, and at first it really didn't seem that strange, I get these kinds of letters all the time. But now, you know, I do wonder: was it all just a ploy?"

"Mum, what are you talking about?"

"I did think it was a bit odd, the amount of e-mails she was sending, but . . . well, you know, she doesn't work, that's clear, I don't know if she's ever worked, really, and she's still in that bloody flat . . . That would drive you crazy by itself. She must have a lot of time on her hands—and right away it was a lot of e-mails, two or three a day. It was her opinion the school unfairly expelled black boys. I did make some inquiries, but it seemed in this case, well . . . the school felt they had a strong case and I couldn't take it any further. I wrote to her and she was very angry, and sent some very angry e-mails, and I thought that was the end of it, but—it was the beginning."

She scratched anxiously at the back of her head-wrap, and I noticed the skin at the top of her neck was raw with irritation.

"But Mum, why would you reply to **anything** from Tracey?"—I was holding the sides of the table—"I could have told you she's not stable. I've known that for years!"

"Well, firstly she's my constituent, and I always reply to my constituents. And when I realized she was **your** Tracey—she's changed her name, you know—but her e-mails have become very . . . weird, very peculiar."

"How long has this been going on?"

"About six months."

"Why didn't you tell me about it before!"

"Darling," she said, and shrugged: "When would I have had the chance?"

She had lost so much weight her magnificent head looked vulnerable on its swan-like neck, and this new delicacy, this suggestion of mortal time working on her just as it works on everybody, spoke to me more loudly than any of the old accusations of daughterly neglect ever had. I lay a hand over hers.

"Odd in what way?"

"I really don't want to talk about it in here. I'll send some of the e-mails on to you."

"Mum, don't be so dramatic. You can give me an idea."

"They're quite abusive," she said, tears gathering in her eyes, "and I haven't been feeling very well, and I'm getting a lot of them now, sometimes a dozen in a day, and I know it's stupid but they're upsetting me."

"Why don't you just let Miriam deal with it? She deals with your communications, doesn't she?"

She took her hand back and assumed her backbench face, a tight, sad smile, suitable for combating questions about the health service but unnerving to see over a dinner table.

"Well, you'll find out sooner or later: we've split up. I'm still in the flat on Sidmouth Road. I have to stay in the neighborhood, obviously, and I won't find another deal like that, at least not right away, so I asked her to move out. Of course, it **is** technically her flat, but she was very understanding about it, you know Miriam. Anyway, it's not a big deal, there's no hard feelings, and we've kept it out of the papers. So that's the end of that."

"Oh, Mum . . . I'm sorry. Really."

"Don't be, don't be. Some people can't deal with a woman having a certain amount of power, and that's just how it is. I've seen it before and I'll see it again, I'm sure. Look at Raj!" she said, and it was so long since I'd thought of the Noted Activist by his real name that I realized I'd forgotten it. "Running off with that fool girl as soon as I finished my book! Is it **my** fault he never finished a book?"

No, I assured her, it was not her fault Raj never finished his book, on "coolie" labor in the West Indies—though he had been working on it for two decades—while my mother began and finished her book, on Mary Seacole, in a year and a half. Yes, the Noted Activist had only himself to blame.

"Men are so ridiculous. But it turns out so are women. Anyway, it's a good thing in a way . . . at a certain point I really felt she was trying to interfere in ways that . . . Well, this **obsession** of hers with 'our' business practices in West Africa, human-rights abuses, and so on—I mean, she was encouraging me to ask questions in the House—in areas I'm not really qualified to speak on—and in the end I think what it was really about, in a funny way, was trying to drive a wedge between me and **you** . . ." A less likely motivation for Miriam I could hardly imagine, but I held my tongue. ". . . And I'm getting older and I don't have as much energy as I did, and I really want to be focused on **my** local concerns, **my** constituents. I'm a local representative and that's what I want to do. I haven't got ambitions any further than that. Don't smile, dear, I really don't. Not any more. At one point I said to her, to Miriam—'Look, I've got people walking into my surgery every day from Liberia, from Senegal, from the Gambia, from Côte d'Ivoire! My work **is** global. This is where my work **is**. These people are coming from all over the world to **my constituency**, in these terrible little boats, they're traumatized, they've seen people die right in front of them, and they're coming **here.** That's the universe trying to tell me something. I really feel this is the work I was born to do.' Poor Miriam . . . she means very well, and God knows she's well organized, but she lacks perspective sometimes. She wants to save everybody. And that kind of person does not make the best life partner, for sure, though I will always consider her a very effective administrator." It was impressive—and a bit sad. I wondered if some similarly chilly epigraph existed for me: **She was not the best daughter, but she was a perfectly adequate dinner date.**

"Do you think," asked my mother, "do you think she's unhinged . . . mentally ill or . . ."

"Miriam's one of the sanest people I've ever met."

"No—your friend Tracey."

"I wish you'd stop calling her that!"

But my mother wasn't listening to me, she was in her own dream: "You know, somehow . . . well, she's on my conscience. Miriam thought I should have just gone to the police about the e-mails in the first place but . . . I don't know . . . when you get older, somehow things from the past . . . they can weigh on you. I remember when she used to come for counseling at the center . . . Of course I didn't see her notes, but I got the sense, speaking to the team there, that there were problems, mental-health issues, even back then. Maybe I was wrong to stop her coming in, but it really wasn't easy to get her the placement in the first place, and I'm sorry, but at the time I really and truly felt that she had abused my trust, your trust, everybody's . . . She was still a child, of course, but it **was** a crime—and it was a lot of money—I'm sure it all went to her father—but what if they'd blamed **you**? At that point it was just best to sever all connections, I thought. Well, I'm sure you have lots of judgments about what went on—you always have a lot of judgments—but I wish you would understand that it was not easy raising you, I was not in an easy situation, and on top of everything I was focused on trying to get myself educated, trying to get myself qualified, maybe too much so in your opinion . . . but I had to make a life for you and for me. I knew your father couldn't do it. He wasn't strong enough. No one else was going to do it. We were on our own. And I had a lot of balls in the air, that's how it felt to me, and—" she reached across the table and grabbed my elbow: "We should have done more—to protect her!"

I felt her fingers pinching me, bony in their grip.

"You were lucky, you had this wonderful father. She didn't have that. You don't know how that feels **because** you're lucky, really you were born lucky—but **I** know. And she was a part of our family, practically!"

She was pleading with me. The tears that had been gathering now fell.

"No, Mum . . . no, she wasn't. You're misremembering: you never liked her. Who knows what went on in that family or what she needed protecting from, if anything? No one ever told us—she certainly never did. Every family on that corridor had secrets." I looked at her and thought: do you want to know ours?

"Mum, you just said it yourself: you can't save everybody."

She nodded several times and brought a napkin to her damp cheeks.

"That's true," she said. "Very true. But at the same time, can't you always do more?"

Five

The next morning my British mobile rang, a number I didn't recognize. It wasn't my mother, or Aimee, or either of the fathers of her children, or the three college friends who still hoped, once or twice a year, to lure me out for a drink before my flight departed. I didn't know the voice at first, either: I'd never heard Miriam sound so stern or cold.

"But you understand," she asked me, after a few awkward pleasantries, "that your mother is really ill?"

I lay on Aimee's plush gray couch, looking out over Kensington Gardens—gray slates, blue sky, green oaks—and found, as Miriam explained the situation, that this view merged with an earlier one: gray cement, blue sky, over the tops of the horse chestnuts, past Willesden Lane, toward the railway. In the next room I could hear the nanny, Estelle, trying to discipline Aimee's children, in that lilting accent I connected with my earliest moments, with lullabies and bathtime and bedtime stories, thwacks with a wooden spoon. Headlights of passing cars at night, gliding over the ceiling.

"Hello? Are you still there?"

Stage three: it had begun in her spine. Partially successful surgery, back in February (where was I, in February?). Now she was in remission, but the last bout of chemo had left her frail. She should have been resting, allowing herself to recover. It was crazy that she was still going to the House, crazy that she was going out to dinner, crazy that I had let her.

"How could I know? She didn't tell me."

I heard Miriam kiss her teeth at me.

"Anyone with any sense just needs to look at the woman to know something is wrong!"

I wept. Miriam patiently listened. My instinct was to get off the phone and call my mother, but when I tried to do this Miriam begged me not to.

"She doesn't want you to know. She knows you have to travel and whatnot—she doesn't want to disturb your plans. She'd know I told you. I'm the only person who knows."

I couldn't stand this vision of myself as a person my own mother would rather die than disturb. To avoid it, I cast around for dramatic gestures, and without even knowing whether or not it was possible offered up the services of Aimee's many private doctors in Harley Street. Miriam chucked sadly.

"Private? Don't you know your mother by now? No, if you want to do something for her, I can tell you what would make the most difference right at this moment. This crazy woman bothering her? I don't know why it's obsessing her so much but it needs to stop, it's all she can think about—and that's not right at a time like this. She told me that she spoke to you about it?"

"Yes. She was going to forward me the e-mails but she hasn't."

"I have them, I'll do that."

"Oh, OK . . . I thought—I mean, she said, at dinner, that you two . . ."

"Yes, yes, many months ago. But your mother is someone who will always be in my life. She's not the kind of person who leaves your life once she's in it. Anyway, when someone you care about gets ill, all the other business . . . it just goes."

A few minutes after I put down the phone the e-mails started to arrive, in little flurries, until I had fifty or more. I sat where I was reading them, stunned by the rage. The force of it made me feel inadequate—as if Tracey had more feeling for my mother than I did—even though it was not love expressed here but hate. Stunned, too, by how well she wrote, never boring, not for a second, her dyslexia and many grammatical errors were no hindrance to her: she had the gift of being interesting. You couldn't start reading one without wanting to finish it. Her central accusation against my mother was neglect: of her son's problems at school, of

Tracey's own complaints and e-mails, and of her duty—I mean my mother's—to push forward the interests of her constituents. If I'm honest, the earliest e-mails did not seem to me unreasonable, but then Tracey broadened her scope. Neglect of state schools in the borough, neglect of black children in those schools, of black people in England, of black working-class people in England, of single mothers, of the children of single mothers, and of Tracey the single child of a single mother, all those years ago. It interested me that she wrote "single mother" here, as if her father had never existed at all. The tone became sweary, abusive. In some of the e-mails she sounded drunk or high. Soon it was a one-way correspondence, a systematic dissection of all the many ways Tracey believed my mother had let her down. You never liked me, you never wanted me around, you always tried to humiliate me, I was never good enough for you, you were scared of being associated with me, you always held yourself apart, you pretended you were for the community but you were only ever for yourself, you told everybody I stole that money but you had no proof and you never defended me. There was a whole tranche of letters that referred only to the estate. Nothing was being done to improve the units the council residents lived in, these units were being left to degenerate—almost all of them now in Tracey's block—they hadn't been touched since the early eighties. Meanwhile, the estate across the road—our estate, which the council were now busily selling off—had filled up with young white couples and their babies and looked like a "fucking hotel resort." And what was my mother going to do about the boys selling crack on the corner of Torbay Road? The closure of the swimming pool? The whorehouses on Willesden Lane?

That's how it was: a surreal mix of personal vendetta, painful memory, astute political protest and a local resident's complaints. I noticed that the letters got longer as the weeks passed, starting at a paragraph or two and expanding to thousands and thousands of words. In the most recent some of the fantasies and conspiratorial thinking I remembered from ten years earlier re-emerged, in spirit if not in letter. Lizards made no appearance: now a secret eighteenth-century Bavarian sect had survived its own suppression and was at work in the world today, its members many powerful and famous blacks—in league with elite whites and the Jews—and Tracey was researching all this very deeply and was increasingly convinced that my mother might herself be a tool of these people, minor but dangerous, who had managed to worm her way right into the heart of British government.

Just after midday I read the last e-mail, put my coat on, walked down the road and waited for the 52 bus. I got off at Brondesbury Park, walked the length of Christchurch Avenue, arrived at Tracey's estate, climbed the stairs and rang her bell. She must have been in the hallway already because she opened the door right away, a new baby of four or five months on her hip, its face turned from me. Behind her I could hear more children, arguing, and a TV at high volume. I don't know what I expected, but what was in front of me was an anxious, heavy-set, middle-aged woman in terrycloth pajama bottoms, house slippers and a black sweatshirt that had one word written on it: OBEY. I looked so much younger.

"It's you," she said. She put a protective hand to the back of her baby's head.

"Tracey, we need to talk."

"MUM!" cried a voice from inside. "WHO IS IT?"

"Yeah, well, I'm in the middle of making lunch?"

"My mother is dying," I said—that old childhood habit of exaggeration spontaneously came back to me—"and you've got to stop what you're—"

Just then her two older children stuck their heads round the door to stare at me. The girl looked white, with wavy brown hair and sea-green eyes. The boy had Tracey's coloring and a springy Afro but didn't look especially like her: he must have taken after his father. The baby was far darker than all of us, and when she turned her face toward me I saw she was Tracey's double and incredibly beautiful. But they all were.

"Can I come in?"

She didn't answer. She sighed, pushed the door open with her slippered foot and I followed her in.

"Who are you, who are you, who are you?" the little girl asked me and before she got an answer slipped her hand into mine. I saw, as we walked through the lounge, that I had interrupted a screening of **South Pacific**. This detail moved me, and made it hard to keep in mind the hateful Tracey of the e-mails or the Tracey who had put that letter through my door ten years before. I knew the Tracey who wasted an afternoon on **South Pacific** and I loved that girl.

"You like it?" her daughter asked me, and when I said I did, she pulled my arm till I sat on the settee between her and her older brother, who was playing on a phone. I had marched down Brondesbury Park full of righteous fury, but now it seemed completely possible that I might just sit on this sofa and pass the afternoon watching **South Pacific** with a little girl's hand nestled in mine. I asked her for her name.

"Mariah Mimi Alicia Chantelle!"

"Her name's Jeni," said the boy, without looking up. I thought he looked to be eight, and Jeni five or six.

"And what's your name?" I asked, cringing to hear my mother's voice in me, talking to all children, whatever their age, as if they were barely sentient.

"My name is Bo!" he said, imitating my intonation, making himself laugh—the laugh was pure Tracey—"And what is **your** story, Miss Woman? Are you from the Department of Social Care?"

"No, I'm a . . . friend of your mum's. We grew up together."

"Hmmm, maybe," he said, as if the past were a hypothetical he could take or leave. He reapplied himself to the game he was playing. "Never seen you before, though, so I got my SUSPICIONS."

"This bit is 'Happy Talk'!" said Jeni, delighted, pointing at the screen, and I said, "Yes, but I have to talk to your mummy," although everything in me wanted to stay on the sofa, holding her hot little hand, feeling Bo's knee resting inadvertently against mine.

"OK, but come back straight after you do your talking!"

She was clattering around the kitchen with her baby daughter on her hip and didn't pause when I entered.

"Great kids," I found myself saying, as she piled plates and gathered cutlery. "Sweet—and sharp."

She opened the oven; it almost scraped the opposite wall.

"What you making?"

She forced the door shut again and with her back to me shifted her baby to her opposite side. Everything was the wrong way round: I was the solicitous, apologetic one, she in a place of righteousness.

The flat itself seemed to draw this submissive role out of me. On the stage of Tracey's life I had no other role to play.

"I really need to talk to you," I said again.

She turned round. She had a proper face on, as we used to say, but when we caught each other's eyes we smiled, it was involuntary, a mutual smirk.

"I'm not even laughing, though," she said, reassuming her face, "and if you've come in here just to start one with me you best just leave again 'cos I'm not up for it."

"I came here to ask you to stop harassing my mother."

"Is that what she told you!"

"Tracey, I read your e-mails."

She put the baby over her shoulder and started jiggling it and patting its back over and over.

"Listen, I live in this area," she said, "unlike you. I see what goes on. They can talk it up in Parliament all they like, but I'm on the ground in here, and your mother's meant to be repping these streets. She's on TV every other night, but you see anything different round here? My boy's got a 130 IQ—all right? He's been tested. He's ADHD, his brain goes so fast, and he's **bored every day** in that shithole. Yeah, he gets into trouble. **Because he's bored.** And all these teachers can think to do with him is expel him!"

"Tracey, I don't know anything about that—but you can't just—"

"Oh, stop stressing, make yourself useful. Help me get these plates in."

She handed me them, put the cutlery on top and directed me back to the living room, where I found myself setting the small, round table for her family, just as I had once set teatime for her dolls.

"Luncheon is served!" she said, in what seemed to be an imitation of my voice. Playfully she slapped both the older children round the back of their heads.

"If it's lasagne again I'm gonna start crying on my knees," said Bo, and Tracey said, "It's lasagne," and Bo assumed the position and comically beat the floor with his fists.

"Get up, you joker," said Tracey, and they were all laughing, and I did not know how to continue in my mission.

At the table I sat quietly while they argued and laughed over every little thing, everybody seeming to talk as loudly as possible, swearing freely, and the baby still on Tracey's knee, being bounced up and down while Tracey fed herself one-handed and bantered with the other two, and perhaps this was how their lunch times always were, but I couldn't rid myself of the suspicion that it was also, on Tracey's part, a form of performance, a way of saying: **Look at the fullness of my life. Look at the emptiness of yours.**

"Are you still dancing?" I asked suddenly, interrupting them all. "I mean, professionally?"

The table went quiet and Tracey turned to me.

"Do I **look** like I'm still dancing?" She looked down at herself and around the table and laughed harshly. "I know I was the smart one but . . . get a fucking clue."

"I—I never told you, Trace, but I saw you in **Showboat.**"

She did not look remotely surprised. I wondered whether she had spotted me at the time.

"Yeah, well, that's all ancient history. Mum got ill, there was no one to look after the kids . . . it got too hard. I've had some health issues myself. Wasn't for me."

"What about their dad?"

"What about their dad what?"

"Why can't he look after them?" I was pointedly using the singular, but Tracey—always alert to euphemism or hypocrisy—was not fooled by it.

"Well, as you can see, I tried vanilla, café au lait and chocolate, and you know what I figured out? On the inside, they're all the fucking same: men."

I was rattled by her language, but the kids—their chairs turned toward **South Pacific**—did not seem to notice or care.

"Maybe the problem is the kind of men you choose."

Tracey rolled her eyes: "Thank you, Dr. Freud! Hadn't thought of that! Any other pearls of wisdom for me?"

I kept quiet and ate my lasagne, still partially

frozen in the middle, but delicious. It reminded me of her mother and I asked how she was.

"She died, a couple of months ago. Didn't she, princess? She died."

"Nanna died. She went to the angels!"

"Yeah. Just us now. We're OK, though. These fucking social workers keep bothering us, but we're all right. Four musketeers."

"We burned Nanna in a big fire!"

Bo turned round: "You're such a idiot—we didn't just burn her, did we? Like we just put her on a bonfire or something! She was cre-ma-ted. It's better than getting stuck in the ground, in some closed-up box. No thank you. That's how I want mine, too. Nanna was like me, 'cos she hated closed-up spaces. She was claus-tro-phobic. That's why she always took the stairs."

Tracey smiled fondly at Bo and reached out for him, which he ducked and avoided.

"She got to see the kids, though," she murmured, almost to herself. "Even little Bella. So I feel good about that bit."

She brought Bella up to her lips and kissed her all over her nose. Then looked over to me and gestured toward my womb: "What you waiting for?"

I stuck my nose in the air, realizing too late that it was a borrowed gesture—one I'd been using for years in moments of pride or adamancy—and that it properly belonged to the woman sitting opposite me.

"The right situation," I said. "The right time."

She smiled, the old cruelty in her face: "Oh, OK. Good luck with that. Funny, innit," she said, exaggerating her accent for effect, and turning to the television, not me: "Rich birds with no kids, poor birds with plenty. Sure your mum would have a lot to say about that."

The kids finished eating. I picked up their plates and took them to the kitchen and sat there for a minute on the high stool, breathing in and out mindfully—as Aimee's yoga teacher had shown us all how to do—and looking out through the strip of window into the parking bays. There were answers I wanted from her, going a long way back. I was trying to work out how to re-enter the living room in a way that would reset the afternoon in my favor, but before I figured it out Traccy walked in and said: "Thing is, what's between me and your mum is between me and your mum. I don't even know why you've come round here, honestly."

"I'm just trying to understand why you would—"

"Yeah, but that's the thing! There can't be no understanding between you and me any more! You're part of a different system now. People like you think you can control everything. But you can't control me!"

"People like me? What are you **talking** about? Trace, you're a grown woman now, you've got three beautiful kids, you really need to get a grip on this kind of delusional—"

"You can call it by any fancy name you like, love: there's a system, and you and your fucking mother are both a part of it."

I stood up.

"Stop harassing my family, Tracey," I said, as I walked purposefully out of the kitchen, pursued by Tracey, through the living room toward the front door. "If it carries on, the police will be involved."

"Yeah, yeah, keep walking, keep walking," she said and slammed the door behind me.

Six

In early December Aimee returned to check on the progress of her academy, traveling with a smaller group—Granger, Judy, her ditzy e-mail proxy, Mary-Beth, Fern and me—without press and with a specific agenda: she wanted to propose a sexual-health clinic within the grounds of the school itself. Nobody disagreed in principle but it was also very difficult to see how it could possibly be referred to publicly as a sexual-health clinic or how Fern's discreet reports of the sexual vulnerability of the local girls—which he had gathered slowly, and with a great deal of trust, from a few of the female teachers, who had taken great risks themselves in speaking to him—could be brought out into the light of the village without causing interpersonal chaos and offense and perhaps the end of our whole project. On the flight over we discussed it. I tried, stumblingly, to speak to Aimee about the need for delicacy, and what I knew of the local context, thinking, in my mind, of Hawa, while Fern, more eloquently, discussed an earlier German medical NGO's interventions in a nearby

Mandinka village, where female circumcision was practiced by all, and the German nurses had found oblique approaches won traction where more direct condemnations failed. Aimee frowned at these comparisons and then took up again where she had left off: "Look, it happened to me in Bendigo, it happened to me in New York, it happens everywhere. It's not about your 'local context'—this is **everywhere**. I had a big family, cousins and uncles coming and going—I know what goes on. And I'll bet you a million dollars you go into any classroom of thirty girls anywhere in this world and there's going to be one at least who has a secret she can't tell. I remember. I had nowhere to go. I want these girls to have somewhere to go!"

Beside her own passion and commitment our qualifications and concerns looked petty and narrow, but we managed to wear her down to the word "clinic," and an emphasis—at least when discussing the clinic with local mothers—on menstrual health, which was its own complication for many girls without the means to pay for sanitary products. But personally I didn't think Aimee was wrong: I remembered my own classrooms, dance classes, playgrounds, youth groups, birthday parties, hen nights, I remember there was always a girl with a secret, with something furtive and broken in her, and walking through the village with Aimee, entering people's homes, shaking their hands, accepting their food and drink, being hugged by their children, I often thought I saw her again, this girl who lives everywhere and at all times in history, who is sweeping the yard or pouring out tea or carrying somebody else's baby on her hip and looking over at you with a secret she can't tell.

It was a difficult first day. We were glad to be back and there was unexpected pleasure in touring a village no longer so strange or alien to us, seeing familiar faces—in Fern's case, people who had become intimate friends—and yet we were all also on edge because we knew that Aimee, though she attended to her duties, and smiled in the photographs Granger was tasked with taking, had a mind full of Lamin. Every few minutes she glared at Mary-Beth, who tried to call again but got only voicemail. In some compounds connected to Lamin through blood or friendship we asked for him but nobody seemed to know where he was, they'd seen him yesterday or earlier in the morning, perhaps he'd gone to Barra or Banjul, perhaps to Senegal to see family. By late afternoon Aimee was struggling to hide her irritation. We were meant to be asking people how they felt about the changes in the village, and what more they wanted to see, but Aimee glazed over if people spoke to her for any length of time and we began moving in and out of compounds with too much speed, causing offense. I wanted to linger: I wondered whether this would be our last visit and I felt some urgency to retain everything I saw, to imprint the village in memory, its unbroken light, the greens and the yellows, those white birds with their blood-red beaks, and the people, my people. But somewhere in these streets a young man was hiding from Aimee, a humiliating feeling, and a new one for her, she who had always been the person others ran toward. To avoid reflecting on this, I could see, she was determined to keep moving, and as much as her purposes frustrated my own, I still felt sorry for her. I was twelve years behind her but I, too, felt my age among all those scandalously young girls whom we met in every compound, too beautiful, confronting us both, that hot afternoon, with the one thing no amount of power or money can return to you once it's gone.

Just before sunset we moved to the very east end of the village, on the border of where it stopped being the village and became the bush once more. There were no compounds here, only corrugated-iron huts, and it was in one of these we met the baby. All very tired, extremely hot, we didn't notice at first that there was anyone else in the small space other than the woman whose hand Aimee was presently shaking, but as I stepped round to make space for Granger to get inside and out of the sun, I saw a baby laid out on a cloth on the floor, with another girl of about nine, at the baby's side, stroking the infant's face. We had seen many babies of course but none as young as this:

it was three days old. The woman wrapped her up and passed the tiny package to Aimee, who accepted it into her arms and stood there staring at it, without making any of the usual comments people feel they should make when holding a newborn. Granger and I, feeling awkward, came close and made these comments ourselves: girl or boy, how beautiful, what smallness, such eyes, such lovely thick black tufts of hair. I was saying these things automatically—I'd said them many times before—until I looked at her. Her eyes were huge, wonderfully lashed, black and purple, unfocused. No matter how I tried to get her to look at me she wouldn't. She was a little God refusing me grace, though I was on my knees. Aimee held the baby tighter, turned from me, and placed her own nose on the child's bud-lips. Granger went outside to get some air. I moved close again to Aimee and craned over the baby. Time passed. The two of us, side by side, unpleasantly close, sweating on each other, but both unwilling to risk moving from the baby's sightline. The mother was speaking, but I don't think either of us really heard her. At last Aimee, very reluctantly, turned and placed the baby in my arms. It's a chemical thing, maybe, like the dopamine that floods through people in love. For me it was a drowning. I have never experienced anything like it before or since.

"You like her? You like her?" said a jovial man,

who had appeared from somewhere. "Take her to London! Ha ha! You like her?"

Somehow I passed her back to her mother. At the same time, in some place of alternative futures, I ran straight out of there with the baby in my arms, hailed a taxi to the airport, and flew home.

When the sun fell and nothing more could be done in the way of visiting, we decided to end the day and convene the next morning for the school tour and a village meeting. Aimee and the rest followed Fern to the pink house. I, curious about what had changed since my last visit, headed to Hawa's. In the absolute darkness I made my way very slowly toward what I thought was the main crossing, reaching out for tree trunks like a blind person, and astonished at every turn by the many adults and children I felt passing by me, who walked quickly and efficiently, without torches, to wherever it was they were going. I made it to the crossing and was steps from Hawa's door when Lamin appeared beside me. I hugged him and told him Aimee had been looking for him everywhere and expected to see him tomorrow.

"I am just here. I have not been anywhere."

"Well, I'm going to see Hawa—will you come?"

"You won't find her. She went two days ago to get married. She is back to visit tomorrow, she would like to see you."

I wanted to commiserate, but there was no right phrase.

"You must come to the school tour tomorrow," I repeated. "Aimee looked for you all day."

He kicked at a stone in the ground.

"Aimee is a very nice lady, she is helping me and I am thankful, but—" He stopped at the line, like a man fluffing a long jump, but then suddenly jumped anyway: "She is an old woman! I am a young man. And a young man wants to have children!"

We stood outside Hawa's door, looking at each other. We were so close, I felt his breath on my neck. I think I knew then that it would happen between us, that night, or the next, and that it would be a commiseration offered with the body, in the absence of any clearer or more articulate solution. We didn't kiss, not in that moment, he didn't even reach for my hand. There was no need. We both understood that it was already decided.

"Well, come in," he said finally, opening Hawa's door as if it were that to his own home. "You are here, it is late. You will eat here."

Standing on the verandah looking out, in more or less exactly the same spot I had last seen him, was Hawa's brother Babu. We greeted each other very warmly: like everyone I met he considered the fact that I had chosen to return once again as some kind of virtue in itself, or he pretended to find it so. To Lamin he gave only a nod, whether through familiarity or frostiness I couldn't tell. But when I asked about Hawa his face definitively fell.

"I was there yesterday for the marriage, the only witness. For myself, I don't care if there are singers or dresses or platters of food—none of it matters to me. But my grandmothers! Oh, she has started a war in this place! I will have to listen to women complaining until the end of my days!"

"Do you think she's happy?"

He smiled as if I had been caught out somehow.

"Ah, yes—for Americans this is always the most important question!"

Dinner was brought to us, a feast really, and we ate outside, with the grandmothers forming a talkative circle at the other end of the verandah, looking over at us occasionally, but too busy with their own discussion to pay us much mind. We had a solar lamp at our feet that lit us from below: I could see my food and the lower parts of Lamin and Hawa's brother's faces, and then beyond there were the usual busy noises of domestic work and children laughing, crying, shouting, and people walking from the various outhouses back and forth across the yard. What you didn't hear were men's voices, but now I heard some very close at hand, and Lamin stood up suddenly and pointed at the compound wall, where, either side of the doorway, half a dozen men now sat, their legs facing toward the road. Lamin took a step toward them but

Hawa's brother caught him by the shoulder and sat him back down, approaching instead himself, with two of his grandmothers at his side. I saw one of the young men was smoking and now flicked his cigarette over into our yard, but when Hawa's brother reached them it turned out to be a quick conversation: he said something, one boy laughed, a grandmother said something, he spoke again, more firmly, and six backsides slipped out of view. The grandmother who had spoken opened the door and watched them walk on, down the road. The moon came out from a cover of clouds and from where I stood I could see at least one of them had a gun on his back.

"They are not from here, they are from the other end of the country," said Hawa's brother, rejoining me. He still wore his bloodless conference-room smile, but behind his designer glasses I could see in his eyes how shaken he was. "We see it more and more. They hear the President wants to rule for a billion years. They are running out of patience. They begin listening to other voices. Foreign voices. Or the voice of God, if you believe this can be bought on a Casio tape for twenty-five dalasi in the market. Yes, they are out of patience and I do not blame them. Even our calm Lamin, our patient Lamin—he, too, has run out of patience."

Lamin reached out for a slice of white bread but did not speak.

"And when do you leave?" asked Babu, of Lamin,

his tone so full of judgment, of blame, that I assumed he referred to the back way, but they both chuckled at the panic that must have passed over my face: "No, no, no, he will have his official papers. It is all being arranged, thanks to you people who are here. We are already losing all our brightest young men, and now you take another. It is sad but this is the way things are."

"You left," said Lamin sullenly. He pulled a fishbone from his mouth.

"That was a different time. I was not needed here."

"I am not needed here."

Babu did not answer and his sister was not there to fill up the spaces between us with chatter. When we had finished our quiet meal I preempted those many child-maids, gathered the plates together and walked in the direction I'd seen those girls go, toward the last room in the block, which turned out to be a bedroom. I stood in the dim light, unsure what to do next, when one of the half a dozen sleeping children in there raised his head from their single bed, saw the load in my arms and pointed me through a curtain. I found myself outside, in the yard again, but this was the back yard, and here were the grandmothers and some of the older girls, crouched around several tubs of water in which clothes were being washed with large bars of gray soap. A circle of solar lamps illuminated the scene. As I came upon them work paused to observe some live animal theater: a cockerel chasing a hen, overpowering her, putting his claw to her neck, driving her head into the dust, finally mounting her. This operation took only a minute, but throughout the hen looked bored, impatient to get on with her other tasks, so that the cockerel's brutal sense of his power over her seemed somehow comic. "Big man! Big man!" cried one of the grandmothers, spotting me, pointing at the cockerel. The women laughed, the hen was released: she wandered around in a circle, once, twice, three times, apparently dazed, before returning to the henhouse and her sisters and her chicks. I put the plates where I was told to, on the ground, and came back to find that Lamin had already left. I understood it was a signal. I announced that I, too, was going to bed, but instead lay in my room in my clothes, waiting for the last sounds of human activity to fade. Just before midnight I took my headtorch, made my way quietly through the yard, out of the compound and through the village.

Aimee had thought of this visit as a "fact-finding trip," but the village committee considered everything a reason for celebration, and the next day, as we finished the school tour and entered the yard we found a drum circle awaiting us under the mango tree, twelve late-middle-aged women with drums between their thighs. Even Fern hadn't been warned, and Aimee was agitated at this new delay to the schedule, but there was no way to avoid it: this was an ambush. The children streamed out and formed a second, huge circle around their drumming mothers, and we, "the Americans," were asked to sit in the innermost circle on little chairs taken from the classrooms. The teachers went to get these, and among them, approaching from the very other end of the school, over by Lamin's maths class, I spotted Lamin and Hawa walking together, carrying four little chairs each. But I did not, when I saw him, feel in any way self-conscious, nor was I ashamed: the events of the night before were so separated from my daytime life that it felt to me that they had happened to someone else, a shadow body who pursued separate aims and could not be forced into the light. I waved to them both—they showed no sign of seeing me. The drumming started. I couldn't shout over it. I turned back toward the circle and took the seat offered to me, next to Aimee. The women began taking turns in the circle, laying their drum aside to dance in dramatic three-minute bursts, a kind of anti-performance, for despite the brilliance of their footwork, the genius in their hips, they did not turn outwards to their audience but instead remained facing their drumming sisters, their backs to us. As the second woman started, Hawa entered the circle and took the seat next to me that I'd been saving for her, but Lamin only nodded at Aimee before sitting himself on the other side of the circle, as far from her, and I suppose from me, as he could manage. I squeezed Hawa's hand and offered my congratulations.

"I am very happy. It was not easy for me to be here today but I wanted to see you!"

"Is Bakary with you?"

"No! He thinks I am buying fish in Barra! He does not like dancing like this," she said and moved her feet a little in echo of the woman stamping away a few yards from us. "But of course I won't dance myself so no harm is done."

I squeezed her hand again. There was something wonderful about being near her, she cut every situation to her own dimension, believed she could adapt anything until it suited, even as flexibility fell out of fashion. At the same time a paternalistic—or perhaps I should write here "maternalistic"—impulse surged through me: I kept hold of her hand, too tightly, in the hope, the irrational hope, that it would—like some cheap charm bought off a **marabout**—confer protection, keep her safe from evil spirits, whose existence in the world I no longer doubted. But when she turned and saw the creases in my forehead, she laughed at me and freed herself, clapping to welcome the arrival of Granger into the circle, who moved round it as if it were a break-dancer's ring, showing off his heavy-footed moves, to the delight of the drumming mothers. After a suitable minute of reticence, Aimee joined him. To avoid watching her, I looked around the circle at all the adamant, inflexible love, sadly misdirected. I could feel Fern to my right, staring at me. I watched Lamin look up every now and then, his glances directed only at Hawa, her perfect face wrapped up tightly like a present. But in the end I could not evade the image of Aimee, dancing for Lamin, at Lamin, to Lamin. Like someone dancing for a rain that will not fall.

Eight drumming women later, even Mary-Beth had attempted a dance and it was my turn. I had a mother pulling each arm, dragging me up. Aimee had extemporized, Granger had historicized—moonwalk, the robot, the running man—but I still had no ideas about dance, only instincts. I watched them for a minute, the two women, as they danced at me, teasing me, and I listened carefully to the multiple beats, and knew that what they were doing I, too, could do. I stood between them and matched them step for step. The kids went crazy. There were so many voices screaming at me I stopped being able to hear the drums, and the only way I could carry on was to respond to the movements of the women themselves, who never lost the beat, who heard it through everything. Five minutes later I was done and more tired than if I'd run six miles.

I collapsed next to Hawa, and from some fold of her new hijab she produced a small piece of material with which I wiped some of the sweat from my face.

"Why are they saying 'too bad'? Was I that bad?"

"No! You were so great! They are saying: **Toobab**—this means—" She traced her hand across the skin of my cheek. "So they are saying: 'Even though you are a white girl, you dance like you are a black!' I say it's true: you and Aimee, both of you—you really dance like you are blacks. It is a big compliment, I would say. I never would have guessed this about you! My, my, you even dance as well as Granger!"

Aimee, overhearing, burst out laughing.

Seven

Some days before Christmas, I was sitting in the London house, at the desk in Aimee's study, finalizing the list for the New Year Party, when I heard Estelle, somewhere upstairs, she was saying: "Dere, dere." It was a Sunday, the second-floor office was closed. The children had not yet returned from their new boarding school and Judy and Aimee were in Iceland, for two nights, doing promotion. I had not seen or heard of Estelle since the children left and had presumed—if I even thought of her at all—that her services were no longer required. Now I heard that familiar lilt: "Dere, dere." I ran up a floor and found her in Kara's old room, in what we used to call the nursery. She stood by the sash windows, looking out on to the park, in her comfy crocs and a black sweater embroidered with gold thread, like tinsel, and a pair of sensible pleated navy trousers. Her back was to me, but when she heard my tread, she turned round, a swaddled baby in her arms. It was so tightly wrapped it looked unreal, like a prop. I approached quickly, reaching out—"You cyan just come up and touch the baby!

Your hands got to be clean!"—and it took a great deal of self-control to take a step away from them both and put my hands behind my back.

"Estelle, whose baby is that?"

The baby yawned. Estelle looked down at it adoringly.

"Adopted tree weeks ago, I believe. You didn't know? Seem to me everybody know! But she just arrive here last night. Her name is Sankofa—don't arks me what kind of name is that because I could not tell you. Why anybody wan give a lovely little baby like this a name like that I must say I don't know. I'm going to call her Sandra until somebody make me stop."

The same purple, dark, unfocused gaze, sliding off me, fascinated by itself. I could hear in Estelle's voice the delight she already took in the child—far more, it seemed to me, than she had ever taken in Jay and Kara, whom she had practically raised—and I tried to focus on the tale of this "lucky, lucky little girl" in her arms, rescued from the "back of beyond," placed "in the lap of luxury." Better not to wonder how it had possibly been managed: an international adoption in less than a month. I reached out again. My hands were shaking.

"If you wan hol' her so bad, I'm about to wash her right now: come upstairs with me, you can clean your hands."

We went to Aimee's gigantic en suite, which had at some point been quietly made ready for a baby:

a set of towels with rabbit ears, baby powders and oils, baby sponges and baby soaps, and half a dozen multicolored plastic ducks lined up along the edge of the bath.

"All this nonsense!" Estelle crouched to examine a kooky little device made of terrycloth with a metal frame that hooked to the side of the bath and looked like a sun-chair for a tiny old man. "All this equipment. Only way to wash a baby this small is in the sink."

I knelt next to Estelle and helped unwrap the tiny package. Froggy limbs splayed, astonished.

"The shock," explained Estelle, as the baby wailed. "She was warm and tight and now she's cold and loose."

I stood by as she lowered Sankofa, outraged and screaming, into a seven-thousand-pound hunk of Victorian porcelain I remembered ordering.

"Dere, dere," said Estelle, wiping a cloth in the child's many wrinkled crevices. After a minute or so she cupped Sankofa's tiny backside in her hand, kissed her on her still-screaming face and told me to lay the swaddling blanket out in a triangle on the heated floor. I sat back on my heels and watched Estelle rub coconut butter all over the baby. To me, who had never so much as held a baby for more than a passing moment, the whole procedure looked masterful.

"Do you have children, Estelle?"

Eighteen, sixteen and fifteen—but her hands were greasy so she directed me to her back pocket and I drew out her phone. I swiped right. Saw, for a moment, the uncluttered image of a tall young man in a high-school graduate's robe, flanked on both sides by his smiling younger sisters. She told me their names and special talents, their heights and temperaments, and how often or not each one Skyped or replied to her on Facebook. Not often enough. In the ten or so years we had both worked for Aimee, this was the longest and most intimate conversation we'd ever had.

"My mudder take care of dem for me. They go to the very best school in Kingston. Next thing he'll be heading to the University of the West Indies for engineering. He's a wonderful young man. The girls they take him like a model. He's the star. They look up to him so much."

"I'm Jamaican," I said, and Estelle nodded and smiled blandly at the baby. I had seen her do this many times, when gently humoring the children, or Aimee herself. Blushing, I corrected myself.

"I mean, my mother's people are from St. Catherine."

"Oh, yes. I see. You ever been dere?"

"No. Not yet."

"Well, you're still young." She wrapped the child back up in its cocoon and held it to her breast. "Time's on your side."

*   *   *

Christmas came. The baby was presented to me, to all of us, as a fait accompli, a legal adoption, suggested and agreed upon by the parents, and nobody questioned this, or not out loud. No one asked what "agreement" could even mean in a situation of such deep imbalance. Aimee was in the throes of baby love, everyone else seemed happy for her—it was her Christmas miracle. All I had were suspicions and the fact that the whole process had been hidden from me until it was already over.

A few months later I went back to the village for the final time, making inquiries as best I could. Nobody would speak to me about it, or offer anything but happy platitudes. The birth parents were no longer living locally, no one seemed to know exactly where they had moved. If Fernando knew something about it, he wasn't going to tell me, and Hawa had moved to Serrekunda with her Bakary. Lamin moped around the village, he was in mourning for her—maybe I was, too. Evenings in the compound, without Hawa, were long, dark, lonely and conducted entirely in languages I didn't know. But though I told myself, as I headed out to Lamin's place—five or six times in all, and always late in the night—that we two were acting on an uncontrollable physical desire, I think we both knew perfectly well that whatever passion existed between us was directed through the other person toward something else, toward Hawa, or toward

the idea of being loved, or simply to prove to ourselves our own mutual independence from Aimee.
She was really the person we were aiming at with
all our loveless fucking, as much a part of the process as if she were in the room.

Creeping back from Lamin's to Hawa's compound, very early one morning, just before five,
as the sun came up, I heard the call to prayer
and knew I was already too late to pass unwitnessed—a woman pulling a recalcitrant donkey, a
group of children waving from a doorway—and
so changed direction, to make it look as if I were
out for a walk for no particular reason, as everyone
knew the Americans sometimes did. Circling back
round the mosque, I saw Fernando right in front
of me, leaning against the next tree, smoking. I'd
never seen him smoke before. I tried smiling casually in greeting but he fell in step with me and
grabbed me painfully by the arm. He had beer on
his breath. He looked like he hadn't slept at all.

"What are you doing? Why do you do these
things?"

"Fern, are you **following** me?"

He didn't answer until we were the other side
of the mosque, by the huge termite hill, where we
stopped, obscured from view on three sides. He let
go of me and started speaking as if we had been in
the middle of a long discussion.

"And I have some good news for you: thanks to
me, he will be with you very soon on a permanent

basis, yes, thanks to me. I am going to the embassy today in fact. I am working very hard behind the scenes to unite the young and not-so-young lovers. All three of them."

I began a denial but there was no point. Fern was always very hard to lie to.

"It must be a truly strong feeling you have for him, to risk so much. So much. Last time you were here, you know, I suspected it, and the time before—but somehow it is still a shock, to have it confirmed."

"But I don't have **any** feelings for him!"

All the fight went out of his face.

"You imagine this makes me feel better?"

Finally, shame. A suspicious emotion, so ancient. We were always advising the girls in the academy not to feel it, because it was antiquated and unhelpful and led to practices of which we didn't approve. But I felt it at last.

"Please don't say anything. Please. I'm leaving tomorrow and that's it. It just started and it's already over. Please, Fern—you have to help me."

"I tried," he said, and walked off, in the direction of the school.

The rest of the day was torture, and the next, and the flight was torture, the walk through the airport, with my phone a grenade in my back pocket. It didn't go off. When I walked into the London house everything was as before, only happier. The children were well settled—at least, we didn't hear from them—the last album was well received. Photographs of Lamin and Aimee together, both looking beautiful—back at Jay's birthday, from the concert—were in all the gossip rags and were more successful, in their way, than the album itself. And the baby had its debut. The world was not especially curious about logistics, as it turned out, and the papers considered her delightful. It seemed logical to everyone that Aimee should be able to procure a baby as easily as she might order a limited-edition handbag from Japan. Sitting in Aimee's trailer one day during a video shoot, eating lunch with Mary-Beth, personal assistant number two, I tentatively introduced the topic, hoping to wheedle some information out of her, but I needn't have been so careful, Mary-Beth was more than happy to tell me, I got the whole story, a contract had been drawn up by one of the entertainment lawyers, a few days after Aimee met the baby, and Mary-Beth had been there to see it signed. She was delighted at this evidence of her own importance and what it suggested about my position in the hierarchy. She took out her phone and flipped through the pictures of Sankofa, her parents and Aimee smiling together, and in among them, I noticed, was a screenshot of the contract itself. When she went to the bathroom and left her phone in front of me I e-mailed the screenshot to myself. A two-page document. A monumental amount of money, in local terms. We spent about the same on household flowers in a year. When I brought this fact to Granger, my last ally, he surprised me by considering it a noble case of "putting your money where your mouth is," and spoke so tenderly about the baby that everything I had to say sounded monstrous and unfeeling in comparison. I saw that rational conversation wasn't possible. The baby cast a spell. Granger was just as much in love with Kofi, as we called her, as everybody else who came near her, and God knows she was easy to love, nobody was immune, certainly not me. Aimee was besotted: she could spend an hour or two just sitting with the child on her knee, staring down at her, without doing anything else, and knowing Aimee's relationship with time, its value and scarcity to her, we all understood what a mighty measure of love this represented. The baby redeemed all kinds of deadening situations—long meetings with the accountants, tedious dress fittings, PR-strategy brainstorm sessions—she changed the color of a day simply by means of her presence in the corner of whichever room, on the knee of Estelle or rocking in a Moses basket on a stand, chuckling, gurgling, crying, untarnished, fresh and new. The first chance we got we'd all crowd around her. Men and women, of all ages and races, but all of us with a certain amount of time racked up in Aimee's team, from worn old battle-horses like Judy, to middle-rankers like me, to young kids straight out of college. We all worshipped at the altar of the baby. The baby was starting from the beginning, the baby was uncompromised, the baby wasn't hustling, the baby needn't fake Aimee's signature on four thousand headshots heading for South Korea, the baby didn't have to generate meaning out of the broken shards of this and that, the baby was not nostalgic, the baby had no memories and no regrets, it did not need a chemical skin peel, it did not have a phone, it had no one to e-mail, truly time was on its side. Whatever happened afterward, it wasn't out of any lack of love for the baby. The baby was surrounded by love. It's a question of what love gives you the right to do.

Eight

In that last month of working for Aimee—just before she fired me, in fact—we did a mini-European tour, starting with a show in Berlin, not a concert, a show of her photographs. These were photos of photos, images appropriated and rephotographed; she had taken the idea from Richard Prince—an old friend from the old days—and added nothing to it except the fact that she, Aimee, was doing it. Still, one of the most respected galleries in Berlin was more than happy to host her "work." All the photos were of dancers—she thought of herself first and foremost as a dancer and identified deeply with them—but I did all the research and it was Judy who had taken most of the photos, as whenever the time came to go to the studio and rephotograph the photographs there was always something else that had to be done: meet-and-greets in Tokyo, the "designing" of a new perfume, sometimes even the recording of an actual song. We rephotographed Baryshnikov and Nureyev, Pavlova, Fred Astaire, Isadora Duncan, Gregory Hines, Martha Graham, Savion Glover, Michael Jackson. I argued for

Jackson. Aimee didn't want him, he wasn't her idea
of an artist, but catching her in a harried moment
I managed to convince her, while Judy lobbied for
"a woman of color." She was worried about under-
representation, she often was, which meant really
that she was worried about what others might per-
ceive as an under-representation, and whenever we
had these conversations I had the eerie sensation of
viewing myself as really being one of these things,
not a person at all but a sort of object—without
which a certain mathematical series of other objects is not complete—or not even an object but a
kind of conceptual veil, a moral fig-leaf, protecting such-and-such a person from such-and-such a
critique, and rarely thought of except when in this
role. It didn't offend me, especially: I was interested in the experience, it was like being fictional.
I thought of Jeni LeGon.

I got my chance during a car ride over the border between Luxembourg—where Aimee had
gone to do a little press—and Germany. I took out
my phone and googled LeGon and Aimee looked
over the images distractedly—she was texting simultaneously on her own phone—while I talked
as quickly as I could of LeGon as person, actress,
dancer, symbol, trying to keep a hold of her wavering attention, and suddenly she nodded decisively
at a picture of LeGon and Bojangles together, of
LeGon standing, dancing, in a pose of kinetic joy,
and Bojangles kneeling at her feet, pointing at her,

and she said, "Yes, that one, I like it, yes, I like the reversal, man on his knees, woman in control." Once I had that "yes," I could at least start on the research for what would appear as text in the catalog, and a few days later Judy took the photo, slightly at an angle, missing parts of the frame, for Aimee had asked that they all be rephotographed this way, as if "the photographer was dancing herself." As far as these things go, it was the most successful piece in the show. And I was glad of the chance to rediscover LeGon. Researching her, often alone, often late at night, in a series of European hotel rooms, I realized how much I had fantasized about her as a child, how fundamentally naïve I had been about almost every aspect of her life. I'd imagined, for example, a whole narrative of friendship and respect between LeGon and the people she worked with, the dancers and the directors, or I'd wanted to believe that friendship and respect could have existed, in the same spirit of childish optimism that makes a little girl want to believe her parents are deeply in love. But Astaire never spoke to LeGon on set, in his mind she not only played a maid, she was in actuality little different from the help, and it was the same with most of the directors, they didn't really see her and rarely hired her, not for anything except maid parts, and soon enough even these roles dried up, and not until she got to France did she begin to "feel like a person." When I learned all of this I was in Paris myself, sitting in

the sunshine, in front of the Odéon theater, trying to read the information off the sun-blanched
screen of my phone, drinking a Campari, checking
the time compulsively. I watched the twelve hours
Aimee had allotted for Paris disappearing, minute
by minute, almost faster than I could experience
them, and soon the cab would come, and then an
airstrip would fall away beneath me, and onwards
we would go, to another twelve hours in another
beautiful, unknowable city—Madrid. I thought of
all the singers and dancers and trumpet players and
sculptors and scribblers who had claimed to feel
like people, finally, here, in Paris, no longer shadows but people in their own right, an effect that
possibly required more than twelve hours to take
effect, and I wondered how these people were able
to tell, so precisely, the moment that they began to
feel like a person. The umbrella I sat under gave
no shade, the ice had melted in my drink. My own
shadow was huge and knife-like under the table.
It seemed to stretch halfway across the square and
to point at the stately white house on the corner,
which took up most of the block and outside of
which a guide at that moment held up a little flag
and began announcing a series of names, some
known to me, some new: Thomas Paine, E. M.
Cioran, Camille Desmoulins, Sylvia Beach . . .
A small circle of elderly American tourists stood
around, nodding, sweating. I looked back at my
phone. And so it was in Paris—I tapped this sen-

tence out with my thumb—that LeGon began to feel like a person. Which meant—I did not write this part down—that the person Tracey had imitated so perfectly all those years ago, the girl we'd watch dance with Eddie Cantor, kicking her legs, shaking her head—that was not really a person at all, that was only a shadow. Even her lovely name, which we'd both so envied, even that was unreal, in reality she was the daughter of Hector and Harriet Ligon, migrated from Georgia, descendants of sharecroppers, while the other LeGon, the one we thought we knew—that happy-go-lucky hoofer—she was a fictional being, born of a typo, whom Louella Parsons dreamed up one day when she misspelled "Ligon" in her syndicated gossip column in the **LA Examiner**.

Nine

The grenade went off finally on Labor Day. We were in New York, a few days away from leaving for London, with a plan to meet Lamin there, his British visa finalized. It was foully hot: the rancid sewer air could prompt a smile between two strangers in the street as they passed each other: **can you believe we live here?** It was like bile, and it was the scent of Mulberry Street that afternoon. I had my hand to my mouth as I walked, a prophetic gesture: by the time I reached the corner of Broome I'd been fired. It was Judy who sent the text—and the dozen like it that followed—all of which were as stuffed with personal invective as they would have been had Aimee written them herself. I was a whore and a traitor, a fucking this and a fucking that. Even Aimee's personal outrage could be outsourced to a secondary party.

A little light-headed, woozy, I got as far as Crosby and sat down on the front step of Housing Works, on the vintage-clothes side. Every question sprouted more questions: where will I live and what will I do and where are my books and where are my clothes and what is my visa status? I wasn't so much angry with Fern as annoyed at myself for not better predicting the timing. I should have been waiting for it: didn't I know exactly how he was feeling? I could reconstruct his experience. Working on Lamin's visa paperwork, buying Lamin's air ticket, organizing Lamin's departure and arrival, his pickups and his drop-offs, enduring the e-mails back and forth between him and Judy at every stage of this planning, devoting all time and energy to somebody else's existence, to somebody else's desires and needs and requirements. It's a shadow life and after a while it gets to you. Nannies, assistants, agents, secretaries, mothers—women are used to it. Men have a lower tolerance. Fern must have sent a hundred e-mails about Lamin these past few weeks. How could he resist sending the one that would blow up my life?

My phone buzzed so frequently it seemed to have an animal life of its own. I stopped looking at it and focused instead on a very tall brother in the window of Housing Works, he had tremendous high-arched eyebrows and was holding up a series of dresses against his thick frame, stepping into a pair of roomy high heels. Spotting me, he smiled, sucked in his stomach, did a little turn and bowed. I don't know why or how but the sight of him galvanized me. I stood up and hailed a taxi. Some questions were answered quickly. All the stuff I had in New York was in boxes on the sidewalk outside

the West 10th Street apartment and the locks had
already been changed. My visa status was linked to
my employer: I had thirty days to leave the country. Where to stay took longer. I'd never really paid
for anything in New York: I lived on Aimee, ate
with Aimee, went out with Aimee, and the news
my phone brought me of the price of a single night
in a Manhattan hotel made me feel like Rip Van
Winkle waking from his hundred-year sleep. Sitting on the front steps of West 10th, I tried to
think of alternatives, friends, acquaintances, connections. All links were weak and led anyway back
to Aimee. I considered an impossibility: walking in an easterly direction down this street till it
met, in some sentimental dream, the west end of
Sidmouth Road, where my mother would answer
the door and lead me to her spare box-room, half
buried in books. Where else? Where next? I had
no coordinates. Unhailed cabs went by, one after
the other, and fancy ladies with their little dogs.
This being Manhattan, nobody paused to watch
what must have looked like a staged reenactment:
a weeping woman, sat on a step, under that Lazarus plaque, huddled by boxes, far from home.

I remembered James and Darryl. I'd met them
both back sometime in March, it was on a Sunday night—my night off—I'd traveled uptown
alone to see the Alvin Ailey dancers, and in the
theater got talking to my seat mates, two gentle-

men New Yorkers in their late fifties, a couple, one white and one black. James was English, tall and bald with a lugubrious voice and a very jolly laugh, still dressed for a pleasant pub lunch in some Oxfordshire hamlet—though he had lived here many years—and Darryl was American, with a gray-tipped Afro, mole-ish eyes behind glasses, and trousers with frayed hems and paint spattered on them, like a student artist. He knew so much about what was happening on stage, the history of each piece, of New York ballet in general and Alvin Ailey in particular, that at first I thought he must be a choreographer or an ex-dancer himself. In fact, they were both writers, funny and full of insight, I enjoyed their whispered opinions concerning the uses and limits of "cultural nationalism" in dance, and I, who had no opinions about dance, only wonderment, amused them, too, clapping after every light change and leaping to my feet as soon as the curtain fell. "It's nice to see **Revelations** with someone who hasn't seen it fifty times," noted Darryl, and afterward they invited me for a drink in the hotel bar next door, and told a long and dramatic story of a house they'd bought, in Harlem, an Edith Wharton—era wreck, which they were doing up with their life savings. Hence the paint. To me it was an obviously heroic effort but one of their neighbors, a woman in her eighties, disapproved, both of James and Darryl, and the fast-paced gentrification of the neighborhood: she

liked to shout at them in the street and push religious materials through the letterbox. James did
an excellent physical impression of this lady, and
I laughed too much and finished a second Martini. It was such a relief to be out with people who
did not care about Aimee and did not want anything from me. "And one afternoon," said Darryl,
"I was walking alone, James was somewhere else,
and she leaps out of the shadows, grabs my arm
and says: **But I can help you get away from him.
You don't need a master, you can be free—let
me help you!** She could have been going door to
door, stumping for Barack, but no: her thing was
James enslaving me. She was offering me my own
personal underground railway. Smuggle me up
into Spanish Harlem!" I had seen them occasionally since, on my free Sunday nights in the city. I
watched them chip away at plaster to reveal original cornices, and fake porphyry by flicking specks
of paint at a dark pink wall. Each time I visited I
was moved: how happy they were together, after
so many years! I didn't have many other models
of that idea. Two people creating the time of their
own lives, protected somehow by love, not ignorant of history but not deformed by it, either. I
liked them both so much, though I couldn't really
call them more than acquaintances. But I thought
of them now. And when I sent a cautious text from
the steps of West 10th, the response was immediate, characteristically generous: by dinner time I

was at their table, eating better food than I'd ever come close to at Aimee's. Flavorsome, fat-filled, pan-fried food. A bed had been made for me in one of the several spare rooms and I found they were like fondly prejudiced parents: however I told my tale of woe they refused to consider any part of it my fault. In their view I should be the angry one, all the blame was Aimee's, none of it was mine, and I went to my beautiful wood-paneled room comforted by this rose-tinted vision.

I wasn't angry until Judy sent the non-disclosure contract over, the next morning. I looked at a PDF of a piece of paper I must have signed, aged twenty-three, though I couldn't remember ever doing so. Within its inflexible terms the things that came out of my mouth did not belong to me any longer, not my ideas or opinions or feelings, not even my memories. They were all hers. Everything that had happened in my life in the past decade belonged to her. Rage rose up in me instantaneously: I wanted to burn her house down. But everything you need to burn somebody's house down these days is already in your hand. It was all in my hand—I didn't even need to get out of bed. I set up an anonymous account, chose the gossip site she hated most, wrote an e-mail containing everything I knew about little Sankofa, attached the photo of her "adoption certificate," pressed send. Satisfied, I went down to breakfast, expecting, I suppose, my hero's welcome. But when I told my friends what I'd done—

and what I thought it meant—James's face turned as grave as the medieval St. Maurice statue in the hall, and Darryl took off his glasses, sat down and blinked at the pinewood dining table. He told me he hoped I understood how much, in a short time, he and James had come to love me—it was because they loved me they could tell me the truth—and that the only thing my e-mail signified was that I was still very young.

Ten

They camped outside Aimee's brownstone. Two days later—to my shame—they were knocking on James and Darryl's door. But that part was Judy's doing, a blind item: illicit affair, "vengeful ex-employee" . . . Judy came from a different era, when blind items stayed blind and you could control the story. They had my name within a few hours, and soon after my location, God knows how. Maybe Tracey is right: maybe we are tracked at all times through our phones. I stayed in bed, while James brought up cups of tea and opened and shut the door to a persistent reporter and Darryl and I watched the tide turn on my laptop in real time as the day went on. Without doing anything different, without taking any action at all, I went from Judy's tawdry, jealous minion to The People's bold whistleblower, all in a few hours. Refresh, refresh. Addictive. My mother called and before I could even ask her how she was she said: "Alan showed me on the computer, and I think it was a really brave act. You know, you've always been a bit cowardly, I don't mean cowardly—a bit timid. It's my fault, I overprotected you, probably, mollycoddled you. This is the first really brave thing I've seen you do and I'm very proud!" Who was Alan? Her speech sounded slurry and not quite her own, more fake-posh than I'd ever heard it. I asked in a light way about her health. She gave nothing away—she'd had a little cold, but it had passed—and though I knew for a fact she was lying to me she sounded so adamant it felt like the truth. I promised her I'd come to visit her the moment I was back in England and she said, "Yes, yes, of course you will," with far less conviction than she'd said everything else.

My next call was from Judy. She asked me if I wanted to get out. She already had a ticket for me, on the red-eye, tonight. At the other end there would be an apartment I could use for a few nights, near Lord's cricket ground, until the fuss died down. I tried to thank her. She laughed her seal-bark.

"You think I'm doing this for you? What the fuck is **wrong** with you?"

"OK, Judy, I already said I'll take the ticket."

"That's gracious of you, love. After the mountain of shit you've created for me."

"What about Lamin?"

"What **about** Lamin?"

"He expected to come to England. You can't just—"

"You're ridiculous."

The phone went dead.

After the sun went down, and the last man on the doorstep left, I abandoned my boxes with James and Darryl and got a taxi on Lennox. The driver was of that deepest shade, like Hawa, and had a likely-sounding name, and I was in the state of seeing signs and symbols everywhere. I leaned forward with my year-off enthusiasms and ragbag of local facts and asked him where he was from. He was Senegalese but this didn't hamper me much: I spoke without pause through the midtown tunnel and out into Jamaica. He beat the steering wheel every now with the hub of his right hand and sighed and laughed.

"So you know how it is, back home! That village life! It's not easy but that's the life I miss! But sista, you should have come to see us! You could have just walked down the road!"

"Actually, the friend I was telling you about," I said, looking up for a moment from my screen, "from Senegal? We just organized to meet in London, I was just messaging him." I repressed the urge to tell this stranger that I, in my generosity, had paid for Lamin's ticket.

"Oh, nice, nice. London is better? More nice than here?"

"Different."

"Twenty-eight years I've been here. Here is so

stressful, you have to be so angry to survive here, you live off the anger . . . it's too much."

We were pulling into JFK, and when I tried to give him his tip he returned it.

"Thank you for coming to my country," he said, forgetting I hadn't.

Eleven

Now everyone knows who you really are.

By the time I landed, our old girlhood dance was out in the world. I find it interesting that Tracey chose not to send it to me until two whole days later. In her vision of things others would know who I really was before I did—but then perhaps they always do. It reminded me of her way with our earliest tales of ballet dancers in peril, how she would correct and edit me: "No: that part here." "It'd go better if she died on page two." Moving and rearranging things to create the greatest impact. Now she had achieved the same effect with my life, placing the beginning of the story at an earlier point so that all that came after read as the twisted consequence of a lifelong obsession. It was more convincing than my version. It drew the strangest reactions from people. Everybody wanted to see the footage and nobody did: it was pulled down wherever it was posted almost as soon as it went up. For some—maybe you—it was borderline child pornography, if not in intention then in effect. Others found it only exploitative, though it is hard to put your finger on who is exploiting whom. Can children exploit themselves? Is it anything more than a couple of girls messing around, simply two girls dancing—two brown girls dancing like adults—copying adult moves innocently, but skillfully, as brown girls often can? And if you think it more than that, then who has the problem, exactly, the girls in the film—or you? Whatever is said or thought about it seems to make the viewer complicit: the best thing is not to see it at all. That is the only possible high ground. Otherwise, this cloud of guilt, which can't be exactly placed, but still you feel it. Even I, watching the video, had the troubling thought: well, if a girl behaves like that at the age of ten, can she ever be said to be innocent? What won't she do at fifteen, at twenty-two—at thirty-three? The desire to be on the side of innocence is so strong. It pulsated out of my phone in waves, in all those posts and rants and commentaries. By contrast, the baby was innocent, the baby was guilt-free. Aimee loved the baby, the child's birth parents loved Aimee, they wanted her to raise their baby. Judy got that message out far and wide. Who was anyone to judge? Who was I?

Now everybody knows who you really are.

The tide turned again, fiercely and with great sympathy in Aimee's direction. But there were still people on the doorstep of Judy's rental, despite all her preparations and the doorman's promises, and on the third day I left with Lamin for my mother's Sidmouth Road flat, which I knew, in all available records, would be registered in Miriam's name. There was no one on the doorstep. When I rang the doorbell there was no answer and my mother's phone went to voicemail. Finally a neighbor let us in. She looked confused—shocked—when I asked where my mother was. This woman, too, would now know who I really was: the kind of daughter who had not yet heard her own mother was in a hospice.

It looked like all the spaces my mother had ever lived in, books and papers everywhere, just as I remembered, but more so: the space for actual living had reduced. Chairs were serving as bookshelves, and all available tables, most of the floor, the work surfaces in the kitchen. It wasn't chaos, though, there was a logic to it. In the kitchen diaspora fiction and poetry dominated and the bathroom was mostly histories of the Caribbean. There was a wall of slave narratives and commentaries upon them leading from her bedroom down the hall to the boiler. I found the address of the hospice on the fridge, it was written in somebody else's handwriting. I felt sad and guilty. Who did she ask to write it? Who drove her there? I tried to do a little tidying. Lamin lent a hand, half-heartedly—he was

used to women doing for him and soon sat himself down on my mother's sofa to watch the same
heavy old TV set from my childhood, kept half
hidden behind an armchair, to make the point that
it was never watched. I moved piles of books back
and forth, making little headway, and after a while
gave up. I sat at my mother's table with my back to
Lamin, opened my laptop and returned to what I'd
spent the whole of yesterday doing, searching for
myself, reading of myself, and seeking Tracey, too,
below the line. She wasn't hard to find. Generally
the fourth or fifth comment, and she always went
at it full tilt, every time, no compromise, aggressive, full of conspiracy. She had many aliases. Some
were quite subtle: tiny references to moments from
our shared history, songs we'd liked, toys we'd had,
or numeral recombinations of the year we first met
or our dates of birth. I noticed she liked to use
the words "sordid" and "shameful," and the phrase
"Where were their mothers?" Whenever I saw that
line, or a variation upon it, I knew it was her. I
found her everywhere, in the most unlikely places.
In other people's feeds, under newspaper articles,
on Facebook walls, abusing anyone who did not
agree with her arguments. As I followed her trail,
the idiotic daytime shows came and went behind
me. If I turned to check on Lamin I found him
still as a statue, watching.

"Turn that down a little?"

He'd increased the volume suddenly on a property-makeover show, of the kind my father had once liked to watch.

"The man is speaking about Edgware. I have an uncle in Edgware. And a cousin."

"Do you?" I said, trying not to sound too hopeful. I waited but he returned to his show. The sun went down. My stomach began to rumble. I didn't move from my seat, I was too intent on my Tracey hunt, flushing her out of the covert, and checking a secondary window every fifteen minutes or so to see if she'd invaded my inbox. But her methods with me were apparently different than with my mother. That one-line e-mail was all she ever sent me.

At six the news came on. Lamin was very affected by the revelation that the people of Iceland were suddenly, catastrophically poor. How could such a thing happen? A failed harvest? A corrupt President? But it was news to me, too, and not understanding all of what the newsreader said I could offer no interpretation. "Maybe we will hear information also of Sankofa," Lamin suggested, and I laughed, stood up, and told him they didn't put that kind of nonsense on the evening news. Twenty minutes later, as I peered into a fridge full of rotting produce, Lamin called me to come back in. It was the closing story on the real news, the British Broadcast news as he called it, and there in the top-right corner was a stock photo of Aimee. We sat on the edge of the sofa. Cut to a strip-lit office space somewhere, with a picture of the frog-faced President-for-life askew on the wall, in front of which the birth parents sat in their country clothes, looking hot and uncomfortable. A woman from an adoption agency sat to their left and translated. I tried to remember if the mother was the same person I'd seen that day in the corrugated-iron hut, but couldn't be sure. I listened to the agency woman explain the situation to the foreign correspondent who sat opposite them all, he was wearing a version of my old wrinkled uniform of linen and khaki. Everything had been done according to procedure, what had been leaked was not the adoption certificate at all, it was only an intermediary document, clearly not intended for public consumption, the parents were satisfied with the adoption and understood what they had signed.

"We have no problem," said the mother, in halting English, smiling at the camera.

Lamin put both hands behind his head, sank back into the sofa and offered me a proverb: "Money makes problems go away."

I switched it off. Silence spread through the house, we had nothing whatsoever to say to each other, the third point on our triangle was gone. Two days ago I had been pleased with my dramatic gesture—fulfilling a duty of care Aimee had neglected—but the gesture itself had obscured the reality of Lamin: Lamin in my bed, Lamin in this living room, Lamin indefinitely in my life. He had no job and no money. None of his hard-won qualifications meant anything here. Each time I left the room—to get tea, to go to the toilet—my first thought upon seeing him again was: what are you doing in my house?

At eight o'clock I ordered Ethiopian takeaway. As we ate I showed him Google Maps and where we were in London in relation to the rest of the city. I showed him Edgware. The various ways you can get to Edgware.

"I'll be going to see my mother tomorrow, but feel free to hang around here, obviously. Or, you know, go off exploring."

Anyone watching us that evening would have thought we had met a few hours earlier. I felt shy of him once more, of his proud self-containment and capacity for silence. He was not Aimee's Lamin any more, but he wasn't mine either. I had no idea who he was. When it was clear I'd run out of geographical conversation he stood up and, without any discussion, went to the box-room. I went to my mother's room. We closed our doors.

The hospice was in Hampstead, on a quiet, tree-lined cul-de-sac, a stone's throw from the hospital where I was born and a few streets from the Noted Activist. Autumn was pretty here, russet and gold against all that valuable red-brick Victorian real estate, and I had strong associative memories of my mother walking through it on brisk mornings like this one, arm in arm with the Noted Activist, bemoaning the Italian aristocrats and American bankers, the Russian oligarchs and the upscale children's clothes stores, the basements being dug out of the earth. The end of some long-lost bohemian idea of the place she'd held dear. She was forty-seven then. She was only fifty-seven now. Of all the futures I had imagined for her in these streets somehow the present reality seemed the most improbable. When I was a child she had been immortal. I couldn't imagine her leaving this world without ripping its fabric. Instead, this quiet street, these gingko trees shedding their golden leaves.

At the desk I gave my name and after a short wait a young male nurse came for me. He warned me that my mother was on morphine and sometimes confused, before leading me to her room. I didn't notice anything about this nurse, he seemed completely nondescript, but when I got to the room and he opened the door my mother pushed herself up in her bed and cried: "Alan Pennington! So you've met the famous Alan Pennington!"

"Mum, it's me."

"Oh, I'm Alan," said the nurse, and I turned round to look again at this young man my mother was smiling at so radiantly. He was short, with sandy-brown hair, small blue eyes, a slightly pudgy face and an unremarkable nose with a few freck-

les over the bridge. The only thing that made him
unusual to me, in the context of all the Nigerian,
Polish and Pakistani nurses you heard talking in
the corridors, was how English he looked.

"Alan Pennington is famous around here,"
said my mother, waving at him. "His kindness is
legend."

Alan Pennington smiled at me, revealing a pair
of pointy incisors, like a little dog's.

"I'll leave you two alone," he said.

"How are you, Mum? Are you in a lot of pain?"

"Alan Pennington," she informed me, after the
door had closed behind him, "only works for
others. Did you know that? You hear about these
people but it's another thing to meet them. Of
course, I've worked for others, all my life—but
not like this. They're all like that here. I had a girl
from Angola first, Fatima, lovely girl, she was the
same . . . unfortunately she had to move on. Then
Alan Pennington came. You see: he is a carer. I
never thought about that word very deeply before.
Alan Pennington **cares**."

"Mum, why do you keep calling him Alan Pennington like that?"

My mother looked at me like I was an idiot.

"Because that's his name. Alan Pennington is a
carer who **cares**."

"Yes, Mum, that's what carers are paid to do."

"No, no, no, you don't understand: he **cares**.

The things he does for me! No one should have to do those things for another human being—but he does them for me!"

Tiring of the subject of Alan Pennington, I convinced her to let me read aloud for a while from a slim book she had on her side-table, a little stand-alone edition of **Sonny's Blues**, and then lunch arrived on the tray of Alan Pennington.

"But I can't eat that," said my mother sadly as Alan lay it across her lap.

"Well, how about I leave it with you for twenty minutes and if you're absolutely sure you can't eat it just ring the bell and I'll come and take it back? How would that be? Does that sound all right?"

I waited for my mother to tear a strip off Alan Pennington—all her life she had hated and dreaded being patronized or spoken to like a child—but now she nodded seriously as if this were a very wise and generous proposal, took Alan's hands in her own shaking, wraith-like grasp and said: "Thank you, Alan. Please don't forget to come back."

"And forget the most beautiful woman in the place?" said Alan, though clearly gay, and my mother, lifelong feminist, erupted in girlish giggles. And they stayed like that, holding each other's hands, until Alan smiled and released her, off to care for someone else, abandoning my mother and me to each other. I had a rogue thought, I hated having it: I wished that Aimee was here with me. I had been at deathbeds with Aimee, four

times, and on each occasion had been impressed
and humbled by her way of being with the dying,
her honesty, warmth and simplicity, which nobody
else in the room ever seemed able to manage, not
even family. Death did not scare her. She looked
directly at it, engaged with the dying person in
their present situation, no matter how extreme,
without nostalgia or false optimism, accepted your
fear when you were afraid, and your pain if you
were feeling it. How many people can do these
supposedly straightforward things? I remember a
friend of hers, a painter who had lost decades to the
severe anorexia that eventually killed her, saying to
Aimee, on what turned out to be her deathbed:
"God, Aim—didn't I just waste so much fucking
time!" To which Aimee replied: "More than you
know." I remember that stick figure between the
bed sheets with her gaping mouth, so shocked she
burst out laughing. But it was the truth, no else
had dared tell her, and dying people, I found out,
are impatient for the truth. I spoke no truth whatsoever to my mother, I just made the usual small
talk, read her more of her beloved Baldwin, listened
to tales of Alan Pennington, and lifted her beaker
of juice so she could suck at it through a straw.
She knew I knew she was dying but for whatever
reason—bravery, denial or delusion—she made no
reference to it in my presence except to say, when I
asked her where her phone was and why she hadn't

answered it: "Look, I don't want to spend the time I have left on that bloody thing."

I found it in the compartment of her side-table, in a hospital laundry bag, along with a trouser suit, a folder of papers, a guide to parliamentary conduct and her laptop.

"You don't have to use it," I said, powering it up and laying it on the table. "But just leave it on so I have a way of contacting you."

The notification alarm started going off—the phone buzzed and danced across the counter—and my mother looked over at it with a kind of horror.

"No, no, no—I don't want it! I don't want it on! Why did you have to **do** that?"

I picked it up. I could see unopened e-mails, dozens and dozens of them, filling the screen, abusive even in their subject headings, all from the same address. I started reading through them, trying to resist the catalog of pain: child-support woes, rent arrears, skirmishes with social workers. The most recent were the most frantic: she feared her children were about to be taken from her.

"Mum, have you heard from Tracey recently?"

"Where's Alan Pennington? I'm not going to eat this."

"My God, you're so sick right now—you shouldn't have to be dealing with this!"

"It's not like Alan not to check in . . ."

"Mum, have you heard from Tracey?"

"NO! I told you I don't look at that thing!"

"You haven't spoken to her?"

She sighed heavily.

"I don't have many visitors, darling. Miriam comes. Lambert came once. My fellow Members of Parliament do not come. You are here. As Alan Pennington said: 'You find out who your friends are.' I sleep mostly. I dream a lot. I dream of Jamaica, I dream of my grandmother. I go back in time . . ." She closed her eyes. "I did have a dream about your friend, when I first got here, I was on a high dosage of this"—she tugged at a drip in her arm—"Yes, your friend came to visit me. I was asleep and I woke up and she was just standing by the door, not talking. Then I went back to sleep and she was gone."

When I got back to the flat, emotionally weak, still jet-lagged, I prayed that Lamin would be out and he was. When he didn't come back for dinner I was relieved. Only the next morning, when I knocked on his door, nudged it open and saw he and his bag were gone did I realize he'd left. When I called I got voicemail. I called every few hours for four days and it was the same. I had been so concentrated upon how I might break the news to him that he must leave, that we had no future together, that I hadn't imagined, not for a moment, that all the time he was plotting his own escape from me.

Without him, without the TV on, the flat was deadly quiet. It was just me and the computer, and the radio, from which more than once I heard the voice of the Noted Activist, still going strong, full of opinions. But my own story was fading, online and in all other mediums, all that brightly illuminated commentary already burned out, puttering to blackness and ash. At a loss, I spent a day writing e-mails to Tracey. First dignified and righteous, then sarcastic, then angry, then hysterical, until I realized she was having more effect on me with silence than I could manage with all these words. The power she has over me is the same as it has always been, judgment, and it goes beyond words. There is no case I can make that will change the fact that I was her only witness, the only person who knows all that she has in her, all that's been ignored and wasted, and yet I still left her back there, in the ranks of the unwitnessed, where you have to scream to get heard. Later I found out Tracey had a long history of sending distressing e-mails. A director at the Tricycle who had not cast her, she thought because of color. The teachers at her son's school. A nurse at her doctor's office. But none of this changes the judgment. If she was tormenting my mother as she lay dying, if she was trying to ruin my life, if she was sitting in that claustrophobic little flat, watching my e-mails line up on her phone and simply choosing not to read them—whatever she was doing, I knew it was a form of judgment upon me. I was her sister: I had a sacred duty toward her. Even if only she and I knew it and recognized it, it was still true.

A few times I left the flat for the corner-shop, to buy cigarettes and packets of pasta, but otherwise I saw no one and heard from no one. At night I picked up random books from my mother's pile, tried to read a little, lost interest and started another. It occurred to me that I was depressed and needed to speak to another human. I sat with my new pay-as-you-go phone in my hand, looking down at the short list of personal names and numbers I'd copied off the old work phone, summarily disconnected, and tried to imagine what form each interaction would take, if and how I could get through it, but every potential conversation felt like a scene from a stage play, in which I'd be playing that person I'd been for so long, who seems to be at lunch with you but is actually turned toward Aimee, working for Aimee, thinking of Aimee, day and night, night and day. I called Fern. The ring was a single long foreign tone and he answered with "**Hola**." He was in Madrid.

"Working?"

"Traveling. It will be my year off. Didn't you know I quit? But I'm so happy to be free!"

I asked him why, expecting a personal attack,

directed at Aimee, but his answer had no personal aspect, he was concerned with the "distorting" effect of her money in the village, the collapse of government services in the area, and the foundation's naïve, complicit dealings with the government. As he spoke I was reminded and ashamed of a profound difference between us. I had always been quick to interpret everything personally, where Fern had seen the larger, structural problems.

"Well, it's good to hear from you, Fern."

"No, you didn't hear from me. I heard from you."

He left the silence hanging. The longer it went on, the harder it was to think of what to say.

"Why are you calling me?"

I sat listening to him breathe for another few seconds until my phone ran out of credit.

About a week later he e-mailed to say he was in London for a short trip. I hadn't spoken to anyone but my mother in several days. We met up on the South Bank, in the window of the Film Café, sitting side by side, facing the water, and reminisced a little, but it was awkward, I became bitter so easily, every thought pulled toward darkness, to something painful. All I did was complain, and though I could see I was irritating him I couldn't seem to stop myself.

"Well, we can say that Aimee lives in her bubble," he said, interrupting me, "and so does your friend and, by the way, so do you. It's possible that it's like this for everyone. The size of the bubble is different, this is all. And perhaps the thickness of the—what do you call this in English?—skin—film. The thin layer on a bubble."

The waiter came, we paid avid attention to him. When he left we watched a tourist boat make its way down the Thames.

"Oh! I know what it is I want to tell you," he said suddenly, slapping the bar and rattling a saucer. "I heard from Lamin! He is fine—he is in Birmingham. He wanted a letter of reference from me. He hopes to study. We e-mailed a little bit. I learn that Lamin is a fatalist. He wrote to me: 'It was **intended** for me to come to Birmingham. So I was always coming here.' Isn't that funny? No? Well, maybe I use the wrong word in English. I mean that for Lamin the future is as certain as the past. It is a theory from philosophy."

"Sounds like a nightmare."

Fern looked puzzled again: "Maybe I put it wrong, I'm not a philosopher. To me it means something simple, like to say the future is already there, waiting for you. Why not wait, see what it brings?"

His face was so hopeful it made me laugh. We got some of our old friendly rhythm back, and sat talking for a long time, and I thought it was not impossible that there might be a future in which I could care for him. I was settling into the idea that I wasn't going anywhere, there was no hurry any longer, I would not be on the next plane. Time was on my side, as much as it is on anyone's. Everything that afternoon felt wide open to me, a kind of shock, I didn't know what was happening in the next few days or even the next few hours—a new feeling. I was surprised when I looked up from my second coffee and saw the day fading and the night almost upon us.

Afterward, he wanted to get on the tube, at Waterloo, it was the best stop for me, too, but instead I left him and chose the bridge. Ignoring both barriers, walking straight down the center, over the river, until I reached the other side.

Epilogue

The last time I saw my mother alive we talked about Tracey. That isn't strong enough: Tracey was really the only thing that allowed us to speak at all. My mother was mostly too tired to speak or be spoken to, and for the first time in her life books held no attraction. I sang to her instead, which she seemed to like—as long as I stuck to the old Motown classics. We watched TV together, something we'd never done before, and I made small talk with Alan Pennington, who came in every now and then to check on my mother's fierce hiccups and her stools and the progression of her delusions. He brought lunch, which she could no longer look at never mind eat, but on that last day we had together, when Alan left the room, she opened her eyes and told me in a calm, authoritative voice, as if remarking on something that was a plain and objective fact—like the weather outside or what was sitting on her plate—that the time had come to "do something" about Tracey's family. At first I thought she was lost in the past, she often was in those last days, but soon I understood she was speaking of the children, Tracey's children, although in speaking of them she moved freely between their reality, as she imagined it, the history of our own little family, and a deeper history: it was the last speech she ever gave. She works too hard, said my mother, and the children don't see her, and now they want to take my children away, but your father was very good, very good, and often I think: was I a good mother? Was I? And now they want to take my children away from me . . . But I was just a student, I am studying, because you have to learn to survive, and I was a mother and I have to learn, because you knew that any one of us they caught reading or writing faced jail or a whipping or worse, and anyone caught teaching us to read or write got the same, jailed or whipped, it was the law at that time, it was very strict, and in that way we were taken out of our time and place, and then stopped from even **knowing** our time and place—and you can't do anything worse to a people than that. But I don't know if Tracey was a good mother, though I certainly tried my best to raise them all, but I know for sure your father was very good, very good . . .

I told her she was good. The rest didn't matter. I told her everybody had tried their best within the limits of being themselves. I don't know if she heard me.

I was gathering my things when I heard Alan Pennington coming down the hall, singing in his flat, off-tune way, one of my mother's favorite Otis tracks, about being born by the river, and running ever since. "Heard you do that one yesterday," he said to me, appearing in the doorway, chipper as ever. "Lovely voice, you have. Your mum's very proud of you, you know, she's always talking about you."

He smiled at my mother. But she was beyond Alan Pennington.

"It's clear as day," she murmured, closing her eyes as I got up to leave. "They should be with you. The best possible place for those children is with you."

For the rest of that afternoon I entertained the fantasy, not seriously, I don't think, it was only a Technicolor dreamsong playing in my head: a ready-made family, suddenly in the here and now, filling my life. The next day, I took a morning walk around the barren perimeter of Tiverton Rec, the wind whipping through the caged fence, carrying away sticks thrown wide for dogs, and found myself walking on, in the opposite direction from the flat and past the station that would have taken me to the hospice. My mother died at twelve minutes past ten, just as I turned into Willesden Lane.

Tracey's tower came into view, above the horse chestnuts, and with it reality. These were not my children, would never be my children. I almost turned back, like someone who has woken abruptly from a sleepwalk, except for an idea, new to me, that there might be something else I could offer, something simpler, more honest, between my mother's idea of salvation and nothing at all. Impatient, I left the path and crossed diagonally through the grass, heading for the covered walkway. I was about to enter the stairwell when I heard music, stopped and looked up. She was right above me, on her balcony, in a dressing gown and slippers, her hands in the air, turning, turning, her children around her, everybody dancing.

Acknowledgments

Thank you to my early readers: Josh Appignanesi, Daniel Kehlmann, Tamsin Shaw, Michael Shavit, Rachel Kaadzi Ghansah, Gemma Seiff, Darryl Pinckney, Ben Bailey-Smith, Yvonne Bailey-Smith and, in particular, Devorah Baum, for encouragement when it was most needed.

Special thanks to Nick Laird, who read first and saw what had to be done with time, just in time.

Thanks to my editors and agent: Simon Prosser, Ann Godoff and Georgia Garrett.

Thanks to Nick Parnes, Hannah Parnes and Brandy Jolliff, for reminding me what work was like in the nineties.

Thanks to Eleanor Wachtel, for introducing me to the matchless Jeni LeGon.

Thank you to Steven Barclay, for a little space in Paris when it was most needed.

I am indebted to Dr. Marloes Janson, whose engrossing, thoughtful and inspiring anthropological study **Islam, Youth, and Modernity in the Gambia: The Tablighi Jama'at** proved invaluable, bringing context where I had impressions, possible answers when I had questions, and providing many of the cultural underpinnings of this story, as well as helping create the feel and texture of certain scenes in the novel. A note on geography: North London, in these pages, is a state of mind. Some streets may not appear as they do in Google Maps.

Nick, Kit, Hal—love and gratitude.